Originally from South Africa, Ph
has spent most of her life living in ru
BSc. in Rural Science and an MA in .
Intervention. She has worked for many years as a Community
Mediator and Restorative Mediation Practitioner, primarily
within the Irish Travelling Community. When not writing,
Phyllida divides her time between lecturing, looking after her
grandchildren and running a small family business.

Also by the same author

'*Yum & Yarns*'

Awards for *Across The Ford*

A winner in the IWC Novel Fair, an international
competition for first novels.

ACROSS
THE
FORD

A story of forgiveness

Phyllida Taylor

ALKIRA
PUBLISHING

Across the Ford: A Story of Forgiveness
Phyllida Taylor
Copyright © 2024
Published by Alkira Publishing, Australia
ABN: 32736122056
http://www.alkirapublishing.com

ISBN: 978-1-922329-68-4

Across The Ford: A Story of Forgiveness is dedicated to my good friend and colleague Anne Redmond, RIP, on whom the character of Bridget is based. Any other likenesses are purely incidental, and I thank anyone who feels they identify with a character for inspiring my story.

PROLOGUE

It was evening time when I drove into the farmyard. The sun was still hovering well above the horizon, and the warmth of the day was in the stones. A cloud of river midges danced in the warm air, and it felt as if summer could go on forever. I had never been to that place before and had never met the farmer, either. I still don't even know his name. He was a craggy old bachelor with squinty eyes and a flat tweed cap that appeared to be felted to his bald head with the grease of a lifetime. Most of his teeth had caved in, which made him hard to understand. His clothes looked as though they had grown old in the same epoch as himself, taking his shape, his colour and his smell. If he dissolved inside them, his whole attire could have just carried on his life without him.

My mission there was to collect a pony for a friend. To access the farmyard, it was necessary to drive over a pebbly ford at the bottom of a long, narrow boreen. I was preoccupied with how to turn the jeep and horsebox, which took up most of the space. It reminded me of one of those move-it-up-and-down monkey puzzles we used to amuse ourselves with on the bus ride home from school. I knew I would have to work it out somehow, because reversing all the way back up to the main road was out of the question.

He greeted me with a sly and knowing grin.

'I've seen you before, girl.'

'Oh, I don't think so. I've never been here.' My voice sounded English and prissy, even to me.

Almost mimicking my accent, he replied, 'Oh, but you have.' He shook his bent and stubby thumb in my direction, as if hitching a ride. 'This day last year, to be sure, I was lifting into town, and you left me standing on the road.'

'You must be mistaken; I know I was never over this way in my life.' We carried on the conversation like that for a bit and then moved on to platitudes about the weather.

The pony was fat and obstinate, but he poked her with a stick and flapped a sack at her hind legs, while I tried to coax her with a carrot, at the sight of which she plunged into the horsebox. Somehow, after much shunting back and forth, I managed to turn the vehicle and extricate myself. Driving into the sun as it slipped behind the hills, I tried to think back to the previous year; but that was another life. When I got home again, I checked my diary for twelve months previously. Lo and behold, on the twenty-first of July, I would have driven right past the end of that lane on my way to meet a work commitment in the next town. My mind would have been fixed on the job at hand; or more likely, day dreaming. I almost certainly hadn't seen him standing in the ditch; even if he had waved his hand at me, he would only have been a fleeting shadow in the corner of my eye. He couldn't have gleaned more than a glance at my face as I whizzed past. Moreover, I had been driving a very old, previous incarnation

2

of the swanky, new, bright yellow jeep I took into his yard that day. Also, my hair had been long and plaited then. A year on, and it was bobbed like a boy to suit my new and far more pragmatic lifestyle. Yet he remembered my face twelve months later, and he knew it.

Now, as I contemplated the great metamorphosis that took place in my life between 1978 and 1979, I realised that for this old farmer, nothing ever changed. It was a rhythm that rolled along, year after year. He talked to the crows that swooped into the fields to gather everything, including loose hair from the donkey's back. He trudged around the farm in old wellingtons with soft hay for socks. He ate his boiled egg, dried out the shells and fed them back as grit to the hens that roosted all over the farm. The plate of crusts went down for the dog to lick clean; washing up was for women, and he didn't have one. He sat by his open range at night, slowly pickling in the smoke, listening to his little transistor, while he searched the dog's matted coat for ticks and fleas. Time gradually slipped by. He spooned baked beans straight from the tin and drank beer from the neck of the bottle, tossing all the empties into the haggard behind the house, where they are slowly becoming the archaeological treasures of centuries to come.

Small wonder, I supposed, that the sight of a girl with plaits, driving an old jeep, was so remarkable that it imprinted itself indelibly onto the canvas of his mind. Our two worlds collided very briefly. The experience has stayed, vividly, with me for forty-four years. I wish I had given more time to talk to him.

Recently, I drove past there to try to call it all back, but the road had been realigned. No trace of the entrance to the lane remains.

3

Some years later, I heard from my friend with the pony that the old man had apparently shot himself. I also read in the local paper, around that time, that a substantial haul of guns and ammunition had been found in the area.

CHAPTER ONE

The aeroplane taxies down the runway, propellers rumbling loudly. It rises like a swaying albatross over the frozen fields of England, which are now rapidly shrinking. The steady drone of the engines does little to settle Katherine's nerves. She tries to doze, as she didn't sleep much last night, worrying about everything. After a while, she gives up, takes a magazine out of her bag and reads the headline 'Declare Yourselves the Free and Liberated Women of Nineteen Sixty-Nine!' A photograph shows a back view of a group of bare-breasted women swirling their bras above their heads, silhouetted against a bonfire. A claw tightens around Katherine's guts as she pictures herself dutifully ironing Harry's shirts, striving for immaculate collars and cuffs, a skill she learned how to perfect at nine years old while in the Brownies. Brown Owl had impressed upon the girls the great importance of 'pleasing your husbands'. She thinks about all the other womanly arts that she has given her adult life to learning in order to delight her husband. Inevitably, her mind rolls into his nightly needs-café, where

Harry is getting more and more difficult to please. That's the hardest part. It was all such a romp in the beginning. Now, like most things to do with Harry, it is tinged with fear, guilt and, ultimately, failure.

Katherine's brain functions in criss-cross patterns, going back and forth over the same ground most of the time. It's a word-search puzzle for clues to the worrisome question of how to be. Lately, it has become even more jumbled up, as if the words are written in code. What once felt so right now seems completely out of step. She tries to apply justifications, like it's what good wives do; it gives her a sense of purpose; or perhaps, more honestly, because it makes her life simpler to stay on the right side of Harry. But she knows that she just isn't keeping up, either with being a good wife or with the world of new thinking and independent, liberated women. It has become a daily meditation; her own 'Great Matter'. She tries to answer it by using different formulae, a series of what-ifs. Whichever way she tries to work it out, she keeps getting entangled, snared by the knowledge that the real life is passing her by. Like that bruise on the back of her head after telling Harry it was fish and chips for dinner because she was breaking out and going to the cinema with some friends.

It is not only Harry who makes her feel like everyone else's shadow, either. She is on this journey to Ireland, but she doesn't understand why. It was just assumed. Her father had summoned her to come home to Suffolk on Thursday and pronounced shortly after breakfast yesterday, 'Katherine will go. She can represent the family.' Looking directly at her, he had said firmly, 'Go and see Pierce, the family solicitor, in Kilkenny. Find out what really happened. For God's sake, don't come back until you've got to the bottom of it!'

For these kinds of situations, her father tends to speak

to her as if she were the dog under the table—benign, impersonal and definitive. One doesn't question him, ever. Her mother has her own way of coping. Georgina tips away in the background, sorting things out so that she gets what she needs, but she never challenges her husband.

There are lots of unanswered questions. It was all such a rush. For instance, Katherine thinks, what does 'died tragically' mean? Aren't all sudden deaths a tragedy? Her father expects her to 'go over there' and 'get to the bottom of things', without giving her any pointers beyond the tip of his finger. Perhaps it's because she was almost certainly the last one in the family to see him alive? But that was some years ago when she was a teenager, full of innocent affection for her batty old Uncle Jack. The big life had eluded him, and he had remained, struggling away, alone on the family farm. She tries to put herself in the picture by imagining the place again, but then, of course, it was always summer when she used to visit. Everything is shiny and green and even cow pats smell sweet in July meadows. She can barely summon to mind her uncle's smiling face as he waved her goodbye at the railway station in Kilkenny amid clouds of steam belching from the engine stack. Now all she has is a fading picture of him returning to the farm alone that day in the tub-trap, which he had borrowed from the Ryans next door. She visualises him humming along gently, reaching out for fronds of honeysuckle from the hedge, sucking the sweet nectar from the flowers and chewing straws of hay plucked from his jacket. The collie dog would have been riding shotgun beside him, anxiously watching out for potholes, as she always did. This image is overshadowed by a gnawing sense of guilt and foreboding.

She gazes out of the aeroplane window. The first yellow shards of dawn have turned to pale blue. The Irish Sea is glistening below. Tiny toy ships pattern the water with white shark fins. Last night, after a few glugs from his hip flask, her father had taken her hand and started to say something. His bloodshot eyes were glistening with a mixture of atropine drops and tears. He changed his mind; the words didn't come. She kissed him goodnight. He grabbed her back, and as if to make some sense out of this little drama, growled in her ear, 'Don't trust them, Katherine, not any of them!' This was followed immediately by a paroxysm of chest-wracking coughs. She tried to ask him what he meant, but he waved her away with an affectionate wince, whacking his chest with his clenched left fist, hocking up globs of phlegm into his handkerchief.

A cold sweat breaks out across her forehead as she tries to remember if she packed any dope. She fumbles in the bottom of her shoulder bag, groping around for the small tin. Her fingertips crawl over the surface, caressing the smooth, familiar patterns of blackcurrant throat pastilles impressed upon the lid. She grips it tightly. All is well.

Eventually, the coastline of Ireland appears in the gaps between the gathering clouds. It looks just like a map in a school atlas with jagged lines of green and grey interspersed with long, yellow curves. She has never seen it from the air before. It is very different from when you arrive by mail boat, pulling into Dun Laoghaire harbour at dawn, feeling queasy and freezing cold, even in the middle of summer. Katherine used to wonder how it happened that the mail wasn't delivered reeking of dead fish, vomit and stale urine, like herself.

Even in late November, the countryside is still green. Between the clouds, she can see many little fields patched across the landscape, outlined with bare hedgerows; brief glimpses of settlements linked by ribbons of road and meandering rivers. They look like dismembered jigsaw pieces.

The great machine shudders, buffeted about by turbulence. Then sinks into a pillow of fluff that blots out the view. It feels like the plane is tumbling out of the sky, shrouded in smoky mist and bumping up and down. Katherine's ears are blocked. All she can hear is a pounding in her head and the muffled roar of the turbines. Too late now to search for boiled sweets. Both hands are needed to hold the seat in front. Suddenly, the runway appears ahead. Bang! The wheels hit the tarmac. The unwieldy beast rumbles to a halt.

Once in the terminal building in Dublin, Katherine enquires about trains or buses to Kilkenny. It seems hopelessly complicated. She decides she needs a cup of tea and a cigarette to settle her stomach and to make a plan. The only other person in the restaurant is a man in a donkey jacket, sitting alone at a table, eating breakfast. He is gazing out of the window onto the runway. It is a Saturday; he probably has nothing better to do. He watches the planes landing and taking off while he eats his bacon, eggs and black pudding. It turns out that he is down a few bob after last night; a bit of cash would come in handy. He offers to drive her all the way to Kilkenny. Katherine hesitates; she knows it isn't wise to take lifts from strangers, but the thought of being driven the whole way is too tempting, at least until she sees his car. It has lines of rust-pitted holes along the side panels. It's just like the old banger that Peter, the gardener's son at home, bombs around the lanes in, terrifying wildlife and game birds and sending cyclists flying into the hedge.

The guy assures her indignantly, 'It most certainly is able for the journey!' He pats the roof and opens the passenger door. With trepidation, and nursing her aching head in her hands, Katherine slides into the front seat. She knows she has given in too easily. She always does.

'You're over on holiday?' he calls out as he chucks her holdall into the boot and slams it shut with such force the car trembles.

'No, not really.' Unwilling to give too much away, she knows she will have to say something. 'It's my uncle's funeral.'

'Sorry to hear that, missus. Lord ha' mercy on him. Was he old?'

'I'm not sure how old he was, really. Sixty, perhaps; he was my father's youngest brother.'

'You going to the funeral on your own, then?'

'My father is a bit poorly, and my mother, well ... she doesn't like Ireland much.' Turning her wedding ring around on her finger, she adds, 'And my husband is too busy with business things.'

'Right, too busy, eh? Where are you from yourself?'

'We live in London, but I'm from Suffolk. That's where my parents still live.' Then, wishing very much to turn the conversation away from herself, she asks, 'How about you?' He is bumping and crunching the gears to get out of the car park.

'Me? Here and there. I'm a citizen of the world, you could say.' He looks across at her. When he catches her eye, he winks. 'I get about, you know, no fixed abode. Paudie's my name.' He reaches out his right hand, across his body, to shake hers.

'Katherine Fletcher.' She takes his great paw and feels her fingers being squashed together like supermarket sausages. She wonders how someone could have no fixed abode. She offers him a cigarette, and they both light up. The car jerks forward, out onto the main road. A van veers across to avoid them, and the driver hoots, sticking up two fingers out of the window. Paudie does the same back.

'What do you do for a living, Paudie?' she ventures.

'Ah sure, you know, this and that. I'm a stringer, I suppose you'd say.'

'Oh, cool.' After a few minutes, the car is full of cigarette smoke. She winds the window down a bit. Freezing spikes of rain bite her cheeks.

'What does a stringer normally do on a wet Saturday in November?'

'Drink, watch the racing, you know, hang out. I like the vibes in the airport. Plenty of "A" listers going through, you know. They often get that starlight flight from London. You'd wonder why people like that are trying to save money, wouldn't you?' He says the last bit with a mid-Atlantic accent. He glances across again. She is not looking his way. He makes as if he was checking in the mirror and adjusts his thick curls.

'Did they have any other family here, your uncle and your old man?'

'No, my uncle was a bachelor. He lived alone on the farm.'

'Oh, I see,' he nods knowingly. 'This'll be your first time in Ireland, then?'

'No, actually, I used to come over to visit him in the summer holidays when I was a teenager.'

He looks over again, directly at her for a couple of seconds, and Katherine is acutely aware of her false eyelashes and wonders if her mascara is running.

'You'll find Ireland a very different place now, you know.'

'Really?' She is thinking that surely nothing ever changes here except the weather and the price of butter.

'Don't you get the news over there? We are on the very verge of another civil war here!' His tone is much changed. He looks at Katherine. She looks away.

'What?' Her mind was comfortably hovering around the

small buttercup-decorated meadows, fat cows and the sweaty pork chops in the village shop in Knocklong, a couple of miles from her uncle's farm. 'What do you mean, "civil war"?'

'Oh yeah! Riots in Derry, bombs in Belfast. You just wait. It'll be Dublin next. Then who-began-it all over the bloody country!' The car swerves unnervingly across the road. He jerks it back onto the left-hand side and swears. When the road has levelled up again, he goes on. 'Never heard of Bernadette Devlin?'

'Who?'

'The queen of the Bogside. The youngest person elected to Westminster in over two hundred years. That's women's liberation for you. She'll shake 'em up, you wait and see! Don't you read the papers at all?' He whacks the dashboard with his left fist.

'Not really.' Katherine doesn't feel she should admit that her mother removes anything about Ireland before her father can get his hands on the daily papers. Ever since he was knighted by Queen Elizabeth for his services to British industry, no one mentions 'home' and 'Ireland' in the same sentence. In fact, Ireland is rarely mentioned at all. And Harry doesn't believe in second-hand news. He doesn't trust the newspapers and discourages Katherine from buying them. 'Bloody waste of money!' The only papers that interest him are the *Racing Weekly* and the *Financial Times*.

'Oh, you're all very snug in your ignorance over there. You'll hear about it soon enough, though. They won't stop at Dublin, you know. Oh no, not at all. It'll be bombs going off all over the British Isles. Full-scale war before it's finished!' He slaps his right hand onto his knee. 'You'll know all about it then, girl!'

Katherine's head throbs. She decides it is time to eat her

bar of chocolate. It seems to her that Paudie is too worked up about the injustices of the past five hundred years to accept a share in her tainted British sweetmeats.

'I was up there, you know, in Derry, when the last riots were on.' His accent changes again to include a northern twang. 'Very rough. Very rough indeed.' After a while, he says, 'What time is this funeral, anyway? What was your uncle's name, by the way?'

'I think the Mass is at two, but I'm not too sure. His name was Jack Butler.'

'Butler, eh? Two o'clock?' He looks at his wristwatch. 'Ah, plenty of time,' he says cheerily.

They stop several times to get a quick drink and to ask the way or check the tyres and let the engine cool down a bit. They munch through a few bags of ready salted crisps and some Irish chocolate bars. Paudie likes to chat with the locals wherever they stop. It is a long drive from Dublin to Knocklong in the county of Kilkenny.

The last few miles of the journey are the worst; small roads with massive potholes and right-angle bends with no camber, surfaces that were laid down for small herds of cattle or donkey carts to travel from farm to farm at a pace quite alien to the motor car. Katherine tries to focus her gaze on the ever-narrowing strip of tarmac bobbing up and down before them. They approach a T junction. In the middle of a field on the hill, right in front of them, stands the skeletal remains of a Georgian mansion.

'I wonder what happened there?' she muses out loud.

'Torched by the IRA, no doubt. The countryside is littered with them places. Bloody eyesores. They should all be levelled and the cut stone used to build decent houses for the people who lived on these estates.'

13

'I wonder what happened to the family who lived in the house? They picked a lovely place to build it, though, didn't they? It seems a pity, a waste.'

But Paudie dismisses that with a sharp 'Hmm!'

The grand entrance is still more or less intact with carved stone pineapples on top of large, limestone piers. A pair of wrought-iron gates gracefully lace the gap between them. It has stopped raining now, and the sun, which is directly ahead, is shining through the bare windows of the charred remains of the house. They pause briefly to let a farmer and his donkey pass. SUNNYHILL is engraved on a marble slab set into the wall. As the light changes, a black sky descends once more. Katherine gets a sudden cold feeling and shivers.

'Can you hack on a bit there, please, Paudie? I don't want to be late.'

'Okay, okay. Not far now, by my reckoning; about two miles down to the left here.'

The road is looking more familiar to Katherine as they pass some landmarks, like the creamery, the pub and the village shop. Her mind plummets back to reality.

The telegram, which arrived a couple of days ago, gave little information about what had happened to her uncle, just that he died tragically and a bit about the funeral arrangements. Her father had mumbled this over breakfast yesterday, as he rattled his false teeth with his tongue and shook the newspaper into shape. She noticed his hands were shaking more than usual.

As if reading her mind, Paudie asks, 'What took him, then, your uncle?'

'Sorry?'

'What did he die of? Heart attack, I suppose?'

'Oh, yes, maybe, I'm not sure really. It was sudden, anyway.'

'They always say that. More men die of heart attacks in this country than anywhere in the world, you know.' He glances over at her and winks. 'Tough lives.' He makes a gesture resembling a glass being brought to the lips. Then he suddenly bristles up and says, 'Wait a minute, what did you say his name was? Butler? He's not the one who blew his head off with a shotgun a few days ago, is he?'

'What?'

'You mean you didn't know? That bloke at the petrol pumps back there was full of it. Yeah, apparently, they found him in the cow byre during the week. That's what they say, anyway. Some people think he was murdered. Did you not know that? Lord ha' mercy on him, anyway.' He crosses himself and slows the car almost to a halt. When it is about to stall, he boots the accelerator, and they jerk forward again. He adds, 'Some sort of local conspiracy, maybe? Which or whether, they are giving it as suicide, anyway.'

Katherine goes pale and thinks she is going to puke. She tries hard not to picture what someone looks like when they have blown their brains out with a shotgun. Although having once seen Peter blast a rat to smithereens at close range, the image is hard to avoid.

Paudie goes on, as if talking to himself. 'Must have been lonely, poor old dickens. That man did say something about the troubles too.' He adds, almost cheerily, 'Could have been an accident, of course. You wouldn't know …'

'What troubles? He didn't have a care in the world.'

This fires Paudie up again. He shouts up to the roof of the car. 'You know nothing, do you? The civil war, girl. It was pretty bad around these parts. Whole families torn asunder. Brother shooting brother, even. Not that long ago, really. It's never properly gone away, always rumbling in the background.

15

You'd want to get wised-up on it before going into God-only-knows-what down here. You could be next! It's not known as head-hunter country for nothing, you know.'

Finally, they drive into Knocklong. The village has changed somewhat in the fourteen years since her last visit. To begin with, Katherine is disorientated. Nothing looks as she remembers it. The old stone chapel, where she used to go to Mass with her uncle, has been abandoned amongst its tumbling tombstones. They drive on up the hill to where the vast, angular structure of a new church resembles a grasshopper crouched in prayer. A new primary school is being built beside it. There are white bungalows dotted here and there like mushrooms that appear in the fields after an autumn night. Paudie drives past the few parked cars and stops right in front of the church, where people are milling around.

Mercifully, the coffin is closed. The funeral, the Mass and interment are taking place on the same evening. With the suspicion surrounding his death unresolved, Jack could not repose inside the church, but he could be brought to the open doors for some prayers to be said there, because, after all, it could possibly have been an accident, and 'nobody wants to speak ill of the dead'.

To Katherine's surprise, Paudie gets out, opens her door, and instead of saying goodbye, he walks through the crowd, nudging her in front of him.

'Come on, I can't let you go into that alone; wouldn't be right.'

Afterwards, when both of them are freezing cold, they try to find shelter in the porch. Paudie stands close beside her, as if he were her brother, hugging his jacket to his chest and nodding earnestly as people shuffle past.

A bitter evening breeze is blowing right up Katherine's

legs. She keeps her knees pressed together and holds the flaps of her coat down with her left hand. The congregation move slowly, and one by one they clutch her right hand and mumble the same mantra.

'Sorry for your troubles, ma'am.' After a while, Paudie starts shaking their hands himself, getting into conversations that Katherine is unable to decipher. Her ear is not tuned in to the Knocklong accent. All she can make out clearly is that, and 'Lord ha' mercy on him' and 'bad business', over and over again.

No one seems willing to look her in the face for more than a brief glimpse. The Ryans, who are the nearest neighbours, take up a position at her left, and they make the appropriate replies. Katherine tries to catch the gist of all their conversations. She can only grasp odd snippets. From what she can get, however, the talk is more about curiosity than sympathy. The coffin is lifted onto the shoulders of a team of pallbearers, recruited from the crowd, who slide it into the hearse. Tears roll down Katherine's face.

Jim Ryan grips her arm firmly and says, 'Sure look't girl, no one knows who their friends are till they're dead.'

Josie Ryan looks wistfully back into the church and shakes her head. She crosses herself, and her pale eyes glisten.

'Sure they don't,' she mumbles and glares briefly at her husband. Her handkerchief is fluttering as she dabs her cheeks. She gathers it up expertly in her gnarled fingers and tucks it into her sleeve.

The whole community stroll along behind the coffin as it makes its way down the hill to the new cemetery. Men, hats in their hands, lead the procession. Women with tightly tied headscarves, some pushing babies in prams and pushchairs, follow, enjoying a brief respite from the sleety rain. They chat away as if it were an afternoon outing. Paudie drives Katherine in stately solitude. The car clunks and jolts, unused to travelling at three miles an hour. It hits the tarmacadam craters in slow motion. By the time they reach the graveyard, the sun is skulking behind the trees and cutting streaks of light like a ladder on the wet road. Feeling awkward to be sharing all this with a virtual stranger and embarrassed that people might think Paudie was her husband, she tells him she can manage on her own from here and gives him a ten-pound note.

'Sure, I'll wait for the tea, anyway,' he says cheerily. 'Never know, there might be a story in it.'

'Oh, heavens, I don't think anyone has organised any tea.' She looks around, trying to imagine from whence all that might materialise. 'I'm sorry.'

'So, what will you do now, then? How about coming for a drink when this is over? I'm in no rush. I can bring you back to the airport, or wherever, you know.'

For a moment, she hesitates. It makes sense. She has no plan, and who cares really what these people think? She has an open-ended return ticket and a roll of ten-pound notes in her pocket, which Harry had handed her at Heathrow. He had squeezed her backside and said, 'Watch out for sharks, girl.' But it is her father's words that are in her head now, and she knows she will have to make some kind of an effort to find out what happened here.

'Thanks, Paudie, but I've got family business to deal with. I'll get a lift into town and worry about the rest after that. You go on before it gets dark and the roads are icy. You have a long drive ahead of you. Thanks all the same.' She is not sure if he looks relieved or sorry. Maybe it is just the way the light is fading.

He dithers for a minute, then says, 'You mean you plan to

stay here? Well, I suppose you are a grown woman. If you're sure you'll be okay?' Then, throwing a glance around the small crowd, he adds gravely, 'Mind yourself now.' He leaves her leather holdall in a puddle beside the road. 'Look't, here's a phone number where you can reach me. My mam takes messages. Call me if you get into difficulty. Anything at all.' He shakes her hand, pressing into it a small piece of card with 'Patrick Finnegan. Freelance Journalist.' and a phone number typed onto it. She slips the card into her coat pocket, feeling a mixture of comfort and trepidation. The car belches and farts as it rattles away up the road. Katherine gives a little wave before turning and facing the next part alone.

The grave has been dug in an unused corner of the cemetery just inside the boundary walls. Surrounded by bright green, virgin grass is a heap of fudge-coloured soil. Katherine stares into the rectangular hole. It looks really deep and final and isolated well away from any other graves. A few wreaths are laid out around it. The most ostentatious one overshadows all the rest. It's a huge ring of white lilies, framed by glossy ivy leaves. Katherine bends to read the card. 'From Your Loving Family'. She wonders how the flowers had arrived before she did, guilty that it wasn't she who had organised it. For an awkward few moments, a hush falls on the graveyard. A murmuration of starlings swirls in the sky above, like a black lace shroud waving goodbye.

When Father Fitzgerald steps forward, his robes flapping around in the wind, everyone closes in. They dip their heads and cross themselves. The old priest opens his prayer book and clears his throat, and they all begin to chant along with him. When he has finished, he closes the black book. He shakes some incense over the hole, lifts his head to face the crowd and says ominously, 'Let this be an end to it.'

19

People start to melt away. Katherine stands, politely bidding them goodbye while slowly losing the feeling in her freezing feet. Although they all look vaguely familiar, she has long since forgotten who is who in Knocklong. Of course, she knows the Ryans and their daughter Marie, who now has a clutch of children, huddling close. Marie's youngest brother, James Junior (always known as JJ), is standing with a group of men over by the gate. Their heads are down, and they are kicking at stones. Puffs of tobacco smoke hover between them. JJ clutches his cigarette in one hand; the other is thrust deep into his trouser pocket. The last time Katherine saw him, he was a gawky weanling whose beard was just a brown fuzz. Now he is a bulky young bull, pulling his head menacingly low between hunched shoulders. He scowls at Katherine from beneath oily curls and thick, misshapen eyebrows. He doesn't come over to talk, just nods when their eyes meet.

Katherine recognises another man in that bunch when he swings around to face her, Nicholas Molloy from the harvest dance in Knocklong many years ago. Normally, Katherine is not good at remembering names and faces, but this one, she thinks, with a tingle of embarrassment, she'll never forget. Her first kiss with a stranger; the awkward clash of teeth, the delicious frisson of passion; especially as he was twice her age and throbbed like an unwillingly bridled colt. She can still hear him crooning into her ear as he spun her around the dance floor, 'Don't worry, girl, the beast is wild, but the fence will hold!' In a dark corner of the parish hall, he had taken her hand and pressed it into his crotch so she could feel the beast. He slid his own hand up her thigh and groped the little piece of flesh between her suspenders and heaven.

Molloy drops his cigarette end, letting it fizzle out in the wet weeds. Weaving his way around the headstones, through the crowd, he saunters over to her. He nods solemnly, shakes her hand and mumbles, 'Wretched business.' There is no smile, no glimmer of acknowledgement; he hardly lifts his head, just keeps staring at his boots as if somehow they are to blame. Then, pulling his overcoat together and doing up the buttons, he walks away.

The air is saturated with the smell of dead and dying leaves. A winter fog is settling in. Katherine shivers and thinks it would be a respectable time to leave. Sorry now that she let Paudie escape, she sizes up the few cars parked outside the wall for a lift into town. Before she gets a chance to approach anyone, two things happen. First, Jim Ryan steps in front of her and insists, in a formal tone of voice, that she visit them before she returns to England.

'I will, Jim, maybe tomorrow. I haven't made any plans yet.'

'Mmm. Well, make sure you do, mind.'

Josie steers her husband away as a tall gentleman in tweeds steps up. Heads turn in her direction. He takes off his hat and his right glove and shakes Katherine's hand.

'Excuse me. Timothy Pierce, ma'am, family solicitor. Sorry for your troubles. Fine old gentleman, he was. Too bad. Too bad altogether.' He hands her his business card and then continues, 'Call to my office. Tonight would be good. We have some family business to settle. I'll be there until six o'clock.' He checks his wristwatch. 'You have plenty of time.' He bows, dislodging the strands of white hair that have been drawn across his bald scalp, and sweeps them back into place as he slips his hat onto his head. Katherine pops the card in her other pocket. For some reason, it doesn't seem appropriate to have his and Paudie's calling cards together in the same one. Divide and conquer is one of her father's many isms, coming into her mind when she least expects them.

21

Katherine glances at the last few vehicles still parked on the road beside the cemetery and asks if anyone is going to Kilkenny. An elderly couple invite her to travel with them. She climbs into the back seat and hauls her holdall in beside her. She sinks her face into the polo-neck of her pullover, breathing through the warm lamb's wool. Lulled by the sway of the car, hunger and a creeping tiredness, she is beginning to wander into dreamland. The car swerves to avoid a giant pothole. She is jolted back to the present.

'Sorry about that, missus. These roads do be desperate bad after the rains we've had lately.'

The driver's accent reminds her of Uncle Jack. It could be him, with one of his crazy bits of rhyming rhetoric like, 'There you are now, up the craggy mountain, down the valley wide, the sheep ain't lost, they're on the other side!' She had bumped her head opening the door of the car, and between the pain of that and this unexpected nostalgia over her uncle, she is overcome. She wants to cry, but in the company of complete strangers, is unable to dislodge the dry lump in her throat. Instead, she giggles and says, 'Oh, whoops-a-daisy, that was a near thing!'

Apart from some small talk about the weather and some touching memories of Jack and his family, 'when there were better days', they travel in silence until they reach the town. The driver pulls the car up in the middle of the high street. He turns around and smiles.

'Ok, missus, this is it, then—the Marble City.' Katherine thanks them both and stumbles out onto the pavement, clutching her holdall like a long-lost friend.

'Mind yourself now,' the woman says with a depth of feeling that surprises Katherine. The Morris Minor lurches away, leaving only a sooty cloud behind it. She sees it disappear into the evening mist and feels a mixture of relief and anxiety.

Even though Katherine is used to having someone telling her what to do next, it is good to be alone just now. Her mind is dithering. She pulls up the velvet collar of her coat and stamps her feet in an effort to bring them back to life. Looking up and down, she searches for something that she might recognise. Cars have now completely replaced the sturdy cobs and their various drawn vehicles that used to clop along the high street, delivering goods to all the shops. The old gas lights have become electric ones, and the shops look different too, brighter and tidier, more enclosed. Instead of turf fires and horse dung, there is a gagging, sulphurous stench of Polish coal. With a twinge of sadness, she remembers a hotel where Uncle Jack used to take her after the cattle fairs in town, where they once ate boiled meat and murdered vegetables, all smothered in brown sauce. She walks up the High Street, finds the hotel is still there, and thankfully, almost totally unchanged.

'How long will you be staying?' the elderly female receptionist asks in her gentle country lilt.

'I don't know. Tonight, anyway.' She follows the gently swinging tweed skirt and the heavy brogues down a gloomy passage past the dining room. There is a resonance of the Ursuline convent school, where she was a boarder for seven years. It is lingering amongst the odours of cabbage and floor polish. She feels the hair rising at the back of her neck, remembering how the nuns would swoosh down burnished corridors, always on some kind of mission, leaving no footprints, just guilt in their wake. The only sound they made was the clip-clop of their leather-soled shoes and the clink of rosary beads against a large ring of keys. Katherine shivers, takes her hands out of her pockets and sharpens her pace.

The room is almost completely taken up with a slab-shaped bed, padded in winter woollens and laid over with a shiny, glaucous robe, like a birthday cake without the candles. The window faces out onto a dimly lit car park. Her breath condenses in white puffs. She closes the curtains. Flopping onto the end of the bed, she looks up into the defiant face of the Monarch of the Glen, ornately framed and staring out from the centre of the wall. There is a hint of cigarettes and old socks, with a vague suggestion of lavender soap loitering about the room. The hands of nuns were always pale and blotchy from too much soap.

By the time Katherine ventures out into the street again, the pavements are perilous with glistening frost. The yellow streetlights shine like lighthouses into the freezing fog. Santa Claus grins and twinkles as he seems to dash from shop window to shop window, amongst the fairy lights and fake snow.

She wonders how it is that Christmas has come so early here. London is stately by comparison. The thought of it makes her long for orderliness and normality; the elegant curve of Regent Street, the old Manor House in Suffolk, even Harry.

Mr Pierce is obviously expecting Katherine, because his secretary, who shows her straight into the inner office, takes no time at all to produce tea and foil-covered biscuits on a round, tin tray and she knows her name.

'You look like you could do with a cup of tea, Mrs Fletcher.' She pours for both of them, slops in a dollop of milk and two spoons of sugar and stirs briskly. Then she looks directly at Katherine and says, 'I'm sorry for your loss, ma'am.'

'Thank you, Mary.' Pierce gets up and holds the door open for her. She looks back at Katherine from the doorway with an expression of motherly concern, which changes rapidly to disdain as her eyes catch sight of the knees and thighs beneath the woollen coat. Katherine shuffles about in the chair, rearranging things so they don't poke through quite as much. Up goes Mary's head and she stomps away. Mr Pierce closes the door quietly behind her. He gives a little smile as if to say, don't mind her, she means well. Katherine is glad she did not wait until the morning to see Mr Pierce, as she had been tempted to do. Now she wants to get this over with and go home first thing tomorrow.

She glances around the office, looking briefly at the faded photographs of the Kilkenny Hunt, meeting year after year on Boxing Day outside the hotel where she is staying; tall, silk top hats on the gentlemen and elegant habits on the ladies riding side-saddle.

She waits to see how it will go if he picks up the cup in his shaky hand, but he says, pointing to the tray, 'Help yourself, my dear. I've already had enough tea for one day.'

Katherine takes a cup and sips the scalding brew. They face each other across the old mahogany desk. Here and there, beneath the mounds of paper, she glimpses ink stains and circular welts scarring the age-darkened, leather surface.

'Well, now, Miss, it's good you called; messy business altogether. Still, he had a good enough old innin's. Anyway, that's that. We have some details to attend to here.'

He looks down as he speaks. His long, knobbly fingers fumble around in the manuscripts before them until he holds up a fresh-looking document. Katherine is relieved that Harry isn't with her. He would have blundered into this situation with some withering remarks about office efficiency, correct protocol and so on, making matters so much worse. He has no concept of nuance, the Irish kind that she has inherited from her father. Harry needs to be right and in control. He always has the last word.

Pierce taps his glasses back onto the bridge of his nose and glances over the parchment that is now quivering in his hands. A white-faced clock ticks steadily on the mantelpiece behind him. An orange light, diffused by cobwebs, glows through the window and, along with the one spotlight on the desk, makes strange shapes around the room. She folds her arms across her body in an effort to stop her stomach rumbling.

'Mmm, yes, mmm,' Pierce observes, before leaning back into his creaking chair. He suddenly lunges forward and thrusts the papers into Katherine's face. 'You'd best read it for yourself.'

Her eyes skate over the legal jargon without comprehending much of it. She sees her name written as Katherine ('Katie') Fletcher, née Butler. Very few people, apart from her uncle Jack and Marie Ryan, have ever called her Kate or Katie. Her mother hates short forms of anything, especially names. Georgina has tried to insist on everyone calling her daughter Katherine (after her own mother), right from the start. Bridget (the nanny, housekeeper and now indispensable family retainer) managed to take the sharp edge off it by adding 'Miss dotey little pet' onto the end, so it all sounded like one word.

'Is this my uncle's will?'

'Indeed, he made it with me here a few weeks before he … well, before he passed.' He starts picking at his fingernails, and Katherine notices, with an unexpected surge of sympathy, that one of them is already beginning to bleed around the edges. 'You'll see it's not unduly complex. You are, er, Katherine Rose Fletcher née Butler, sure you are?' He looks up briefly and, not waiting for a reply, goes on. 'John Butler, otherwise known as Jack, left everythin' to you. No other beneficiaries.'

She stares up into his face so as not to draw attention to the reddened fingers. He nods and glances across the room to where his name is painted backwards on the frosted glass window of the office door.

'A decent little farm, bit of hill and rough grazin', some tillage, perhaps, a few useful outbuildin's—in all, around the seventy acres. The dwellin' house is in need of some renovations, I would imagine. He led a simple life. The poor old divil.'

Katherine isn't really taking it in. Already her mind is wandering, picturing Uncle Jack sitting in this very chair, telling Timothy Pierce he was leaving the farm to her. His cap would have been twisted into a rope on his lap, blobs of sweat gathering on his freckled brow. She can imagine him pulling back the sleeve of his jacket to wipe his forehead with his grubby old shirt cuff; wondering if the buttons held where she sewed them on with that coarse thread you could buy in the village shop. The remains of Jack's gingery-grey hair would have been moulded to his head by the sweat and grease around the inside of his felt hat. Pierce, turning his attention back to his fingernails, mumbles on about death duties and some insurance policy that Jack had taken out to cover all that.

'I advised him myself,' he concludes, in a very satisfied tone of voice, pursing his lips and locking his hands together on the blotter. Then something pops into Katherine's head.

'But surely insurance companies don't pay up if ... well, what I mean, I suppose, is won't there have to be an inquest?'

He passes a nicotine-stained finger across his lips, leaving a faint trail of blood. The tip of his tongue slips out and licks it off. In a conspiratorial, hushed tone, he replies, 'Look't, child, the less said about all that, the better. An unfortunate—some would say even tragic—accident. The death certificate was signed. I saw to that too. No need to start any hares in the corn at this stage.' He coughs, causing his eyes to bulge. He takes a cigarette from the little silver case on the desk, taps the end of it on the back of his hand and lights it, then offers one to Katherine. She wants to be ladylike and say 'No, thank you', but her hand reaches out and takes it anyway. While leaning across the desk for a light, she inhales a strong and salty whiff from Mr Pierce. It reminds her of horses sweating in the parade ring at a point-to-point.

It isn't that Jack left the farm to her—he didn't really have anyone else, after all—but her father is a magistrate, and she knows there should be an inquest. She can sense a conspiracy, but is not able to nail it. She sucks deeply, as if by drawing the smoke into every fibre of her body, she can somehow imbibe the wisdom she will need to deal with this and everything else that is now careering towards her like a bolting horse.

'I'll make all the arrangements for you. It shouldn't be too hard to find a buyer with two strong farmers up agin' you there. Molloys, for instance—good bet, safe money; maybe Ryans? Anyways, you just sign this paper here.' A new document seems to appear like a white rabbit out of a hat.

'What's that for?'

'It's the Power of Attorney enablin' me to act on your behalf.' The sheet is pristine; the ink fresh and shining. He points the blunt end of a fountain pen towards her.

She stares at the paper and takes the pen. The nib is glinting invitingly, a wee droplet of ink beginning to form in its cloven tip. Like a hare at a gate, she sees her escape route and is about to sign, when she suddenly remembers her father's words, 'Act in haste, repent at your leisure'. Katherine stubs her cigarette into an ashtray and lays the fountain pen carefully on the desk beside it. She stands up. Using her mother's imperious tone and upper class, colonial accent, she looks him in the eye and says, 'This is all a bit sudden for me. I'm going to need time to think about things. I'll have to discuss it with my father. But thank you for your kind offer.'

She puts her hand out to meet his, shakes it and is about to reach for the door when Pierce replies, 'Don't sit on it too long—people will get suspicious, talk, that kind of a way. Could make it awkward to sell in the heel of the hunt.' His hand is on the brass doorknob. 'Better to sell and be done with it quickly, before too many gets wind of the thin'.'

His smoky breath is warming the back of her neck. He hovers there, with Katherine pinned between him and the door, for several seconds. Then he steps back a little. He pushes out his lower lip, exposing little purple capillaries, criss-crossing the pink flesh inside.

'Mmm, well, how and ever, if you're sure.' Opening the door, he moves aside and nods as she leaves the office. 'You know where to find me, anyway.'

She walks across the tiled hallway and out into the cold fog. Standing on the marble steps leading down onto the street, she has an uneasy feeling that she should have taken that sheet of paper. Her signature is easy to forge; Harry does it all the time. She knows she should have brought both that power of attorney and a copy of the will away with her. She can almost feel Harry's finger stabbing at her chest, his eyes bulging, as he shouts at her, 'You stupid girl!' Deciding to go back, she turns around, but the heavy, blue door has been closed behind her. She hears the lock turn. Dithering, she stands on the pavement, looking up and down the street at all the Georgian doorways with cracked glass fanlights and polished brass mountings. She determines to return and collect them in the morning.

Her cold feet, clad in Italian, red leather boots, begin to walk. Although it is empty, a tearoom is still open. Katherine sits down in a corner and wraps her fingers around a mug of instant coffee. A doughnut squints up at her sympathetically, with its one, jammy eye. She bites into it, feeling the sugary sweetness oozing between her teeth, hoping the raspberry seeds don't lodge themselves where she'll never be able to fish them out. The hot liquid scalds her throat. So many things plough through her mind, turning old pastures into fertile ground, where, like bindweed and redshank in wheat fields, almost any thought can grow rampantly.

She gazes out of the steamy, café window, pondering on the thought that love doesn't look or feel the way you expect it to. The vision of her uncle waving goodbye flashes back into her mind. She wonders whether she had put her arms around him and given him the hug she wants to give him now. Who knows? That was some years ago. At sixteen, you don't think much about the needs of old men.

She looks up when the waitress calls from behind the counter, 'Will that be all, missus?' The girl is ringing up the till and looking at the clock.

Katherine's legs unfold beneath the table. She stands up, smiling benignly and nods, 'Yes, thank you, that was lovely.' She leaves a ten-shilling note under the plate.

As she walks outside, smog catches her in the back of the throat. She coughs and holds a handkerchief over her mouth. Once she is safely inside the hotel, she takes a hot whiskey and a fistful of coins into the phone booth halfway up the stairs.

'Hello, Daddy? … I think I'll have to stay for a bit to sort things out … No, I don't know anything … I'll let you know when I find out … Can you tell Harry I'll ring him tomorrow? Say hi to Bridgie for me, and Mama. I love you,

Daddy. Oh God, there go the pips again. I haven't any more half-crowns, sorry. Thanks.' With that little lie still on her lips, she goes into the bar. Even though she is now past being hungry, she orders the roast beef as a gesture, a nod to better days with Uncle Jack. It looks and tastes just the same as it did back then, only now it comes with a few lettuce leaves, a sprig of parsley and a pile of chips.

Eventually, Katherine lies on her bed trying to make sense of everything that's happened today. She goes over the known facts and weighs them against various theories and possible conspiracies. Mr Pierce and the people of Knocklong are behaving like tired hounds after a day's hunting; game's over, time to lick the wounds and move on. Don't look back. She is beginning to feel a bit like that herself. 'And let this be an end to it.' Only it isn't, is it? She locks the door, rolls a small reefer and lights the twisted paper at the end.

CHAPTER TWO

The night brings a savage change in the weather. When Katherine wakes up, the world outside is being lashed by sleet and hail. The room is stuffy with the stale smell of hash. She lifts the window from the bottom, and sleet hits her in the face. She can't even see the far end of the car park, just the hotel sign thrashing about on its gibbet. Now she is wide awake and ready to tackle breakfast. The journey home starts to take shape in her head. She has an open return ticket; maybe she could ring Paudie and get him to pick her up from the train and drive her to the airport ... She knows that she needs to go to the farm and see for herself what kind of state it's in, and perhaps then she'll get inspiration. She'll have to face Mr Pierce again. Those documents will have to be retrieved. Whatever she decides to do about the farm, it needs to be her own decision, of that, she is sure. A sharp pain digs in between her ribs. She is not going to consult Harry on this one.

She doesn't fancy her chances trying to hitch out to Knocklong in this weather, so after breakfast, she asks the receptionist about taxis. At first, the woman looks blank. Katherine puts a fiver on the desk.

'Would this help?'

The woman's eyes light up, and her fingers start whizzing around the switchboard, talking to this one and that, until eventually she finds a man who will take Katherine out to the farm. She hands the fiver back to Katherine and says cheerfully, 'You'll be needing that to pay Mick O'Rourke!'

O'Rourke parks right at the front steps of the hotel and blows his horn.

'Shocking awful day, missus; where are we going?'

Katherine's hair is flailing around her face, and her coat is blowing out in all directions. She scrambles into the passenger seat and gives him the address, repeating it several times, just to be sure. The gears crunch, and the car lunges forward. Water from a huge puddle sprays up and leaks in under the door. The city streets are almost deserted. Bits of wet litter hurtle around in the wind. As they drive out into the countryside, Katherine looks at bunches of cattle crowding miserably into the corners of muddy fields on either side of the road. A small flock of sheep is marooned on an island of high ground surrounded by water. They are huddled together with their humped backs turned into the squalls of driving rain.

A dismembered branch comes scudding in front of the car. O'Rourke swerves violently, releasing a string of curses, most of which Katherine has never heard before. The car lurches out of control, ricocheting from verge to verge, finally coming to rest with the bonnet embedded in the offside bank. It's facing in the opposite direction. He steps out into the full blast of the gale, which by now is ripping the air to shreds and shouts back in at Katherine, 'Ah, Jaysus, we're beached!'

Nursing a few new bruises and with her heart still

pounding, Katherine struggles out to have a look. 'Couldn't we push it?' she yells, trying to shove her thick hair under her collar.

He looks at her with a mixture of disdain and pity and shouts, 'God, no! Are you mad, girl?' Then, with a twinge of pride, he adds, 'Sure, look't, she's nearly banked the ditch!'

The two of them set off on foot with the wind and rain chasing them fiercely from behind. O'Rourke knows of a bar nearby where they can surely get some lads to give the car the heave-ho.

'If she hasn't launched herself into a lake by then!' he jokes merrily.

Muddy liquid is becoming a fast-flowing torrent covering the road. They slosh along. In minutes, both are soaked to the skin. A van drives past, and a tidal wave splashes up their legs. A bit further on, the van stops, and O'Rourke tugs at Katherine's arm and says, 'Be Jaysus, we're made up, girl. Come on, hop in there, you.' He nudges her into the front seat and squashes himself in beside her. The three of them begin to steam with the heater rattling away on full blast.

As it turns out, the pub is a couple of miles away. The driver shouts across that his name is Fonsie Hayes. He agrees to join them for a 'quick one'. When they open the pub door, it swings back and crashes against the wall. The wind rushes in behind them, bringing with it a gush of water and dead leaves. A few old men look over and glare at them from their high-stools at the bar. Another gust slams the door shut, and the whole building quivers. Smoke from a turf fire swirls around the room. The three soaking wet figures stand and shiver as pools of water gather in the sawdust at their feet. Katherine hands O'Rourke a wet banknote. He orders whiskeys all round. He and Fonsie sink two or three of them in quick succession. Fonsie begins to quiz Katherine. The other men just keep staring. When it emerges that she is Jack Butler's niece, they all look to the ground, crossing themselves and mumbling.

Fonsie says quietly, 'Sorry for your troubles. Lord ha' mercy on him, the poor old divil.' After what seems like ages, he adds soberly, 'Come on, I'll take you the last leg of the way myself.'

Katherine tries to give O'Rourke some money for his car repairs and so on when they say goodbye, but he backs off as if she is trying to give him leprosy.

Fonsie opens his coat and stretches it over her head and shoulders. Huddling close, he hustles her out of the bar, opens the van door for her with his spare hand and when they are on the road again, he says, 'Don't mind them. Feelings run deep in these places. They don't mean any harm by it, not really.'

He knows the way. It isn't far. They drive along with just the rattle and hum of the van and the scritch-scratch of wipers, which are barely able to keep up with the torrents lambasting the windscreen. Occasionally, a question breaches the awkwardness.

'You staying long?' Before she has a chance to grapple with this one and think up an appropriate reply, he bounces on. 'London very busy at this time of year? I was there once, in the fifties, working on the buildings.'

At the mouth of the boreen, Katherine is suddenly unsure. She recognises nothing. It is all so wild and hostile. The hedges are bare, gaps exposed, and nothing is as she remembers it. Trying to picture how the van will make it down to the farm and back up to the main road again, she says, more bravely than she feels, 'You can leave me here.'

'Ah sure, not at all, may as well go the whole way now we've come this far.'

They bump along, over the rise and down the narrow, pockmarked track, towards the river. What lies ahead is almost obscured by swirling, sleety rain. The bare tops of leafless trees appear and disappear, as do glimpses of old stone buildings and the chimneys of the farmhouse. When Katherine sees that the ford is flooded and the river has taken the road, her eyes fill with tears.

'Is this it, then? How in God's name do you get to the house? I don't fancy your chances on that foot bridge! Are you sure you are going to be all right here on your own? You've seen it now, why not let me bring you home to my place and the missus'll get you a nice hot cup of tea? Then I can take you safely back to your hotel.'

For a few minutes they sit in the van, looking at an old, rickety wooden bridge. Katherine tries to weigh up the options. The vehicle is swaying a little in the wind, sleet smacking off the tin roof. She is hunched up, trying to find some solace in her soaking wet coat.

'Would you not come back tomorrow when the weather picks up a bit?'

Whiskey fumes coming in waves from Fonsie's breath frighten Katherine more than the prospect of being alone at this place in a storm. She giggles a little, nervously. Looking away, she opens the door quickly, before she has a chance to change her mind. 'You'll have to reverse up to that gateway and turn. I can go over the footbridge. Thanks very much for the lift.'

She clambers out, landing in a mushy puddle, sending freezing slop right up over the tops of her boots. A gust of wet wind wraps her hair around her neck.

'Look't, I'll come back for you in an hour or so, or you'll get pneumonia!' he shouts through the window. Relieved at the thought of this and suddenly touched by his kindness, she tells him she'll be at Ryan's next door, thanks him and turns to face the past—and the future.

The van bumps and crunches, trying to reverse into a gap. It revs up loudly in an attempt to release the back wheels from the grip of the mud, sending showers of muddy sludge spraying out behind. Finally, it lurches forward with a jerk and begins the ascent up the lane. With a bip from the horn, the van disappears over the brow of the hill and away into the gale.

Katherine slithers across the mossy footbridge, the river gushing beneath her. She has never even imagined the place like this. In bygone summers, the ford was a pebbly ripple over the road, where brickeens scooted around, glinting in the sun, and flies swarmed, vying for a place to lay their eggs on the surface of the water. Now, in spate, it is a force to be reckoned with. The words of her riding teacher pop into her head: 'Look up, heels down!' It gets her to the other side.

The house is huddled in amongst lanky ash and sycamore trees, all reaching upwards, clambering for light. Hampered only mildly by tangled branches, the wind swoops around the back of the buildings and ravages its way along the riverbank. Katherine contemplates going into the house, but a quick glance at its lifeless eyes is enough to deter her. She reaches forward to take hold of a drover's blackthorn stick. Her uncle must have left it against the wall, tucked snugly beneath the eaves of the porch. The bark is smooth from his hand's grip. It almost feels like it is still warm, as if he had just left it down for a moment while he lit his pipe or scratched his head.

Water sprays out of the gutter, which is blocked by the corpse of a dead bird and other debris. Somewhere inside the house, a door is thumping against its jamb. She cannot believe she was foolish enough to let Fonsie drive away and leave her here alone. Those brave notions she had this morning, to go out there, question the locals, assess the situation and so on … have melted away. Now she just wants to go home. She tries to shelter there in the porch. Her mind is working on contingency plans. The icy rain pouring off the roof is spraying everywhere and going down her neck. She wonders how long she would be waiting for a lift back to town if she walked up to the main road and stuck out her thumb. She can't even picture how you get to Ryan's from here. It's all so long ago, so different.

Even though she is freezing cold and the rain has seeped right through all her layers of clothing and is chilling her bones, some unseen force seems to be holding her enthralled. She is trying to transpose her memories of a jolly, bustling little farmyard in midsummer, wild flowers popping up everywhere, bees and butterflies and the tinkle of shallow water, onto this bleak and hostile scene. Nothing matches. Now all this is her problem. She knows that, somehow, she will have to deal with it.

A walleyed collie creeps out from the shadows and approaches, keeping close to the ground, hugging the buildings on its way round. It crouches at her feet, wagging its tail, but at the same time curling back its top lip, showing crusty teeth. It looks up at her, hungry and abandoned. Katherine bends down, and the thick, oily coat warms her hands. The panting breath smells of dead rats. As she looks around her, she notices tyre tracks in the mud like rivulets that are spitting back rain. They are swirling about in all directions as if from three-point turns, maybe several different sets of tyres, perhaps even a small tractor. Her head starts to spin. The tracks come alive and twirl in front of her. She steadies herself with one hand on the edge of a stone trough, from which the water is splashing over. The other hand is resting on the dog's head. It is panting gently, reassuringly. Scanning the farmyard, her eyes are drawn towards the cow byre. She stares into that gaping, toothless mouth and tries to beat off thoughts of her uncle going in there for the last time, holding his loaded shotgun.

A sudden lash of wind catches a gate and clatters it against the stone pillar behind her.

'You came, then.'

Katherine whips round. Jim Ryan is standing in the gateway. He is leaning forwards, struggling with a bale of hay slung over his shoulders. He has a bucket of meal in the other hand. At the sound of his voice, two white-faced cattle poke their heads out over a shed door on the other side of the yard. A black cow moos through a hole in the wall, its face shining from the rain cascading off the roof. He drops the bale and sets the bucket down beside it.

'Someone had better feed them few cows. No sense in leaving them to starve.'

Katherine sits on one corner of the bale.

'You may get off that now, before it gets full of muddy water.'

'Oh yes, sorry. I just …' She retreats into the porch and watches Jim as he swings from one shed to the next, dispensing fodder, wondering if she should be helping him, but knowing that would be ridiculous. A couple of crows swoop down from their lookout in the trees and snatch up the odd grains, then lurch once more, swaying into the gale.

For a brief moment, the wind subsides, the rain stops and, from beneath a heavily bruised sky, the low sun slices sharply across the yard. Wet branches, slated roofs and pools of water are lit up vividly and gleam with an orange glow. A perfect rainbow is set in a shallow arc over the farm. There is another reflected faintly above it, with the colours going in the opposite direction; red on the inside and violet fading out on the upper rim. Katherine stares at it, wondering how she has never noticed that before.

'Come on, girl, you're coming with me.' Jim catches her by the arm and shoves her through the gate, swinging it shut behind them. He herds her along the riverbank. Once they leave the farm, the wind begins to rev up again. It licks the surface of the water into waves and cows the saplings along the far side so violently that they are forced to dip their heads and kiss the swell. Katherine's urban, leather boots slip and squelch in the mud. Her coat billows out behind her like a sail, tugging her backwards. She bends into the wind, catching clumps of turf to steady herself as she scrambles up the bank, onto a stone bridge and out on the road behind Jim. By this time, she is not only soaking wet and shivering but also weak with hunger. The last few hundred yards along the tarred road are a blessed relief. Eventually, the Ryans' house comes into view.

A bunch of raggedy cats lurk around the back door, looking for a chance to dive into the kitchen. The same straw mats, boots and general debris litter the porch as they always did. The face of Jesus with his Sacred Heart, exposed and bleeding, is still on the wall to greet those who enter; only now, at the right hand of Christ, sandwiched between him and the new pope, smiles the tanned face and white teeth of

John F Kennedy. Each is illuminated by its own flickering red bulb.

Josie is in her den, humming. She thwacks a wooden spoon against the inside of a mixing bowl, pounding dough. A dog growls from between her legs. She gives it a kick, and it cowers back behind the door. When she hears them come in, she wipes her hands on her thighs and puts both arms out to greet Katherine.

'Well, will you look at yourself? Come here to me, girl, till I get those wet things off you. You're like a half-drowned cat what's been pulled from the river!' Josie peels the wet outer garments from a shivering Katherine and drapes them skilfully on chairs in front of the range. She wraps an old coat around Katherine's shoulders and folds her into an empty seat. In no time, Josie has swept the papers and rubbish into the corner of the table and laid out a rudimentary meal. Hot tea permeates Katherine's insides. Josie is a 'feeder'; everyone knows that. She plies bread, eggs and chunks of greasy bacon into Jim and Katherine until they are exhausted from eating.

Suddenly, Jim throws his cap onto the table, spinning a crust into the waiting jaws of the hungry dog, which darts forward and catches it on the wing. 'It's true he left it to you, then?'

Katherine, bewildered by this sudden attack, turns to Josie for help, but Josie, having had a good idea what was coming, has retreated to the far side of the table and is moulding her dough into loaf shapes, keeping her eyes down. Jim seizes his chance and goes on. 'Look't, girl, we'll give you a fair price for the place.' He grabs his cap, punches it with his fist and then he slaps it over his knee. 'I can't say better than that!'

Katherine is beginning to shiver again and longs to be

curled up out of sight on an old blanket beside the range, like the dog. Keeping her eyes focused on the oilskin table cloth, she replies, 'Thanks, Jim, you've been very kind. I don't know what I'm going to do yet. I'll have to go back into town and talk some more with Mr Pierce. He said something about Molloys and other neighbours being interested as well. He must mean you, I suppose.'

Already Katherine thinks she's stupidly shown her hand too soon, and she can hear Harry chastising her for not keeping her cards closer to her chest.

Jim grunts. 'Bah, that Pierce and his fancy ways. Tell your Mr Pierce from me that I can match any of his offers!'

'I don't know if I want to sell the place yet.' It just slipped out, as if from nowhere.

'Ah sure, in God's name, don't be daft, girl! What would a hippie like you be wanting with the place? I need it.' Then, changing his tone a bit, he goes on, more gently, 'I ask you this, what did Molloy or any of the other neighbours ever do for Jack Butler, only pester him senseless to get out of the place? If he'd wanted Molloy to have it, he'd have gev it to him, or sold it to him, while he was still able. He could have spared himself, and you, a rake of hardship.'

'And maybe he'd still be with us, the poor old divil,' Josie chips in, while putting the bread into the oven. She farts when she bends down and smacks her backside with her spare hand, as if it were a bold child. Jim seems to take this as a signal to ease off.

'Maybe he didn't care what happened in the finish of it. Either ways, he hardly expected you to live there and farm it yourself, did he now?'

'Well, he took that to the grave with him, and now it's between him and our Lord,' Josie adds firmly, 'and you won't be long after him, girl, if you don't get right into bed and stay there. I never saw anything look as poorly as you do this minute!'

Whereupon Katherine chunders into the ash bucket.

What follows is a bleary haze to Katherine. She sweats and shivers in Marie's old attic bedroom at the back of the Ryans' house. Josie puffs up and down the stairs to her with hot-water bottles and watery soup for some days. Katherine is only vaguely aware of her coming in and out with trays, laying freezing cold hands on her brow and rearranging the bedclothes. She thinks a doctor might have come at some stage. She's not sure, because in that lost time, Katherine hallucinates. It is a strange bioscope of images, like Jack, pleading into a void, aching with anxiety. He is not the jolly, twinkly eyed farmer she remembers him to be, but hollow cheeked and gaunt. Things aren't right. He is out of his depth and frightened. Her father is there too, looking the other way while some kind of war is raging all around him. Her mother, the passive observer, laughs emptily. Worst of all are the fits of uncontrollable rage, in which Katherine repeatedly smashes bits of antique furniture over Harry's head. No matter what she does or how much she hits him, he just remains infuriatingly calm, picking up the pieces and arranging them neatly into a pile, where they rematerialise as sheep, hopping out through an open window. Eventually, the torments subside, giving way to peaceful sleep.

Katherine is roused by a distant bell calling early Mass and the sounds of the farmyard waking up. A cockerel repeats his reveille in urgent bouts. Bit by bit, the whole farm joins in, encouraged by dogs yapping, geese honking and hungry calves bawling. An outburst of gaggling from the turkey shed drives the cacophony to a rousing crescendo, orchestrated by Jim and Josie. They are clanking around with buckets of meal, shouting at each other and the animals, more out of habit than anger. Their fighting days are done. The farm is a graveyard of buried hatchets. In the main, they crank along together like cogs in a mill wheel, no highs, no lows, just an endless intermeshing, one keeping the other turning.

She lies still, listening to the world below. Her eyes are getting accustomed to the light. Gradually, the pieces come together and a picture takes shape. There are more questions than answers. Inevitably, she thinks of Harry and how it would be if he was here now. What would he do? With a familiar sense of panic tinged with relief, she knows that he would be agitating to get her out of here and on the next plane home. She looks at her watch to find the date, but being unwound for days, it has stopped ticking.

She longs to talk to someone from home, Bridget perhaps. Bridget is always the loving voice of reason. She is the only person in the world that Katherine feels completely safe with, now that Jack has gone. She wonders if the telephone is working in this house. Would they let her ring home? But what could she say? She is not ready to give up. She scrabbles around in the murky places at the back of her head, trying to find an object of certainty. Her eyes circle the room for clues. She knows the place now. It is where she and Marie used to hide out and pretend to be lost orphans, waiting for the cruel man to come and find them and drag them away to an institution, to live like Oliver Twist. They taunted each other with visions of how bad things could possibly be, until eventually hunger and the smell of Josie's baking would always bring them back to reality. For now, though, it must be the map of mould on the wall and the smell of urine from the cracked chamber pot in the corner that induces a sudden flashback to her honeymoon.

Sorrento, 1964, five years ago. That room had smelt faintly of damp and stale piss as well. They were on the fourth floor of what called itself a four-star hotel. The magnificent view of the Bay of Naples must have been on the other side of the building. Harry refused to let Katherine do the bookings, even though her Italian, albeit a little rusty, had been more or less fluent at one time. When they arrived, he was so anxious to get down to business that he couldn't be bothered about complaining; he could deal with all that later. It was a sultry September evening; a thunderstorm welling up, with purple clouds lying on the terracotta rooftops. The full-length window was wide open, and a net curtain billowed into the room on the tail end of a breeze, which was blowing up from the sea. Harry mounted, naked, but for a pair of French knickers around his neck. He was squealing and grunting like a rutting boar and trying to hold Katherine's legs over his shoulders. As she clung onto the side of the bed, she happened to glance out of the window. The street was narrow, and directly opposite, standing on a little wrought iron balcony, an old woman was staring at them. Just for a fleeting moment, Katherine can recall the woman's wry smile. She winces at the memory of young love. Those were the days when her mission, her one goal, was to please her man. Nothing else came near.

Katherine stretches down into the bed. Her foot touches and then recoils from the cold rubber of last night's hot-water bottle. The room is dimly lit through a crack between the heavy curtains. Her hand pats the bed and rests when it feels her clothes, laundered and folded neatly on the frayed and faded patchwork quilt. She pulls them on quickly without getting out of bed. A trick she learned as a small child, in their

freezing manor house on the Suffolk coast. Standing on the
lino beside the bed, her legs weak and her feet tingling, she
tries to get her bearings. She looks for a mirror, but it's on the
other side of the room. Anyway, there is no place in her life
now for daubing and scraping or plucking, manicuring and
false eyelashes. They belong in the other world. She tries to
unravel her hair with her freezing cold fingers, but gives up
and rolls it into a knot at the nape of her neck.

She pulls the cover from the bed, wraps it around her
shoulders and goes tentatively down the wooden steps from
the attic and across the dark landing. Holding the banister
rail with her spare hand, she descends the final staircase. She
stands silently on the bottom step, a little nervous about
opening the door into the kitchen. The radio is on, and there
are voices too. She waits until she hears a door closing and
guesses that Jim and JJ have gone out to attack the farm.

'Well! Will you look at you, all up and dressed and
everything, and not even a sup of tea brought up to you?'
Josie comes towards her with welcoming arms. 'How are you
at all? You need to take it easy now, you've been very poorly.
For God's sake, don't overdo it, or you'll be back in that bed
again before you could say "Bonjarvey".' Josie opens the oven
and takes out two loaves. A swirl of hot steam briefly fills the
room, along with the intoxicating smell of roasted wheat. She
drops them into tea towels and wraps them tightly, leaning
them up against the side of the breadboard to let the air
circulate beneath them. She is facing the window, sawing at
the heel of yesterday's loaf and pouring tea.

While not having to look Josie in the eye, Katherine takes
her chance. 'I've made up my mind, Josie. I've decided to stay
at the farm, at least for a while, anyway. It seems like destiny.
I want to give it a go. I need to know what happened to my

uncle. I think I might get a better sense of it if I stay there and try to feel the vibes.' She can feel her heart pounding. Even to her, this pronouncement doesn't ring true.

Josie turns towards her and puts down the cup and plate. Leaning her weight on her two hands, she shakes her head slowly from side to side. Bits of chaff fall onto the table. She purses her lips and makes a soft moaning sound. Shaking some more hay out of her grey curls, she mumbles, 'In God's name, child, you can't be in your right mind. That is just so much as I rove out! Here, drink your tea and eat a cut of bread. Vibes, indeed! You'll get plenty of those in that place.' She sits down opposite Katherine and looks at her and then past her to the door, as if willing the men not to come in right now.

'If I do decide to sell, I'll give Jim the first refusal.' She steadies herself on the edge of the table. 'Well, anyway, I'm going to think some more about it before I go back to London. I need to make a proper plan.'

'Take care of yourself, for God's sake; you know things aren't always … Well, good luck to you, girl. That's all I can say now.' The farmer's cracked mug looks all wrong in those fine-boned, pale, white hands.

'Would you not stay here with us, at least until you are on your feet again?'

'It's very good of you, Josie, especially after you have been so kind to me already. But you know what they say in the Girl Guides, "giving in is giving up"! I must go back to the farm and try to find out what has been going on there.' Unsure of her feet, she walks around the table, holding on with one hand. 'My father will never forgive me if I don't.'

Josie has closed her eyes and is swaying gently from left to right, muttering, 'You don't have any idea what you are blundering into over there. In the name of Jesus, come to your senses, girl, while you still have the chance. A farm isn't just for Christmas, you know!'

At this, Katherine sits back into the chair. Her eyes are smarting.

Josie sits opposite her and reaches across the table for Katherine's delicate, little hands. 'What do you hope to find out, anyway? The death certificate was signed, you know that. It's hard to think about, but Jack Butler took his own life. That's an end to it, really.' After a respectful pause, she goes on briskly, 'Anyways, look't, if you are determined to go back there, come over if you … well, if things … you know what I mean. You are always welcome here, whatever, sure, you know.' She pushes the plate of buttered bread towards Katherine, who eats without much relish.

She finishes the sweet tea and looks up at Josie. 'Do you think I could borrow a pair of wellingtons?'

Josie puts one of the fresh loaves, butter and a few eggs, along with milk in an orange squash bottle, into a Bolland's biscuit box and hands it to Katherine.

'You're welcome to them. Take Marie's, and take these with you too. And remember, the door's always open here. Don't mind Jim, his bark is worse than his bite.' She adds, mumbling and turning away, 'Just watch out for the others.' As Katherine is putting her feet into Marie's gumboots, Josie remembers something. 'Fonsie Hayes called for you the day you came in here. He said he was to give you a lift back into town. He had a fill of whiskey in him, so I told him you weren't here.'

Jim drives Katherine back to the farm in the Morris Minor and parks at the edge of the ford. The water has subsided a good deal since last week, but still he won't risk his car. She lets him cross the bridge first, unsure if it will take the weight of both of them at once. He sets about feeding the animals. The crows are squawking and squabbling in their high roosts above the house. Apart from that and the mooing of cows, grateful to see fodder coming their way, the place is still and quiet. A wispy fog floats over the river and drifts out along the valley. The mud in the yard is frozen into crisp peaks. The bright morning sun gives her courage. She tries the kitchen door. It yields inwards with a whine. She stumbles and nearly falls down a shallow step into the shadows. Katherine stands, motionless, for a few minutes. There is a strong smell of damp soot. Water is dripping into a stone sink in the back kitchen. Tap, tap, tap. The light, from low in the sky, shines directly in through the window opposite the door, catching dust she has disturbed from the flagstone floor. She moves a little further inside. Shivers ripple down her spine, starting at the nape of her neck and running right through her. The dog is breathing warm air onto the back of her leg.

Jim startles them both. From the open door, he shouts, 'Right you are, then, all done. I'll be over later to feed 'em again, after the dinner. Sure you won't come on back with me now? It's not too late to change your mind and see some sense.' She draws breath to answer, but he nods in the general direction of the farmyard and quickly goes on, 'Well, good luck now, missus, and if you needs help before you goes back t'England, you know where we are.' He is in the room now and right beside her. She can feel the warmth from his body and smell the years of farming beneath the freshly laundered Sunday shirt. His eyes are scouring the room. His heavy, smoke-filled lungs are wheezing in the damp air.

'I do, Jim, and thank you for your help. It's really cool. I expect I'll be over later.' She giggles nervously as usual. The collie is crouched behind Katherine now, pressing itself against her leg. Jim stuffs his cap onto his head and ducks slightly as he backs out through the doorway, skilfully avoiding tripping over the step. Katherine asks him, 'By the way, Jim, what is the dog's name?'

'That one? Never known as anything, only Katie.'

CHAPTER THREE

Katherine stands in the kitchen, clutching Josie's warm parcel. The only parts of her that seem to be working are her eyes, her beating heart and her muddled memories. Her limbs have lost their willingness to move, and if her breath was not visible in pale white puffs before her eyes, she could nearly believe she's stopped breathing too.

Jack's chair by the range, like the form of a hare in a summer meadow, is still holding the shape of his body; but it gives no clues about what was going through his head. His faded tartan slippers, the impression of feet pressed into them, await his return. Katherine studies the strange way they have been left, not side by side and the right way up, more like they have been kicked off in a hurry. Or in a rage. Or moved subsequently?

The dog is panting loudly with her tongue hanging from the corner of her mouth. Katherine bends down. She breaks off a small corner of bread and offers it. The dog sniffs it warily as if she fears being poisoned by strangers, but hunger drives her, and she takes it from Katherine's hand. Skulking into a dark corner of the room, she wolfs it down in several gulps, then laps up the milk that Katherine pours into a tin bowl. Droplets of white spray onto the flagstones. The bell for the midday Angelus is ringing in the distance.

Gradually, Katherine begins to wander around, feeling like a voyeur poking through the detritus of her uncle's life, picking things up and putting them back down again. There are all kinds of boxes in piles here and there. Memories start to come back to her as she uncovers little snippets of his life. Jack had many intriguing ways to beat the system. He didn't like to throw anything away. 'You never know, like the ten good virgins, when everything will be called in.' For instance, keeping his beer-bottle tops to flatten them out with a hammer and use them for fixing holes in the soles of his working boots. The empty bottles he stored up and took back to the pub, where each one could be turned in for a thruppenny bit, a down-payment on another pint to bring home and drink while he listened to the shipping news, dreaming of faraway places like Rockall or Finisterre.

Foreign postage stamps had been his favourite treasures. Most of them carried a solemn depiction of the British monarch, King George, 'that fine-looking man with the dithery voice'; or, more recently, the profile of a 'fresh-faced young queen wearing the crown, as if she'd been born in it'. Stamps had a magic quality. For a few pennies, that expressionless profile guided home the news of Jack's diaspora of brothers and sisters, living in the wide reaches of the Commonwealth. Envelopes would arrive in the post, enclosing sheets of fine, blue paper, covered with the evenly spaced and beautifully symmetrical flows of ink. Stories of children and grandchildren, new and better houses, bushfires, floods and hurricanes, the price of lambs and fleeces or descriptions of machinery used to harvest the Canadian prairies. Some very lyrical prose, like how an Australian sunset looked when it glowed through the corn dust. Some were illustrated with primitive sketches of wild animals and exotic birds. Josie read the letters to Jack over a cup of tea. They usually finished with the fond wish to return home someday. One by one, as his siblings lost interest in home, or perished in their new lands, the letters dwindled and, eventually, stopped coming altogether. Some of them still have the smudges of cow shit and rhubarb jam from Jack's thumbs and fingers, which folded them neatly and placed them into rusting biscuit tins. Josie held the secrets of Jack's family close to herself, where they merged with all the other confidences that the people of Knocklong, for whom schooling had failed, bestowed upon her; while she plied them with cups of tea. All these tales eventually melted into a compost heap in the back of her brain.

The less frail, brown envelopes that brought bills and government bulletins, farming regulations and so on, Jack saved for storing small objects like stray buttons and pieces of labels from feed bags, or dockets from the creamery and green shield stamps, of which he had thousands. These, more prosaic, envelopes were stowed in cardboard boxes. Some, laced by paper worms and snails, fall into small pieces when Katherine lifts them; the rest are slowly moulding into oblivion in corners of the kitchen. He used to fold up scraps, like dud sweepstake tickets and small paper bags, and stuff them into empty sardine tins. When well-soaked in fish oils, he would tie them into bundles with rubber bands to be used as mini fire-bombs with which to light the range. Binder twine, saturated as it once was in creosote, was wound into ropes and twisted up to form little knots. They bubbled

53

and fizzed any damp twigs or turf into a quick blaze. The butt ends of candles, which had been a lifesaver during the endless power cuts that occurred every time the wind blew too strongly, or the linemen went on strike, would be placed into empty matchboxes on the back of the range. There, they melted down into incendiary devices that could be stacked neatly in Fig Roll wrappers and stored for use in the cold, dark days of winter. Josie often joked that if farmers ever have to keep accounts and pay taxes like everyone else, there'd be some fun retrieving any evidence from Jack Butler!

There is no sign of Jack's stash of firecrackers now. Apart from mouldy boxes and biscuit tins, so rusty that the lids are welded on, all Katherine can see are random piles of stuff littering every surface. Rancid butter papers, used matches, sliced-pan wrappers—some tortured into weird shapes, dotted here and there all over the place. It is like the *Marie Celeste*, as if he had just walked out and would be back at any minute. In the centre of the table, an egg-smeared teaspoon stands to attention where it has harpooned the empty shell. She folds the waxed bread papers, smoothing them out with her fingers, shaking dried-up mouse droppings onto the floor, wondering vaguely why Josie and Marie hadn't cleaned the place up.

The range is stone cold. There are little rodent footprints in a pile of ash on the weeping flagstones. Teardrops of moisture glisten on the cast-iron range. Katherine leans across and peers into a pot at the back—something is fermenting within. She recoils from the stench and quickly replaces the lid. The frayed remains of a gingham curtain jump around in the draught that is blowing in through a crack in the window. She remembers Bridget sewing those curtains on Josie Ryan's treadle Singer one summer evening while they all sang romantic ballads in the parlour. Jack had thumped the floor with his right foot and whooped 'fine girl, ye'are!' while Josie pounded on the piano and the sewing machine clattered and whirred. The girls used to swirl around the room, flinging their legs in the air, like fairies in a spring wind.

Katherine's eyes keep going back to the armchair, glazed with a fine dusting of green mould. She can almost feel him crumpled into it, as he stared into the hearth; his long legs stuck out in front of him, his big toes forcing their way through the tips of his worn-out socks and slippers. She lights a cigarette and sits on a wooden seat with a wobbly back leg. As she exhales, the smoke is sucked towards the chimney and snakes up into the darkness. Then it occurs to her, if the cigarette smoke will go up there, so will smoke from a fire. She jumps up, gathers the waxed papers from the table and stuffs them into the grate, grovels around in a butter-box in the corner for some bits of turf and a few twigs and is glad of her old Zippo to set fire to it all. It heaves and belches out clouds of smoke before settling down to a dim smoulder.

Using a piece of cardboard for a shovel, Katherine scoops the ashes into a bucket and heads out into the yard to look for something more substantial to burn. She is startled to find a white and blue Ford Anglia parked at the far side of the river, with two uniformed Gardaí sitting inside it. They seem surprised to see her too, and one of them jumps out of the car and approaches via the footbridge. He holds up his right hand.

'Garda Sergeant Dawson, ma'am. Are you, or have you seen, Mrs Katherine Fletcher?' The use of her married name stings like a warning.

'Yes, that's me. Is something amiss?' All kinds of thoughts are rushing through her head. Something wrong at home, or have the neighbours put the police onto her as a way of getting her to go away? Is it some new information about Jack's death, perhaps? What has she done wrong?

'You could say that.' A rueful smile creeps across his jaw as he eyes her small frame, from her fiery red hair down to Marie Ryan's huge wellington boots. 'You've caused quite a commotion. Where have you been for the last week?' he shouts, moving carefully on the slippery boards, clutching the hand rail.

Apparently, when Katherine didn't return to the hotel after two days, they had notified the Gardaí. She had neither checked out nor paid the bill. Now she is officially a missing person. The Gardaí didn't concern themselves too much with this at first, assuming from the description the receptionist had given that she was a dizzy hippy gone walkabout. She'd turn up sooner or later. However, when Harry returned from his business trip in Manchester and found that Katherine had not been in touch with the family since the day of the funeral and no one seemed to know where she was, he began to kick up a fuss.

A bunch of bullocks are pushing and shoving at the gate on the other side of the yard, bellowing. Everything in her life has changed, and she forgot to tell her husband. The bullocks are jostling each other, snorting steam clouds. She wonders if the gate will hold them in. She knows that once roused, nothing will hold Harry Fletcher back.

Dawson had called out to the farm several times only to find the place deserted. He had apparently tried Ryans', but they were tight-lipped. Katherine was their secret hostage. Spurred on by the superintendent in Kilkenny, who was by this time getting twice-daily telephone calls from England, they had planned to start house-to-house searches today. A team of volunteers is ready to begin investigating the river, as if tragic deaths run in the family.

'You'd better come along with me and sort out some of the problems you've left in your wake, girl. You can phone from the barracks and let your husband know that you're okay, and then I imagine someone can take you back to your hotel.'

'It's okay, thanks, I can phone from the hotel.'

'You don't know who might be listening in on that line. No, we'll stop into the barracks on the way. Safer all round.'

~

Despite the high ceiling and formidable, dark wooden counter, the Garda barracks in Knocklong is a cosy little place. There are lots of notices on the walls about such things as bicycle lamps, sheep-dipping regulations and so on. It is the notice about gun licenses that draws Katherine's eye particularly. Images come rushing into her head: the cow byre, blood on the walls. She wants to ask if they know yet what really happened, but she hears her father's voice in her head: 'Hold your whisht, girl.' She says nothing.

Two uniformed officers are sitting in armchairs in front of a coal fire, drinking mugs of tea and toasting their stockinged feet. They look around and nod. Some newspapers are strewn about. She sees the headlines: 'Heiress Goes Missing.' There is an old and almost unrecognisable photograph of her trying to look mature and serene. Glancing at it, she remembers it is the one that was taken by a studio photographer in Ipswich, on the announcement of her engagement to Henry Fletcher. Georgina had wanted to give the impression that her only child was marrying well. Katherine cringes.

Sergeant Dawson is working his way through the various telephone exchanges to get a line to England. He hands the receiver across the counter to Katherine.

'There you are—it's ringing.'

'Hello? Harry? Is that you? It's a really bad line … Yes, I'm fine now, but I've been laid up with some kind of … What? … Yes … Yes, I know … Well, this is going to take a bit of sorting out.' She can feel the ears in the room all tuned to her every word, straining to hear Harry's end of the conversation as well, which isn't hard because he is shouting. She remembers the phone closet in the hotel; it can hardly be less private than this one. 'Harry, look, I really can't hear you, it's a terrible line … don't freak out … I'm sorry. I'll ring you when I get back into town … Yes … Bye for now.'

Sergeant Dawson hands her a cup of tea, stirs in two heaped spoons of sugar and nudges a packet of Kimberly Micados across the counter towards her. 'You look like you could do with a good feed.' He offers to drive her into town to sort out her affairs with the hotel.

The receptionist shows no surprise to see Katherine, just smiles politely, gives her the bill and calls a lad to bring out the bag. Dawson, who has followed her into the lobby, takes the holdall back to his car and opens the passenger door for her, nodding to her to get in. They whizz along, the windscreen wipers scraping back and forth, moving the mucky mist, which is spraying up out of thawing puddles, from one side to the other and back again, leaving rainbows of dirt.

'You not staying in town, then? You're hardly going back to that farm on your own? How will you manage? I imagine your husband is coming over to sort things out?' And finally, 'Would you not be nervous, a girl on your own in that place?' He looks around at her as if expecting her to wince.

'Should I be?'

He shrugs his shoulders and glances in the mirror before

turning into Knocklong. They pass the Sunnyhill ruins. She wants to ask him about it, but something stops her.

'That depends. Some would be very nervous. Some would have reason to be, too.' He pulls up outside the village shop. 'You'll be needing a few messages before you go back up there, then. I'll wait here for you.' He lights a cigarette, winds down the window and watches the smoke dissipate slowly.

It seems that the entire population of Knocklong is staring at her as she struggles back out to the Garda car with her shopping under both arms. Katherine nods hither and thither, thinking it best to try to be friendly at least. Dawson leans across and opens the car door for her. After a few bangs and chugs, the car starts up again, and they pull away from the curb.

Of course, everyone knows well who she is, and each has their own version of the story. Jack Butler shot himself after discovering he couldn't pay his bills anymore; was drunk and fell over his shotgun while trying to kill rats; had some kind of accident doing target practice for shooting stray dogs; perhaps, he was murdered by intruders looking for beer money, for such things did happen; or worse, in whispered tones, by someone in the locality with an old grudge. If the IRA is mentioned, all go silent.

The postmistress knows more than most people. As the one in charge of the main switchboard, she receives, intercepts and redirects all the telephone calls in and out of the village, including those from the Garda station. But she has learned the wisdom of holding her tongue. They were all at the funeral, had shaken the soft, white and manicured hands that now clutch brown paper bags in the passenger seat of the panda car speeding into the distance. They had all peered briefly into those green eyes and thought how like her uncle she looked, same red hair, same freckles; but oh, what a hippy; how exotic. And that mini skirt!! Here today, gone tomorrow. Everyone is still asking, 'What will become of the farm?' Now this one is doing her shopping and wearing wellington boots, like anyone else. Surely, she can't be thinking of staying out there, in that place, on her own? They all now know that Katherine is the daughter of a very wealthy man who grew up in Knocklong like the rest of them, but that he disappeared to England after the civil war, when the going got really rough. There is plenty of talk about how he really made his money and similar amounts of outrage that, after all they had fought for, he took a knighthood from the British queen. It was in all the local papers, when Katherine had gone missing. Some stringer had picked up the story, and it had made it into the national news.

Sergeant Dawson, bobbing along behind the steering wheel, feels the need to mediate in some way between Katherine and the wagging tongues. The long hairs in his red ears are almost twitching.

'Bit of an ordeal, that? You'll have to get used to that kind of thing if you intend staying around here at all. You are a bit of a celebrity. Don't worry; it'll wear off in time, you know; if you last that long, of course.' He splashes straight over the ford, spraying the river right up to the windows. With the engine coughing and spitting water, he yanks on the handbrake in the yard, jerking all the groceries onto the floor. As Katherine is grovelling around, trying to gather them up again, he slides his hand along her thigh and breathes onto her neck. 'Need any help there?'

'No, thank you, I'm fine! Thanks for driving me around. No need to get out. I can manage.' Grabbing her holdall and most of the shopping, she bolts from the car, leaving a few baked bean tins rolling around in the soggy footwell.

She doesn't turn back. She just opens the kitchen door with her shoulder and kicks it shut behind her. Leaning against the inside of it, she listens. The car engine begins revving its way out of the mud and eventually fades off up the lane, leaving Katherine with a thumping heart and shaking hands.

She relives Harry's part of the conversation in the Garda station. 'What on earth is going on? Your parents are frantic with worry. I can't let you stay there on your own. You're letting me down. You've abandoned me. What are you playing at?' He would probably have said a lot more if she had not cut him short; something she could only do with the safety of the Irish Sea between them. She is glad she didn't call him from the relative privacy of the hotel phone booth. She might have weakened and appealed to him for support, asked his advice even.

Something in his tone of voice reminds her now sharply of the one time she was pregnant. Harry really didn't want children until he had established himself more securely, if he even wanted them at all. He said he needed his wife to be able to look after herself by day and him by night, not throwing up every morning and bursting into tears all the time. As it happened, she had tripped and fallen down the great oak staircase in the manor house, breaking her arm. Sometime later, she had a day of agonising cramps and a small dead baby slipped into her hands over the toilet bowl. From that dark day, through weeks of lonely tears, eventually, life returned to normal; although never quite the same. It wasn't spoken of again.

She resolves to write to Harry later on tonight, when she has got the place sorted out a bit. She knows, however, that the lack of writing paper won't be the only reason why she puts it off.

The range has gone out. Lighting it again proves a lot more troublesome than before. She has used most of the bread wrappers, and all the remaining kindling is too damp to raise more than a sad whimper in the grate. She blows into the firebox, trying to coax a spark out of the dying embers. More smoke goes into her lungs than up the chimney. Coughing, she flops into the armchair, which smells of mildew, making her gag again. Katherine shivers and shrinks inside her woollen overcoat, trying to imagine herself in a better place; probably sitting by the Aga in the manor house, drinking tea and joking around with Bridget, or maybe swinging merrily down the Kings Road, looking in shop windows. She gives it another go, kneeling in front of the range with a folded hessian sack between her thin knees and the cold flagstones. She tries to blow the last bit of oxygen from her hegging chest into the obstinate lump of rusty old cast-iron.

The kitchen door swings open. 'Well, praying to that thing won't bring it to life, you daft girl.'

Although by now the evening is drawing in and the room is full of smoke, she can just make out JJ Ryan standing on the threshold.

'Come inside. Don't stand there letting in more cold air.'

'Better to let some of that smoke out. What are you doing in here, anyway? That old range is bet out. What are you wasting your time at it for? That uncle of yours was forever messing with it, trying to humour the bloody yoke. God only knows what's stuck up that chimney.' He moves a little closer and peers up into it over her shoulder. The smoke makes him cough violently. He leans out of the door and hocks phlegm into the yard.

'I have the animals fed, and I'm heading on home now.

Mam sent these over for you.' He holds out a billycan of milk, another hunk of bread wrapped in a cloth and a golden ingot of butter, folded neatly into greaseproof parchment. When he sees her tears, he says, 'Ah there, don't be crying, now.'

'I'm not. It's the smoke getting into my eyes,' she lies.

'Oh. I saw on the paper where you're an heiress? Quite the star, now! I suppose you don't need money. Is that what's on you that you won't sell?'

'It isn't to do with money. This was my father's family home, and I feel I should …' Even to her own ears, this sounds unconvincing.

'Hah! Some family home! Bloody misery, that's all it is, and all it'll ever be.'

'Well, if it's so miserable, why should you or anyone else want it so badly?'

'That's different. Don't you know, girl, land is land, whatever; and it belongs to the people what's gonna farm it.'

'It's more than just a piece of land to me.'

'There isn't anything more than land! We'll soon see how you feel about it after a few weeks of bone-shrinking winter in it!' The fast-escaping light of evening becomes a hazy gloom in the old kitchen.

'It's no life for a girl on her own. You should come back with me and get a decent meal into you.' He is looking at the tin of spaghetti hoops on the kitchen table. 'We can have a go at that chimney in the morning.' The thought of Josie's thick beef stew and suet dumplings pulls her strongly. 'If you like, I'll call back later and see how you're fixed then. Well, whatever, please yourself, girl. Lock that door after me, though.'

'I'll be all right if I get the fire going. Do you know if there is any store of turf in the sheds out there?'

'I wouldn't say Jack had what would keep his pipe going.

He left nothing to feed them animals on either, poor old divil. He never really thought much past next week. We've been foddering them all from beyond since he ...' He switches on the naked light bulb. Moving more into the room, he faces Katherine directly. 'How do you think you're going to keep them going? Ye'll starve, the lot of ye!' His shadow is swaying over her.

'I'll buy some more food for them.'

'Will you? As easy as that? You'll just nip out and buy a few thousand bales of hay, straw, meal? What do you know about that kind of thing, a city girl like you?'

'I'm not a city girl!'

'Well, ye're no farmer, are ye!'

'I can learn. I'm grateful to you for all your help, and I will pay your dad for the fodder and whatever that you've used already. If you could help me out for a few more days, I'm sure I can get it organised; just while I think about what to do next.'

'And maybe you'll come to your bloody senses! We'll keep doing them jobs around the place, the few bits and pieces, till you do. Can't let animals go hungry for the want of a bit of common sense.' He grunts and leaves without saying goodbye. The light bulb swirls in the draught from the door but does little to dispel the encroaching shroud of evening.

Katherine sits on her haunches until her ankles and knees start to sting. She leans towards the smoking range and tries again to puff some life into it. When her lungs hurt too much to go on, she decides to try another plan for relighting it with some bits of binder twine she picked up earlier. It fizzes and sparks briefly. More smoke blows back into her face.

There is a knock at the door. The dog growls, cowering under a chair.

Katherine peers out of the window. In the dim light, she can just make out Fonsie Hayes, standing back a little from the door, stamping his feet to try to warm them up, or maybe to give a polite warning.

'Well! You're a bit of a celebrity, you know. Everyone's been out looking for you this last week. I called up a few times to see if you were here, but no sign of life at all. And Josie Ryan said you weren't there. Now Dawson tells me you intend moving in?' He humps some neatly baled briquettes of pressed turf into the room and drops them by the range. 'Brought you over something for a house warming. These old places do be terrible damp in winter. Here, look't, let me kickstart that thing for you.' Fonsie unwraps a packet of firelighters that he has folded up in newspaper. He riddles the grate vigorously.

Once lit, Fonsie's fire takes off like a bonfire on Guy Fawkes night on the village green in Suffolk. Soon the huge black kettle is chuffing like a steam engine. He takes it into the scullery and immerses all the grimy cups, plates and mouldy pots in steaming, soapy water.

'Here, we'll get all this delft washed and the place cleaned up a bit. There must be a long-handled brush about someplace. You look in that press behind the door there. Give the room a bit of a sweep. Use that old box in the corner to stick the rubbish in.' He hums away with his arms up to the elbows in soap suds. When he comes back into the kitchen, he grins, 'That's a right job now. Looks much better! Shove that kettle on again there, you, and we'll have an old cuppa tea.'

Katherine wipes two cracked tea cups with the hem of her skirt and is about to pour milk into them, when Fonsie exclaims suddenly, 'Whoa, never put the milk in first! It's a dead giveaway; only the English do that. You're going to have to go a bit native now, missus!'

'Why not milk in first?'

'Takes the edge off the tea.' He picks a few mouse pellets out of the sugar bowl and tosses them into the fire, winks, scoops three spoonfuls into his cup and stirs it vigorously. When he is satisfied with the colour and smell, he tips half of it out into the saucer and carefully lifts the rim to his lips.

'What about your husband? He's not coming over too, then?'

'That remains to be seen, Fonsie. He's never been to Ireland.'

Fonsie nods a few times. 'Never been to Ireland?' He hangs around for a while, making small talk, probing gently into Katherine's future plans. He soon appears to realise that the past is a much more interesting subject. Katherine has no plans for the future. They both munch through Josie's bread and butter, and Katherine eats cold pasta straight from the tin. She thinks, perhaps, Fonsie is someone who could be her friend. But she keeps a safe distance, just in case.

When he has left, she drapes a heavy old jacket, from a hook on the wall, over the window and shoves a bale of briquettes up against the door. Eventually, she pulls her woolly hat over her eyes and falls asleep with the light on, swathed in her coat and a blanket, as near to the range as feels safe. She wakes up several times, chucks a few more bits of pressed turf into the firebox and tries to get comfortable, but whenever she stirs, shards of cold air shoot in under the damp wool. At one point, she looks across the room and sees a rat peep out from a hole in the cupboard door. She thinks it'll scuttle off when it realises she's sitting there, but it just saunters across the floor. Not even the sight of the dog deters it. She tucks her feet up under her and shouts at it, but the rat just puts its nose in the air and wiggles its whiskers as much as to say, 'What's that strange smell in my kitchen?' Katherine throws a slipper at it. Mildly startled, it trots out of sight behind the range.

After that, there is no further hope of sleep, so she decides to stoke up the fire and try the radio. The batteries are dead. There are lots of old ones at the back of the stove where Jack used to store things like that, in the hope that a bit of warmth might revive them, like sick lambs. She tries each one. They are all defunct. She makes a mental note to add batteries and 150-watt light bulbs to her next shopping list. When she realises that it is still only nine o'clock at night, she wonders if she would make it down to Ryans' without falling into the river. A warm bed, hot breakfast in the morning, Josie crooning, Jim crowing. Without as much as a torch, that seems like a fairy tale. She finds a saucepan among the pots that Fonsie has washed and left neatly stacked in the scullery, pours some milk into it and puts it onto the range. She watches until small bubbles start to break the surface, makes a mug of cocoa and settles back into the armchair. She remembers her little blackcurrant pastilles and goes searching in the bottom of her handbag. There is the usual moment of panic when she can't find it until her fingers touch the familiar ridges. 'You're addicted to that stuff,' Harry keeps telling her. She always denies it: 'I just like the taste in my mouth, and it soothes my nerves'. She never smokes it in front of her parents and only recently brought Bridget into her little secret. 'Why not? Everyone else does, and anyway, it keeps me off the fags a bit.' Katherine knows that when the dope runs out, she will be in trouble. She crumbles the flakes into some Dutch tobacco and rolls it into a joint.

CHAPTER FOUR

Now that the river is passable again, Jim Ryan can plunge over it in his Morris Minor with the trailer bouncing along behind and the day's fodder hopping up and down. He has a particular grunt that precedes his tap-tap on the kitchen door. Katherine would prefer if JJ came, even though she is a little frightened of him. He is more entertaining than his father and not as gloomy. Jim has a way of breathing death or disaster into everything. He has a few regular mantras: 'Terrible weather, they're giving snow and ice till after Christmas. Nothing, only rain after that', before he really gets into his stride. 'Them sheep won't stay long on the hill before they start to break out into the forestry beyond.' His cheerful greeting today is, 'Water butt is nearly empty, only ice in it now; they'll all perish with the drought if you don't find a way of lagging them pipes, girl.' He shouts gleefully across the yard. Then, as Katherine starts to struggle into her wellies and a coat, 'You leave this to me, girl. You'll only break your ankle in that mud!' he growls.

'But I need to learn how to do these things, Jim.' Her feet feel like the ice that seals the water butt. Josie has given her a woolly hat, but it is too big, and when she's outside, she has to hold it down with one hand. She is waiting till Friday, when Jim can give her a lift into town, to buy some more suitable clothes. Her Chelsea wardrobe is beginning to give up. For sure, she will take over some of these jobs when she can get a sturdy pair of Levis, a few work-a-day woolly jumpers and a proper waterproof jacket. She teases herself with the promise that if she can stick it till Friday, she will treat herself to a new pair of gumboots that fit properly and a night or two in the hotel. A nice hot bath, roast beef; they might even have fixed the television in the residents' lounge …

'You feed the hens, then. Here, give them some of this,' he says, handing her a tin plate with meal on it. The fowl all rush the gate when she goes into their run. Some escape, but when she puts the plate down, they scamper back and all start pecking frantically, like they were never fed before. She backs out quickly in case they finish and beat her to the exit.

'Bloody waste of good meal feeding them hens. They haven't laid an egg for weeks, or if they did, they have 'em well hidden. I'd wring their necks, the whole lot, and stick 'em in the pot, if they were mine.' It is remarks of that kind that make Katherine determined to stick it out. At least until she has something to say to her father about what really happened to his youngest brother. Till then, she knows it means scooping buckets of water out of the river and keeping the range going for boiling kettles to thaw out frozen pipes. Today, she plans to try to find ways to fill gaps in porous fences.

Like everyone in Knocklong, Marie Ryan is appalled but also intrigued at the notion of the prim and proper Katie Butler, with the prissy accent, who she knew so well as a shy teenager, staying alone in that spooky farmhouse in the tall trees. No one, not even Marie Ryan, believes she will last beyond a week, if that. Although, unlike the rest, Marie knows the heiress has a very stubborn side to her apparently passive nature. After all, who was it who insisted they walk home from the village pantomime in the middle of the night, rather than taking turns on Billy Rafter's crossbar? And in those ridiculous shoes as well. Who would only eat potatoes if presented to her without their skins and brushed her teeth three times a day? No one in Knocklong knows Katherine like Marie Ryan does. She is noticing the deterioration in Katherine's appearance; she has slipped, in the short while that she has been in Ireland, from being a stylish sixties swinger with magnificent, waist-length, red hair and false eyelashes, into a country colleen with a wild and dishevelled look. Those pale, manicured hands that shook the hoary old fists of Knocklong, beside a fresh grave, are now rough and chapped with chipped nails. She has tangled locks and cracked lips. Marie is convinced she sleeps in her boots. If she sleeps at all, that is. She doesn't believe that Katherine has even ventured upstairs, never mind taken her clothes off or washed herself. And she is right.

Marie offers to help clean the place up a bit and make it more homely, but is relieved when Katherine puts her turned-up-nose in the air and says defiantly, 'No, thank you, Marie. I've asked Fonsie to come and do a few jobs for me.' Then, responding to Marie's sniggers, she goes on, 'He's going to put in a proper lavatory and shower for me next week.'

'Mmm, inside facilities? There's posh!'

As Jim predicted, the fences don't hold fast, and Katherine spends hours every day trying to find new ways of tying up gates and filling gaps in ditches by dragging around bits of broken machinery and so on. However, Fonsie is as good as his word. He installs a rudimentary bathroom downstairs. He borrows a tractor to dig a big hole in the calves' field, some yards behind the house, 'for the waste'. He puts some loads of slig, which he gets from a small quarry on the farm, into the hole and, more or less, fills it back up again. Apart from a stench pipe and drain that he sinks into the ground and connects to the house, there is nothing beyond optimism to inspire confidence that this arrangement will work.

'It'll keep you going for the time being, at any rate,' he says with his usual cheeriness. 'Now stick the kettle on, you, and we'll drink to it!'

Katherine tries to quiz Fonsie about her uncle's death and what might really have happened. He knows nothing. Not only that, but he is not much interested in gossip about it either.

'Let sleeping dogs lay, girl,' he says with a wistful look out across the haggard.

The nights are long and cold. Even though Katherine has more or less mastered the range, and having cleaned the chimney, Fonsie keeps her stocked up with logs and briquettes, the house still feels hostile; full of shadows and strange noises. She doesn't stray far from the kitchen. And never goes upstairs. Her supplies of food, she stores on the table, pulling back the chairs so that rodents can't leap up and steal it, or in the makeshift fridge that Fonsie has fixed up. It is basically just a perforated tin box placed in front of the cracked window in the scullery. Some days, it is colder in there than outside.

The light is left on all night. The nearest she comes to sleeping is after smoking a joint, curled up in Jack's armchair, with Josie's woolly hat pulled down over her eyes. She is getting used to the scratching of rodents, the dog snoring and the sound of the wind whistling through the cracks.

Day fifteen at the farm dawns, and there is an almighty racket in the yard. The dog starts barking and clawing at the back door to be let out. It sounds like someone is strangling the hens. She thinks for a moment it might be Jim, with the final solution. Too terrified to go out and investigate, she is stuck to the chair, shivering. Gradually, morning begins to creep through the window. Katherine pulls on her coat and ventures outside. There are feathers and blood mashed into the mud. A few terrified hens are huddled high on a roost. The rest of the flock are either mangled and dead, or missing. She tries to tie bits of wire across the hole, the futility of which becomes apparent when, later that morning, in the murky light, she meets a vixen skulking through the farmyard with another hen squawking, flapping like a child being chased with a wooden spoon, between its jaws. Yelling and running after it does no good. The beast doesn't miss a beat, just gathers pace, as it disappears off across the field. The pitiful screeching gradually subsides, leaving Katherine face down in the mud.

As if the whole village has heard the commotion, Marie happens to call 'to check up on things'. She sings triumphantly, 'When that starts, you'll never stop them. Come on, we'll kill the last few. At least you'll have a bit of meat for the dinner!' With which she grabs an already traumatised hen from where it is cowering on its roost. The cockerel bolts, flapping its wings. It flies up onto a rusty hay rake, crowing like there would never be another dawn. Meanwhile, Marie is grappling with one of the two remaining hens. Holding its feet in one hand, she yanks downwards on its head with the other, breaking its neck with a swift and decisive click. The wings flap, and the whole carcass shudders for some seconds before she throws it onto the kitchen table and stomps out to catch the last one.

'Oh, please Marie, leave that one alone! I can't eat two chickens, anyway.'

'What do you mean? If you don't eat it yourself, the old fox will!' She adds with relish, 'It's not as if they are fat, either. You'd need a half dozen to make a bowl of soup out of them!'

'But surely we could fix the hen run a bit better ...'

'You might as well be up a dog's arse laying out a picnic for pups!' Whereupon she grabs the last hen and dispatches it in the same manner.

'Put the kettle on there, you, and we'll pluck 'em now.'

Marie plunges the birds into scalding water, and with deft, even strokes, she whips the feathers off them both. Her fists are full of feathers, and they are sticking to her forearms, making her look like Bird Woman from the village carnival freak show. She pushes her skilful midwife fingers into the rear end of each carcass, and, with a squelching noise, draws out their guts and a whole necklace of unlaid eggs in various stages of development. Katherine wonders if she will ever be able to eat a boiled egg again, as Marie drops the gizzards and all the unlaid eggs into the dog's dish on the floor. She tosses the two bodies into a basin of freezing cold water and wipes her blotchy, red hands across the cheeks of her backside. The hens sink to the bottom and loose feathers float around on the surface. Katherine looks away, distracted by the dog scoffing in the corner.

Marie has selected some of the guts and put them into a saucepan. 'You can make a bit of soup out of them for your tea.' She looks satisfied; a feeling enhanced by Katherine's disgusted wincing and the certain knowledge that Katherine will give them to the dog as soon as her back is turned.

'You get some twine, and we'll hang 'em behind the door in the back kitchen for a couple of days—these old birds do be terrible tough. We'll get dad to fix that hen run with new wire, and you can buy some pullets when the weather warms up a bit. Mammy'll give you eggs till then, I'm sure.'

'You believe in me, Marie? You think I will stick it out, don't you?'

The naked birds are hanging by their scaly feet from a nail on the back door. Four red eyes are bulging, and the few remaining neck feathers fluff out like the war bonnet of an Indian chieftain. Blobs of blood congeal on the flagstones.

'Sure. Why wouldn't you stick it out?' Marie is doing a brief reconnoitre of the kitchen and scullery. 'I see you've done a few bits and pieces to the old place already?'

'Fonsie still comes up most days and does this and that. He's repapering my bedroom and got the fire up there working again. Soon I'll be able to go upstairs to bed. Then I won't have to sleep by the range anymore.'

'Fonsie Hayes? He's up here most days? Well, he's okay, I s'pose; you can trust him, I'd say. You're not paying him too much, are you?'

'Twenty quid a day.'

'What? He saw you coming! I hope he's bloody well worth it.'

'He's worth it to me. I even have a flushing loo now and a shower that works most of the time. Besides, it makes me feel safer having him around.'

74

'Flushing toilet! What'll it be next? A gold-plated seat on it for that money! At least you will be able to have a wash, anyway. So it's all going famously here now, then. Soon you'll be living like anyone else.' She turns her eyes to the farmyard once more. 'You got that fodder for the cattle sorted out, I see?'

'Yes, I bought a few hundred bales of straw and hay from Nicholas Molloy and some bags of meal from the creamery. Your dad still comes over most days and gives me a hand. It's all taking shape now.'

'Bet Molloy charged you three prices for that hay? Do you still fancy him?' Marie's eyes twinkle.

'Hey, cool it, Marie. That was a long time ago. He's too old for me, anyway. Besides, I am actually married now, you know.'

'So what? Where's your hubby now when you need him? Not much of a marriage if you are here and he's over there. What kind of a setup is that?'

'I don't know. It's scary, though.'

'Scary? What's scary about it? You're here and he's yonder. What about it? If he's any kind of a husband, he'll come over here and fetch you home. Won't he?' She isn't looking at Katherine. She is poking sticks into the range with the violence of the mildly frustrated. Then she turns around, and she isn't smiling. 'You would want to mind that Molloy, Katie. He'll soon get his feet under the table if you don't look out. He is not to be trusted. And did you say he helped you calve that old cow of yours too?'

'I couldn't have done that on my own. He just happened to be here, delivering hay at the time.'

~

It was in the evening when Nicholas Molloy had rumbled into the yard on a little putt-putt tractor with a trailer-load of bales. He had found her worried and fussing over a cow that was stomping around the barn, mooing. In minutes, Molloy had stripped to the waist and buried his arm into the end of the animal. Man and beast groaned and strained and heaved, until at last a pair of little hooves appeared, and he tied a rope on each one. He gave one end to Katherine and said, 'Lean on that and pull when I tell you.'

They pulled, and the calf inched towards them. When its nose appeared between the forelegs, the tongue was lolling out of its mouth. Molloy tugged and heaved and shouted at Katherine, 'PULL!' She couldn't see how anything would survive that kind of brutality at birth, and it had seemed completely lifeless when it landed in a heap on the straw in front of them. He splashed cold water into its ears, and then, holding it by the hind legs, he swung it in a wide arc several times before he dropped it beneath its mother's head. The cow licked it into life. Soon it was shaking the water out of its ears and staggering up onto its wobbly legs.

'You should sell that one on the cow now. No money in suck calves on their own,' he remarked, as he wiped his arms on a twist of hay and pulled his shirt and jumper back over his head. He followed her into the kitchen and took the mug of whiskey she offered him.

'It's so cute, though. I might keep the cow and milk her. I could sell the calf when it gets a bit bigger.'

'Oh Christ! You hardly plan on staying here, do you? I'll give you a fair price for the farm, you know. Has Ryan made you an offer? Whatever it is, I'll better it.'

'Jim Ryan says exactly the same. He reckons you pestered Uncle Jack to sell you the land.' Katherine could feel the whiskey loosen her tongue.

'I didn't pester your uncle, girl. That was them Ryans. They had him driven half demented with their wily ways. No wonder the poor old dickens shot himself.' Molloy hefted his leg over the seat of a wooden chair and leaned his arms on the back of it.

Katherine asked him, 'It wasn't an accident, then?'

'Who knows? What do you think yourself?'

'I heard he was shooting rats in the cow byre and he tripped. There was no inquest, even.' By now, she is pretty sure that Jack's death wasn't accidental, but it's a story, one that's easier to live with than the alternatives.

'You just mark my words, and mark them well, girl. When the time comes, and it will come, you'll see, I'll give more for this farm than they will.' He shook himself and said in a lowered voice, 'This place isn't half creepy.'

The smell of his body, warmed by the smouldering range, filled the room. He leaned forwards, bringing his face nearer to where Katherine was sitting. 'Tell me, what do you think about Bernadette Devlin getting elected, then?'

She had a sense that this was a trick question, that a lot depended on her answer.

Before she could think what to say, though, he growled, 'An innocent man beaten to death in his own living room, by the RUC, right in front of his family! One thousand, five hundred Catholics forced out of their homes in Belfast and Derry? You wait; it's only just beginning! The Provos'll shake 'em all up!' He threw back the dregs of the whiskey and thumped the mug on his knee. Then he pointed up to a faded press cutting pinned onto the charred beam above the range. 'Remember that night? Only time a Brit was crowned harvest queen in Knocklong! You were quite a looker in them days; mind you, you're still a whole lot better looking than Miss Bernadette Devlin!' Then, moving his eyes slowly around the darkening room, he asked her, 'Are you not nervous in this place on your own?'

'I have my dog.'

He swung out his long arm, knocking the mug to the floor, where it smashed into sharp pieces. Patting the dog on the head and laughing cynically, he said, 'Yeah, you have the dog.'

CHAPTER FIVE

I t is now mid-December. The days are very short and grey, but colder and calmer after some of the stormy weather in November. Although things have settled down, every day brings a haunting sense of loss as the year slips away. Katherine tries to concentrate on overcoming the constant challenge of the unexpected. Little targets help to mask the overwhelming obstacles ahead. For all that, though, a kind of routine is beginning to take shape. The hardest thing is fighting off the feeling of useless endeavour that Jim Ryan paints, like battleship grey, over everything. All that stuff about fences, frozen water, impending starvation and the hidden threat implied in the ubiquitous rhetoric: 'You'll never stick the winter', 'Where's that husband of yours now, then?' and 'Rats don't go away. They just hide.' And the most unnerving of all: 'You not afraid, all alone in that place?' Implying by his tone of voice that if she isn't, then she ought to be.

Most days are structured around simple needs: keeping the range going, helping to feed the cattle, putting out hay and checking on the sheep; then drinking tea and eating fig rolls with Fonsie. He calls often to check his gin-traps around the scullery and dispose of any mutilated victims into the ditch outside the haggard before settling comfortably into the armchair.

'You can't live with rats. Dirty beasts. Still 'n all, even the smell of dead rats fades eventually, eh?'

Katherine enjoys his visits. It's a chance to be normal, to let her guard down. The daily highlight now is milking the black cow. It has taken Katherine many attempts to get it right, and Fonsie wasn't much help. Not his thing. In the beginning, her hands ached, her back ached, and for the first week or so, it took such a long time that the cow, having finished her meal, grew restless and kicked the bucket over as she wandered off, mooing for her calf. In the end, Katherine bought a halter in the creamery, and now she ties the cow by its head to a ring on the wall, the same way she would tie a pony that refused to stand still to be groomed. Having mastered the technique of gripping the teats at the top and working the milk downwards between her fingers, it flows freely, frothing into the pail between her knees. Her hands are raw and sting, but it's the one time in the day when she feels warm and productive; in control. She massages some yellow unction into the udder and into the cracks in her fingers. The warm milk is her prize. When successfully retrieved, she cradles the bucket in her arms and places it in the scullery to cool.

She bought a bicycle from an advert in the local paper, and most days, on her way home from the village, she does a little detour to visit Josie Ryan. The womblike warmth of the Ryans' kitchen has a magnetic effect on her. Josie is always at home. Except on Fridays (when everyone goes to

town), Mass on Sundays and all local funerals, weddings and
First Communions. Otherwise, if not around the farmyard
attending to calves and hens, or standing in gaps while the
cattle are moved around, Josie is either in the scullery or in
the kitchen. Sometimes she is just sitting at the table, staring
into the middle distance, with the radio crackling away loudly
from the shelf. More usually, though, she is engaged in several
different duties simultaneously, like baking bread, scones and
pies, while also doing the washing.

When Katherine walks in today, she finds Josie in the
scullery, stuffing clothes through the wringer with a pair of
wooden tongs. The scalding suds froth into a soapy soup in a
basin on the floor. She abandons the laundry when Katherine
appears and turns her attention to making tea.

'How are you sleeping? Are you sure you're getting enough
to eat? Here, have another cut of bread and some rhubarb jam.
You're fading away, and God knows there wasn't too much of
you to begin with!'

Katherine asks her, 'Josie, what are the Provos?'

Josie slumps into the chair and drops her head into her
open hands. She closes her eyes. 'The start of something very
bad; bad things leading to more bad things. They are stirring
all that old stuff up again. As long as it stays up north, it's
nothing for us to be worrying about down here,' she says with
a grunt and reaches for the teapot to pour them both a warm-
up. 'Now, tell me, how's that black cow doing? Did the dairy
instructor call out and show you how to milk?'

'Not yet. I think I have it now, though. I'll need her help
if I ever get round to making butter.'

'Did you give her a name? The cow, I mean.'

'Mary.'

'Oh that's nice, after Our Lady.'

81

'No, after Bloody Mary, the black-haired queen. She was such a tyrant in the beginning. Anyway, who are they? The Provos, I mean?'

'It's all about history, the border and a long struggle between one type of worship and another, and one type of government or the other. The Provisional IRA are just the same crowd with a new name to make them sound better. You'll stay out of it if you know what's good for you.'

'But why should it affect me?'

'People have long memories. Families were split in two. Your family were head, neck and heels into it, one time. Your poor uncle tried to keep out of it. So should you.'

'But what about the rest of my family? What did they do?'

'Look't, Katherine, as I said, this was a divided community not too long ago. People did things they can't go back on now. Old wounds don't just go away.'

'So what happens then?'

'They go underground or get sugar-coated in politics. Either way, it's not something you want to get tangled up in.'

Katherine cycles away from Ryan's with a belly full of new bread and jam. The world looks better. The bike spins on freely towards her own farm, as if it's also been thoroughly oiled with sweet tea. She had arrived at the Ryans' house with a knot of worries torturing her insides. Now she can see the beautiful colours that the low afternoon sun picks out on the hills and pastures. The gold and russet coloured leaves that still cling to oak and beech trees, glowing against the watery sky. She passes through an ancient birch grove in the bog that looks like mankind has never touched it. The delicate lattice of white branches is sprayed with a purple haze that she has never noticed before. A cold wind pricks her cheeks.

Josie's motherly way of smoothing things over takes

the sting out of life. Marie is more like her father, telling Katherine she's just replaced a life of luxury with one of miserable drudgery.

Marie loves her husband, in her own pragmatic way, has lots of children to keep her busy. She had a worthwhile career as a nurse and midwife until she got married and had to give it up. And to top it off, she's got Josie, who steps in whenever help is needed. They are all part of a team that pulls together. But for Marie, money is the answer to everything. Only yesterday she said, while on a visit to the farm, 'If I had your money, I'd be travelling the world in the Q.E.2, or sipping a pina colada in the Costa Brava. Not grubbing around in the mud, living alone in that haunted house, in the perishing cold!'

'But money doesn't make people love you or take care of you when you most need it. It just makes everyone jealous and nasty. It brings out the worst. There's no challenge in it, either. When you run out, you just go to the bank and get more.'

'"You just go to the bank and get more"? Will you listen to yourself, girl? How many people can do that? Doesn't someone have to work for it in the first place? Either that or it's got through crime. Or you just fall in for it, like you have.'

'My father worked hard all his life. He's definitely not a criminal!'

'Not that kind, maybe. Didn't he have to run for it after the civil war, with a massive great price on his head?'

Katherine winces. 'I don't really know what happened at that time, Marie. But I know he was clever, and he worked hard.'

'And didn't he marry money as well?'

'That business wasn't going anywhere when he married my mother. He brought it back from the brink of bankruptcy and built it up himself. Anyway, how do you know so much about my family? Stuff I don't even know myself!'

'Well, you should. Everybody else does.'

There is a lull in the village activities around half-past nine in the morning when the children are in school. Everyone who is going to work has left and the corner-boys haven't yet taken up their positions beside the hardware shop. The post office is quiet, and this is when Katherine usually slips into the phone booth with a bag full of coins to ring Harry. Mostly, he asks her the same things: 'What's happening about selling the farm? When are you coming home?'

He tells her that her father is not good, chest still at him, weather cold, etc. He might tell her the hounds were meeting at the Dog and Duck and the shooting is picking up, as much as to say, 'Look what you are missing out on.' Katherine manages to deflect issues about selling the farm with references to Mr Pierce and his management of the situation. She shivers when he asks her if she is any nearer to finding out 'what happened there'.

'No, not really. It's complicated,' she replies and tries to move things on by asking about her mother, Bridget and Elvis, her cob, who in any other year, she would be hunting every weekend by now.

Harry says he is coming over soon to see for himself what's going on, to sort things out once and for all. Her thighs and her teeth clench. He goes on, undaunted by her silence. 'You can be sure I'll get to the bottom of it pretty quickly. Scurrilous lot.' She takes a few short breaths and says goodbye, and that's it for another couple of days.

Katherine finds it easy to picture Harry in Pierce's office with Molloy and Jim Ryan. He would, probably, also have an auctioneer there to speed things up. Harry would decide who got what and they would wrangle over the price. He would be in his element. He might even bring in a second solicitor in case Pierce was double-dealing with the locals. Katherine can hear him relaying this manoeuvre to her parents over Sunday dinner. Her father, while not really wishing to pour cold water on Harry's success, would ask if there hadn't been any other potential buyers, and was he sure he got the best price? Harry would make up some arguments about neighbours having to have preference over land deals, following the land acts of whenever. On occasions like these, in the past, Katherine's father would look at her, trying to read her reaction, searching her face and demeanour for the secret signs of acquiescence. He would be more concerned not to fall out with Katherine than to agree with Harry, whom he does not trust. He sees too much of himself in his son-in-law. He has little faith in Katherine either, but at least she is flesh and blood. Her mother, Georgina, would probably say, limply, 'Oh, you are clever, Henry, and now you have Katherine back home to look after you. Jolly good, well done. Let's all have a stonking good tea to celebrate!' She would smile benignly at her daughter, while listening out for the daily bringing in of the sandwiches, scones and Dundee cake.

But that fantasy trails off into a mass of frayed ends; living happily ever after has lost its meaning for Katherine. She is off the path and running free among the briars in the undergrowth now.

~

Milking the cow is a job for early in the evening, while there is still light enough to cross the yard without a lamp and before it's so cold that her feet scream out for mercy. She is scared of the shadows and dark corners and especially of the gloomy cow byre, where she never goes. The small barn is directly opposite the door, just a short skip across the yard. She can make it in one breath, dodging potholes and cow pats. Her gleaming white bucket is scalded with boiling water. She takes this, a hot damp cloth and a bowl of barley meal to where Queen Mary is standing, up to her knees in straw. She puts the feed in the trough and ties the cow's head securely. Using an upturned butter box to sit on, she washes the udder. Working the teats rhythmically and firmly, listening to the jet of milk hit the side of the bucket, stopping occasionally to shake out her aching fingers, her other worries all melt away. With her head resting against Mary's soft flank, she listens to the ruminations gurgling inside. It's a harmony between the munching of the meal and the frothing of the milk being the base guitar, while the various stomachs and tubes deeper within provide a simple riff. She hums along, 'Hey Jude, don't make it bad, sing a sad song and make it better …' She never really knows the words, but that doesn't matter. It's better than 'Mary had a little lamb', which she knows ends badly and which reminds her of lumpy semolina.

When she has enough milk for herself and the dog, Katherine unties Mary and opens the dividing gate, letting the calf in to finish off. He is much rougher than she is. He sucks hard at the udder until the cow lets down more milk, then, with his tongue tightly around the teat, he sucks for all he's worth. His tail goes up and dribbles of milky foam fall into the straw. Katherine retrieves the milking bucket from the safe corner where she had left it and straightens up to face the rest of the evening.

A car is driving into the yard. The door opens and bangs shut again. It's the heavy thud of an expensive vehicle. It is nearly dark now. After a few seconds, footsteps approach the barn.

'What in God's name are you doing?'

Katherine's heart starts pounding when she hears the familiar voice. She spins around. He is standing in the opening, yet she can barely make out his features. But the short, blocky shape and square head are unmistakable. His hands are resting on the gate. In two steps, she would feel his breath.

'Oh, Harry, you gave me such a fright! How did you get here?'

'Well, that's a nice way to greet your husband, isn't it? Here, let me take that for you.' He reaches out and lifts the bucket over the gate. Looking at the two or three pints at the bottom of it, he remarks with a slight smirk: 'Is that all you get?'

They embrace a little stiffly in the yard with all the animals, including the dog, staring at them.

'Kat, this is dismal,' he says as he ducks his head to get through the kitchen doorway. He looks disparagingly at her creamery dungarees and gumboots, which are two sizes too big. 'Do you have any decent clothes? Come on now, get into something respectable, and we'll go into town and get a meal. And for God's sake, comb your hair!'

Katherine changes into her funeral outfit, which is damp and smells of mould. She sprays a liberal amount of scent around her, loops up her hair with a big clip, and manufactures a smile.

Watching from the bedroom door, Harry says, 'Right, you're ready, then? That'll have to do for now. Let's go. We can try to see that solicitor of yours and get all this sorted out. It's high time you came home.'

She slides reluctantly into the hired car.

He has already picked out a hotel on the Dublin Road. It has some symbols on a big sign, which also declares 'Off season rates'.

'We can leave seeing that solicitor till the morning.' He gives her bottom a squeeze. 'I'm too tired and hungry to deal with all that now, anyway. That's a frightful journey over from London!'

Apart from a couple of travelling salesmen and a very young couple staring shyly at their plates, they are the only people in the restaurant. Katherine is trying to whisper.

'I've done a bit of research. I telephoned that Pierce fellow last week,' he bellows into the silence. 'He reckons the place is worth about forty or fifty grand, at best. It's not a very popular locality, it would seem, but the neighbours are keen to get hold of it and would bid each other up a bit above the odds. He thinks you've been stalling for some reason?'

She has no reply ready, so she throws in a question, a trick she learned in school when the nuns found you out and you were standing in front of the Mother Superior with no believable excuses for muddy footprints on the dormitory windowsill.

'What does Daddy think?'

'He's been poorly lately. Your mother doesn't want me to trouble him with things like that.'

'What do you mean, poorly?'

'Oh, you know, that chest of his.' The waiter is standing at the table with his notebook and pencil ready. Harry orders for both of them.

Katherine has not had a square meal for weeks. She can't believe how good it tastes but how little she is able to eat. Harry points a forkful of meat at her and says, 'This beef is like old shoe leather,' as if it was her fault. She is sure that Harry is going to call for the chef and send it back, like he usually does. He is too hungry; he lets it pass. He tastes the wine, winces and says, 'It'll do.' He drinks most of it and then the best part of a second bottle as well.

'What's really the matter with Daddy?'

'He's getting old; everything is starting to wear out. He worries about you.' Harry yawns loudly. He is beginning to go a kind of hunting pink around the jaws. 'Let's skip dessert and go to bed. We have some business to catch up on.' He reaches under the table and pinches her knee.

Harry has already booked a room, but he's not happy with it and spends some time fussing around, harassing the receptionist and then the duty manager. Eventually, he comes back to the lounge and says, 'Oh, come on, Kat, it'll have to do. It's only for one night. We're going home tomorrow.'

The room is small. The breezeblock walls are painted the same green as a Neapolitan ice cream. Harry puts a coin in the television meter, and it comes to life. He quickly turns it off again when he realises that it doesn't have the BBC. He gives it a kick.

'Stupid bloody thing. I wasted half a crown on that!' He tries the shower, but after a battle with the 'useless taps', he gives up.

He appears in the room. He is still wet and tries his usual trick of balancing the hand towel like a flag on his upturned mast while prancing around. He does two laps of the room and then remembers something.

'I brought you something, sweetie.' He takes a little packet from his trousers, which are neatly folded over the back of the chair, and opens it. With a magician's flourish, he waves a piece of black satin. 'Some silk panties.' He poses in front of the mirror with them stretched across his groin. He gives himself a quick rub with them and then tosses them across the bed to Katherine. 'Put them on.'

Harry is watching her undress and struggle into the French cami-knickers. He starts to tear at them with his teeth, growling like a bear in a Disney film. 'Don't squirm so. I can't get a proper grip.' The silk is cutting into her groin. 'Hold still, girl, for God's sake!' He takes a fist of her hair and fastens her head to the pillow. His teeth find her breast.

Yellow light is leaching through the curtains. Katherine tries to keep as still as possible. She watches his shadow moving on the wall. Then he flops sideways and releases her. She remembers a friend telling her years ago, 'deep breathing helps'. She tries that.

'Not bad, considering I'm out of practice.' He grunts, rolls over and goes to sleep, smiling.

~

Harry wakes up the next morning with a hangover. He reaches for Katherine, fumbling around for something that might arouse him sufficiently, but she has left the nest and taken the knickers with her. He tries the feeling of the polyester sheets, but they are too abrasive, and he gives up, rolling onto his back and staring blankly at the dabbed icing effect on the ceiling. Then he realises it's after ten o'clock. He puts his hand over his face and groans. He tries to relive the final few moments of last night, but they, too, are slipping away from him. 'Oh God, how does she manage to slip through the net like that?'

It is very stuffy in the room. The mustiness is the same as the tenement flat he shared with his mother and three sisters, in number 56 Bartholomew Lane, EC 14. It was in an alley behind the shop where his mother worked as a dressmaker. She used to do running repairs and alterations with a sewing machine in a dingy back room by gaslight. The kick and whirr of the treadle and the clickety-clack of its well-oiled workings; the stench of hot starch off the iron and cheap coal nuggets smouldering in the grate. There had been a faded photograph of his father on the dresser, in varying tones of grey and brown in his naval uniform, smiling optimistically beneath his moustache.

When he finally stumbles out of bed and goes to the mirror, Harry finds Katherine's note, scribbled on the back of a docket from the creamery. 'Sorry, tried to wake you. I'll get a lift out to the farm. I have to feed the animals.'

He skips the 'Full Irish' and refuses to pay for it too. On the way to Knocklong, Harry pulls up outside Johnny's pub. It is cold. A drizzling mixture of sleet and mushy hailstones insinuate themselves through his Crombie overcoat, and even with the collar turned up, they slither down the back of his neck. A group of old men are sitting beside a small fire. The smell of their bodies and the turf smoke catches Harry in the back of the throat. He nods, but they just look, as if to say, 'We know who you are and what you've been up to.' He orders and downs a shot of scotch and then a chaser or two. He stares at a handwritten sign on the counter beside an old clock, which says: 'SORRY, NO TICK'.

Climbing back into his hired car, Harry mumbles to himself, 'Bugger it anyway, that whiskey was so cheap I could have bought them all a round or two with the change from a tenner and had them singing like songbirds, with all the gossip about Katherine and her family.'

He heads on, determined to confront Katherine about

this farming nonsense. Apart from anything else, he will have to account for her behaviour to her family and what on earth would her parents make of him if he went back without her?

Katherine is on her haunches in a shed, trying to get a lamb to suck from a ewe that isn't cooperating. She and the woolly beast are grappling shoulder to shoulder in the corner, and the lamb is between her legs. She hears the car drive into the yard, but ignores it, although it is difficult to deny her pounding heart. She hears him open the kitchen door, shout for her, and then a few minutes later, his grumbling swear words as he picks his way across the puddles. It isn't hard to find Katherine, because the dog is barking. He stands at the half-door of the stable, watching her for a few minutes, enthralled.

'Ah, there you are,' he says, as if he thinks she is hiding from him. She doesn't look up. 'Katherine, you know your father is not at all well. I think he is starting to give up ever since you went away.' The ewe escapes. Bounding out over Katherine's shoulder and flattening her onto her back, it turns to glare at her from the far corner, trampling the bleating orphan on its way. 'That's not her lamb, is it?'

'No. Close the bottom door, for goodness's sake, Harry!'

'Where is her own lamb?'

'Over there.' She points to the dead body in the straw. He looks at it for a moment and then back to the lamb in Katherine's arms.

'What happened to the mother of this one?'

'She has triplets, and Jim Ryan, he's the neighbour that's been helping me, reckoned she wouldn't have enough milk for them all, so he brought the smallest one in here early this morning. She's not going to take to it, though.'

'I think I can help you there. Get me a sharp knife.' She pulls a pen knife from her pocket. Harry tests the blade on his thumb, surprised to find it razor sharp. He takes off his coat and jacket, rolls up his sleeves and deftly skins the corpse, tossing the flayed body out over the door. 'You hold it still there for me.' He ties the wet skin over the little triplet with a piece of twine. 'That should do the trick. It's crazy having them lambing at this time of year, anyway. There mustn't have been any management on this farm at all!'

He has the ewe wedged into the corner with his knee against her shoulder and is holding the lamb's mouth up to the udder. After a while, it latches on, and he slowly loosens his grip on the ewe. She sniffs the pelt of her dead baby suspiciously, and then begins to lick it, bleating gently and nudging the little cuckoo in underneath her shaggy fleece. 'Come on, we'll leave them to it. You need to get cleaned up.' Then, looking at his hands and the knees of his neatly pressed, grey flannel trousers, he adds, 'And so do I.'

'That's really far out, Harry. Where did you learn a neat trick like that?'

He looks across at his wife's brazen hair, backlit by the low winter sun, forming a wispy halo around her freckled face. He swore long ago that he would never tell her or any of her family about the war and the deprivation of the few years that followed it.

Harry was eleven when he and his four siblings were evacuated from East London in 1944. They had already survived the blitz in 1940 by going every night with sleeping bags and gas masks into the air-raid shelters in the underground station near their home. As twilight fell in war torn London in September 1940, everything went black. His job was to batten sheets of cardboard over the windows to protect the glass and make sure that not a smidgen of gaslight could escape and attract the wrath of the Blackout Warden. His mother and his sisters made the sandwiches and filled flasks with soup and tea. The street was completely dark; no lamps, no traffic lights, no lights in shop windows. Even car headlights were reduced to a slit like the pupil of a cat's eye. They stumbled and tripped over sandbags on the pavement as swarms of people filed down the stairs into the bowels of London, where they slept the night on the underground platforms. No one knew what they would see when they scrambled out like rabbits in the morning. Would their tenement block still be standing or have been bombed into a pile of rubble in the night? They didn't even know if they would be able to get out of the tunnels or if they would find they had been buried alive.

Mr Churchill said, 'Never before in human history was so much owed by so many to so few.' And so it went on. Sometimes the bombing was worse than others. Miraculously, their street wasn't hit.

Harry's mother spent the war sewing uniforms for soldiers. His father went to the front several times. The last time he didn't make it back. The telegram was neatly folded and placed on the dresser beside his photograph.

Then Hitler decided to have another serious go at bombing London in 1944, with V1 flying bombs and V2 rockets. This time, all the children were evacuated to the country. Harry and his three sisters stood in Liverpool Street station with the other children from their road and hundreds more besides, herded by volunteers from the Women's Institute acting as the billeting officers. Harry, like all the rest, had his name on a sheet of thick paper hung around his neck. All the children carried cardboard boxes containing their gas masks. No one went anywhere without one of those. The luckier ones had a little suitcase full of clothes; others, just a shopping bag with their few belongings. Everyone had been given a list of basics that they had to bring. Harry's mother, being a seamstress, made sure her children had decent clothes, and this was the first year that Harry was given long trousers. The mothers were all held back behind a barrier, their eyes searching the crowds for a farewell wave from their disappearing ducklings.

There were no toilets on the train. It took four hours to chug and puff its way up the east coast to Norwich. By the time they fell out into the station, most of the kids had peed in their pants, and the train stank like cattle trucks. The children were taken from there, in lorries and bread vans, to the town hall. They lined up against the wall, where local families and farmers came to look them over and make their choice. Harry and his younger sisters went to a big estate some miles out of town, and two old ladies took the older girls to a village not far from Norwich.

They were driven through mighty wrought-iron gates and swept away up into the mansion, and Harry went to the steward's house down by the farmyard. They met nearly every day in the estate schoolhouse for lessons with the teacher from their old school, who had been billeted in the big house along with them.

Quite a few children from the East End of London had their schooling in this freezing cold but brightly lit classroom, sitting on wooden forms and writing on their laps. The younger children of the gentry attended the lessons as well. They sat on proper chairs and had wooden desks to themselves. The well-bred girls also had fur mufflers for their feet and hands. Jessica de Montfort took a fancy to Harry, which she showed by teasing him about his 'thuper' cockney accent. Before the evacuees arrived, she had never heard anything like it. She was a robust girl of ten with a thin, lispy, little voice and rosy cheeks. Harry longed to be able to speak like she did, who, even as she squeaked, had big round Os and sharply pronounced pointy Is. 'Harry' in East End cockney came right through the nose, dropped the H and almost missed the Rs as well. Jessica was able to make the two perfect syllables sound like the smooth, sweet-clover honey that she gave him on slices of pure white bread at tea time. Sometimes she brought him in through the servants' entrance of the big house, up the narrow wooden back staircase, along endless, dusty corridors to the nursery wing, where she let him play with her brother's lead soldiers and clockwork trains. As Harry played, enthralled by the perfectly crafted miniatures, Jessica would sit on the window seat and watch him. His beautifully tailored trousers and waistcoat, cut and remade from his father's Sunday-best suit, fascinated her. He looked a perfect gentleman. As long as he didn't speak, no one would ever have known.

Mrs Teasel, the steward's wife, was an industrious and frugal woman who made soap and candles out of mutton fat and paraffin wax, which she steeped together in a huge wooden bucket with old citrus peels gleaned from the big house kitchens. One bar of soap had to last Harry for the remainder of the war, however long that would be. He washed in the cold water from the pump when he had to, but mostly used the soap to catch the tormenting fleas, which came in swarms from the fens and lived in the warmth of his flour-sack, calico sheets and felted wool blanket.

Mr Teasel, along with the shepherd and all the other able-bodied men who normally worked on the home farm, had been called up or volunteered and were gone to the war. The estate was being farmed by a few old retainers and a platoon of hearty Land Girls dressed in jodhpurs and thick, green, flannel shirts. In the early morning, a gang of pale German prisoners-of-war arrived in an army truck, marshalled by soldiers from the Home Guard. They were fed by Mrs Teasel at the deal table in the back kitchen, where she had laid out wedges of grey bread, thickly larded with lamb dripping and Blackwater River salt. The Germans devoured it, believing it would line their miserable stomachs and shield them from the constant threat of starvation.

The merry troupe of Land Girls, most of whom were billeted in the big house, were well fed by the time they arrived for work. Ten of them set forth with buckets to milk the fifty pedigree shorthorn cows twice a day. The children could hear their sweet voices singing patriotic harmonies in the cowshed near the schoolroom.

When he wasn't in school, Harry had a whole litany of jobs, like bringing in logs for the range, skinning rabbits, trapping pine martens and searching for vipers that might kill lambs or eat the duck eggs. During the lambing season, he went with the shepherd's dog out into the night to hunt for newly lambed, black-faced, Suffolk ewes. He could only see them if he happened to catch their emerald green eyes glinting in the beam of the Tilley lamp. He moved silently over the frosty grass, listening for the grunt of a ewe that might be lying in the lee of the hedge, having singled herself out from the flock, to give birth on her own. His job was to bring them back to the hurdle pens, where they could be watched and minded. Many nights he spent alone in these lambing pens with nothing but a hissing lamp and the breath of the sheep dog to keep away the fox and the freezing east wind. Harry became an expert on the calls of the night. Thus it was, working with the few old men left in England, that he had learned the tricks of the shepherd's trade.

'Oh, I don't know, Kat; I guess it's a kind of race memory. It makes sense though, doesn't it? The ewe seems to know her own smell.'

Harry follows Katherine back into the kitchen and puts the kettle on the range. She takes some tobacco from a pouch in her pocket and rolls it skilfully, mixed with dried marijuana flakes from her dwindling stash, into a thick reefer. She lights it, sucks hard and then offers it to Harry. He takes the joint between his finger and thumb, puts it to his lips and pulls lightly. He passes it back to her without inhaling. This goes on for a while, the two of them sitting by the range. Katherine is drifting, and Harry, biding his time, is waiting for the right moment. After a while, Katherine's head is lolling back and her eyes are rolling around like poached eggs swilling in a pan of simmering water.

~

He stands up and leans over her. 'Katherine, wake up! You'll have to come home with me now.' She stares up at him through the smoke. 'Get your things together. If we get going now, we can catch the flight back tonight.'

Katherine begins to laugh. She looks at him with bleary eyes through the mellow haze. 'Cool it, man.'

'Snap out of it! You didn't really think you could stay here on your own, did you? Why do you think I'm here? I'm taking you home. I didn't come all this way to skin lambs and smoke dope!'

'Whoa there, cool it. Chill out. I'm not ready to split here.' She smiles blissfully and giggles a bit more. Her voice is like soap bubbles blown through a tiny hoop into the air.

'Goddamn it, girl, what d'you mean, 'not ready'? What are you waiting for? What mad, harum-scarum schemes are you thinking of now? Your mother is right. You haven't the brains of a bloody 'edge'og!'

It is at moments like these that Katherine can hear Harry's own mother speaking. The combination of whiskey, dope and frustration unleashes the faintest betrayal of cockney, revealing everything he has struggled all his life to conceal.

Harry straightens up. He thumps the beam over the range.

'I'm telling you, Katherine, this is madness. You are coming back to England with me right away!'

He opens the door to let the freezing air from outside hit her in the face and bring her to her senses. She is still drifting, wondering why Harry is shouting again. She is floating over endless horizons; the comfortable, folding hills of North Kilkenny where the sun lingers forever, lighting up the sky with scarlets, pinks and purples; and the absolute blackness of the night, against which every star in heaven shines out.

'For God's sake, pull yourself together!' He snatches the remains of the joint from between her fingers, throws it into the firebox, grabs her by the shoulders and starts to drag her towards the door. She puts up her hand and tries to push him away, but he catches her hair and pulls.

'You stupid girl, you can't stay here. What in God's name are you thinking of? Come to your senses!' He hits her full across the face with the back of his hand.

The dog leaps out of the shadows, barking loudly. It catches his trouser leg and tries to tug him away from Katherine. Harry kicks out at it. He loses his balance and trips over the chair, falling against the edge of the table, bringing Katherine down as well.

With a bleeding lip and a head that feels like it doesn't belong to her, she staggers to her feet and runs out into the yard. She heads for the barn, where it's dark and she can hide. She crouches behind the barn door, holding the dog's mouth shut. She listens for Harry coming after her, but hears nothing except the beat of her heart as its pulse thumps against the inside of her skull. She shivers in the shadows for what seems like ages. All she can hear is Queen Mary chewing the cud and the bleating of lambs. Eventually, she hears the kitchen door open. She holds her breath. The car is starting up, turning around. The tyres crunch in the frost. It is driving over the ford, fading away up the hill of the boreen. She waits a while longer just to be sure he's really gone.

The blood has dried into a crust on the side of her face. She sits in the gloomy kitchen, lights another joint and tugs the dog up onto her lap. She understands well that Harry knows better than to fight unwinnable battles, but she isn't sure if he has decided not to wait around or retreated temporarily and plans to come back for another round later on. She spends the night on watch, with the dog close by and the light on.

~

Driving into the evening sun, Harry curses mildly about the money he's wasted on an air ticket for Katherine, and when he gets there, he haggles at the Aer Lingus desk to get it open-ended for another time. He grinds his teeth, swearing at his wife as if everything in Ireland was her fault. What angers him most, although he doesn't care to admit it, even to himself, is the way she has a knack of reminding him of who he really is. She knows nothing about all that, especially the time just after the war was over, when he and his sisters had gone back to the bombed-out East End of London. No one will ever hear the stories of the utter desolation Harry and his family had suffered. Nothing was ever the same again. Their mother was worn out, their father gone forever, to the bottom of the

100

sea in the belly of a troop ship sunk by a German U-boat. London was in heaps of rubble, and everyone around them was hungry and sick. Some of the things he did to get money or food to keep his family alive, he will never repeat; most especially what it felt like to bend over for an old poof, just to get the price of a few vitals or a couple of extra meat vouchers. However, no matter how bad things were in 1945, Harry had glimpsed the far side of the mountain by then. He was able to settle into grammar school, to face the teasing about his cockney accent and his 'down home' style of clothes. He knew that education and a hard neck were the way out and, more importantly, the way up. No matter how high and mighty the other boys appeared, everyone was shaken by the war. No family was left untouched. Harry was one of the lucky ones; he had lived both on the mountain and in the valley, and he had made his choice.

He had been about seventeen when a letter arrived from Mrs Teasel, inviting him to come up to Norfolk again to spend his summer holidays with them on the estate. Mr Teasel had returned from the war, shaken, aged and impotent. They had no children of their own, and Harry turned out to be just the 'reviver' they needed. He found the place had a very different atmosphere in peacetime—no sparky Land Girls singing in the meadows, and no ghostly German prisoners to do all the donkey work either.

The Suffolk punches, with their gleaming chestnut coats burnished with dapples like copper coins scattered across their broad, rounded backs, were out to pasture now. Living in retirement, the horses watched their work being done by a team of stuttering machines. The hay was no longer forked up onto tripods to ripen in the fields for weeks, but turned and tossed behind a tractor and buck-raked into stacks. The cows that had once been crooned through the milking by the hum of soft voices and the strong hands of Land Girls and milk maids, were now hitched up to a pulsating apparatus that sucked the milk from them in a quarter of the time.

Mrs Teasel had mellowed slightly. She asked Harry to do things with a 'please', and now that sugar rationing was easing off, she could coax him with Ginger Parkin, sweet talk and Chelsea buns. During this post-war deep breath, no one had to eat dried eggs or chew on Horlicks tablets to get their protein levels up anymore. Teasel himself didn't do a lot. Come rain or shine, winter or summer, through lambing and calving and harvest time, he sat at a coal fire in the steward's office, shuffling piles of paper and smoking his pipe. In the morning, after breakfast, Harry, with the other estate workers, was sent to Mr Teasel to get his instructions for the day. It didn't take Harry long to complete the list of tasks. The rest of the time he spent either at the river with a group of lads from the village, trying to work out how to coax trout to bite their bait, or lying in the sweet new hay, with chubby, delicious Jessica de Montfort. She always took the bait.

While Harry and Jessica languished in the barn, the swallows and martens swooped in and out, feeding first one and then a second clutch of fleshy little squabs. The two teenagers idled away many summer evenings listening to the distant sound of wood pigeons gurgling and cooing, while trying to follow the dust fairies, which danced in the shafts of sunlight bursting through the splits between the clapboards. At first, he had thought Jessica would be his route out of oblivion, but after a while, she became tiresome and demanding. He diverted his energies back into his education. Against the odds, Harry obtained a scholarship to Cambridge. From then on, he aped the upper classes by day and sustained himself by doing shift work in a canning factory at night. He graduated with an honours' degree in politics and economics. Mr and Mrs Teasel were invited to his graduation, and then he took up a job in the city of London.

Geographically, this had been not too far from his old haunts in the East End, but it might as well have been in China, because, by this time, Harry had focused his eyes in the opposite direction. Sometimes after work or on a Sunday, he would saunter along the Thames and even up into the back streets to have a peep at his childhood home from the safety of his pin-striped suit. He carried on meeting his family occasionally, but only if they came to visit him in his apartment and only when his flatmates were out. He had, however, kept in regular contact with the Teasels and sometimes went up to Norfolk on the train for a weekend visit. Jessica had long since done her season in London and was now engaged to a rosy-faced and chinless gentleman with huge front teeth and bugger's grips—the eldest son of a minor peer from a nearby estate. She was delighted by Harry's metamorphosis, feeling in some way responsible, and, on one of his visits to Norfolk, she invited him to join her party at the Hunt Ball.

The group stood around awkwardly, shivering in the great hall, dressed in dinner jackets and stiff, satin ballgowns, sipping mulled wine and discussing the hunting. Harry was doing his best to keep his mouth shut as much as possible and to blend in. He was introduced to Miss Katherine Butler. Everyone had been a bit unsure what to make of this diminutive, red-haired heiress from Suffolk, whom Jessica had met at finishing school. Jessica whispered to Harry that Katherine's father was a very successful and well-connected industrialist; although Irish, apparently. When Harry heard she was the only child of a millionaire, he took a deep breath and smiled so widely that the gap between his two front teeth was all Katherine noticed about him. Henry George Fletcher never looked back. After a year, they were engaged, and by the time Katherine was twenty-two, they were married. Soon they were comfortably housed in Chelsea, and Harry was brought in as accountant to the family business. He took a tight grip on the books, determined to turn Bagshot Construction, Ltd, which had begun to slide into the business doldrums, into an international PLC. It is now one of the largest construction companies in the UK. Harry is a director and the chief accountant.

He slides into his seat on the plane, smiles at the air hostess, hoping his thick fringe will cover the gash on his forehead. With the *Financial Times* on his lap, he slips one hand between his thighs, the other deep into his trouser pocket. He thinks about last night. After a while, he starts to work out a story that he can tell to Katherine's parents.

CHAPTER SIX

For a few days after Harry's visit, Katherine's head hurts. She remembers little of what happened between them. She knows that it ended badly. Somehow, she is still here at the farm. She has an uneasy feeling about the whole encounter, because, when it comes to rows with Harry, she does not normally win. If anyone bolts, it is usually her. Blood is on the kitchen table, a chunk of her hair is on the floor, one of her front teeth is chipped and she has a swollen black eye, but other than that, it is all blank. The not knowing is nearly worse than remembering. It is a group of scenes from a strange drama: like Harry skilfully skinning a dead lamb. She cries when she sees it there, lying in a puddle in the yard, the miserable little corpse with fluffy legs and head but no skin on its body. The crows have already pecked out its eyes. When she pulls herself together, she takes it out into a wooded area and leaves it for the foxes.

Until Jim Ryan took the withered pelt off the cuckoo lamb yesterday, it still had the scraps tied around it like a makeshift shepherd's costume in a nativity play, reminding her that this really happened. It was so out of character for Harry. Not only had it worked, but somehow, he had known it would. And the smell of whiskey on his breath; Harry doesn't drink whiskey, and certainly not in the morning. It torments her that she cannot remember anything she said, nor anything Harry said either. She is half listening all the time for the hired car swooshing back over the ford as if he never went home but has been staying in Kilkenny, doing deals behind her back. When he comes again, she knows he'll be full of vengeance; maybe even bringing reinforcements: Pierce, the guards, who knows? Harry has to have the last word.

She ventures out little and spends a lot of time brooding in front of the range. Among other things, she tries to remember if she had the nerve to ask Harry to send over some more dope. It's unlikely, even less likely that he would do it, anyway. All is not lost, though; she has other sources. She sends a coded message on a postcard to a contact in London and watches out for the postman.

As the flagstones weep and the days close in tightly, Harry begins to fade. Life, once again, becomes more about the daily struggles and trying to find out what happened to Uncle Jack. Katherine is increasingly preoccupied with a string of rhetorical questions that are going round on a loop in her mind. How did he live like this? So alone, steadily losing the battle with nature and getting old. What happened to him, that he finally couldn't take it anymore and shot himself? Or did he? The known details roll over and over in her head. There are very few of those. No one seems to know anything, and nor are they willing to talk about it. He shot himself. That's the one thing on which they mostly agree. Why? How? It doesn't seem to matter to anyone, except to Katherine. It is as if they all expected it to happen sooner or later. It's a whispered tragedy. What about Sergeant Dawson's hypothesis that it could have been an accident? But murder? That is a possibility that, when mentioned, leads to a silence more profound than a radio with dead batteries. Evidence? There isn't any. Or at least, what evidence there might have been is no more. Not even a note. This little detail in particular chafes at Katherine. Why would someone steal the last words of a dying man? And if it was an accident, how could that happen? Marie said he was shot in the side of the head with his shotgun. How could you do that? The barrel of a shotgun is nearly a yard long. How could you even hold that, pointing at the side of your head, and pull the trigger? You would have to have very long arms or someone else to do it for you. She tries tipping her head sideways and holding her right arm out as far as it would go. Maybe if you used your thumb? And where is the gun now? Katherine resolves, there and then, to go to the Garda station tomorrow and find out. Surely it belongs to her, along with the rest of Jack's estate? If she holds the gun, it might, somehow, imbue in her a sense of what happened. Anyway, it's a loose end that she can't leave dangling.

Sergeant Dawson makes Katherine feel as if ants are running up and down her legs. It's not the fact that he leers at her or the way he leans across when he opens the car door. Men in Knocklong all seem to do that kind of thing, but he is the only one doing it from the safety of a uniform. This feeling is not eased by the way he quizzes her about her black eye. She is standing in the Garda barracks and has asked for the return of her uncle's shotgun.

'That's a right shiner, missus,' he says with a questioning rise at the end of the sentence. Katherine turns away from him and stares at the floorboards. 'Had a run in with a gate?'

Pause. 'Heard you had a visitor?' When she turns to face him again, his eyes don't meet hers; they are looking directly at her chest.

Katherine tugs the two sides of her coat so that they cross over and cover everything beneath. Dawson takes out his biro and starts filling in a form.

'He shouldn't have kept that gun at all, silly old fool. These are dangerous times.' The word 'dangerous' rolls around his tongue as if there are twenty r's in it. He looks across the counter at the red-haired English heiress all the men are talking about every night in the pub, wondering which of them might have swung a haymaker in her direction. Or was it the visitor in the posh car?

'You'll have to sign for that now; it's evidential, you know.' He is pretending to look at the top of her head as she bends over the paper to sign, but as her coat falls open again, he's trying to get a peep down the front of her jumper, at the way it clings to her curves.

'You mean you are still investigating what happened?'

'Ah, well now, I didn't say that.' Short pause, then before she could ask any more awkward questions, he goes on, 'It would be a lot safer here in the barracks under lock and key, you know.'

'Maybe it would. I don't know. I would like to have it, though, as it belonged to the family. My father has one just like it,' she lies. Her father's gun is a beautiful, well-oiled Purdey, nothing like this very workaday gun that apparently shot poor old Jack.

'You mind where you keep it now, well out of sight. Store the cartridges in a different place too.'

Having failed to persuade Katherine to leave the weapon in the Garda station, Sergeant Dawson makes a big deal of showing her how to carry it, broken open, over her arm. She is tempted to tell him that having helped out at many shoots on the estate at home, she is familiar with guns. He tells her again to keep it well hidden in the press under the stairs.

'You'll need to take out a new gun licence too. If you really intend staying for a while, that is. Here, look't, leave it with me, and I'll drop it over to you later.' But Katherine is determined. She stuffs it into a meal bag and ties the bundle to the handlebars with twine. When he sees her mount up, he just laughs.

'That apple didn't fall far from the tree. She's Jack Butler's niece, all right,' he says to the other two Gardaí watching from the fire place.

Katherine speeds off homewards, trying to avoid the potholes. Normally, she gets off at the hill because she doesn't trust the brakes, but today all she can think of is getting home as quickly as possible. When she reaches the safety of the porch, she unties the parcel and takes it quickly into the house. Unwrapping it on the kitchen table, she tries to picture Jack holding it. It's such an awkward thing. Cold steel, dark wood. So final. This thought keeps going backwards and forwards through her mind. She just can't see him doing it. She lifts it to her shoulder, wraps her finger around the trigger and squints along the barrel. This reminds her of something that happened here many years ago.

She had been about fourteen years old. She was going with Jack one summer night out onto the ridge. He was so tormented by dogs chasing his ewes that he had decided to put an end to it once and for all. They set out together that night with the heat of the day still glowing faintly in the western sky. The two of them had moved quietly, feeling their way along a warm dry-stone wall, trying to stay downwind of the tormented flock. Katherine's job was to swing the torch in an arc, every ten minutes or so, until she caught the eyes of the dog in its powerful beam. Then, like two errant stars that had fallen from the sky, she saw them gleaming straight at her. Jack put the shotgun to his shoulder. There would be no second chance. An almighty crack echoed around the valley below. They walked briskly to where a large dog lay twitching in the damp grass, its own blood running freely over that of the mauled udder of a lame ewe. Jack said there was bound to be an accomplice. Alerted by the shot, it would by now be running swiftly somewhere away into the night.

'He'll be back. The scent of fresh blood will be too much for him. We'll wait here and bide our time.'

The second cartridge finished off the savaged and quivering ewe. The stench of congealing blood sullied the fresh dew. The rest of the flock were huddled tightly in the corner of the field, their pointed noses forced upwards against each other, their sweat and heaving breath forming a rising cloud around them. He dragged the dead dog away and slung it out of sight. Then the two of them crouched down in the lee of the wall and waited silently as a thin, yellow moon slid above the horizon. He pulled two cartridges from his back pocket, cracked open and reloaded the gun.

Jack thought nothing of sitting on some boulders for hours in the chilly night, smoking his pipe and whispering to Katherine about this and that. All kinds of anecdotes about the sheep and anything and everything that came into his head, none of which she can remember now. She huddled into the oily Aran sweater that Bridget had knitted her for Christmas. From time to time, Jack took a small flask from his breast pocket, and they both had a swig of fire water. The night passed without sleep, and eventually, shivering, she had watched the dawn begin to snake across the sky in the east. As it rose to meet the horizon, the sun lit up the mottled clouds; streaks of fluff glowed with an iridescent pink. By now, the flock had settled back to chewing the cud and wandering around, making patterns in the dewy grass.

'Look at that, girl; "red sky in the morning, shepherds' warning". No chance that villain will come back now. We'll make good the morning and check those night lines at the river. Come on.'

He retrieved the dead dog and, holding it by one hind leg, lobbed it over his shoulder. Katherine followed him down to the silvery water where the baited lines were tied and secured with balls of lead in various dark pools at 'The Dead Man's Hollow', just near to where the railway embankment meets the old metal bridge. The river was low, and they slithered down the bank to the water's edge. Jack knew exactly where his lines were tied to whippy little saplings. He lifted them one at a time and drew them in. Four fine trout were dangling from the various threads and hooks. They twinkled like coloured tinfoil in the first slithers of sunlight as they broke the water.

'That's our breakfast now! You put them in your gansey, and I'll bring this old scoundrel.' He gave the dog a nudge with his boot as if to make sure it was properly dead.

Katherine made a pouch out of the front of her sweater, lined it with a few handfuls of damp grass and laid the trout on top. Just as they were about to set off back along the riverbank, Jack stopped.

'Wait now, we'll cook 'em here. They'll taste better like that.' He arranged a few stones in a ring on the ground. 'Give me them fishes there, you. Now go and gather some sticks and some rushes, and we'll start a wee fire here by the riverbank.'

He gutted two of them with a pocket knife, chucking the

innards back into the river. Then impaled them on sharpened
sticks and built a gantry of twigs on which to roast them. It
took a few goes to get the fire to light, because the rushes were
green and fresh with the morning dew. Jack pulled a twist of
tarry string from his pocket, and that did the trick. They sat
together in the moist grass, eating the catch. The mottled
brown skins were blackened and crispy on the outside. The
creamy flesh peeled off the spikey little bones in juicy chunks.
It tasted of the earth, the grass, the river and much more.
Katherine knew that nothing would ever taste as good again.

They had stayed there by the river until the sun was well
above the trees.

'Why is it called Dead Man's Hollow?'

'Mmm, there's a question now. That was all a long
time ago.'

'Tell me, please,' Katherine had insisted.

'Back in the day; bad old days.' He pulled on his pipe,
and a dreamy look came into his eyes. 'Maybe you'd better
ask your father to tell you about that one.' And then just
in case she might ask again, Jack said brightly, pointing his
pipe towards the eastern horizon, 'Only for that red sky this
morning, we could have knocked the meadow today.'

'How will you do that?'

'You are all questions this morning, girl. Let's go back and
see what we can do today. You bring them other two trout.
We'll fry 'em later for our tea. I'll bring this scoundrel.' And
with a heave, he threw the stiffening carcass of the dog back
over his shoulder. Blood was oozing from its nose, and its
eyes were still open, as if watching warily for another shot.
Katherine picked up the gun from where he had laid it in
the weeds.

'Mind, that's still loaded.' She put it down again carefully, but never forgot how it felt in her hands; cold, brutal and surprisingly heavy.

It was always like that with Jack and food. You ate when you could. He seemed to be able to go for days without a square meal. He bought brown soda-bread from Kitty in the local shop and butter in the creamery in the morning. After that, they had to rely on any eggs they could find around the farmyard, praying they were fresh ones, seeing if they would sink or float in a basin of water, just to be sure. Or the odd hare or rabbit unfortunate enough to stumble into one of Jack's many snares; a few cabbages and loads of potatoes from his patch in the haggard and those beautiful brown trout from the night lines. As the summer merged into autumn, she guessed, there would have been the apples in the orchard and the bountiful harvest of blackberries and damsons in the hedges. He always had a jar of honey from Josie Ryan on the go; it was thick and crunchy and tasted of the summer flowers. As long as there was grass, he had milk from the cows. Katherine couldn't imagine what he lived on in the winter months, since he gave up killing a pig and hanging the haunches in the chimney breast to cure in peat smoke. Little wonder he was a mere whippet of a man himself.

He hauled the dead corpse home and left it behind the house till the maggots had more or less picked the bones clean of flesh and the smell had completely dissolved into the grass. Katherine had long since gone back to England before the owner came looking for his dog. She always wondered who that was. Jack seemed not to care. But that was Katherine's mistake. He knew well who owned it. Before that summer was out, he had shot its comrade too. Jack, who normally held dogs in high esteem, was never sorry about these two. They were vermin, and so was their owner.

113

Jack listened to the radio, foddered and tended his cattle and sheep, made a few acres of hay and sowed some drills of cabbages, turnips and potatoes. His social life took place sitting on the donkey cart with his one or two churns of milk, in the long queue at the creamery, every morning, or over a couple of scoops of beer and a game of cards in Johnny's on a Saturday night. Sometimes, if the mood took him that way, he went to Mass on a Sunday morning, calling to Ryans' for a cup of tea on his way home. Josie would always have a Sunday dinner put by for Jack, just in case. He never owned a car. If he needed to go somewhere that was too far away for the donkey and cart, he just stood out on the road and put up his hand at any vehicle that passed. They were few and far between, but they always stopped for Jack. Sooner or later, someone took him wherever he wanted to go. The summers were good and the winters bleak.

Katherine is sure that if he had shot himself, Jack certainly would have chosen September to go, while the leaves still held a resonance of summer and a soft mist greeted every morning and every night. He would not have waited until November, when the days were closing tight around him and the west wind came hurtling along the river and whipped in under the kitchen door, like a blade in the kidneys.

One evening, a week or so before Christmas, Katherine sets out for a walk up on the ridge to check the sheep and feel the wind blow out her hair. It is a wild, blustery day. The sun is shining up from the valley and lingering in a stack of yellow clouds. Everything is glowing with an eerie, citric light. She strides along with her dog at her heels, listening to the hungry ravens croaking as they circle overhead. The Irish vultures on the lookout for a ewe that might have rolled onto her back, like the one she found last week with its flank pecked open and its guts pulled out.

'They don't last long like that, poor divils,' Jim Ryan had told her with a gleam in his eye. 'If the scavengers don't kill 'em, they'll die anyway, lying upside down, like sailors marooned at sea.' He came over to the farm later that day and put it out of its misery with a bullet in the head.

She likes to walk up here because the air is thinner and colder, and the stinging in her lungs reminds her that all life is precious. She checks the walls on the boundary fence and sometimes stops to replace a stone that has become dislodged. Not today, though; it's too cold, and the evening is gathering in. On her way back to the house, she clambers warily over the gate into the yard, careful not to put her weight on its weak spots, lest it collapses beneath her. She whistles for the dog, who's been distracted by a new scent. Jim Ryan is standing with his back to her and his hands in his pockets, looking into the cow byre.

'Oh, there you are. Just came to say Josie asked if you would care to come down in the morning to give a hand killing the turkeys.'

'I've never done anything like that, Jim.'

'Time you learned, then. Them birds don't do 'emselves in, you know.'

When Katherine cycles into the Ryans' yard the next day, the massacre is well underway. A bunch of huge, fat birds are huddled in a corner, not shielded in any way from the full view of their imminent fate. Feathers fly in all directions, and a thick sweat is gleaming on Josie's face. Her mighty arms are working like the hind legs of a horse pulling a plough. Josie was once a poultry instructor. When it comes to turkeys, she is an expert in death. The hens are dispatched by pulling their feet upwards and their heads downwards. A quick, anticlockwise twist with the right wrist, and the neck is broken; there is a short bit of flapping around, and the bird is on its way to Christmas dinner. The cockerels are too big for this. Josie's arms aren't long enough to accomplish the fatal jerk, so they have to be finished off by putting their heads under a broomstick, which she secures by standing on it, and then yanking the feet upwards. The really tough birds have to be dispatched with a hatchet, which is very messy, and Josie's face is smeared with streaks of blood from wiping back her hair with bloody hands.

Now and then, the Ryans' dogs dart across the yard and take a few slurps of the turkey blood, oozing slowly into the central drain, before Josie gives them a kick and sends them yelping away. The bald and scalded bodies are hanging by their feet on a row of nails along the stone wall. Their heads are swelling with blood and their eyes are beginning to bulge. The pointy remains of their wings hang open and limp. Marie's job is to try and pluck the birds while they are still warm and the feathers yield easily. Sitting on a wooden kitchen chair in the arched doorway of the barn, she holds a half-plucked turkey across her lap.

Katherine, her stomach quaking, hopes for a quick escape on some pretext, but Marie soon has her installed on a seat beside herself, plucking away. The tiny chest feathers are the worst. They get into everything; up her nose, in her hair. The smell is strange, sticky and pervasive. Marie is able to tear out fistfuls at a time, but Katherine pinches them between her thumb and forefinger, nervous that she will skin the bird as well. She doesn't accomplish the same satisfying ripping sound that comes from Marie's victims. The feel of the warm flesh, the graceful curve of the mighty chest of a well-fed cockerel, makes her empty stomach gurgle and heave. Marie pulls out

116

the innards with a sucking, squelching sound and drops them into a bucket by her feet. Later on, she will put the livers, necks and other useful gizzards into plastic bags and stow them in the fridge. These will be stuffed back into the washed-out cavity from whence they were wrenched before the birds are taken into the turkey market in town. The occasional random lump of guts is chucked out for the dog, along with some wedges of yellow fat.

Marie, chatting merrily, tells Katherine that when it comes to slaughtering the geese, the livers will be carefully separated for making pâté to sell to shops or give to friends. All the soft under feathers will be stored for restuffing pillows. Those from the tips of the wings will be tied together like witches' brooms, for getting dust out of awkward corners when Josie starts the spring cleaning before Easter. But the goose fat is prized above all else. It will be rendered in a huge pan, mixed with herbs or oil of wintergreen and potted in sterilized jars. Unction to be kept for use as a salve for chapped hands, a liniment for sprains and a balm to soften cold winter udders at milking time. Josie will keep an earthenware jar of pure goose fat in the larder for basting the turkey and roasting the potatoes when it comes to cooking Christmas dinner. Today, however, the geese are still grazing the upper lawn field, peacefully unaware of their destiny and the value of their big breasts and livers, their perfect white feathers and their fatty parts.

After the turkeys have all been killed, plucked, eviscerated and hung, Josie sluices down the yard with boiling water, and Marie and Katherine sweep up the feathers into a soggy heap. Josie wrings her blotchy, red hands into the hem of her apron and offers tea to the girls. This is no ordinary tea; this is 'Turkey Tea', with loads of sugar, thick blobs of cream and a hefty dollop of whiskey.

'That husband of yours was over, then?' Josie looks across the kitchen table to Katherine.

'How did you know that?'

'People talk.'

'What people?'

'He isn't too shy about selling the place, anyway,' JJ growls from his seat in the corner.

Katherine thought he was asleep. She ignores him and turns back to Josie. 'What do you mean?'

Then Marie chips in from across the room, 'She doesn't mean anything, do you, Mam?'

Josie shrugs her shoulders and looks at the globules of butterfat floating around on the surface of the tea. 'You'll be going home for Christmas?'

'Who told you that? This is my home now. I'm going nowhere.'

'Ah whisht! Will you go away out of that, girl? What about your lovely home in London and your folks back in Suffolk?'

'Who told you about my house in London?'

Josie waves a muscular right arm in front of her face, as if swatting a fly. 'No need to get all worked up, you. It's just talk, that's all; no one means anything by it.'

Marie pours out another round of 'Turkey Tea' and heaps in spoonfuls of sugar, along with a good lashing of whiskey and thick cream. She hands one each to Josie, Katherine and JJ.

Josie settles down in the chair again and, returning to her normal chirpy voice, insists, 'Drink that and you'll be more yourself. You'll have your Christmas dinner here with us, then. No argument, do you hear me?'

~

Katherine takes a different route home, just for a change. The lane winds along, away from the river, bisecting an ancient oak plantation. She is gaily singing Christmas carols out loud. The bike is wobbling precariously because she is not getting up enough speed to keep it straight. Deep in the woods, she is suddenly surrounded by an encampment of gypsy travellers. Three brightly painted barrel-topped wagons. A couple of flat carts, shafts up in the air with all manner of things stored underneath, strung along the road. She navigates her way around some piebald ponies hobbled and grazing along the side of the road and a bunch of strong-smelling goats lurking around the trees. She has to stop and get off her bike to avoid running over a small flock of young game birds, sparring at each other in little spats. Women and children stare at her but keep their distance. A few men are squatting around a fire on the edge of the tarmac, smoking. There isn't a puff of wind. Wood smoke lingers in the air. She walks as briskly as she can, nodding politely, right and left.

Some women start to come after her, and one calls out, 'Ha' ye a penny for the baby, missus?'

At first Katherine doesn't understand. She stops, using the bike as a kind of defence barrier. She asks the woman to repeat it. At this, they all crowd around her and start up a chant along the same lines. Her shaking fingers begin to jingle the change in her pocket. One of the men shouts something, and they all retreat, like a wave being sucked back into the sea. Katherine mounts up and pedals fast, looking straight ahead, minding the potholes. Her heart is racing so much that her eyes are blurry. A small band of scrawny lurchers bounds after her, barking fiercely, snapping at the wheels of the bike. The wet hem of her long skirt is smacking against her legs, making it difficult to pedal.

Eventually, clear of the woods, she hops off the bike to regain her breath, which, by now, is scratching and rasping her chest. She looks back. The trees have swallowed all signs of life. There is not even a wisp of smoke to give the encampment away.

Katherine feels dizzy. She rests on the handlebars, trying to steady herself. Her stomach heaves, and she pukes up gallons of turkey tea. The sour taste is sweetened, only a little, by the soft scent of winter grass and wet earth. When she finally manages to steady herself and remount the bicycle, her legs feel heavy and slow. The air is lifeless. Huge blankets of cloud, weighty with sleet and snow, are closing in around the farm. There is an eerie stillness in the valley. The light of the evening is leaking out onto the horizon.

Fresh car tyres have made a criss-cross pattern of tracks in the farmyard. By now, it is nearly dark, but she can still make out where a vehicle has been driven through the gateway into the back field. There are footprints where a man obviously got out to open and close the gate. She is unable to see clearly, but it seems that whoever it was has made several passes, back and forth, through that gate. She stands motionless, listening for engine noises or gumboots thumping the ground. Large snowflakes drift out of the darkened sky and settle in her hair. Gradually, they begin to white out any traces of intrusion. All that breaks the silence is the interminable squawking of manic crows, fighting over roosts, high up in the sycamore trees.

She sings loudly while she milks her cow. When she has about six inches of frothy milk in the bucket, she lets the calf in to finish off and retreats to the kitchen. She jams a chair against the door and lights up a joint, willing the warm smoke to soothe her tangled nerves, to quiet the voices in her head.

~

Before Katherine has thought of making any preparations, it is Christmas Eve. In a dope-induced haze, she drifts back to Christmas at home. Her mother, Georgina, only ever cooks one meal a year, and that is the Christmas dinner—a task which takes her two days to accomplish. She needs the whole house completely to herself. Dressed in a blue and white striped apron, her perfectly manicured fingers struggle to force sausage meat and chestnut stuffing under the skin and into the cavity of the raw turkey. When satisfied that it's as stuffed as it can possibly be, she neatly sews up all the orifices with twine and a carpet needle. She cuts little crosses in each of the Brussels sprouts and pops them into cold water and shaves the potatoes, sculpting them into perfect, matching ovals. The routine on Christmas Eve has always been that her father would take Katherine and Bridget to London in the Bentley to see the lights; thus clearing the decks and enabling Georgina's masterpiece to take shape.

There was a time, for a bleak few years back in the fifties, when Bridget used to struggle home to Ireland for Christmas. It was a terrible journey in the winter, involving a train to Liverpool Street, bus to Euston, another train to Holyhead, changing at Crewe, a 'God-forsaken place', at two in the morning, to catch the mail boat to Dun Laoghaire. It stank of stale fish and vomit and rocked Bridget's guts to ribbons. The freezing cold wait on the windswept quays, praying the train into Westland Row would be running that day, was almost a welcome relief and a break before hauling her stuff onto a train and then a bus to cross the city of Dublin to Heuston Station to wait for the connection down to Kilkenny. The final part of the journey involved thumbing-it out to the family home in Graney, with a suitcase, presents and a leaking plastic mackintosh. The whole thing could take up to three days, depending on the conditions and connections. It leached so much out of Bridget and left Christmas so threadbare in Suffolk that these Christmas visits have long since been phased out.

With all fires extinguished for the night, the old manor house was a chilly place in the early hours of Christmas morning. The east wind, coming directly off the North Sea, slithered under the front door and insinuated its way all around the house. A candle, standing in a tall glass vase in the front hall, was barely able to hold its own against the draught swirling it around, causing gothic shadows across the beams in the high ceiling. Frank and Georgina would retire to bed, exhausted, after Midnight Mass, but Bridget and Katherine usually sat at the kitchen table, huddled beside the Aga, drinking cocoa with a thick layer of cream on top, wrapping up the presents and trying to guess what Father Christmas would bring.

Christmas Eve in Knocklong is very different. Katherine curls herself into the armchair beside the smouldering range, wrapping a heavy cardigan around her shoulders and gripping a mug of tea. It's so quiet in the house that she can hear the faint echo of the church bells ringing in monotone peals. She stares blankly at the smoke from her reefer twisting into ghostly shapes as it is wound around by the various air currents in the room. There are no cheery Christmas carols on the radio when she turns it on; it's just Santa making enormous promises to children all over Ireland. Uncle Jack seems to be in the room; she can feel his presence, almost hear him coughing. She tries to console herself with the thought that in those years when Bridget came home to her own family, she surely would have called to visit him, brought him a bottle of whiskey and news of his favourite niece. The mice scratch behind the huge wooden dresser.

There is a timid knock on the kitchen door. The dog crouches, her hackles up, growling deep in the back of her throat. Katherine opens the door. Standing there in the frosty morning is a traveller woman, a shawl around her head and shoulders and a small baby nestled in the crook of her arm.

'The blessin's 'a' God on you and all your people. Would you have something for the baby this Christmas?'

'Come in from the cold.' Katherine tries to draw the woman into the kitchen, but she just stands there on the doorstep, emanating a strong smell of wood smoke, goats, earth, urine, who knows; it's unlike anything Katherine has ever experienced before.

'Would ye have a bit of food for the childer, for the Christmas?' The woman's skin is brown and deeply lined. 'A sup 'a' milk? Bread? Whatever ye have to spare.'

'How many children have you?'

'Sixteen living.'

'Sixteen! Good grief!' Katherine quickly gathers a few groceries together and stuffs them into a paper bag.

'I'll say a wee prayer for ye an' wish ye a very happy Christmas, ma'am.'

'You too.' Then Katherine boldly asks, 'Are you in that camp in the woods outside the village?'

The woman nods and adjusts her shawl as the baby begins to squeak. 'We are that, ma'am'.

In an unexpected surge of Christmas spirit, Katherine says, 'I might come by that way in the morning with some more bits and pieces, if that's okay?'

'You will be very welcome. The blessings 'a' God on ye, ma'am.'

The woman bows, nods and backs away. Her shoes are only barely holding together. She finds it hard to get a grip on the icy path. Katherine watches as the old woman clambers up onto the back of a flat cart, trying not to drop the baby in the yard. With a crack of the whip, and a few 'huppyas', she is driven away over the ford and up the boreen.

Marie calls round later on and is horrified to hear that Katherine invited a tinker into the house.

'What were you thinking of? She could have taken anything!'

'What on earth would she take?'

'Well, I don't know, the radio, your handbag, anything. Was she alone? You know what they do is one keeps you talking at the door while the others sneak round the back and take whatever they can find.'

Katherine's mind peruses the heaps of broken beer bottles and rusty, baked-bean cans, dog bones and all the other detritus of Jack's life in her back garden.

'Old buckets or bits of scrap metal. You never know. Anything. You didn't give her any money, did you?'

'She said she had sixteen children, Marie.'

'At least! I bet she can't even count them!'

'I wish I had given her some money now. She wouldn't even stand in the warmth of the kitchen.'

'That's something, anyhow. Look't, don't be such an eegit girl; they'll never leave you alone if you give them money. They'll keep coming back forever, like hungry dogs, like that old fox that took your hens!'

'The baby was so tiny and miserable. She looked old enough to be its great- grandmother.'

'God knows what she's feeding it on. Mangy old goats' milk, probably.' Then Marie adds brightly, 'Come on, I know where there's a holly bush with berries on it,' and adds as an afterthought, 'Make sure you lock that door after us!' But Katherine has no key for it.

The two women are tramping up the hill behind the farmhouse when Marie spots a ewe.

'That one's in trouble.'

'How can you tell?'

'Have you ever heard anything grunting like that and it's all right?'

Katherine expects it to jump up and run off when they get near, but instead it keeps groaning and panting. There's a little patch of green around it where the frost on the grass has thawed. The ewe suddenly throws back her head and thwacks it on the ground with a plaintive bleat. Marie points to an angry-looking scarlet bulge, which is protruding from behind.

'See that? Prolapsed uterus. You keep an eye on her, and I'll go home and ring the vet.'

Katherine crouches down beside the animal, making soothing noises. A waxing moon is rising slowly through the mist. A jumble of unconnected thoughts chase each other around in her head while she is trying not to think about her numbing feet. She is wondering, among other things, what Harry would make of this situation. The last dregs of light are lingering on the western horizon. There is an uncanny stillness. She walks around in small circles singing any Christmas carols she can remember the words to, but she can't get beyond the first two verses of any of them; she just sings those over and over again, adding a few foll-derol-dolls to the tune. She hugs her chest with her arms crossed, the clenched fists pressed so hard against her that her biceps begin to hurt.

Eventually, a vehicle comes bumping over the field, through the fog, towards her. It isn't completely dark yet. The last dregs of light are lingering in the mist. Katherine sinks her fingers into the warm, oily fleece and holds the ewe tightly as it struggles to get to its feet.

'Well? You're in bothers here, I believe?' The vet is a stumpy fellow dressed like the Michelin man in tiers of rubberised garments. 'Lucky I was over at Ryans' when Marie here told me what was going on.'

Marie is puffing up the hill on foot with a bucket of steaming water in one hand and a stout bottle in the other. The vet calls over to her, 'Good girl, Marie, put that down and give me a hand here. Might be able to save this one.'

Katherine stares, astonished at the sight of Marie holding the ewe upside down by its raised hind legs, while the vet, using the flat end of the bottle, tries to maul the bulge back inside.

'Some fucking Christmas, eh?'

'Oh, give it up, Paddy, that's what you're paid for.' Marie is struggling to stay upright, with her legs as far apart as her tight skirt will permit, her heels dug firmly into the frosty grass. She's leaning backwards against the weight of the ewe.

'Nothing could pay you for this kind of thing on Christmas Eve.' Paddy grunts, wiping his bloody hand on the ewe's back. 'She isn't helping much. If only the stupid bitch would stop forcing.' His face is glistening with sweat in the silver headlights. 'You can let her down there, Marie, just about done now.'

They all smoke a cigarette, and then he kneels down beside the ewe. After a considerable amount of swearing, he draws out two lambs. 'There you are. Another little Christmas miracle,' he says, as the second one lands on top of the first. 'Who's in charge here now, anyway, Marie? It's mad having ewes lambing at Christmas.' Marie and Paddy both look across at Katherine, then at each other, and smile.

'That one? Are you serious? What does she know about farming?' Paddy mumbles to Marie. The huge jumper seems to make Katherine look even slighter than she usually does.

Marie shrugs. 'For now, anyway.'

'I suppose this old girl won't get up and feed them two now, after all that!' He nudges the ewe with his boot a few times and wipes his arms dry on her wool, then stabs a syringe full of antibiotics into her neck. 'Good luck now.' He gets into his Land Rover. 'And Happy Christmas!'

'We'll get a lift down with you. You can drop us off at the house.' The two girls scramble up into the front seat and squash together for warmth. Marie has picked up the lambs and is rubbing them vigorously. 'Not much point in leaving these two little beggars out in the frost for hungry foxes. We'll bring them in and give them a head start by the range.' She stuffs them both up inside Katherine's jumper. The jeep revs, then slides and slithers down the hill. The women climb out into the farmyard.

'Thank you for coming out, Paddy. What do I owe you?' Katherine calls back into the cab, trying not to drop the lambs.

'Oh for God's sake. A glass of whiskey perhaps, girls?' he replies. This time Katherine isn't the only one to notice the glint in the eye.

Marie pushes Katherine out of the way and firmly slams the jeep door. She shouts through the window. 'I'll fix up with you next time I see you. Good night!'

Paddy drives away, smashing through the ice crust at the edges of the ford.

'God, men! They are all the bloody same!' Marie says as they come into the kitchen.

She sets about organising a nursery of hay in cardboard

boxes for the twins and settles it in beside the range. She sends Katherine back out with a lamp and a billycan. 'Here, you go and get some beastings off that ewe. Go on! They need it. This old cow's milk isn't the real thing for them at all.' Marie is trying to entice the stronger lamb to suck from a rubber teat on the Murphy's Stout bottle. Its chin is resting in her wide palm and her forefinger is in the corner of its mouth, urging it to try harder. Milk is dribbling over her wrist and onto the floor.

Katherine takes the lamp out into the dark. She clambers over the gate and heads off up the side of the hill, swinging the light around until she spots the ewe, more or less where they left it. It's still lying down, so she kneels to feel for the udder. It is cold and torpid.

She returns to the house.

'Where's the beastings?'

'She was dead, Marie.'

'For God's sake, girl, that's no reason not to milk her! Go back out there, you, and have another go before it turns to ice cream in her! Oh, here look't, give me that can, I'll do it.' She thrusts her feet into Katherine's new, green gumboots and stomps off into the night. Katherine runs after her in her slippers, waving the lamp. Marie pulls up her skirt, throws her legs around the corpse and begins to pump its bulging udder. Her yellow curls hop up and down. A dribble of gluey fluid oozes out. The flesh of Marie's thighs swells over the tops of her nylons. Her suspenders are straining.

'Shit! We've left it too late for this. Come on, we'll have to make do with what we've got.' Then she looks up into the lamplight and smiles. 'Don't be too hard on yourself, Katie. Everyone's got to start somewhere.'

Having fed both lambs with the remains of the evening's

milk, they settle them down into their cardboard crib beside the hearth. Marie pulls up her stockings and smooths out the wrinkles on her skirt, dabbing here and there with a damp cloth in an effort to remove the slime and blood from her Christmas outfit.

'I suppose you don't have a mirror anywhere here?' She struggles to force a comb through her hair, then, after some rummaging, she finds a small powder compact in her bag, flips it open and peers into the glass. She pastes pink lipstick onto her pursed lips and dabs some powder onto her cheeks. Finally, she tosses a few sticks into the firebox. 'Keep that fire lighting now and feed them lambs again in about four hours.'

'But I haven't got any more milk!'

'You can milk that cow again later, can't you? I have to go to town now and get the last few bits and bobs for the Christmas.' She is just about to leave when she turns back and says to Katherine, 'By the way, dinner'll be after second Mass in the morning, about half-twelve or that. Mammy'll be expecting you.' She plucks a bottle of clear, unlabelled spirit from her bag and plonks it on the table.

'Moonshine—keeps out the cold; go easy on it, though, it's nearly one hundred percent proof! You won't need curlers in your hair after a few shots of that stuff. Not that you ever needed them things, anyway.'

~

Katherine has several other callers that evening. The first is Nicholas Molloy.

His eyes light up when he sees the bottle.

He lifts it, removes the cork and sniffs the contents, then, reeling back a little, holds it up to the lightbulb, turning it slowly and peering into the oily swirls.

'Poteen! Where did you get that?'

'Oh, Marie brought it.'

He uncorks the bottle again with his teeth and pours a shot of the liquor into two delft teacups, which are slightly chipped around the lip and brown inside from years of strong tea. Katherine is uneasy, not so much at the way he takes over, more by his familiarity. He stands too close, looks down at her, picks a few bits of grit out of his teeth with a fingernail. She is sorry she doesn't have any cut glass tumblers to hide behind. The cups expose her lack of style and add to the informality.

'Sláinte.'

'Cheers.'

She takes a brave swig, and a jet flame swirls around her throat, shooting right down to her feet. Her brain seems to separate from her skull. Her eyes water. She swoons into the chair.

'Far out, man, that's really cool.'

'Here's to the harvest queen, and still the most beautiful woman in Knocklong!'

He chucks the rest of the cupful into his mouth and pours another shot. Katherine leaves hers. She'll have it later when she's going to bed; it'll help blot out the night.

Molloy watches her scald the milking bucket and follows her out to the stable, tripping a little and stumbling over tufts of frozen weeds. It's a beautiful night. Now that the mist has blown down river, every star is shining like it knows that it's Christmas. There is one especially bright star, high in the eastern sky. It makes Katherine think of the wise men enticed by the star's bewitching beauty, being drawn by her dazzling light all the way to Bethlehem. She ducks her head and goes into the stable, hanging the lantern from a nail on the wall.

The cow's head is in the meal bucket, and Katherine settles herself onto her butter box. She rinses the udder, palpating it with warm, soapy water. Soon the streaks of milk are frothing in an even rhythm into the bottom of the pail between her thighs. Nicholas leans against the cow's flank, looking down at her. His cap is tilted back on his head; black curls form a pie-frill around his face, which is marbled with shadows.

'What do you do this for?'

'I need the milk. I've got orphan lambs to feed.'

'That's daft, why couldn't you just give 'em powder like everyone else?'

'It wouldn't be the same.'

'It doesn't seem right. You weren't cut out for this malarkey.'

'How do you know what I was cut out for?'

'I'm just thinking about the loneliness, the cold, the hard work, for a few miserable pints of milk. Is it just to make a point?' He peers into the pail. The amount is meagre. 'You're fuckin' mad!'

He follows her back into the house. The lantern throws moving shadows in the frost.

'You'll be out of here before the New Year. You'll see.'

'I heard you'd been laying bets on how long I'd last?'

'Who told you that?'

'You tell them not to be wasting their money. I'll go if and when I'm good and ready. I'm here for a reason, surely you know that?'

'It'll end in tears, girl, mark my words. Your tears.'

'Why do you say that, Nicholas?' She pours warm milk into the bottles and tries to fix on the teats.

'You want to soften them teats in hot water; they'll go on easier if you do. You're in over your head. You should go home to your husband, where you belong.'

His tone is beginning to sound a little menacing. He takes another swig from the bottle of firewater and jams the cork back down into its neck. He swings it around his head and then points the butt end at Katherine.

'You know, girl, men died for this land. Men are still dying for it, and many more will die before it's sorted. You don't understand how people feel.'

He slams the bottle onto the table and doesn't even shut the door properly after him. Unable to resist the breeze, it swings open again with a squeak. She kicks it hard and jams a chair up under the door handle.

Katherine paces around the kitchen, sensing once more that she isn't alone. It's not a bad feeling, just strange. Even the dog is restless, standing at the foot of the stairs, its hackles up. Katherine peers out of the window into the gloom. She can hear the raucous bark of a vixen in the distance and the nervous growl of the dog at her heels. She switches on the radio, hoping for something cheerful. It's either Mass from the Pro-Cathedral or Santa again, warning all the boys and girls to be good, because he is loading up his sleigh, and he and Rudolf and all the other reindeers are getting ready to set off on their great trek around the skies. She keeps trying to retune it, searching for the jolly rousing chorus of the congregation in Kings College, Cambridge. She and Bridget always listened to that while they stuffed presents into shiny wrapping paper and drank Irish Coffees before they all walked down to the village for Midnight Mass.

Harry isn't a believer. He plays the part, especially at Christmas. He knows the prayers and the gestures. He pretends he knows when to stand and when to sit in Mass, surreptitiously following Katherine's lead. 'So-called believers are misguided, naïve, simple people needing simple metaphors

132

and basic rules by which to live and have an excuse to die. That's why religion is so successful. It doesn't justify a genuine belief in God. Nothing does.' He mostly keeps his religious ideas to himself. All that belongs to a time he has just about obliterated, and the only prayers he feels comfortable with are the simple ones that the head boy recited soothingly in assembly every morning in grammar school, followed by an old-fashioned Anglican hymn, like *Onward Christian Soldiers*.

Uncle Jack was completely the opposite. He took everything on trust. 'If you don't believe in God, where are you?' For Jack, living was God, Heaven and Hell and Purgatory all at once, all going on right here, for anyone to know and everyone with half a brain and a pair of eyes to see. When he reached out his bony, brown arms, they seemed to go right on up into the branches, part of the trees, part of the leaves, part of the wood pigeons cooing and the blackbird singing her shrill little warnings. He would wave them in an arc around him, taking in the whole farm with one sweep; shiny green grass, rusty wagon, turnip chopper and donkey cart. Lambs, cows, calves were all gathered up in that big gesture of stewardship. He surrendered them all to God. Heaven was all around him. However, on the rare occasions when he alluded to his family and things that happened in the distant past, Jack betrayed that he had also had a glimpse of Hell.

Just when Katherine is starting to dissolve into a pool of loneliness, Fonsie taps on the door.

'Ho, ho, ho,' and then, 'It's only me!'

He is clutching an iced fruitcake and some little fluted mince pies that his missus has made. 'Beware of Greeks bearing gifts!' he chuckles, laying them on the table. Katherine offers him poteen, but he just shakes his head.

'God, no! Still got far too much to do to start into that

stuff. I should have put a proper Yale lock on the inside of the door for you.' He is looking at the chair that Katherine has dragged away from the door. 'I'll do it straightaway after the Christmas.' Before he leaves, he ties a holly wreath to the outside of it.

'Couldn't get any with berries on, birds have 'em all gone now it's turned so frosty. But how and ever, better than nothing, eh? You mind yourself now, do you hear? Shove something more solid than the old chair against that door after me. A happy Christmas to you!'

Katherine doesn't go up to bed. She stays in the kitchen to nurse her two little babies. The fire keeps blazing and crackling late into the night. A smell of singed wool rises from the cardboard nest. She turns Mrs Hayes's cake over and pours some of the fiery liquid into its rich brown underside; a trick she learned from Bridget many years ago. She sees no reason why, in the absence of all her family and other witnesses, she should have to wait until Christmas Day, so she cuts a slice. The knife cracks the crisp white snow on top and sinks through yellow marzipan into the deep and fruity earth below. She wants to make a wish, but all she can think to ask for is Bridget, the one person of whose love she is absolutely certain. So she prays for that and courage to face tomorrow, as always. Katherine bites into the cake. She mumbles 'Cheers' out of the side of her mouth. With the bits of the fruit still lodged between her teeth, she falls asleep in the chair.

It's dark and very cold when she wakes in the night. She can hear the dog breathing beside her, the usual rodents scratching behind the dresser. The fire is reduced to glowing ash, and her Christmas candle has burnt to the saucer. Katherine doesn't move. Her eyes search the shadows for something familiar. She sees only amorphous shapes that could be anything. That presence is still here. A disembodied voice resonates inside her head.

'Be careful, Katie. They mean you no good.'

She strikes a match. Its brief flare illuminates shadows before it fizzles out. She sits for a while in the dark, listening to the beat of her own heart. Through the window, she can still see the guiding star.

After a while, Katherine stretches her stiffened limbs and sets about rekindling the fire. She warms milk for the orphans, who, by now, are standing up on wobbly legs, bleating over the edge of their cardboard box.

When they are both fed and settled, she takes the Christmas card from the beam above the stove and reads it again. 'I hope you have a happy Christmas, my dotey little pet. Make sure you keep off the cold, and say hello to Josie Ryan for me. Love as always, B. xox PS Your mum and dad send their love.'

Christmas morning is much like any other except that Katherine is up particularly early, feeding lambs and scalding the milking bucket. The church bell is pealing out with renewed vigour. There has been a heavy frost in the night, and the tap in the yard is frozen. She has to whack the ice on the barrel with the bottom of a bucket to break it to draw out some water.

She thinks of those children living on the side of the road, deep in the woods nearby. The dark, expressionless eyes of that tiny baby, nestled into a smelly old shawl. She makes a resolution to do something for them on this holy day. When all the jobs are finished, the yard resounds with the contented sound of cattle munching hay. Katherine puts on a long, woollen skirt, throws a cape around her shoulders and sets forth with a bundle of clothes and slices of Christmas cake in a wicker basket on the front of her bike. In her pocket, she stashes a bag full of half-crowns that she's been saving for telephone calls to England. The thump of the money against her thigh increases the bruise every time her leg rises and falls with the bicycle pedal.

The way is hazardous, with frozen puddles concealing treacherous potholes. Several times she catches herself thinking up reasons to turn back. Humming simple tunes keeps her mind away from perils unknown. Like Winnie the Pooh climbing the tree with honey bees buzzing around his head, she tries to fix her thoughts on a greater goal. She turns into the woods, and after a while, she reaches the encampment. There is no one to be seen. Some whippets and terriers are tied up beneath the wagons, glaring at her menacingly. Two goats are tethered to trees, and a couple of piebald cobs are grazing the verges, their forelegs spanceled together with rope hobbles. A brightly coloured game cock throws back its head and crows on top of a flat cart. Smoke rises from a small campfire where a blackened kettle sways gently in the heat. It is suspended from a metal spike, bent in a way that resembles the end of a shepherd's crook, leaning over the flames. Spits of boiling water fizz.

As she draws near, she can hear noises from one of the wagons. Smoke is puffing out of the chimney. She is reluctant to get off the bicycle, because then she'll be committed. A terrier runs out and challenges the front wheel in such a way that it forces her to stop and dismount. Katherine bends down and offers her hand for the dog to sniff, then pats it on the head. This small gesture of connection with the dog and the fact that she can see the black Morris Minor, which she knows belongs to old Father Fitzgerald, parked at the side of the wagon, give her courage. She leans the bike against an upturned shaft and mounts the wooden steps in trepidation. Clutching her bundle under her cloak and feeling like Little Red Riding Hood, she knocks. The door is opened slightly. She starts to wish them 'Happy Christmas', but the man puts his finger to his mouth to hush her. She tries to back away, but when he sees the basket, he draws her in.

The wagon is stuffed with people, little and large, kneeling, crouching and sharing laps. Men and boys on one side; women, girls and babies huddled on the other. The young curate from the village is standing with his head bowed, saying the rosary. All are mumbling along with him. Katherine slips in beside him, dips her head and joins in with the prayers she knows so well. When he's finished, everyone crosses themselves and the half-doors of the wagon are thrown open. Men and children spill out onto the frozen grass and set about making a huge cauldron of tea at the fire. The women, shrouded in woollen shawls, stare at Katherine, mumbling to each other in a language she doesn't recognise. They gesture to her to sit down amongst them. The curate sits beside her, and they all wish one another a happy Christmas with nods and smiles. The baby is swathed in a shawl and sweating in a box beside a blazing stove.

Katherine sneaks a glance around the wagon. Shelves are neatly stacked with the chattels of daily life, and any other space is adorned with holy pictures and statues. Every surface is painted in bright red, green and yellow patterns. Although it is all clean and neat, she finds it hard to breathe through the overpowering smell of bodies. It's an earthy mix of pungent odours, acrid, smoky, like rancid dripping. By the way the curate is edging towards the fresh air coming in through the gap in the half door, Katherine guesses she isn't the only one struggling. After a few awkward moments, she singles out the woman she thinks she met in her kitchen yesterday and hands the bundle to her.

'Just a few things. Nothing much, I'm afraid. My name is Katie, by the way.'

'The blessin's 'a' God on ye, missus. Hannah is my name.'

The young priest smiles timidly and offers Katherine his hand.

'Father Noel. I'd best be getting along. Father Fitzgerald is a bit old to be doing Christmas on his own.'

'Oh! No, Father, not till you've had the sup 'a' tay!' one of the younger women says. She leans out of the door and shouts something to the men, who have already fled back to their campfire. Her thick grey hair is scooped high on her head and partially secured with a brassy clip; the rest tumbles over her bare shoulders. Her wrinkled breasts are hoisted and bulging from a tight bodice. Two huge golden hoops are swinging from her ears. She shouts again. Katherine catches Father Noel's eyes as his glance retreats. Hannah takes two beautiful, green lustre cups down from the dresser, wipes them on her apron and scoops sugar into them. The milk is already in the teapot. They all watch as Katherine and the fresh-faced curate sip politely. The tea smells strongly of goats. Hannah stands up and takes a plate from the cupboard above her head. She unwraps a few slices of dark-coloured bread from an old biscuit tin and places them on the plate, offering it to the visitors with a nod. The two smile as they clink their cups together and nibble the bread. Smokey barley and wild honey. They offer a toast to 'many more'. The women mumble something that neither of the outsiders can make out.

138

Father Noel crosses himself and says, 'Indeed, God willing.'
Then they all drink tea and eat from the one plate.

'And a happy birthday, I'm guessing, Father Noel?'
Katherine holds her cup for another clink.

'Thank   you. It was yesterday. How did you know?'

'The name is a bit of a giveaway.'

Father Noel blushes.

Katherine stands up to leave. She beckons to one of the
older children and asks him to gather the others. On the steps
of the wagon, she is surrounded by smutty, black-haired and
dark-eyed little people and a host of dogs. As she reaches into
her pocket, many grubby hands are thrust out in front of her.
She gives them all a coin, trying to distinguish which ones
are coming back for more. It's impossible; they push in closer
and closer and start scrabbling at her clothes, making strange
noises. Their shoeless feet scramble up the steps as they shove
each other out of the way. She throws the last few coins into
the lane, and as the children run to grab them, she makes her
escape. Before she is ten yards down the road, the children
are fighting over the money, the men are shouting at the dogs
and the women have retreated into the dark places to pick
through the bundle.

Katherine had often trotted quickly past the Gypsy
Diddy-Coys on the lane near her home in Suffolk, praying no
one would speak to her and the dogs wouldn't scare her pony
into bolting home. She wouldn't have dreamed of starting
up a conversation with one of them, never mind going into
the wagons. That was totally taboo. Only Bridget did that;
taking them cast-offs and little treats from the kitchen. Now,
Katherine is ashamed of having been such a coward and
cycles away out of the woods and into the bright sunlight.
No matter how vigorously she pedals, she can't shake off the

pangs of loneliness that begin to overwhelm her. She is lonely
for Bridget, Daddy, Mama, Harry, Father Christmas, even
her old cob Elvis and the Boxing Day meet at the Pig and
Whistle; lonely for everything that goes with Christmas at
home. She looks up and turns her face to the sun, which
is shining directly into her eyes. 'If you stay facing the sun,
the shadows will always fall behind you,' Bridget's voice rings
sweetly in her ears. Her hands are so numb with cold that
she can hardly grip the handlebars, and her tears are almost
freezing onto her cheeks. She pushes on, standing up and
forcing all her weight down into every turn of the pedals.
She is determined to feel better by the time she arrives at the
Ryans' house. As she gets nearer, she starts to anticipate the
warmth of the welcome in their kitchen and the prospect of
Josie's Christmas dinner. It will be her first proper meal since
Harry's visit.

All the Ryans are shocked as Katherine tells the story of
her encounter in the tinkers' encampment. When Marie hears
how much she gave the children, she shrieks. 'Half-a-crown!
Each! Dear God, girl, have you lost your senses altogether!
They must have thought all their Christmases had come at
once! They'll never leave you alone now. Didn't I warn you
NEVER to give them any money?'

Then Jim adds for good measure, 'The men'll drink
the lot.'

'How do you know that?'

'Because the women and children have no way of spending
it! They'll get hunted out of any shops they go into.' Josie's
voice is full of irony.

'And what else would the men have to spend their
money on, anyway, only booze and fags?' Marie adds for
good measure.

The parlour is musty. Even a log fire and a Christmas tree laced with tinsel can't really brighten it up. Josie has laid a linen sheet over the table and placed a brass candelabrum in the middle, with some holly twisted around its stem. Marie lights the candles just before Jim says Grace. The children fidget and giggle, and Marie gives the eldest one a kick under the table. Then Josie sets about carving the turkey. Creamy white slices fall over the knife onto the plates and sink into a swamp of gravy. The crackers look out of place, very grand. As the meal goes on, Katherine recognises other things from the hamper she ordered as a Christmas thank-you present to the Ryans. None of them has ever tasted brandy butter. They all prefer custard with their Christmas pudding.

The evening begins to liven up once they get onto the Irish coffees and the card games. One of Katherine's hidden talents is a genius beyond mere fluke when it comes to whist. Soon, the Ryans realise that freckle-faced Katie is going to clean them out of small change, so they move on to poker. JJ and Marie's husband, Pat, take over and start to win it all back. Once everyone is mellow with drink, the singing begins. Josie bangs out some jigs on the old honkey-tonk piano, which hasn't been tuned for years. Slowly but surely, they descend into maudlin melodies about patriots, emigrant ships and the Four Green Fields. The men turn on Katherine and start accusing her of being a cuckoo in the nest, an interloper, and finally, a British spy.

She slips away into the frosty night, switches on her bicycle lamp and pulls her sleeves down over her hands. The bike skids and slides on the ice. Avoiding the woods, she takes the most direct route home. By the time she scrunches over the ford, large snowflakes are drifting from the sky and settling into mysterious shapes as they cover everything in white.

There is an eerie, artificial kind of lightness in the house. The dog paces restlessly around the kitchen, snarling from time to time as it passes the foot of the stairs. For some reason, there is a light on in one of the rooms upstairs. It was Jack's room and one that Katherine never goes into. She is surprised there is even a lightbulb in there. At first, she decides to ignore it, but then, as the evening goes on, and with the courage of a few swigs from the bottle of moonshine, she ventures up to have a look.

The room is chilly and smells of mouldy bedding and a dead rat under the floor. She walks across the bare boards to the window, avoiding the rug, which is littered here and there with rodent droppings. The metal hooks scratch the curtain rail as she draws the drapes together, closing out the night. She looks back into the room, taking in the rusty iron bed with some blankets barely covering a thin horsehair mattress. A naked pillow still retains the imprint of a head. There are some bits of clothing draped over the end of the bed; a shirt or two and some grey pants. She goes to the chest of drawers. A few pieces of paper are secured to the surface with a jam jar full of small brass coins. They look like receipts from the creamery; nothing very interesting. Katherine is about to turn and walk away when her eye is drawn to some scribbles on a sheet torn from a child's copybook, which is peeping out from the bottom of the pile. She carefully removes it, not wishing to disturb everything else.

Her initial instinct, to gather everything up and straighten the room out, is overwhelmed by a sense that she is invading her uncle's privacy. Even the dog hasn't come into the room behind her. It lies on the threshold, eyeing her every move. Katherine switches out the light and closes the door behind her.

In the better brightness and relative safety of the kitchen, she smooths out the sheet of paper and studies the hand drawn scribbles. They make no sense, just lines going hither and thither. It reminds her of the primitive maps she used to draw as clues for Bridget to find her when she had run away from home, after one of her many rows with Georgina. It was at a time when she had been about six years old, and although she cannot now remember what any particular issue was about, she just recalls feeling guilty for not being the way her mother wanted her to be. It wasn't the kind of thing you could say sorry for. She was who she was and knew no other way. Running away always seemed to sort it out. Bridget would come to find her, hug her and tell her she was the best dotey little pet in the whole world. All would be well until the next time.

Katherine turns the paper this way and that, trying to see which way is up and which is down. It has a familiar naivety about it, as if drawn by someone who feels excluded from a hostile world but knows that there is a person who wants to find them, and will eventually be able to. She folds it carefully and slips it into the drawer in the kitchen table.

Apart from the clicking of the dog's toenails on the flagstones, the silence is broken only by the rhythmical dripping of a tap in the scullery and the ticking of the kitchen clock.

Katherine knows that she is banished from the bosom and the hearth of her family by her own stubbornness. She doesn't want the radio. She doesn't want visitors. She is trying to embrace the tendrils of loneliness that creep around her as she begins to exhaust her own inner reserves. A deep sadness wells up from inside her over-extended guts, helped along by a few more swigs from the poteen bottle. Is this what Jack meant by 'really living'?

One of the lambs has expired during the day, and now the other one is up and ready to suck, pucking about in the cardboard crib, trampling all over his dead sibling. Katherine warms the milk, soaks the teat in hot water for a few minutes and slips it onto the bottle. She gently cups her hand underneath the furry chin and coaxes the teat into the lamb's mouth. As it begins to suck and milk dribbles down her wrist and into her sleeve, her mind goes back to the black-eyed faces around the steps of the wagon.

She takes the dead lamb outside to lay it beside its mother's body, wondering as she stomps uphill, with the snow falling gently round her, how farmers get rid of dead sheep, thinking that maybe the vixen will have a Christmas dinner this year. Some feral creature has already started into the flank of the ewe. Katherine's stomach heaves, and she chunders most of its contents into the snow. She tries to kick the white mush over it to smother the evidence of her own gluttony, but the warmth from her insides melts a little hole in the snow, exposing everything. She looks around the bleached landscape, wondering at the shadows from the moon. Gradually, strange shapes become the familiar patterns of hedges, leafless trees and the scattered bodies of sleeping sheep. The lights of farmsteads are twinkling around the valley here and there below. The village is a glowing patch of warmth from whence the church bell is still ringing out. Instinctively, she crosses herself and begins to mumble Hail Marys. Then she remembers that she gave all that up years ago, wraps her cloak around her cold shoulders and stomps back down the hill.

Just when she is sinking below the threshold of bearable sadness, Fonsie calls around to check up on her. His shoulders are flecked with snowflakes, and his cheeks glow from the cold air and the 'few whiskeys'.

'Called to see if you survived the Christmas,' he chirps merrily, casting a knowing eye around the kitchen, looking for signs of well-being or otherwise.

'Still got one lamb to keep you company, I see.'

'Yes, I think I should have come home from Ryans' earlier to feed them. The other one died during the day.'

'Ah, can't be helped. This little fellow will feed you for Christmas next year. If you are still here, that is. Only a lunatic would have ewes lambing at Christmas time. May as well make the most of it! You'll have to get some manners on them rams and keep 'em away from the ewes for a bit longer next year, though.'

'Fonsie, do you think I'm an awful fool trying to do this on my own?'

'Well, now, I think I know what your uncle would have said, if he was here to speak for himself, that is.'

'What's that?'

'You're a Butler, aren't you! Besides, I've got money on you, so don't go and let me down.'

'So they really are taking bets, then? Who's keeping the book?'

'Jim Ryan.'

'Well, the scurrilous old toad! What are the odds?'

'At the moment its fifty-to-one you'll last till the New Year.'

'And what are the odds I won't?'

'No gambling on Christmas Day.' He winks at Katherine and grins, taking a swig from the bottle on the table. 'Christmas is for food, doing nothing and drinking moonshine.'

For an awkward moment, Katherine thinks Fonsie is going to make a lunge for her. She stands with the table between them and tightens the blanket around her shoulders. He grins, keeping his hands on the table to steady himself. There is a bald patch on the top of his head, which is scattered with freckles. He hiccups a few times and then gathers himself together, replaces his brand new woolly hat and wishes her a happy Christmas.

Just as he is going out into the night, he turns back and says, 'Shove a chair up agin' that door after me, won't you?' and then, as if to justify this remark, he adds pointedly, 'There are tinkers just up the road.'

After he has left, all cheer is completely exhausted; only a few fingers of poteen are left in the bottle and the fire is dwindling away to nothing. Katherine throws in the last few dry sticks and some of Fonsie's briquettes. She watches the flames eat into the edges, forcing apart the layers of pressed turf. She drains the kettle into a hot-water bottle, carefully letting out a blistering burp, before screwing down the cap. Hugging the boiling rubber to her chest, she trudges up the stairs to bed. Katherine knows she is not alone this night. The dog hasn't had any moonshine, and she knows it too. There is another presence; unseen, unheard, but Katherine is no longer afraid. Then as she rounds the corner on the stairs, a chill catches her in the back of the neck. A voice in her head warns her again, 'Don't trust them, Katie. Not any of them.'

She lies for a long time, staring out through the gap between the curtains. Fresh snow has made white frames around the little window panes. The dog tries to climb under the blankets. Eventually, Katherine gives in. The two snuggle into the valley in the bed and sleep.

CHAPTER SEVEN

By morning, the snow has ceased falling and has set like the frosting on Mrs Hayes's Christmas cake. Katherine's breath hovers in clouds before her face. The windowpanes have a delicate trace of ice on both the outside and the inside. The dog growls from deep beneath the blankets, causing the bed to rumble. When Katherine lifts the covers, it leaps out, bounds down the stairs and barks hysterically at the kitchen door. Katherine pulls a dressing gown over her nightdress and goes down to see what the commotion is all about. Even through thick socks, the flagstones are freezing cold.

Before she opens the door, she can hear singing outside. For a moment, she hesitates, but then curiosity gets the better of her. There are three men hopping about on the doorstep. All are dressed in old clothes, with raffia skirts, raffia frills below the knees and tall straw hats. Their faces are masked with balaclavas, slits cut out for the eyes and holes for the mouths. The singing stops, but the drumming on the tight-skinned bodhran keeps pounding. Manic, without rhythm, shape or form. The drumstick is flying in all directions. The demented dog barks, howls, yelps and darts at the jiggling feet. They kick out at it. The wild beat gets louder. They push past the dog, past Katherine, and surge into the kitchen. The singing starts up again. Amid the frantic yapping of the dog, she can barely make out the words.

> *'We three kings from Bally-go-far,*
> *'Hungry, cold and needing a jar,*
> *'Don't speak a word, you'll never be heard,*
> *'And you'll never know who we are.'*

This is followed by some more verses in Irish and finished off by one of them, who is backing Katherine into the room and growling right into her face, with no attempt at tune and a strong smell of whiskey on his breath.

> *'The wren, the wren, the English wren,*
> *'Taste the blood of Irish men.*
> *'We'll give her a shock,*
> *'With a Fenian cock.*
> *'Maybe then she'll go home again!'*

She tries to break free and run for the door, but he grabs her. Spinning her around, he thrusts the arm up between her shoulder blades, keeps pushing her forwards, till she is right up against the table. Her legs are off the ground. The rim of a cup bites deeply into her cheek as she is driven face downwards onto the wooden surface. The cup smashes on the floor. He is tugging at her nightdress. The lamb is bleating, dog barking, drum pounding, voices urging. Suddenly, it stops. The drumming stops. The dog is silenced.

'Sweet Jesus! What the hell's that?'

The three men gape at the stairwell. Whatever they see there sends them scrambling for the door. They run out, leaving it open to the white world.

Katherine drops her lower jaw to scream. No sound comes. Even her breath has deserted her. The blood is congealing in streaks on her face. Poteen burns the wounds. She wants to flee up the stairs, but her legs don't move. Then they begin to shake uncontrollably.

Snow dissolves into puddles on the flagstones. Her socks are wet. Both feet numb. She turns and looks out into the bleached farmyard. About to slam the door, dizzy and dazzled by the snow, her eyes hit on a maze of footprints. Crazed patterns of flying birds. Wild geese, left frozen into the snow by a pair of new boots. Scarecrows all gone.

Katherine is shivering violently now. She jams a chair up against the door. Can't remove her stinking gown. Can't wash the blood from her face. She glares at the firebox; it's dead. The lamb has given up bleating. It lies without motion. It could even be dead too. Katherine quakes in the chair for a long time, an old blanket wrapped tightly around her. Squashed into a ball of bruised limbs, numb. Everything rolls over and over in her sore head.

It is a hard-and-fast rule: you don't smoke dope on an empty stomach, and certainly not first thing in the morning. You don't drink before six in the evening either, not until the sun is over the yardarm. But this is not the time for rules. Katherine opens the gin bottle and lets the poteen vaporise up her nose. She puts the cold glass to her lips and gulps a burning swig of firewater. Her head spins, but she has enough control of her hands to roll a joint.

Sometime later, Katherine remembers the lamb. She has

to get milk to feed it. It's lying slumped on its chest in the box, but it is still breathing. She scalds the milking bucket, pulls a coat over her nightgown, puts on a dry pair of socks and steps into her wellington boots. She heads out into the bright morning light, pulling the door closed behind her. The clear blue sky and the pristine crunch of fresh snow feel safe and new. Katherine stands motionless for a few minutes and listens. She guesses from the angle of the sun that it must be about midday. A demented crow is squawking and hopping from branch to branch as if to draw her attention. She looks again at the wild geese impressed into the snow. The cow is bawling for its calf.

It isn't easy to avoid the footprints, frozen into boot-shaped fossils like a herd of prehistoric humanoids, all going out over the stream. Whoever they were, they seem to have abandoned their car on the far side, a little way up the hill, not clearly visible. It looks a bit familiar, but she does not want to inspect it now. Cars are often parked there when men with guns and dogs go out across the hill to shoot rabbits or pheasants or to trap hares for coursing. Too icy this morning to drive back up the hill, she guesses. She keeps focused on the barn door. Going into the darkness, her eyes gradually adjust to the different light. Queen Mary is in the far corner, trying to break down the dividing gate to get at her frantic calf.

Katherine searches the shadows for the milking stool. A hand grabs her from behind. Covers her mouth. Holds her firm. A distorted voice growls in her ear.

'What kept you? Did you think you would get off that lightly?'

She fights to get away, swings the bucket of scalding water backwards. It hits a leg, then flies across the barn and smashes against the far wall. Her hooded attacker grunts and grapples her, face down, into the straw. Her legs are forced apart. Her body yields unwillingly, like a beech log to the axe. The breath is pounded out of her. She is suffocating, fighting to get away. But the struggle is useless, and the deed is done.

He releases his grip sufficiently to pull a sack over her head and ties her hands behind her back with twine. He leaves her trembling in the straw. By the time she manages to turn over and sit up, he has gone. Her heart is pounding in her ears. She can just make out the distant revving of an engine reversing up the boreen. Crows are still cawing outside; a different call now. The cow is still calling for its calf.

Katherine begins to weep into the musty hessian covering her face. It takes her some time to get thoughts to follow each other. She shakes the sack off her head and looks around the barn. At first, she still thinks she will milk the cow, but of course her wrists are hobbled from behind. Her dog is barking frantically inside the house. She must have shut the door in its face. Now she can hear a car, footsteps in the yard, the back door opening. The dog leaps out across the yard and into the barn. It starts to lick her face. She is terrified it will give her away to another intruder. She tries to shush it with soft, soothing words. The unmistakable blocky shape of Marie Ryan appears, silhouetted against the sky.

~

'What the hell's going on here?'

Unable to speak, Katherine just laughs, with tears burning the backs of her eyes but refusing to break through. She is shaking uncontrollably.

'Oh, shit! What in the name of Jesus? This looks bad, Katie. You're a mess. Your face!' She kneels down and gently touches the swollen eyes, the bruised cheeks. She sits beside Katherine and gathers her into her arms, picking bits of straw out of the tangled red locks. 'Who was it?'

Katherine moves her head a little from side to side. They sit together in the straw, Katherine hegging and Marie stroking her hair. Then she realises that Katherine is tied up, and she struggles to untie the knot and remove the twine from her chaffed and bleeding wrists.

'Come on, Katie, we'll get you inside and then decide what's the best thing to do. You must be frozen. What possessed you to come out here in your nightdress? How long have you been here?'

But Katherine seems too confused and frightened to say anything except, 'Can you let the calf into the cow, please?'

Sitting in the kitchen, Marie surveys the mess: chairs tossed around, broken china scattered on the floor amid puddles of water and bits of straw. She pictures an intruder, a scuffle, Katherine bolting outside and then … but that can't be, because she has her boots on and the milking bucket is there, upside down, by the barn wall. It doesn't make sense.

'So what happened?' She doesn't really expect any coherent responses from Katherine, who is by now huddled into the comfort chair with blankets. A cup of tea, heavily laced with poteen, is quivering in her hands.

'Christ, you really are in a bad way! Those bloody knackers, was it?' She tries to wash Katherine's wounds, dabbing gently with a warm cloth and mumbling, 'Fucking tinkers should all be shot at birth!' Then, after a short pause while her eyes scan the room again, she goes on, 'Is anything missing? What did they take?'

Katherine shakes her head. 'No, not them, not that smell. Whiskey, wet straw, new boots, demented scarecrows.'

152

Marie looks at the bits of straw scattered hither and thither and begins to put two and two together.

'Wren boys?' Then Marie gets the tell-tale smell of fresh semen rising. 'Oh, God in heaven, you've been, you know, haven't you?'

Katherine is swaying her head around. 'New boots …' She repeats it a few times. Then, after a pause, she asks, 'What's a Fenian, Marie?'

'A Fenian? Why?' The very word sends cold shivers down Marie's spine. She knows a good few of them.

Katherine laughs again, laughs and cries. No more words are there to form and be spoken.

'Glory be to God, whatever put that into your head? I don't know what to say. I wasn't expecting this! I just came over to tell you that after you left yesterday, there was a phone call for you. Bridget O'Connor wishing you a happy Christmas, and that husband of yours was on too. It's bloody brass-monkeys-freezing outside now.' She kneels in front of the fire and huffs into it, stabbing it with bits of sticks until it blazes up. Trying to divert Katherine away from the thought of Fenians, she goes on, 'That lamb is really weak. It won't last much longer under this kind of regime.' She is wondering if it's worth feeding it at all, but hasn't the heart to say that now.

Katherine is still quaking, watching Marie fussing over this and that nervously. 'It's my own fault, Marie. Look at me. I'm hopeless on my own. I thought I could do it.' The tears break through and start rolling down her cheeks.

'Don't be so stupid, girl! This isn't your fault. It *never* is. Bloody men!'

Katherine gropes in her bag and retrieves her stash of dope and tobacco.

'I can't cope. I'll never be able to live here on my own. I'm only fooling myself. You're right; I am stupid. I've never done anything on my own before, and look at me now. I couldn't even go to Switzerland on my own. They had to pay an escort to take me to finishing school in Lugano!'

'Oh, Katie, don't be talking like that! Come on, we'll get you dressed, and I'll take you over to Mam's. You can ring your Harry or Bridget or whoever. I'll send Daddy across to do the foddering and all that. Then we'll decide what to do. And look't, we'll take the lamb too. Mam'll get it going again; she's a genius at the kiss of life.'

'Oh God, no! Marie, I can't face anyone right now.' Katherine glances around the room, her frightened eyes lacking focus. 'Oh Marie, I—I … Oh God! I don't know … Not the men, I can't face the men …'

'They are all out on the lash today, and then they are going coursing later, so you won't see anyone, except Daddy, maybe.'

'I don't want to speak to Harry either.'

'Well, never mind about all that now. Let's just take care of *you*.' She manages to coax Katherine into some warm clothes. She wants to give her a good wash, get rid of that awful smell. She knows you shouldn't do that. Evidence or something. You see a lot of this kind of thing in the Gorbals of Glasgow or on the district in the Coombe. Nothing ever comes of reporting crimes like that, anyway.

The two of them bundle the half-dead lamb into a sack and jam the door shut behind them.

~

When Josie sees the girls, she takes a motherly look at Katherine and says, 'Come here to me, crather. What's after happening to you at all, girl?' She glances at Marie over Katherine's shoulder, and they make faces at each other. Katherine is still dizzy and thinks she's going to puke.

'Marie, take this wee one upstairs and put her into a hot bath with plenty of salts in it, while I heat the turkey soup and see what can be done about that lamb.'

The thought of soup is the last straw, and Katherine throws up into the pig bucket by the cooker. It is empty retching, slimy, acidic dribble. Her stomach convulses over and over again. Josie holds back Katherine's hair, and her fingers catch in lumps of congealed blood. She gently strokes her back and croons with sympathetic noises from the heart.

'Go on, the pair of you, before it gets any worse. Here, take a few sips o' this.'

Katherine has no idea what it is, but it works. As they are going carefully up the stairs, she can hear Josie on the phone. 'I know it's Stephen's Day, but I don't care! You may come now. She can't be left there on her own any longer. No, she is NOT fit to travel! Listen here to me, Bridget O'Connor. I don't know for sure what's after happening, but tell that husband of hers that she's had a fall or something. For God's sake, don't let on to no one what I suspect. She'll need time to deal with that herself ... No, don't send him to get her. Come yourself, get an aeroplane. Yes, someone will come to the railway station to fetch you, don't worry. I'll come myself if needs be.'

Waiting for Bridget. The next few days pass in a blur. Katherine is either sitting by the cooker in the Ryans' kitchen, cradling a mug of sweet tea, or pacing around their attic bedroom, turning everything over and over in her head. The family try to behave normally around her, but talk in hushed tones. JJ is sent to stay in Marie's bungalow at the other end of the farm, and Jim keeps out of the way as much as possible. He swallows the comments he is so tempted to make. No one mentions going to the Gardaí.

There are whispered conversations when Katherine is out of earshot.

'It wasn't one of ours, I hope,' Josie mumbles.

Marie adds dismally, 'I wouldn't put it past them.'

'Please, God, they wouldn't go that far.'

From then on, that particular issue becomes the subject of the big silence.

Bridget arrives. Everything begins to change. They go back to the farm together. Bridget holds Katherine's hand when they shove open the door and go into the kitchen. Apart from the damp smell, it looks normal. The Ryan women have been in and erased all visible signs of the intrusion. It is both clean and tidy. The holly wreath is still on the door, and there is a little vase of green leaves and berries on the kitchen table.

Straightaway, Bridget takes over. She organises Fonsie to get them a car. She commandeers the cheque book and goes off to the sales. She buys new curtains, delft, soft furnishings, bed linen, electric blankets and a gleaming, plug-in kettle. She throws a few bottles of whiskey into the shopping basket for good measure. Soon she has instigated a routine of three proper meals a day and clean underclothes every morning. It doesn't take her long to master milking the cow, and she gets the men mucking out sheds and reorganising the animals into manageable groups. It's Mass every Sunday, mince on a Monday and fish on Fridays. She trims Katherine's hair, clips the dog's claws, darns blankets and starts knitting warm socks and woolly hats. All visitors, except the female Ryans and Fonsie, are kept out of the house.

Bridget demands to know why 'the incident' has not

been reported to the Gardaí, but then, after discussions with Marie and Josie, she can grasp the futility of that. Not enough evidence. No chance of a conviction. In fact, very little chance of being either believed or taken seriously, especially as it wasn't reported right away and all the evidence has been done away with. If the Gardaí did believe her, they would surely say she must have asked for it.

It was Marie that put the situation in perspective. 'Do you remember what happened to that young widow—one over in Ballybooley that time? They tried to blame that on the tinkers too, and when none of them could be got to own up, even after a good thrashing in the cells, they said the woman was mad. She knew full and well who it was, the full forward on the local hurling team, after getting a proper skin full. She saw his face and told the Gardaí that, but they didn't want to hear it. There was such a swell of bad feeling against her after that she left the area anyway. I think she sold the place to a Protestant family in the end.'

Bridget asks with pertinence, 'Yes, but was she, well, you know, interfered with?'

'Yes, that's the point, Bridget,' Marie insists. 'It was all too shocking, and the parish closed ranks against her. The scandal would have finished him. She was only a blow-in, anyway.'

'So that made it all right, did it?'

'Well, that's all history now, but you wouldn't want them to do that to Katie, now, would you? And let's face it, she says they were masked, and she couldn't positively identify any of them, and the one what done it to her, she couldn't say who that was either, cos he came at her from behind. She never got a look at him at all. So what hope have we?' Marie leans back against the kitchen wall, her hands on her hips.

Bridget finally concedes that it might be better to let

sleeping dogs lie for now.

'We'll probably never know now who it really was, thank God,' says Josie firmly.

Katherine drifts around like a tormented ghost. She whimpers a lot and tries to take her mind off it by smoking dope. At first, she refuses to listen to any talk about going back to England; that would be giving in too easily. Like falling off a pony and refusing to get back up again right away.

'I can't just let them win, Bridgie.' But Bridget thinks that they have probably won already.

'Your father isn't the best at the moment. You're on the mend, but he's going downhill all the time. If you don't go soon, your Harry will surely come back and fetch you out of it, anyway.'

'Does he know? What happened, I mean?'

'He knows you aren't well. He thinks you had a bad fall down the stairs on Stephen's Day. He knows your father isn't well either.'

'But did you tell him about … you know?'

'Of course not, Katherine!' she says, eyes averted. 'Men are funny about things like that. He could take against you if he knew. I've heard of it happening.'

'Maybe he's taken against me anyway by now. Who could blame him, really?'

Bridget gives her that 'only a mother would love you' look.

'Ah, now, come on. He said he missed you at Christmas, and he hopes you'll come home when you've worked things out here.' She lies with professional skill, learned from years of practice.

'Really, Bridgie? He said he misses me?'

'Of course he misses you. We all do—did—well, you know what I mean. He's lost without you. Your poor old father misses you too. And I'm sure your mother does as well, in her own way.'

Katherine's mind has become a muddy river, but she can still see Harry's face, like an angry carp, when she told him she was not going home with him, when he shoved her against the wall, and for the first time, she hit him back. She searches around in that image for traces of love or compassion, but all she can see is rage and righteous indignation. She knows there will, inevitably, be revenge. Harry's toys have been snatched away from him, and he will want to get them back, by fair means or foul.

~

Bit by bit, Bridget hatches a plan to bring Katherine home. It's a plan that is frustrated by the fact that the dotey little pet is never well enough to travel. She does not seem able to keep any food down for long. It is getting worse, not better. Bridget and Marie tell each other it's the shock and the dope, although she is so sick now that she can't even smoke anymore. As the winter softens and the daffodils nose their way up through the thawing soil and begin to bud, both come to terms with the cause of Katherine's sickness.

Bridget has never forgotten that helpless retching as you try to expel everything, including the cuckoo in your womb. She had been fifteen years old when her mother sent her to work for the housekeeper in the priest's house in Kilkenny. Her job was to do everything—washing, starching and ironing, scrubbing tiled floors, blacking the cooker, cleaning out and laying the fires. Father Dalton had a small cast- iron fireplace in his bedroom. That was Bridget's demise. She had tried so hard not to waken him in the early morning, creeping across the room to scuttle out the ashes and put a match to a new fire. But he watched her through half-closed eyes. Then one morning, he called her over with his croaky old voice and said he was cold, very cold, and wanted her to warm him up. He told her to get into his bed and warm his feet. But it wasn't his feet that were cold.

After a few months of this, Bridget was sent to a convent in England 'to work out her time'. That way, she wouldn't be causing a scandal at home. Her baby boy was whisked away by the nuns just after the birth. She had no more than a brief glimpse of him before he disappeared. The next day she was called for to wet-nurse a baby girl whose mother was very sickly and unable to feed it herself. It was okay; the family were Irish and Catholic, she was told. The father in the family came originally from very near to Bridget's own village. So it was that Katherine became her baby. Bridget has been with the family ever since.

Every time Katherine throws up, the smell and the sound of it cuts stripes into Bridget's heart. She is still able to conjure up the image of the little round face of her son before they snatched him away. She thinks she must have signed papers at some stage, but does not remember them. Georgina was completely uninterested in her own beautiful, sweet-smelling little girl, whose twisted birth nearly killed her and the care of whom she left entirely in the hands of the 'plain-faced heifer' from Ireland.

One bright morning in March, Bridget makes her move. 'Katie, my little peteen, I spoke to your mother on the Ryans' phone yesterday. Your poor father is going downhill rapidly. If you don't see him now, you might never see him again.'

'What do you mean?'

'I mean, pet, that he is very ill, and they don't think he has too much more time left.'

Bridget has packed her bag and one for Katherine, been to the travel agent and bought two plane tickets to Heathrow, and organised Fonsie to take them to the railway station. Jim is happy to look after the farm 'for a while'; confidently believing that he has seen the back of Katherine. Marie is not so sure, and Josie, as always, hopes for the best, whatever that may be.

'Don't be worrying about a thing, you, do you hear me? You spend a bit of time with your father and come back to us when you are good and ready. Take care now. You've more than yourself to think about.'

'What is she on about, Marie?' But in her heart, Katherine knows. She still can't speak the words that snake around in her head. On the train, Bridget broaches the subject with her own kind of directness.

'You know, you will have to make Harry believe it's his. You can't ever tell anyone the truth. That kind of truth doesn't work for us women.'

Katherine is tight-lipped. She stares out of the window, thinking the cattle look hungry and miserable. Grubby little fields; junk and old cars slowly rotting in gaps; mud and slobber everywhere. It's like someone has taken a paint brush and sloshed a watery wash of panes grey all over everything. To Katherine, it feels like a woman whose fertility is laid bare to be rained on and pecked over by crows. Ravaged, like herself. She doesn't respond to Bridget, who, cautiously, tries again.

'You'll have to work on it, Katie. Your baby needs a father and a mother.'

Once the words are spoken, it isn't so hard to face. Katherine turns towards the bleached blond hair with greying, brown roots beginning to emerge, the scarlet lipstick and the already-leaching mascara. It's what she loves most in the world. It's all there, in that one, large, powdered face. She buries her head in the soft mass of Bridget's bosom, smelling as always of sweet soap and honeysuckle. Those long arms close around Katherine. Everything will be all right.

CHAPTER EIGHT

As she steps out of the tube station in Sloan Square, Katherine pulls up her green velvet collar, shoving her hair inside. The same way she did the day she stood in the graveyard in Knocklong and watched her uncle Jack being lowered into the ground. Her collar smelled of perfume; now it smells of mould and Ireland.

She begins the long walk from the underground along the King's Road. Her fingers search deep into the satin recesses of the side pockets and curl around the key to the front door of her house in Woodcock Close. Her red, knee-length boots, in spite of Bridget's spit and polish, are so much the worse for having suffered a winter in Knocklong. They clip along the pavement. Mary Hopkin singing sweetly, 'Those were the days, my friend, we thought they'd never end,' and the whiff of incense drifting out through shop doorways. The Psychedelic Café has been repainted, the paisley wash over the windows has been revamped with pictures of Che Guevara and some other Cuban rebels. In the shop next door, Marilyn Monroe is now pouting back at her with lipstick of a deep cherry red and eyes that tell only of last night. Katherine realises that she no longer wants to look like that. She has moved on. That isn't where it's at anymore. She walks on past, not bothering to avoid the cracks in the pavement. Nothing worse can happen now.

The daffodils are already in flower in the little patch of garden in front of her house. They smile up at her as she swings open the wrought-iron gate. The lock still knows the key. The door yields smoothly, and Katherine steps into the hall. Pot-pourri? No, an unfamiliar perfume. It catches in the back of her throat.

Standing in the hallway, she sways a little and drops her holdall onto the ground. It takes her a few seconds for her eyes to adjust to the dim light, the shapes and all the stuff of her old life. She stares at her collection of miniature glass animals in the bow-fronted cabinet, wondering who on earth could have thought they resembled living creatures as they prance around like characters from a Disney cartoon. She glides through the house and into the kitchen. A resentful twinge pecks her when she notices a new electric kettle on the countertop. Harry always insisted she use the gas hob to boil water. Electric kettles are too wasteful. She plugs it in and then finds that even the tea has changed. Not dusty black leaves decanted into the wooden box, but musky Earl Grey paper bags in a black and gold Fortnum and Mason's tin caddy. Her stash of dope that she hid at the back of the cupboard is untouched. She reaches for it, opens the old biscuit box and peels back the thick brown, greaseproof paper, just to be sure. She inhales deeply the powerful smell of the resin. A wave of nausea snatches away the craving. She wraps it up carefully again and closes the lid, pushing it right back behind the bottled frankfurters and chocolate Bath Olivers. Then she has a second thought. She retrieves it from the biscuit tin and shoves it deep into her bag. She left a message with Harry's secretary to say that she would meet him in London, and they could travel down together. It had seemed easier to deal with him alone, here in her own home. Now she is wishing she had gone straight on to Suffolk with Bridget.

Katherine stands for a while in the sitting room, gazing at the watercolours of East Anglia: seagulls chasing the plough, children winkling on the mud flats around the mouth of the Blackwater estuary. All painted at various times by Stella, her godmother, on one of her visits to the manor house. They haven't heard from Stella for years, not since she fell out with Georgina, her only female cousin, over something silly to do with domestic arrangements, about which Katherine knew nothing at all. She had written a few times from Tuscany; sent sketches of her new home there and her new man sitting on the terrace beneath a vine of purple grapes, or maybe wisteria; it's a little vague. That was some years ago. Katherine is sorry she let the thread of the relationship get too thin to revive. It wouldn't be so bad to visit her now; she could do with an old-fashioned godmother. Bridget could come too. She wonders briefly what life in a sun-bleached villa would be like and how some people always managed to land in the jam, while her own life is tumbling further into the mincing machine.

The spring sun has warmed a patch of the Persian carpet in the middle of the room. Katherine lies on her back so it can warm her too. She closes her eyes and begins to drift.

The carriage clock on the mantelpiece chimes delicately, one, two, three. Deciding that Harry can go to hell, she telephones for a taxi to Liverpool Street and rings Peter, the farm worker and gardener's son. He agrees to bring the car to the station. She catches the next train to Ipswich. Peter is there with the Bentley, as always. For a brief moment, she nearly gives him a kiss on the cheek but withdraws just before she is committed; although the rough stubble around his languid smile is hard to resist. He opens the passenger door for her, and she climbs in. The soft cream leather seat feels cold but deliciously familiar, always associated with her father, even though it is really Georgina who insists on such displays of opulence. Frank would be quite happy to drive around in the old Land Rover. Peter starts the banter, glancing across to Katherine, grinning away as usual.

'She 'ad a boy, Maisey 'epworth did'.

Katherine grunts, feeling too sick for conversation.

'She married that old dolt, Teddy Archer, but called the nipper Peter. Could you beat that? Bet 'e weren't best pleased.' He laughs heartily.

She closes her eyes and tries not to think about anything, but the picture of Mumsie Maisey from the village in a wedding dress cheers her up.

'You don't look too 'ot yourself, though, lost weight, an' you 'as always skinny, any road. You gone and got yourself up the duff? Bloody 'ell, girl, you didn't 'ave to run off to Ireland to do that!'

She looks at him. For two pins, she would have told him everything, but then he went on, 'What you have to marry that jumped-up, Johnny-come-lately cockney for, when you coulda 'ad me?' He grins. His teeth gleam out like pale topaz rocks.

'Peter! That's a dreadful thing to say.'

'True, though, innit?'

Katherine thinks back to when she and Peter were teenagers. He was the heartbreaker all the girls wanted. Except

166

her. She knew him too well, and her father would never have agreed to her marrying the farm boy. In fact, he was probably the reason Katherine was sent to finishing school in Switzerland. She makes a joke of it.

'No one stood a chance with Maisey Hepworth on the scene. She was all any of you could think about. You should have married her yourself. She'd have been a great wife. Much better than me, anyway.' After a short pause, she asks, 'Is Elvis fit enough to ride, do you think?'

''e won't complain if 'e gets a go 'atween your thighs, girl!' He chuckles and puts out his left hand and gives her right leg a little squeeze. It feels good, reassuring. Some things can be relied on.

No sooner are they out of the town than Katherine feels an urgent need to pee.

'Can you pull into that gap there? I need to hop over the gate for a minute.'

She tries to open the heavy five-barred wooden gate, but it seems to be stuck in the ground. She starts to climb over it, cross that she is no longer able to vault a gate. Her tight skirt is making it impossible to swing her leg over. She wriggles it up to the top of her thighs.

Peter leans across to the passenger's window and calls out, 'Need any 'elp there?'

'You look the other way!' She tugs the skirt down again and bellyflops over the gate into the field. His eyes are piercing the hedge as she squats in the headland and the east wind whips her naked loins. The smell of the sod makes her long to be young and muddy, free and innocent. Peter's voice reminds her of the feeling of grass on her bare skin, of ants and worms and thistles. She tries to savour the bite in the wind, the sounds and sights of a Suffolk evening. Like the seagulls squalling overhead, flashing brightly against the darkening sky. They are following a tractor tilling away in the distance, swooping in unison, like a sheet flapping around on a washing line, snatching the freshly turned-up grubs in the newly raddled soil. She listens for the scratch of a disc harrow scraping through flinty clay.

Peter beeps the horn and then comes to the gate and leans over it. 'Come on, lovely, it can't be that difficult!'

He is over six feet tall with feral blond curls that flop around his bushy sideburns and ruddy cheeks. He catches Katherine around the waist and lifts her back onto the road. He still doesn't bother with warm clothes, and his shirtsleeves are rolled up from his afternoon's work on the farm. Streaks of cow muck flatten the hairs on his forearm. He oozes a reassuring smell of sweat and the milking parlour. Those huge hands feel warm, solid and comforting. She wants to fall against his waistcoat and sink back to the way things were before she left home, got married, did the other grown-up things. Before it happened. She wants to wriggle through to the back seat and snog till it feels like her teeth will come out through her cheek and her whole body tingle with raw lust. She guesses Peter wouldn't say no either.

The car crunches onto the drive, which sweeps around the front of the manor house. Everything looks exactly the same. Only now the lawn is bright yellow with daffodils on either side all the way up the chase. Finches and tits are pecking at crumbs on the bird table, like there will be no tomorrow.

Having taken the luggage and caught an earlier train, Bridget arrived only a few hours before Katherine.

'I thought you were planning on staying the night in London? What happened to all that 'I need a decent haircut and some new clothes before I go home' and your big intentions to sweeten up that husband of yours and tell him your news?'

'I want to tell Daddy first.'

Bridget smiles. But Frank has already retired to bed.

'Tell him in the morning, pet.'

Georgina is taken aback to see them arriving one after the other.

'We weren't expecting you tonight. I'm not sure if the dinner will stretch.' Her powdered cheek is cool as she slips it briefly past her daughter's. Her hair feels soft and fluffy. Her perfume is the same as always, Dior.

Katherine rushes for the bathroom and throws up with a violence that leaves her reeling.

She stands beside her father's bed, watching his chest rising and falling gently, as his breath goes in through his nose and out in little puffs between his puckered lips. The light through the open door catches the top of his head and shines on a few wisps of white hair. His fingers curl around the bed cover. Big knobbly talons with brown shapes like tea stains seeping across them. She wants to take and hold them. She wants to kiss his pale, papery skin. She wants to say she is sorry for not loving him the way he has always loved her. What could she tell him about Ireland? About what happened? How she has failed? Failed in her marriage, failed the farm, failed to find out what really happened to Uncle Jack, but most of all failed even to look after herself? The thought of that brings a lump into her already sore throat. Bridget draws her away.

Sitting on Katherine's bed beside her, Bridget gently brushes the copper curls just as she always used to do.

'Will you tell your mother?'

'Tell her what?'

'About the baby, of course!'

'Why?'

'She's your mother.' Bridget puts down the brush and walks towards the door. 'You get some rest now. You are going to need all your strength.'

The darkness mellows as a bright, spring moon rises in the eastern sky, peeping in and out behind fast-moving fronds of cloud. Katherine opens the window to inhale the sea air. She can hear the breakers crashing against the rocks protruding from the bottom of the dunes. Huge waves tumble in and out like oxygen being inhaled and exhaled. Stones and shells rattle in the froth as they churn over and over, gradually being worn down into grains of sand. She can feel the rolling pulse of the North Sea, the whack of the water biting into the coast, reclaiming more and more each year. With every wave comes a new cleansing, a new beginning and a new end. Hope comes in, fears recede. Katherine supposes that, eventually, a big wave will take the manor house and wash it out in millions of tiny pieces to join the salty soup of the sea.

It was down there, in that smuggler's cove with the eternally changing turmoil of water, rocks, stones and sand, that Harry proposed to Katherine. They were sitting together under the sandy cliffs, watching gannets dive, counting the seconds till they bobbed up again. He managed to persuade her that she needed to be rescued, and he was the only one who could keep her safe. Marriage seemed like such a mature thing to do. She laughed and cried with the salt breeze lashing her hair across her cheeks. Harry opened his jacket and sucked her into it, picking the sodden strands away from her face and twisting them into a knot behind her head, tidying, sorting, in control.

At the back door, Katherine pulls on an old coat and a pair of wellingtons before she slips outside. She uses the moonlight to find her way through the garden. Her feet know the path to the sea. She stands close to the edge, hypnotised by the rocking of the earth and the magic of the night; the rippling light on the surface of the water below and the wild squawking of seabirds. It would be so easy to let herself go. She is already floating on clouds of despair. They could carry her over the edge and away into oblivion. Everything has come to nothing. Unable to sustain her marriage, but failing in her attempt to break free. The resolve she felt so strongly earlier in the day, when she swept out of her London home, grasping independence like the tinkers snatch at coins, has dissipated. Now she knows she is being sucked backwards into the milieu of old familial roles: daughter, wife. But it's not the same now. She has been violated. Breached. There is no going back. She is hovering precariously at one of the most easterly points of the British Isles, leaning into the wind, longing for weightlessness, for the breeze to lift her wings and carry her out over the North Sea to a place where no one can ask her questions or make her be what she can no longer be.

It is not a voice. It is not the ghostly echoes of lives lived long ago. What Katherine hears and feels now is an intangible presence, an invisible but perceptible shape, an inaudible but soothing sound resonating deep inside her head. 'Step back, Katherine. No more harm will come to you. You are not alone. You will not be alone. This is your destiny. The baby is real. He lives in your womb.' All at once, this is the only reality of which Katherine can be sure. She feels the quickening flutter; she is a mother now. This moment is the most important thing, and all that really matters is to cherish it, to live it and to give it life.

She turns for home. Grey shadows float over the path. She tries to walk through them, but they dance ahead of her, coaxing her feet onwards, enticing her to embrace the life that lies ahead. She knows with a strange twinge of excitement that as every minute passes, nothing can ever be completely the same again.

With the moon and the North Sea behind her and the taste of the salty east wind seasoning her craw, Katherine climbs back into a warm bed and sleeps.

CHAPTER NINE

When he discovers that Katherine is home, Frank makes a grand plan to take her and Bridget on a drive along the coast, have lunch in a hotel, motor around and do a bit of sightseeing. In reality, however, he is not well enough for any of that. Bridget organises a picnic, with a gingham tablecloth, in the conservatory. Frank is sitting in a large wicker wheelchair shrouded in rugs, his terrier, Digger, on his lap. The early vines, climbing along just below the glass, are in flower overhead. A bright morning sun is warming his blotchy face, giving it a slight vestige of colour down one side. His voice is weak. It started somewhere in his chest, but now the tumour is clamouring up his throat and slowly strangling him. A wheezy cough comes in paroxysms, making it hard for him to snatch some breath and start again. Katherine leans in close to him and breathes warm words onto his face.

'Daddy, I have some good news for you. I'm going to have a baby.'

A bony claw comes out from underneath the blanket and

clutches hold of her hand.

'That's the best news ever.' He gropes around and produces a silver hip flask of cognac from within the woollen recesses. 'Cheers!' He takes a swig from the flask and offers it to Katherine. 'I'm dying. You know that, of course.' He waits for a reaction; all he gets is a horrified look on his daughter's face. 'One in the departure lounge, and another steps into the waiting room, eh?' Then, seeing the tears welling into her eyes, he leans forward a little and changes his tone, 'Well done, Katherine. I couldn't have wished for more from you.' He flops back into the blankets. A frail, reptilian membrane of skin slips over his eyes. 'Take care of that child. Soon it'll be all you have of me. I'll be gone before the swallows swoop in over the cliffs again.'

He chokes and spits a blood-streaked glob of spume into his handkerchief. He coughs again. It wracks his whole body. He takes a few more slugs from the flask and then pecks at his chest with his fist. Digger hops down, shakes himself and stretches his limbs. When the coughing fit is over, he hops back up and curls into the rug once more, positioning himself to make the most of the sun's warm pool. Frank stares out of the window towards the mown yew walk. His eyes can now only see as far as the first few pairs of trees. He can't make out the early Himalayan roses that scatter their dark green foliage with shocking pink dots or the blackbird frantically pecking its bright yellow beak into the wet turf, foraging for worms and keeping a wary eye out for the ginger tomcat.

Bridget appears in the conservatory with a hot drink and rattling a little silver tray of tablets. 'I hope you aren't stressing him now, Katherine, my dotey little pet. He's not a well man, you know.' Katherine watches the way in which Bridget cajoles him into taking sips from the mug and pops the pills into his mouth one at a time. He smiles up into her big, round face. Bridget has sent the private nurse to change the linen in Frank's room. She has taken charge again now. No one, not even Georgina, will challenge that.

'He can't stay out here much longer. It's getting cold. We'll have that picnic in the dining room. We can light the fire in there ...'

Her streaked blond curls and sharp blue eyes turn to Frank.

He just smiles and shrugs his shoulders. 'It's okay, Bridget, she won't kill me. That's going to happen, which or whether. Maybe you could make some of that soup for me? You are the only one who can do that.' He reaches out his hand for her and she pats it tenderly.

Bridget goes off to check the lunch, but not before she has rearranged the blankets over his knees and managed to ease the last drop of liquid into his crinkled mouth. Katherine's belly tightens. Tears begin to fall in great dollops. She lets them flow, dropping like salty pearls, into her lap.

'Oh, Daddy, please don't talk like that. It can't be as bad as all that, surely? I need you, Daddy, now more than ever, and my baby needs a grandfather too.' She snivels and blows her nose.

'Some things can't be helped, I'm afraid, Katherine. When the Almighty calls you home, you have to go. I've had a good life. I've been lucky; it's up to you, now, to carry on.'

'Was it always good, Daddy? Why did you leave Ireland and never go back? There are so many unanswered questions.'

He starts coughing again. His eyes bulge as he throws his head forwards, almost falling out of the chair. Katherine grabs him and settles him back again, shocked by how light and lacking in substance he feels. Digger, as if outraged by being unsettled again, yaps a few times and goes off to the kitchen to sit beside the Aga instead.

'Not now, Katherine. Don't fret about those things; it's all in the past. Someday, you can ask Father Fitzgerald to explain, if you really need to know. But wait till I'm gone. Then maybe you'll come home to your husband and live in peace with your child.' He added, almost as an afterthought, 'I'm sorry I asked you to go over, now. It wasn't fair. We'll let sleeping dogs lie.'

'But Daddy …' She sees the pleading in his eyes. 'Okay. Well, maybe later, when you feel a bit better.'

~

The sense of impending doom in the house is claustrophobic, and people have begun to speak in whispers. In sharp contrast, the east wind stings her cheeks as Katherine throws her leg over Elvis and begins to canter down the wide verge that flanks the chase. Spikes of bright yellow forsythia point at her from all directions. Daffodils are swaying to the gusts from the east, bending their heads almost to the ground and then nodding back upright to try again. She leaves the soft, mown grass by the east gate and keeps cantering alongside the sea wall. She has thrown all the rules out with the wind and chucks her riding hat into the grass so she can feel the squall making ribbons of her hair. The tide is right up to the base of the dunes. White-fringed waves are breaking into a high spray of mist against the rocks. Black-headed gulls are swirling around, swooping to the water and spiralling up again, screeching, anticipating a great feast of small fish to come in on the new tide. She pulls up where the path begins to veer away from the sea and turns the cob to face the water. Any other time she would have lit a joint and smoked it lying in the coarse sea grasses, trying to read the clouds.

Or she would have sat on the wrought bench, which was placed there many years ago by her mother's father, who loved to sit and contemplate the world from there while he smoked his curved pipe. Katherine's English grandfather was a landed country squire, unable to join the army because of various physical disabilities he had acquired during the first war, but who, against the odds, had hit lucky shortly after that with his entrepreneurial building schemes. She remembers him only vaguely as a rather formal man with big whiskers and a knotty walking cane, which he waved around a lot when mimicking Mr Churchill, for whom he had little regard. 'That warmongering old narcissist', he called him. How different he was from her other grandfather, Francie, whom she knew only by legend. The poor man had died young and hungry, having fathered eight children. His family, apparently, had been rent asunder in some kind of patriotic bloodbath in the twenties; alluded to occasionally, when Frank might have drunk too much at Christmas.

Elvis is so unfit that he is heaving for breath, and his hair is sticking to his neck in thick curls of sweat. Katherine takes her feet out of the stirrups and lets her legs dangle. She drops the reins so that he can graze. He doesn't want to, though; he also gazes out over the dunes, as if awestruck by the mesmeric roar of the North Sea. She buries her face in his thick mane and drinks up the salty smell.

Katherine knows very few facts about her father's early life. What she does know is that he was clever, hardworking and eventually married the boss's daughter. A similar story to Harry's in many ways, another tale that is also a mystery to her. For Katherine, Frank's real life started on this side of the water. The rest seems to have belonged to someone else. Now, he is too sick for her to badger him with all the things she wants to know, needs to know; must know, if she is going to piece together the frayed ends of Jack's last weeks and find out what is really going on there in faraway Knocklong.

She sits for a long time, watching the herring gulls and turning things over in her head. She stays until the sun has been swamped by heavy grey clouds, leaving only a sea mist rising and a biting wind whipping over the sea wall. Even the gulls have given up their squawking and the tide has skulked away into a dark abyss. She hacks home along narrow lanes, taking the long way round.

When she comes into the house through the back door, the place has grown dark. She hovers in the kitchen for a while, drinking tea and trying to imagine Frank coming into this fine Elizabethan manor house as a young man and courting his mother; much as Harry had courted her. She has seen many photos of him, tall and upright with an Edwardian moustache. He seems not to belong in the plus-fours and deerstalker, like someone who was doing his best to hide, while scheming behind a façade of gentility. Now, he is a knight of the realm, titular head of a multi-million-pound corporation, respected by businessmen and politicians from both sides of the house. There are no photographs from his Irish life, nothing that would give him away, just his name, the remnants of his red hair and his faint Irish lilt.

Georgina has returned from wherever it is she goes to 'get away' and is sipping gin and tonic in the drawing room. Harry is there too. Both look very surprised when Katherine walks in. For a moment, she is utterly thrown by the sight of the two of them standing together in front of the fire with their elbows on the mantelpiece. She hesitates in the doorway, unsure what to do next.

'Katherine! Are you not going to say hello to Henry?'

Georgina takes a long pull on her cigarette holder and then throws her head back and exhales through pursed lips.

'Yes, of course.' Katherine goes over to him and gives him a kiss on both cheeks. 'Where's Daddy?'

They look at each other and Harry says, 'He was very tired. Bridget has taken him up.'

After dinner, Harry is snoring in an armchair. Katherine goes to Bridget's room. She slips into the bed beside her and lets the warmth seep through her clothes, through her skin, into all the cold places within.

'I can't face Harry tonight.'

'You'll have to face it sooner or later.'

'Not now, please.'

'Come here, pet.' She takes Katherine into her arms.

'I felt it move last night, Bridgie. I'm sure it's a boy.'

Bridget gives her a squeeze and kisses the back of her head. The two of them fall asleep together as they have hundreds of times before.

Katherine wakes in the middle of the night. It takes her eyes a while to make eerie objects look familiar. Moonlight throws weird, sepia shapes around the room. The wind is blowing hard, and although the window is shut, the curtains balloon into the room, inflated by the draught hissing through all the gaps in and around the old leaded windows. She can't move because Bridget has rolled onto her back in the middle of the bed and thrown her arms out sideways like the branches of an oak tree. Katherine has to pee, but she's too cold to get out and venture into the corridor. She remembers what it is like having to go in the middle of the night in Knocklong, squatting over a plastic basin so she didn't have to brave it down the narrow, wooden stairs or face whatever she might see in the shadows outside her room.

Eventually, the need becomes too urgent to ignore, and Katherine decides to make a dash for it. The old house never sleeps. It is filled with the sounds of creatures scuttling around, floorboards creaking and the growling of the wind harmonising with Bridget's rumbling snores. Even the plumbing gurgles and hisses a nocturnal tune that Katherine has forgotten in her months away. With her heart thumping from the exertion of the nursery stairs, she slides back between the sheets and presses her cold feet onto Bridget's. After some time, she glides again into the embrace of sleep and dreams about being in a little craft, all alone, out in the North Sea, tossed around in the wind, never to reach the shore.

'I brought you a cup of tea and a few cuts of toast, pet,' Bridget purrs softly into Katherine's ear.

'Why? What time is it?'

'It's nearly eleven o'clock.'

'Oh, good grief!' She sits straight up and declares brightly, 'Do you know what, Bridgie? I don't feel sick anymore. I can't wait for breakfast. I suppose everyone is up and about? How's Daddy today? Is Harry still here?'

'Whoa, stop firing them questions at me and drink your tea. Eat that toast now before it colds and you can't face it anymore.' She laughs and goes on, 'And look at you, still in yesterday's clothes!'

~

Katherine makes several attempts to capture her father alone so she can quiz him about Uncle Jack and the family history. It is hopeless; Bridget is always foostering around him like a clucking hen, seeing off all challengers. Katherine goes instead to search for Harry in the offices around the manor house.

Eventually, she finds a note in the kitchen: 'Hi Babe. Didn't like to wake you. Gone to London on urgent business. Hope you get some rest; you look peaky. Henry.' She notes that he is now signing himself 'Henry'. Gone is the Harry who courted her in the gardens of this very house, who walked her along the stony beach and huddled with her beneath the overhanging dunes, watching exhausted waves dissolve and sink back into oblivion, like a sigh. The midnight skinny dipping and slugging back scrumpy in the garden shed are all memories that might, or might not, have happened.

Katherine realises with some impatience that Bridget is not going to let her near Frank because 'he gets so fussed'. She passes some time riddling around in the drawers in her old bedroom, looking for some clothes to take back to Ireland. Her skimpy, flowery cottons and velvets, that all smell of patchouli oil, are now too tight across the bust. She observes that her belly is beginning to swell. She holds them up to herself in front of the mirror, wondering if anything will ever be the same again.

She moved out of this room after her wedding. Georgina preferred to have the 'young couple' in the spare room on the first landing. It saved the daily having to hump linen, flowers and so on, all the way up to the top of the house. Katherine still hankers for the first morning sun, which seeps into the east-facing room in the nursery wing, high up in the back of the manor. From spring to autumn, it managed to reach all the way across to her rickety, four-poster bed, bringing the morning rays of hope and promise that used to give her the incentive she needed to struggle out from underneath her eiderdown and bounce into another day. Harry became very skilled at the stealth and deception needed to pass Bridget's half-open door in the small hours and make it back to his room again before dawn. It was sweaty spice in muffled murmurs and the constant issue about how to get rid of used condoms. In those days, Harry and Katherine were mates. Everything was about fun or tears.

She sits on the side of the bed and quarries into her memory, trying to resurrect those exhilarating, original thoughts of youth and the raw emotions of fresh love. She bites her lip until it bleeds.

~

Katherine's chance with Frank comes when Bridget goes into the village for some groceries. He is asleep in the library. She stands over him for a while, just to see if he is really breathing. She doesn't want to wake him, but knows she won't have too long before Bridget gets back or the day nurse comes in to check on him. But he wakes up suddenly, coughing and thrashing his arms around as though he has fallen into the sea. She jumps backwards. He catches her by the wrist. 'Ah, there you are, Katherine. I thought you were gone.'

'Daddy! Are you all right?' She holds him tightly and wraps his blanket around his shoulders again. When he has settled down, she says, 'I want you to tell me why you really left Ireland.'

'Never mind that now. It's all in the past, where it belongs. Sit with me for a while. I won't be here much longer. Please.'

He closes his eyes and starts to recite a poem he loves. It sums it all up, love, ambush, and the desperation of inequality.

> 'The wind was a torrent of darkness upon the
> gusty trees,

'The moon was a ghostly galleon tossed upon
cloudy seas,
'The road was a ribbon of moonlight looping the
purple moor
'And The Highwayman came riding,
Riding, riding,
'The highwayman came riding, up to the old inn
door …'[1]

He can't go on. He is doubled over again in another paroxysm of coughing. He begins to go blue, and Katherine wallops him on the back. She realises that it isn't doing any good. He is flailing his right arm in the direction of the small table, but she has no idea what he wants or what those frantic gestures mean.

She runs into the hall in a panic, screaming for help. Bridget is just coming into the house. She drops the shopping and rushes in to where Frank is falling out of his chair. She catches him and shouts at Katherine to get the inhaler off the table. It takes a few minutes to revive him. Katherine looks on helplessly.

'You go and put the kettle on, pet. We'll have a hot drop. We'll all feel better then.'

The tea restores the women, but even after a few swigs from his flask, Frank is still very shaken. Bridget insists on taking him to hospital for the night. She sends for an ambulance, and following a series of phones calls, she summons Georgina. By the time he gets to the hospital, Frank has recovered his composure but not his colour. He lies in a pallor, breathing shallow, soft puffs. Georgina arrives shortly after Bridget and Katherine. The three women take turns to

---

1   *The Highwayman* by Alfred Noyes

sit with him until he gets fed up and sends them all away. He likes being in hospital. It makes him feel safe to have all the breathing apparatus pulsating beside him and the nurses fussing around him.

'Why don't you go to London and try talking to that husband of yours? Your father will be in the hospital for at least a week, maybe more. Once they have their hands on him, they won't let him go that easy.'

'I don't want to leave Daddy. And besides, Bridgie, I don't know how to tell Harry. I don't know how to go on.' She whimpers, tears watering her eyes.

'Well, don't tell him the truth, anyways! Try rubbing his knee a bit, you know yourself.' Rubbing Harry's knee is Bridget's solution to everything.

~

Katherine is trying to talk herself into it on the train to London. She is thinking of a candlelit bistro dinner, a bottle of Beaujolais, a bit of dope, maybe, then gently working up to the big news. But she won't rub his knee. She will think up an excuse for him to sleep in the spare room.

All goes quite well. By eleven o'clock, they are sitting in the car outside the house in Chelsea. Harry is breathing heavy breaths of garlic and lust. His hands are beginning to grope Katherine's thighs.

'Wait till we get inside, Harry, please. I've got something important to tell you.'

'Oh God! Not more stuff about your old uncle, I hope?'

She opens the car door and dives into the safety of the house. Harry does not seem to be in such a hurry now, and she has time to roll a joint and light up before he is standing behind her in the kitchen.

'Well? What is it, then?'

When the moment comes, she is unable to turn around and look him in the eye. She stares instead through the window into the sulphurous light of London.

'I'm pregnant.'

'What do you mean?'

Katherine imagines he might even be smiling, but she can't see his face. It sounds as if he is not smiling.

'How could that have happened?'

There is a short silence. The edge in his voice makes her nervous. He spins her around to face him. She puts her arms across her chest, thinking for a moment that he is going to punch her.

'We can talk about this in the morning, Katherine,' he snaps through clenched teeth. 'Let's not waste any more time now.'

'No, Harry, I can't. I've been told by the doctor that it's not safe.' Surprised and impressed by her own lies, she presses on. 'I don't know how it happened, Harry, except you were pretty drunk in that hotel in Kilkenny. Maybe you weren't careful?'

After that, it is easy. Harry thinks it would be better if he slept in the spare room.

'Does that doctor know how much dope you smoke?' His parting shot is weak but targeted well, and Katherine puts out the joint.

When she wakes up in the morning, Harry is sitting on her bed. His silk dressing gown is tied loosely around his waist, and he is sipping coffee.

'Katherine, how could you have got yourself pregnant? Have you been sleeping around?'

185

'Harry! How could you say that? It must have been those Johnnies you brought with you to Ireland. I had the feeling it might have burst that night in the hotel. I didn't like to say anything at the time. Hoping for the best, I suppose.'

'They don't just pop, like sticking a pin into a balloon, Katherine.'

'Well, I don't know. You were very enthusiastic that night.'

'God, this is a disaster. I'm not ready to be a father. I don't want a bloody child right now. You'll have to have a termination.'

'It's too late for that, Harry. I can feel it moving. And besides, it's not that easy.'

He puts his head into his hands and groans.

'I have to go to Glasgow on business today. I'll decide what to do when I come back. One thing is for sure, you can't go back to Ireland in that state!'

When he's gone, she rolls over to face the wall, and the crying begins. She weeps and sobs and howls, reliving everything that's happened, right back to Jack dying alone in a shed. She is crying for herself, for her father, her baby, her dissipated family, Uncle Jack, even Harry. When she is completely cried dry, she lies in a hot bath, trying to remember if it's gin or quinine you take if you don't want the baby. They don't have either in the house.

She lies there, looking down at her belly. 'You poor little thing, in there. Well, even if he doesn't want you, I do!'

There is a pink dressing gown hanging behind the bathroom door, but it's too big for her. She looks at herself in the full-length mirror; red hair and pink fluff don't work. It must belong to someone else. She drops it into the wicker wash basket for the daily to deal with. Then retrieves it, thinking to use it as evidence. When she follows that thought, it ends in more tears, so finally, she stuffs it into a plastic shopping bag and puts it into the bin.

She rings Bridget. 'But Bridgie, I know I'm not wrong! I just know.'

'You've got to stick to your guns. You can't back down now. Your baby needs a father.'

'What kind of a father will he be if he doesn't want it and he's having an affair with someone else?'

'You don't know that now, do you? At any rate, he has to be better than no father at all, believe me.'

'I want to go back to Ireland.'

'Ireland's no good to you now, pet. You've got to sort things out at home first.'

'I can't stand to be with him, and don't tell me to rub his knee! It's horrible.'

Bridget hates having conversations on the phone; it's a piece of equipment she avoids like Spanish flu. She needs to see the expressions on a person's face. There is a long, awkward silence. 'Don't you think it would be better to stay where you are and fight for your marriage? I can't come back to Ireland now. I have to be here to take care of things, your father being the way he is.'

'I'll miss you. How can I go on my own?'

'Are you sure you aren't just running away? What happened to the Dunkirk spirit? Yesterday, you were going to make it all up and be nice to him. You were going to ring Ryans' and get Jim to take care of things for a bit longer.' After a short silence, she goes on, 'He even promised to feed and take care of the dog, remember? And I'm sure Fonsie will pop over and check up on things. He did say he would.' Katherine does not respond. 'You were going to give that marriage another chance, weren't you? I'll ring Ryans' if you like. Are you still there? Kate?'

Katherine fights the temptation to put the phone down. She's never done that to Bridget.

'How's Daddy today?'

'He's still in the hospital. He's in good hands. Your mother, or that nurse, the fat one, is there with him most of the time. But they think it might not be too much longer now.' Bridget slips in that last piece, even though no one has said it as bluntly as that. There is another silence. Katherine tries to imagine Georgina in the hospital.

'How bad is he, really? Do you think maybe I should come home again instead?'

'What are you going to do about Harry?'

Katherine gives a long, low moan that Bridget can remember from years ago, when the little girl was made to sit at the table and eat rice pudding. She used to look at Bridget, pleading for a way out, and eventually, when Georgina had lost interest, Bridget would swipe it off the table and dump it in the bin.

'I don't know.'

Slowly, it sinks in that her father is really dying. She packs her stash of dope back into her bag, puts a few clothes and her Paddington Bear on top of it and takes the train back to Suffolk.

~

Georgina sits calmly beside Frank's hospital bed. If the panic crawls up her chest and catches her in the back of the throat, she can press the call button, knowing that, in minutes, a competent nurse will rush in and take over. Everything is clean. Except for the paraphernalia of medical attention, there is no clutter around the place. No flowers; they make him cough. No grapes; he doesn't eat fruit, never has done. The light is drawing dim. Georgina gets up quietly and pulls down the blinds. There is an unusually warm glow in the room from a red bulb. It's like the infrared ones they use on the farm for foundling lambs and young pheasants. There is a whiff of lightly singeing blankets, just like lambs' wool when they forget to lift the lamp after Peter brings the orphans into the kitchen and puts them by the Aga.

She settles into a tubular steel chair beside the bed and stares at her husband. She counts the gurgling breaths in and out. It's an uncertain rhythm. It reminds her of a midwife counting the seconds as the whip of labour lashes around you and bites you in half. Katherine is twenty-seven now. Georgina gave birth to her here. In this very hospital, in a room quite similar to this one, except that it was all a bit more primitive then. The war was in full swing. Everyone was on red alert all the time. No fruit then or fat nurses either. Everything was rationed, except common sense, ingenuity and gas masks. All the women were thin, and most of the fathers and husbands were either far away fighting, incarcerated in German prison camps or lying in unmarked graves, somewhere, over there.

Frank, being Irish, could not be called up to fight and spent the war feathering their nest in her father's family business. He had many ingenious ways of turning pennies into pounds. His ingenuity ended when it came to the birth of their only child. He had stomped about outside the delivery suite as the nightmare of childbirth deepened. Georgina's father had also pounded up and down the corridors, whacking his cane off the walls when he heard her cry out. He smacked his gaiters with it during the silences between her screams, claiming loudly that the bloody army had stolen all the best doctors.

She had nearly chewed through her own knuckles. Her mother was squeezing out towels and dabbing at Georgina's tortured face, trying to avoid the gnashing teeth. Buckets of blood followed Katherine into the world. The tiny head was horribly misshapen from the forceps' spoons, and Georgina was ripped to pieces. Neither was expected to live. While all the attention was on Georgina, trying to stop the haemorrhage and to call her back from the depths of exhaustion and acute anaemia, a quiet little Catholic nurse was breathing life and hope into the baby. Georgina remembers wafting in and out of consciousness. White faces, white coats, white lilies and white walls. By the time she revived, some days had passed. To stop the bleeding, they had removed her womb. No more children. No son. Just a little girl, gone now to the other breast of the Irish wet nurse, Bridget O'Connor.

Frank is breathing with a deathly rattle, and Georgina watches helplessly. She is holding his cold hand. The fingers are no longer strong and directive. Bones held together by blotchy skin, like the hoary old feet of a rooster.

'I'm sorry, Frank. Please don't think badly of me. I did my best.'

The fingers move and close around her hand. He opens his eyes, and a smile of serenity widens across his face. After a while, she presses the red bell.

'I think he's gone, Nurse.'

The nurse tries for a pulse. She reaches forward and gently closes Frank's eyes. 'God rest him,' she whispers and crosses herself. She turns off the infra-red lamp.

Georgina sits in the chair as the gloom gathers around her. Tears threaten but don't appear. A priest is among the people who come and go. He stares at her, unsure if she is Catholic or not, but then mumbles on regardless. Bridget and

Katherine come in, holding each other in grief and weeping. Harry arrives soon after with cups of tea. For a long time, the dimly lit room is full of people. Harry and Bridget make all the arrangements. Georgina's mind slips into freefall, unable to grapple with the logistics of a funeral.

~

The dining room table is draped in black. It is heady with the scent of lilies and hothouse roses. Frank looks like a waxwork masterpiece from Madame Tussaud's, lying in his satin-lined casket. His hands are locked together over his chest with his mother-of-pearl rosary beads twisted through his fingers. Someone has given him a haircut and trimmed his whiskers. What little hair he has left is neatly combed down with Brill cream. The candle on the sideboard smokes from burning unevenly as it yields to the draught from the open door. The great, gilded mirror over the mantelpiece is covered with a shroud 'just in case'. Bridget thinks of everything.

People file past to pay their respects and drink whiskey. Bridget and the gardener's wife keep up an endless supply of tea and sandwiches. Georgina avoids the dining room and hides in the study, relying on Harry to call her if anyone important arrives. Finally, she throws in the towel and slinks off to bed.

Poor little Digger crouches under the table, growling occasionally at the feet that shuffle past. No one visits after ten o'clock. Bridget and Harry keep vigil, trying to stay awake by telling stories and drinking coffee. Katherine wants to stay with them, but Bridget urges her to go to bed. 'You need your sleep, pet.'

They all manage to crawl through the night.

Georgina chain-smokes all the next morning, fretting about the funeral arrangements and going back over their life together, feeling the pinch of guilt that goes with every bereavement.

The burial is bleak with the east wind swirling the winter wheat. Blackthorn blossoms, the eager, spring virgins that appear on thorny branches even before the leaves unfurl, duck and dive on their rigid boughs. Peter and Harry are the chief pallbearers. It all has to be balanced up by the undertakers, because Peter is over six feet tall, and Harry, well, he's short and stocky. The gardener and the farm workers fill in the gaps. Long faces, long black coats. Georgina tries to stop her skirt from clinging to her legs and her umbrella from snapping inside out. Bridget weeps on, stopping only to blow her nose before starting up again. She and Katherine huddle together inside a tartan car rug. Bridget nudges Katherine, and they both turn round together to see a group of figures standing back from the crowd beneath two withering elms. They are dressed in khaki fatigues, black berets and dark glasses. They are raising rifles to the sky. In unison, they fire off a volley of shots and then disappear before anyone has time to raise an alarm.

'The IRA,' Bridget snivels into Katherine's left ear. 'He was much respected.'

There is a minor scuffle. People scream and dart around. Then it's over. A seemingly endless string of politicians and dignitaries, including the Irish ambassador, pay their respects. They call her 'Your Ladyship'. Georgina shakes their hands weakly, as if being Irish is contagious. There are many things she does not understand. She feels with relief that she no longer has to try.

Frank has left his wife relatively little apart from the house, which was hers anyway, and the income from the farm, which was also hers and returns to her, with the portfolio of stocks and shares, which were the rest of her dowry. They are now significantly swollen by his shrewdness and his extraordinary Midas touch. It is more than enough to keep her household in luxurious comfort for the rest of her life. Apart from a modest bequest for Bridget, a small token for Harry and some obscure trust fund, which no one knows anything about except Frank's solicitor, he leaves the rest of his considerable fortune to Katherine.

~

The weeks that follow are a strange mixture of awkward grief and frenzied bursts of activity. No one feels they should be getting on with things except Harry, who not only continues to run the business empire unchallenged, but assumes the role of estate manager as well, making the sweeping changes he's long dreamed about. Georgina is happy to let him take over everything while she mourns quietly, getting thinner, paler and more withdrawn. In an unusual reversal of roles, Katherine is comforting Bridget, who is even more lonely and distraught than she is herself.

The ghosts of Knocklong, and her Irish family, preoccupy Katherine. The funeral disturbs her memories of Jack's strange burial; all those unanswered questions, hanging in limbo. It torments her that her father died so quickly, before she managed to find out anything significant about the past. There is an aching sense of unfinished business. Like Jack, he went too quickly and took everyone, except Bridget, by surprise.

~

Harry is so involved with all his new responsibilities that he has no time to concern himself with Katherine, the baby or all the weeping and moping around that is going on in the house. He hardly seems to notice the wind changing. Katherine and Bridget are packing trunks and preparing to leave. One morning, when the May sun is warming the front of the house, he walks into the hall and finds the two women sitting on their suitcases, waiting for Peter to bring the Bentley to the front door.

'Where are you two going, then?'

'I told you Harry, I have to go back to Ireland to finish what I started there six months ago.'

'You didn't tell me you were thinking of going back there now, though!'

'I've been telling you for weeks, but you don't listen to me. You have so many other things on your mind these days.'

Bridget presses her leg hard against Katherine's, urging her not to get into a row, reminding her they had agreed she wouldn't bring up anything contentious, especially not about a possible affair. At least not until they had more to go on and the Irish Sea between then. Harry does not read the secret language. He looks at the two women, unable to fully grasp the situation.

'You said yourself that the spring would be a better time to sell the place and sort things out,' Bridget says, trying to distract him from staring at all the luggage.

'And who's going to keep house here?'

The car crunches the gravel outside and stops. The boot clicks open, then there is a sharp knock on the heavy oak door. Katherine looks at Bridget for reassurance. Bridget nods and squeezes her hand gently.

'I'm sorry, Harry, I have to go, and I need Bridget to go

with me.' She smiles her best smile. Bridget has no smiles for Harry today.

'Maybe you could get a temporary housekeeper till we come back? It probably won't take too long to finish off sorting things out over there.' The lie slips easily out of Bridget's lips. She never disliked him as much as she does this minute.

'You seem to be taking a lot of stuff with you.' He kicks the suitcase that Katherine is sitting on, just missing her leg. Then, pointing at her belly, he goes on, 'And what about that baby? You'll need to see a doctor, I'm sure. How will you manage that over there? In that tuppenny ha'penny backwater?'

Bridget stiffens and stands up. She looks him straight in the face. 'Do you think there are no doctors in Ireland?'

'It's little more than a banana republic! Oh, go on then, but don't say I didn't warn you.'

Peter nods at the two women and quickly takes out the bags.

CHAPTER TEN

The countryside is smiling when Bridget and Katherine return to Knocklong. All the grey sliminess of winter has dissolved into the past. The tall hawthorn hedges are muffled in white froth, fading here and there to a soft Victorian pink. Left and right, the verges sway with the creamy blossoms of cow-parsley. All the tears of hardship have turned into daisies and buttercups, freckling the glossy, green meadows. The last few ewes have lambed and the early babies are growing up and getting fat. Jim Ryan has organised them into the fields, along the inches beside the river. Rusty old cars and iron bedsteads fencing the gaps in the ditches are overgrown with brambles and brightly flowering purple and yellow vetch. The black cow and calf are out to grass with the rest of the cattle, some of which have also calved, and the yard is no longer overlooked by hungry faces. Dandelions and early grasses are once again blooming gaily around the house, and the nettles and bindweed are beginning to reclaim the haggard. The dog rushes out of a shed to greet Katherine and Bridget as they clamber down from Fonsie's van.

Marie has been to the house and opened the windows, made up the beds and lit the range. She has checked and double-checked. Everything looks normal. There is no trace of anything having happened there since the two women left a couple of months ago. No smell of pipe smoke in the kitchen. No stub ends of Woodbines on the floor. Any number of covert meetings can have taken place here, but you wouldn't know.

They dump the bags and cases outside the kitchen door and stretch their limbs in the midday sun. Katherine scoops some clean water from the barrel into the dog's dish and pulls a few stalks of cocksfoot from their sheaths to suck the sweet juice from the soft ends.

Before Fonsie turns and drives away, Bridget tries the car, but the battery is flat, so he takes it away to be charged up. The two women decide to postpone going into the house, and instead they leave the cases in the porch and take a walk along the river, anticipating a cup of tea with Josie.

'The bump is growing nicely now, I see. How have you been? I heard your father passed away some weeks back. Lord ha' mercy on him.' She crosses herself and then reaches for the teapot.

'How did you hear that, Josie?'

'This isn't Outer Mongolia; we get the papers, you know! There was a long obituary in the local paper too. I kept it for you; I'll get it after. Didn't realise he was a real "sir". Knighted by the queen, indeed! How's your poor mother? And that husband of yours?' She saws off chunks of fresh, brown bread and lathers them with butter and damson jam. Bridget asks for news of her own family, and the two older women gossip away merrily while Katherine reads the obituaries from the various papers that Josie has saved for her.

They tell how Frank had been involved in quite a few skirmishes and ambushes during the civil unrest, apart from 'the great train arms heist' and the burning of the mansion at Sunnyhill. He was also reputed to have been a senior commander in the Old IRA. He left Ireland in 1923 under suspicion for many 'misdemeanours', including a possible involvement in the death of George Rolt of Sunnyhill. The papers made a big thing of his 'vast wealth', his important influence on the Labour government, his having been very friendly with Harold Wilson, how he used his position in industry to further Wilson's left-wing agenda and to gain a knighthood. Apparently, the two men had fallen out eventually, probably over the devaluing of the pound in 1967.

Katherine wonders how it is that some journalist in Ireland knows so much more about her father than she knows herself. She reads the name Patrick Finnegan at the top of the article. She doesn't make the connection until Josie says, 'Isn't that the fellow who brought you to your uncle's funeral? I remember him enquiring locally, that time, about your family's history. He was around here looking for you. He thought to do an interview, said he would come back sometime in the summer.'

Katherine can remember Georgina's utter disdain for 'that horrid little man, Wilson', his working-class origins, his 'ghastly accent' and how she had always maintained, within the family at least, that Wilson was a communist and a Russian agent. Katherine knows that Harry has kept up the important contacts and built many more alliances besides. He has the knack of being able to manipulate all the political instruments at once and play them like an orchestra.

Marie arrives after a while with two of her little girls, who scamper around teasing the dog. They laugh and throw freshly gathered buttercups at each other. She lays her midwife's hands on the growing bump and asks, 'Plenty of movement, I hope?' Then, with her slate grey eyes looking straight at Katherine, 'How did your Harry take to the idea of being a father, then?'

Bridget and Katherine exchange looks. Katherine shrugs her shoulders. 'He'll get used to it. He's got a lot on at the moment, managing the economy, building his empire!' They all laugh.

Jim comes into the kitchen. He shows little sign of surprise to find the visitors there. He eyes the tea cups and the crumbs.

'Well? You've come back, then?'

'Thank you so much, Jim, for looking after the farm for me. The animals all look well; the lambs are getting fat,' Katherine says nervously and produces a bottle of whiskey from a carrier bag.

He nods. 'Aye, and them sheep will soon be full of maggots too; they'll have to be dipped before there's nothing left of them. How do you think you'll manage all that now, in your condition?' He looks at the bump. 'All on your own.'

Bridget stands up and leans over Jim, who suddenly looks very small. 'She is not alone.'

Jim moves sideways and points his cap at Katherine. 'I hoped you'd have come to your senses, girl. I'm still willing to buy the place.'

'For goodness's sake, Jim, would you ever leave Katherine alone? Give her a chance to settle down, and then she can decide what to do.' The sharp tone in Bridget's voice startles everyone, except Katherine, who feels the warming breath of unconditional love at the back of her neck. Bridget ushers her towards the open door.

Josie gives them one of her bundles of bread, butter and eggs cosseted in a linen towel and a billycan of fresh milk. Marie drives them back to the farm. She wants to be there when they open the door, to assess their reaction to the way things are in the house.

It feels quite different. Apart from being warmed through by the early burst of good weather and the gently smouldering range, there is a new calmness. Katherine no longer feels an ominous presence in the rooms. Maybe Jack has finally found peace. The thought whispers through her veins. It's like a prayer that chants warmly to the rhythm of her heart. The familiarity of the place now has its own embrace. The baby kicks. It feels right.

~

Word soon spreads that the hippie girl and Bridget O'Connor are back, and the visitors start calling again. Nicholas Molloy finds her digging a vegetable plot in the haggard one sunny morning when Bridget has gone to Grainey to visit her own mother. A small transistor radio is blaring away, 'Obla di, Obla da, and Molly was a singer in the band.'

Katherine swings with the groove. The world is good. The soil is soft and a deep brown, enriched by years of rotted hay, dung and other vegetation. She thrusts the spade downwards, stamping on it with her foot and tossing the sods out onto the grass. The smell of the earth as it crumbles off the spade is sweet and rich. She shakes it off the roots and chucks the weeds into a wheelbarrow. A grain of soil gets into her eye, and she pulls down her eyelid to try to shift it.

For a short while, Nicholas stands, watching her from behind, the light cotton of her skirt swaying with the movements of her body. The sun, shining through the fabric, outlines her slender legs and thighs. The dog rushes round the side of the house, barking. Katherine blinks into the sun; her back is stiff from bending down. She is wearing a sleeveless tee-shirt, and as she leans back to ease the stiffness, Nicholas stares at the curve of her belly. There is a small patch of taut skin visible between the lilac of the vest and the elastic waistband of her skirt. Her arms are tanned, her face a mass of freckles and her green eyes are glowing with lusty, good health. Katherine is standing with her foot on the shoulder of the spade and her hand in the small of her back, accentuating her fullness.

'I believe it now; you English do dig with your left foot! Should you be doing that? Digging like that in your condition, I mean?'

Katherine is startled and spins around. Something in his voice always makes her uneasy.

'Why ever not? It's a really cool feeling.'

'What happened to that husband of yours? Shouldn't he be here doing that for you?'

Then Katherine laughs at the good of it. 'Harry, digging a garden! He's an industrialist, not an agrarian. But he'll be back and forth to see how we are getting on here. The summer in London is too hot and stuffy for me at the moment.' She bends to turn the radio down. Her breasts are almost bursting out of the top of the tee-shirt. 'Fancy a cup of tea?'

Just at that moment, tea is the very last thing on Nicholas' mind, and the thought of being alone in the kitchen with Katherine is making him tremble. 'Where's Bridget O'Connor these days?'

'She'll be back shortly. She never leaves me alone for long. Why don't you go in and put the kettle on and I'll finish off this row?'

'Look't, you put on the kettle and I'll do this for you. Here, show me that spade.' As he reaches across to take the spade, he realises that he's not familiar with the scent of a woman's sweat straight off her warm skin. He is forty-five years old. Apart from the occasional, or shameful, skirmish, the only woman he has ever known at all intimately is his mother. Her body is shapeless, crumpled and creaking with arthritis. The daily nurse and he himself help her with all kinds of personal tasks. It's a mechanical process; he doesn't see her as a woman, but as a series of barely working parts; a comfort blanket for him, an aching prison for her. She smells of talcum powder and salves, masking bodily functions.

'That's far out. I could do with a rest now anyway.' Katherine hands over the spade and gives him a glorious, wide smile, showing him her perfect teeth. 'Thanks.'

'Tell you what,' he says briskly, 'why don't you bring the tea out here, and we'll have it in the sun?'

'How do you like it?'

'Like what?'

'Your tea, of course!'

'With whiskey and spice and all things nice...' His voice trails off as he realises he is going too far, too fast. 'Milk and three sugars and ginger biscuits. Please.'

Katherine sits down in the kitchen for a rest while the kettle boils. She surveys all the little bits of treasure she dug up yesterday that Bridget has washed and put to dry on the range. Some chips of blue and white crockery, a few with intricate patterns; the handle of a tea cup, the edge of a soup bowl. There are some little blue or green bottles that were filled with soil, a few bits of clay pipe and lots of bones. Fonsie said those were all the dogs and rabbits shot by Jack over the years. To Katherine, it's the archaeology of her family. 'It's quite a museum of rural life, that,' Fonsie joked last night when he called to see how they were getting on with the garden.

She watches Nicholas out of the scullery window. Flies are buzzing against the glass. He has opened his shirt to the waist. His skin is white beneath the thick black curls on his chest.

By the time she brings out a small tray of tea and Bridget's buns, Nicholas has dug the whole row and two more.

'That's so cool, man. You have nearly finished it! Bridget will think I did it all myself.'

'What are you doing this for, anyway?'

They sit with their backs against the warm stone wall, facing the sun. Their shoulders are almost touching; her knees are bent and relaxed and her skirt falls in a valley between them. He tries to concentrate on the tea, to keep his eyes from following the little rivulet of sweat that's trickling down her cleavage, from imagining the salty taste of it. He spoons sugar into the cup and stirs it, conscious that his other hand is covering his groin, just in case.

'I love it. This is the life for me.' She reaches up and sweeps her hair away from her face. Even her ears are tinged with the brown glow of the sun. 'Can't you see that?'

The smell of her labours lifts enticingly from her armpit. He bites down hard on a fairy cake and washes it into his throat with scalding tea.

'I can. I can see it now, all right.' Then, looking away, he says, 'I wouldn't leave you alone here with just a dog and Bridget O'Conner if you were my wife.'

A cuckoo's call echoes from the hill behind the house, and a swarm of bees leaves the roof. They dart around frantically, more and more of them circling out from under the eaves, gathering into a frenzied whirlwind. The demented cloud swirls past and disappears into the orchard below the haggard.

'Why did you cut your hair?'

Katherine shakes her head of bobbed red curls.

'Oh, I don't know. I did it the day after my father died. I prefer it like this; it's more practical.' As she says it, she realises the real reason was because she wanted to hurt Harry and to annoy her mother; it's all she could think of to get her own back at them. The power of the hair. It works. She would not have done it while her father was alive. He was so proud of it. He said his mother's hair was just like that, and he often described how she wore it in a plaited coil around the crown of her head. How even as she grew older, it never lost its lustre. 'I suppose you didn't know my father. Did you?'

'No, I was born the year after he left here. My parents knew him all right. Most people did. He was a bit of a legend. He started something, you know. Pity your uncle didn't feel the same way.'

Katherine does a quick mental sum and is shocked to realise that Nicholas is nearly twenty years older than she is. She tries to think of reasons why that doesn't matter.

'How do you mean, "pity he didn't feel the same way"?'

'Ah, you know, Jack went the other direction. There was a lot of hardship in them days. He wanted an end to it, I suppose. Ireland was divided, you know the way, politically as well as geographically. They should never have signed that treaty. Dev was right. Look at the mess they've left behind them. It's only starting now; the real battle is still to come.' He has leaned in and shifts a little back to his original position. 'Ah sure, that's the way now. No need for you to get involved in that kind of thing. And Jack should have kept his nose out of it while he had the chance.'

Just then, the car splashes over the ford. Molloy jumps up as if caught shoplifting. 'I must go. Thanks for the tea.'

Before Bridget had even opened the car door, he vanished

the way he came, over the wall and out onto the cart track at the back.

~

Fonsie is very excited about the bees, and as soon as Katherine tells him they are hanging like an enormous bunch of grapes, humming in the apple tree, he grabs a butter box, pulls Bridget's jelly muslin over his head and tucks it in well under the lapel of his jacket. Then he stalks up to the swarm, places the box directly under the bees and gives the branch an almighty whack. Most of them fall into it with a thud. He throws a sack over them, fighting off the stragglers, which are by now darting around in an angry turmoil and beginning to get through the defences. He puts the box into the shade, calling triumphantly, 'We have 'em!' He is hitting at his head and flailing his arms around. 'They'll settle down after a bit. That's honey for the winter, girls! You know what they say: "A swarm of bees in May is worth a load of hay".'

Later on, Fonsie comes up with a conical basket and transfers the bees into it amid a cloud of smoke from some burning cardboard that he waves around them. The skip sits upside down on an old table at the bottom of the orchard. There is a small gap where Fonsie has propped a stick underneath it, from whence the bees dart in and out, busily foraging in the blossoms and flowers that bloom abundantly for the rest of the summer.

~

The sheep are shorn by two men from the other side of Kilkenny. They come every year around the same time. Their visit is preceded by a postcard, which says simply, 'June 15th, weather permitting. Have sheep in, ready and dry for shearing and two men to help.'

It gives Katherine a start to see Jack's name on the card. For a strange few seconds, she pictures the postman cycling over the ford, whistling away, the dog giving him two or three cursory barks; Jack stamping his feet into his boots as he comes out into the yard, coughing and blinking in the morning sun, which is shining on his white whiskers; his shirt tails are not properly tucked in at the back, and the braces are holding it all together. The two old friends exchange some words about the weather, and the postman reads the message to Jack. She can even feel the rush of excitement as he anticipates the yard full of sheep; Josie coming over with dinner for the men, pulling a few bottles of beer out of the crate in the river where he keeps them cool beside the milk churn, the kitchen humming with stories from around the valley.

Tears burn the backs of her eyes as she realises she never knew Jack with white whiskers. Even though he had always seemed old to her, the last time she saw him, he was still in his fifties, fit and ready for anything. Now, both Jack and Frank are dead, and all the other siblings raised here in this place are gone to the other side of the world. She doesn't know if they are dead or alive, if she has cousins or uncles and aunts. She knows nothing except that she is here now and has to keep things going for all of them. She is here for her own son to know this place, to know he's Irish, and, of course, to find out what really happened to Jack.

Bridget organises a feed for the shearers and the Ryan men who come to help. She boils a gigantic ham and a mountain of spuds. Three beautiful spring cabbages, plucked this morning from the garden, are chopped and tossed into the greasy, salty water that has boiled the meat. She has baked soda bread and pies made with rhubarb stalks from a thicket at the bottom of the orchard. The fridge is stocked with pints of beer and bottles of barley water.

Even Josie Ryan is impressed. 'B'dad, Bridget O'Connor, you can come over to my place next and do the same all over again if you like!'

'Whisht, go away with that, Josie Ryan, I'm only barely trottin' after you!'

The sheep are huddled in the yard, heaving and panting in the heat. The two shearers are stripped to the waist. One is cranking the machine, round and round, clickety clack, clickety clack. The other one is hauling the beasts onto their haunches and peeling off the creamy fleeces as smoothly as Bridget skinning potatoes with the little paring knife she keeps just for that. Jim grabs the ewes and drags them forward out of the huddle. JJ rolls up the wool into neat, round bundles and tosses it onto a few sacks in the corner. The whole operation takes most of the day, and by early evening, they are sitting around the kitchen table, eating for Ireland.

'What happened to old Jack, then?'

Bridget and Katherine are in the scullery washing the dishes when this starts up. They look at each other. Bridget holds a soapy finger up to her lips.

'Shot himself. Last November,' Jim Ryan says, trying to make it sound normal. The two shearers cross themselves and mumble things.

'Silly old fool was shooting rats in the cow byre. Must have tripped over his bootlace and shot himself instead,' adds JJ with a touch of glee.

'They al'us say that, don't they?' says one of the lads as he picks up and sinks his charred teeth into another slice of tart.

'So the young one's doing the farming now, then, is she?'

'Ha!' Jim scoffs, spooning custard onto the pastry and shovelling it all into his mouth at an angle so that his few remaining good gnashers can get a grip on it. 'She don't do much. Sure look at the state of her! Can't think what's keeping her here. It's the daftest thing I ever saw.'

'Some woman, all the same!' says the younger of the two lads. 'Wouldn't mind a bit of that after dinner!' They all laugh.

'Where's the husband, then? Or is there one?'

'That's what I don't understand,' says JJ. 'How could a man let his wife off on her own, here, in her condition? He mustn't be too pushed about her, anyway.'

One of the shearers jibes, 'I know what I'd be doing with her on a summer's day if she was my wife, pregnant or not!' He wipes his mouth on his sleeve and takes a swig of beer.

This is too much for Bridget; she stomps into the room, drying her arms and offering around more tea. 'Before you go', she says briskly.

~

Jim and JJ come over a couple of days later and gather up all the sheep and throw them one by one into a vat of evil-smelling, cloudy liquid. Sergeant Dawson leans on the fence and makes a pretence of counting them and entering it in his pocket notebook. Jim marks a few of the heftier lambs with a big, coloured stick and tells Katherine that he'll be back next week to take them to the mart.

'We won't let in the rams till autumn; we'll have a bit of order on the lambing next time.'

Rows of onion sets start to shoot out long, green stalks in the vegetable patch, and Bridget plants more ranks of cabbages to keep them company. Sometimes in the evening, Katherine goes down to the river and lays out night lines, just the way Jack had shown her many years ago. Using fat worms from the garden to bait the hooks, she ties the fishing wire to low-hanging sally branches and sinks them into the still pools with little lead weights. She likes to linger on the riverbank, watching for trout to break the surface, causing rings on the water as they snap at flies. Occasionally, she sees the shock of electric blue as a kingfisher flashes past, or, as the light fades, she might glimpse an otter glisten as it skims along the far bank.

One evening, while walking through the water meadows beside the river on the extremities of her land, Katherine finds the ruins of what must have been, at one time, a cosy farmstead. It is dressed in vines of ivy, with some rampant sycamores and elders, which have grown in hapless camouflage, creating a kind of secret shrine to a lost family life. Very little of the cottage remains, just the two gable ends and bits of rubble walls. She stands for a moment, trying to get a sense of where the door might have been. It is possible to make out a row of post holes where the rafters would have joined the side walls. Some wood pigeons have nested there in the crevices, and as she approaches, one flies out, flapping past her head. She stumbles and nearly falls on the ground where the floor would once have been. There is no trace of it now, nor windows; nothing beyond the remnants of a chimney breast that could be linked to human habitation. Hairs bristle at the back of her neck, and a cold shiver creeps up through her body. The baby gives a few kicks; her womb tightens reassuringly around it.

She picks her way through the tangled briars, and holding her arms up to avoid the stinging tips of nettles, Katherine inspects what is left of the outbuildings. One is in remarkably good order with a corrugated tin roof. Scrambling over heaps of stones hidden in the long grass, she makes her way to a clearing that has recently been clipped back. There is a trodden path through the wilderness to a sturdy wooden door.

She tries to open it, but it's barred and padlocked. There are wheel tracks going to and fro, leading out through a fringe of bracken beyond. She nearly trips over the smouldering remains of a small bonfire on a bare patch of soil. Around the heap of ashes is a halo of singed straw and cloth, some bits still holding the shape of masks and tall hats. Katherine takes one up to have a closer look, then chucks it into the centre, pokes it about a little with a long stick and watches it catch and burn. Blue and yellow tongues lick along the stalks, biting into the fabric. She kicks the rest of the debris into the fire before going back to the shed to see if she can open the door.

Peering in between cracks in the planks, she can make out very little. It looks like crates are stacked up, but it's too dark in there to see clearly. Her heart is thumping, and the dog stays close to her leg. Knowing in her gut that she has stumbled onto something sinister, she wants to bolt but is immobilised by her own curiosity; that, and a deep and unexpected sense of violation; familiar and unwelcome.

It rained a few days ago; there are footprints in the soft ground, unusual but distinctive patterns. She has seen this before. It looks like wild geese, out of formation, lost their way, going all over the place. Katherine takes the shortcut back across the fields.

When she gets home, she rummages in the kitchen table drawer, retrieves a neatly folded sheet of paper and smooths it on the tabletop. All of a sudden, the random lines and shapes make sense to her; it is a map. The square shape with the 'X' in the middle is the shed. She shows it to Bridget.

A few days later, when Katherine is resting in the heat of the afternoon, Bridget tucks the sheet of paper in her apron pocket and takes a walk to see for herself what it is that so alarmed the dotey little pet, stealing her sleep away, the night she came back from setting the fishing lines in the river. A swarm of midges torments Bridget as she yomps along the path that fishermen have travelled for generations. She takes a stick and pokes at the brambles and wild angelica growing innocently enough alongside the fronds of hemlock and water dropwort, beating them all out of her way. She looks out over the gently flowing water, imagining all kinds of demons lurking below the ripples. A black water rat hops over her foot and slips into the current. She takes a swipe at it and nearly falls in after it. She catches a sally branch and pulls herself back upright, cursing out loud. She keeps plodding on, following the track until she comes to the place that Katherine described.

It is even creepier than she had imagined it. There are legends surviving about Katherine's great-uncle Daniel who built this cottage himself in the days when, if you could build a house and get the roof on in twenty-four hours, you could call it your own. The story goes that, during the troubles, Daniel captured a great haul of guns and ammunition and shot a few of the Black and Tans in an ambush at the old metal railway bridge, a little further downstream. He was hounded by the militia, and finally hanged upside down with his throat slit at the mass rock in the woods beyond. Bridget glances up to get a feeling for the lay of the land. They say his wife Peggy was tortured to death right here, by the Tans, forced to tell where Daniel was hiding. Even that the baby was carved out of her belly, and she was nailed to the kitchen door. No one is quite sure what Frank's part in the arms ambush was, but he was surely involved. Mercifully, no one talks about that kind of thing nowadays.

At the clearing, Bridget takes out the map and compares the layout with what she can see here. She doesn't waste time lingering around the cottage ruins, but goes directly to the locked shed. She pulls a screwdriver from one pocket and a torch from the other. With violent little stabs, she enlarges a small hole in the planks and then shines the torch through it. There are crates, all right. One near the door is open. Bridget's heart starts to race when she realises what she is looking at. She sits on a tree stump for some time, waiting for the thumping to subside. A cold sweat sticks her blouse to her chest.

'Oh, God in heaven, what have we blundered into?'

She tells Katherine she's bored with trout and not to bother setting the night lines anymore.

~

They watch the men save a late cut of hay. Bridget no longer invites them in for feasts. She and Katherine stack the boot of the car with bottles of tea and piles of sandwiches and drive it out to them in the meadows. They look on as the men toss the sweet-smelling, sun-dried grass into huge cocks and tie them down with sacks and rope and wooden tent pegs hammered into the ground.

Slowly, the leaves begin to turn, and the hedges are full of blackberries and rose hips. Bridget tries to divert Katherine from fretting by tempting her with the joys of crab-apple jelly and blackberry jam.

They go for drives in the car. Sometimes, they stop in towns along the way to browse the shops for baby clothes or nappies. They weed around the vegetables, pick fruit and struggle over knitting patterns. Bridget is crocheting a lacy, ivory-coloured shawl from skeins of soft wool. Daily, it grows larger and larger; anything to occupy her hands and keep the dotey little pet from thinking about those sheds and what might be in them and turn her mind to the baby instead.

Jim has more or less completely taken over the farm work again. Katherine gives him a roll of pound notes every now and then. They do not call it wages; it is all put down to expenses. Very little money comes back in. Whatever there is gets swallowed up almost immediately by bills for fodder, seeds, artificial insemination, the vet, and so on. Jim does not clutter up Katherine's life with 'unnecessary paperwork' and apparently tells her as little as he thinks he can get away with.

CHAPTER ELEVEN

One morning in September, Bridget receives the news that her own mother is not well. She hasn't been well for years, gradually dissolving into the next world. It's one of the many reasons Bridget uses to justify their prolonged stay in Ireland. However, she has now taken a fall. Bridget has to go.

'I'm cool with it, Bridget. You go to your mother for a bit; of course I'll be all right. Anyway, since you got the phone put in, I can always ring Marie if I need help. I know you won't be too far away. Jim is here every day doing the farm, and Fonsie will keep calling, for sure. You know what he's like. I think he's nearly more excited about the baby than you are! Certainly more than Harry is. I don't know if it's nervousness or lack of interest, but he never mentions it when I do get to talk to him on the phone. He just says, "Well, as long as you are okay" and "When are you coming back?"'

'He's just in denial. He'll come round before the baby is born. You'll see.'

'Well, it's not due for a month or so anyway.'

Bridget does some mental arithmetic. 'Mmm, well, I'm not sure. I just need to be there when Mam comes out of hospital.'

Once all the evening jobs are done, Katherine drives Bridget up to Grainey. The house is a little cement council cottage, built with its gable end facing a quiet road, on a remote hillside. These days, when the sun is slipping away earlier and earlier, leaving only a memory of itself in the evening sky, there is a smell of harvest and dew-damp stubbles blowing up from the valley. A dusty old dog is lying across the doorstep of the cottage. Bridget leans down to pat its head. She looks up at Katherine.

'You go on home. I'll be back as soon as my sister gets here from Scotland to take over in a couple of days. She can get the train from Dublin. Then we'll pack up and go back to London.' The two women hug as tightly as the large belly will allow.

'Mind yourself, now, you; no digging and no chasing sheep. Lock the door at night. Don't tell no one you're on your own, do you hear me?'

Katherine tries to peer into the house, but Bridget is not sure what she'll find when she goes in and doesn't want to upset the dotey little pet with unpleasant sick-bed scenes. The two women look at each other for a brief moment, and then Bridget gives Katherine another quick hug and sends her on her way with a tender smile.

'You take care of yourself now, d'you hear me?'

Combine harvesters gobble and chunder their way through the standing corn. Everywhere the sound of engines has been droning on into the night. The harvest is so much later here in Knocklong. At home in Suffolk, by now all the corn will be in and sold and the ploughs already preparing the soil for sowing winter wheat. The hounds will be cub-hunting early in the mornings. Katherine can nearly hear the mellow call of the horn echoing through the kale plantations as the huntsman urges the young hounds to seek and scatter the fox cubs. Peter will be cleaning and testing out the guns in readiness for the shooting season to begin, and the young pheasants will be out of the pens, scattered all over the estate, making the most of their short lives.

Here in Knocklong, one or two small combines harvest all the little fields in the area. To make the most of the last few chances, when there is sufficient time between the dew rising in the morning and falling heavily again at night, they chomp along all day, every day. No one still uses a reaper and binder in this part of the country. The hedges are alive with wrens and sparrows and finches, gorging themselves on the surfeit of berries and small grubs and insects. Teams of rabbits scuttle about, gleaning the headlands.

A second clutch of swallows is gathering on the phone wires, ready for their first great southern adventure. It hasn't rained for some weeks, and the ford at the entrance to the farm is a tiny tinkle of water, barely darkening the stones. Everywhere there is a general heaviness. This morning, an autumn mist had hovered just above the surface of the stream, giving it a ghostly air. Now, as evening closes in, black clouds begin to bleed up along the valley.

Katherine finds it hard to sleep. The baby is pressing on both her lungs and her bladder. She lies awake, listening to the sounds of the night. The dog is breathing with its nose against her cheek.

Yesterday, Jim mentioned something about sheep breaking out and new fencing being needed at the far end of the farm. She wants to see it for herself, but Jim is insistent. 'Not at all.

Don't even think of it in your condition. Stay here and try not to fall over that dog!'

There has been a lot of coming and going with his putt-putt tractor and trailer. For some reason, they need to do this work late at night, long after Katherine has locked up and gone to bed. Now, though, all she can hear is the scraping of rodents in the skirting boards and owl fledglings mewling like kittens as they get a bit big for the nests in the sycamore trees across the river. She tries to pretend that she is not alone in the house; that Bridget is snoring in her room as usual. The night is interminably long. Katherine eventually falls asleep as the dawn is forming a bright rim around the curtains.

~

Sunday is heralded as usual by a distant church bell calling the faithful. She decides it is time she showed her face to God again. She brushes her hair, puts on her tweed coat and starts up the car.

Father Fitzgerald hurries through the prayers until he gets to his own homily. He climbs slowly into the pulpit, grips the front of it firmly and, with a wheezy breath, addresses his congregation. 'Now is the time for the faithful people of Ireland to stand together once again!' He speaks of terrible oppression and our dark past, how we fought for every crust we now share before our Lord. How we must rise up again and support our brothers and sisters in the north, in their hour of need.

After the mass is over, Katherine, bewildered by this powerful call to arms from the fatherly old priest, asks Josie what it was all about.

She just nods and says, 'Oh, that old man! He gets carried

away by times. It's more than likely because of all the stuff up north. Don't mind him. It's time for you to look after yourself.'

She looks at Katherine's bump, protruding so much that the coat buttons won't do up in front. Katherine is tempted by the offer of lunch with the Ryans, but she is tired and can't face sitting round the table and fielding all the leading questions from the men. She drives home instead. She is also hoping that Bridget might be back when she gets there; but the house is empty and still, with just the dog guarding the door.

In the afternoon, the tractors and combines are quiet, and even the sky seems to be resting on its cushion of grey clouds. Katherine decides that whatever Jim says, she is going to have a look at the new fence for herself. She walks out along the track that follows the river until she comes to the place where the work has been going on. The men have built two substantial pillars out of stone and hung a brand new tubular-steel gate. Even to Katherine, this seems excessive for keeping a few sheep in, especially as beyond it, on the other side, are just those ruined remains in a swampy wilderness of gorse and bracken. The gate swings easily with a musical squeak, unlike all the other gates on the farm that are tied with wire and bits of twine and can only be opened with the greatest of care, lest they fall to pieces at your feet like a heap of bones. She bolts the gate behind her and, following the dog, she plods on.

As she comes nearer to the old homestead, Katherine sees a black car through the trees. The boot is open. In the shadows, it isn't possible for her to be sure if she recognises it. She picks her way over rocks hidden in the bindweed and long grass, moving closer to the tin-roofed shed between the trees and the river. The shed door seems to be open as well. A man is moving stuff from there to the car, or the other way round; she can't really be sure which, because the car is backed right up to the shed door. She keeps out of sight by crouching a little down the side of the riverbank, camouflaged by the rampant hogweed and nettles. Her heart is quickened to a pounding thud. The dog has her hackles up, but, responding to Katherine's hand, stays silent and close to the ground.

Katherine doesn't realise how near she is to the edge of the water. Clambering awkwardly through the reeds, her foot gets caught in a tangle of briars, and when she jerks it free, she stumbles backwards into the freezing water. She clings onto a bunch of rushes. Her feet can't get a hold. The roots are coming away. A swirling current is sucking her in. The dog's frantic barking is slurped up with water in her ears. She swallows a gulp of muddy stew and starts to choke, gasping as the cold water steals her breath away. Screams only materialise in her head. Mouth, throat and lungs submerged. Ears are gurgling. The world closes over her. She thrashes about, trying to swim upwards, but her waterlogged boots are dragging her down.

Suddenly, an arm is around her neck, tugging her backwards up onto the bank. The river is pulling at her feet. A muffled sound of heaving as a man's fist is pressing on her chest. He rolls her over so her face is in the grass and pounds the liquids out of her. She vomits slime and muddy water. He turns her onto her back again. His lips cover hers, and the warmth of his breath begins to fill her lungs. She coughs, belching up more mud and murk. Her body shakes. Her eyes are stinging, but she can see the blurred outline of a hooded head. She can make out broad shoulders silhouetted against the darkening sky. The wordless figure rises and backs away. She tries to call out to him, but her throat is bubbling still. Her vision is obscured by muddy water. Car doors bang. The engine revs. Then all Katherine can hear is her own shallow breath returning, her heartbeat in her ears and the dog panting in her face, licking it with a warm, raspy tongue. Her hand goes to her belly. She waits for the reassuring kick from within. She waits. And waits. Then it comes, all of a sudden; the little feet and arms flail around, as if he too was drowning. She can feel a knee pushing out, a heel under her ribs, an elbow somewhere lower down. She imagines the child clinging onto the umbilical cord. Her womb tightens reassuringly, like a lover's embrace. All is well.

Katherine hauls herself to her feet. They squelch inside her wet boots. It takes her a few moments to get her balance, so she sits for a while on a pile of stones, letting her sodden hair fall between her knees. Her brain feels like it is slopping around in her skull. The dog shakes itself, and a muddy spray surrounds it. Sodden clothes and water weeds cling to Katherine with the smell of the river. She begins to shiver.

The evening is closing in, and the sky has disappeared behind purple curtains. A sharp but eerie light flashes sideways, shining up the branches against the darkening horizon. It is chased by a boom of thunder. A few heavy drops of rain plop into her lap. Then a bolt of lightning splits the sky, and the crack is so loud the ground shudders beneath her. She puts her hands to her ears.

Electric shocks fizz through the firmament, followed almost immediately by whacks of thunder. Every few seconds, the ruins and all around them light up in brilliant electric colours, trembling as the thunder crashes. A raging war in the skies gathers momentum, and rain tumbles down in torrents. Wind rushes through the trees, like the ghost of a herd of mad bulls. Katherine looks for some shelter and sees the outhouse door has not been completely locked. She wrenches it open and dives inside.

Rain is pounding the tin roof so loudly that her ears begin to hurt. She stumbles around in the darkness, reefing her leg on the sharp edge of a box. As she throws out her hand to save herself from falling, she grabs something cold, smooth, metallic. With one almighty bolt of lightning, hundreds of guns and crates of ammunition are lit up in vivid shades of green. She stumbles outside, kicks the door shut behind her and struggles back to the path she knows.

There is water everywhere. It is coming down with such velocity it makes dents in the ground. It could be forcing its way through her skin. She can see no more than a few feet in front of her. Huge puddles are merging into ponds all around. The river is like a tidal wave being forced through a narrow gorge by a hurricane. She puts her head down against the force of the rain and wind and sloshes through it, slithering in the mud, holding her belly with one hand and tugging her sopping wet coat up over her head with the other. The dog bravely leads the way.

Eventually, she makes it home; pulls off most of her saturated clothes outside the house and falls almost naked into the armchair. The tempest is beating at the door and windows.

Katherine folds a blanket around herself and begins to shake violently. Everything aches and hurts from pulling and dragging, banging and pounding. Her lungs are stinging, and her throat is clogged with the taste of muddy water. The worst pain is in the small of her back, where it feels like her insides are being forced through the wooden rolls of Josie's clothes wringer.

The storm has taken out the electricity. The only light in the house is from intermittent flashes that sear through the room in jagged streaks. She tries the phone. It's dead. She manages to torch a candle. In an effort to steady the

221

tormented flame, she settles it into an empty jam jar. Every time she moves, the pain in her back fires up and lashes like a bull whip, tightly round her loins. The thunderstorm, which seemed, briefly, to have moved away along the valley, has turned and comes charging back. It is now right overhead. It splits the house with streaks of lightning and shakes it with booms of thunder.

Katherine throws some cushions onto the floor and rolls around in them, moaning, trembling, calling out to God for help. She is a small craft alone in the ocean, tossed about in massive waves, being rhythmically thrashed to shreds. Once again, she is sucked beneath the swell; she tries to anchor herself by clinging to the back of the chair. In a brief moment of peace, she realises she is not alone. The figure that has been standing quietly in the shadows moves towards her. She tries to speak. A few simple words form themselves before she is wracked once more.

'Nicholas?' She reaches out her hand. Her body is quivering. He settles the loosened blanket around her again and guides her gently back into the armchair.

'What in God's name ...? What can I do to help?'

'Freezing, light fire. Clothes, upstairs.' She flails her arm in the direction of the stairwell.

He quickly rustles up a good blaze in the firebox of the range and looks towards the stairs. All his worst fears come crowding round him. He knows what he saw there in a moment of shame. He is unable to move towards it.

'Please. Clothes ... on my bed. Anything.' Katherine bends over and emits a deep, animal moan.

Nicholas dives into his nightmare and bounds up the stairs. He lights a match to get his bearings. It dies in the draught. He lights another and goes through the first open door he comes to. He feels around in the dark, gathering up whatever comes to hand, and races back down the stairs. Thinking aloud, he says, 'You should be in hospital, girl, but I've no way of getting you there except on the tractor. That rain is still coming down in torrents. The river is in spate, the ford impassable by car. I suppose I could go out and try to get an ambulance ...' He dithers about in the scullery, filling the kettle and groping around for anything to make a cup of tea. 'I really don't want to leave you alone. Where's Bridget O'Connor, anyway?'

Katherine struggles with the garments, managing only to pull a big jumper over her head, before being rent asunder yet again. She is not ready to answer questions. She lets out an almighty howl. Nicholas runs back into the room.

'What now?'

Warm liquid is seeping through the fabric of the cushions and leaching onto the flagstone floor. Nicholas gathers whatever might be useful from a pile of clean linen on the shelf at the back of the chimney breast. He sits beside Katherine, and her head drops onto his chest.

For a few minutes, there is peace. Then, up on her knees, brighter and sharper, she starts bossing him around, 'Here, give me that towel. Go and wash your hands. Get the first-aid box from under the sink. Quick!'

He rushes about, doing what she tells him, fumbling in the candlelight.

'The baby. It's coming now!'

Katherine throws back her head and sucks in a very long breath. A sonorous groan resonates through the room. She draws deeply on all her strength and begins to push. One almighty heave, bone on bone. Nicholas is there, on his knees behind her. The tiny purple body drops gently into his towelled hands. She flops forward against the chair. The infant squirms between her knees. Nicholas is rubbing it gently as it starts to breathe and lets out little, high-pitched cries. He swaddles her son gently into the towel and hands the bundle to Katherine, the umbilical cord still intact. The baby's eyes are open, and in those first few moments of life, they lock on to their mother's gaze. The two stare at each other.

'I'll put the kettle on,' Nicholas says. 'This is your moment.'

'No, wait, share it.' Katherine smiles up at him. Her cheeks are shining and her eyes sparkle. He is engulfed by a rush of alien feelings. He has never known anything as beautiful, as glorious or as radiant as this mother and child glowing in the newness of human life, the dim candlelight shining in a corona around them. This is the Madonna. He sits down on the floor beside them; a nugget of stolen gold in his guilty hands. Tears are running down his face.

She lifts the swathed bundle to her breast, and the tiny mouth begins to nuzzle in. Nicholas fumbles around with the scissors and buttonhole thread. After some time, Katherine passes him the child. She stiffens her back, stretches up her chin and howls as her womb closes tightly again, expelling the placenta onto the floor. It's over. The torture of the long night no longer matters. She is cast adrift from all pain, all hurt, all anxiety. She has a son. She did it herself. She didn't need Harry or Bridget or Marie or any doctors. She doesn't even want a smoke. This is her golden moment. It is her own glory, and nothing, no one, can take that away.

The storm has passed over. Apart from the gentle sound of rain on the windows, the house is quiet, warmed by the flicker of candles and the light of the fire. Katherine is curled into the big armchair, a blanket around her and the infant asleep in her arms. The range crackles sweetly beside her. The kettle is beginning to chuff like a steam train on the hob.

After some time, it occurs to her to ask Nicholas the big question, the one he has been dreading more as each minute goes by, but for which he has not prepared a reply. 'How did you come to be here on such a night, Nicholas?'

He had made a deal with the Almighty. If she was alive when he went back, he'd come clean, tell her everything. All that promising to God was yesterday. Now, he has lost his nerve. How on earth can he explain that not twelve hours ago he pulled her from the river, pumped muddy water out of her lungs and left her there to live or die and weather the storm alone? How he had got stuck in the flood driving back across the fields, walked three miles through the thunder and lightning, returned with a comrade and a tractor to pull the loaded car out of the mud in the teeming rain; how his only concerns had been his precious load and the fear of discovery. Then the relief he felt when he got back and found she was gone from the riverbank. He knew that in his haste to avoid discovery, he hadn't properly locked the shed. There were difficulties with fallen trees, the swollen river, which came out right over the bridge, and so forth; all to protect a guilty secret. That seems so insignificant now. The truth that has been searing his conscience all night seeps away from him. Things have changed.

'I was out checking sheep nearby with the tractor, worried about them getting marooned in the low-lying meadows in that rain. I thought of you women here on your own; wondered if you were all right.' He stands up and walks to the window, half believing his own lies. Looking out, he says, 'It's like Noah's ark here, surrounded by water.'

'Thank you, Nicholas. You are a good friend. I nearly drowned earlier, in the river. Someone pulled me out. I don't know who it was; they had a hood on. Left me there on the riverbank, and then the storm … And now look at me—a mother!'

He swallows hard. 'You'd have been okay, which or whether. You're a real woman, Kate.' Then, slipping further away from his promise to God, he adds, 'Look't, I'd rather you didn't tell anyone I was here tonight.'

'Whyever not? I'll have to tell them something.'

'It can be our own special secret. It's important to me.'

In her present state of euphoria, Katherine doesn't care about anything, any secrets, any promises; it's all stuff that doesn't matter anymore. She has found her power.

Katherine and her new baby are tucked into her bed with hot water bottles.

The dog is lying on guard between them and the door. She is drifting in and out of sleep, intermittently reliving the birth, the storm and coughing up muddy water. Her mind bounces over one thing after another. Who was it that pulled her out? Why did he leave her alone there, struggling to suck the life back into her lungs? Images dart through her mind, like a hare leaping around, looking frantically for a gap in the ditch. The first spectacular flash of lightning, the feeling of cold steel on her wet hands, the river filling her airways and glugging away her breath; all yesterday. She tightens her grip on the sleeping bundle in her arms and thanks God that everything has safely passed and today is a reality.

~

Marie comes bouncing into the yard on the back of the tractor with Jim. She stands in the kitchen, taking in the remains of the drama. Wet cushions, bloody towels, the milking bucket sitting in the corner; instead of milk in it, there are stale blood clots and the fleshy afterbirth. Scissors and sewing thread beside a bottle of brandy on the table. Two tea cups, two glasses. She bounds up the stairs calling, 'Katie, where are you?'

By now, mother and baby are sleeping. The morning sun is shining across them, warming the room. Marie stands in the doorway of the bedroom. She is heaving to get her breath back. The scene reminds her of attending home deliveries in the slums of Glasgow, where the babies were swaddled, sometimes in a linen tablecloth, used only once before to adorn the wedding breakfast. There were no clothes for the newborn; they grew too quickly to warrant such a waste of resources. Once they graduated from the linen cloth, babies were wrapped in a knitted shawl passed around the newborns in the area. No nappies either, just chopped-up flour sacks or old towels torn into squares. If the father's drinking wasn't too much to endanger the baby, it slept in the parents' bed; otherwise, a bottom drawer was padded with an old pillow and a folded blanket, and that would be the crib. Twins slept end to end. Triplets weren't an issue; they never survived. In such homes, the mother would rarely be left alone; there was always some old crone on duty, with cups of tea and various salves for mother and child. They tried to keep the father out of the bed as long as possible. But the babies kept on coming.

Marie closes the curtain in an attempt to prolong Katherine's sanctuary. She tiptoes out of the room, goes back to the kitchen and puts the kettle on. She has a look at the afterbirth, turning it over in the bucket, mauling it around, inspecting it for possible lesions that could cause a haemorrhage or other problems later on. When she is scrubbing her hands in the scullery sink, she sees a man's cloth cap, still wet from a drenching in last night's rain. She studies it, searching for signs of familiarity, but she fails to identify it.

Some man had phoned her this morning. He was disguising his voice. 'You might want to call on that hippy one; she could do with some help up there.' That was all he had said before hanging up and leaving the dial tone purring in Marie's ear. She had tried to phone Katherine right away, but the line was dead. Everywhere is water. Fields are lakes, roads are rivers. Farmsteads are either perched on little hills or popping out of the landscape like boats in the sea.

Marie puts a pot of tea, some toast and two boiled eggs onto a tray and climbs back up the stairs. When she opens the curtains, the sun floods in through the dusty window, rippling sparkling rivulets across the bed. She gently prises the child from his mother's arms and lays him at the foot of the bed where the warm rays can welcome him into the world and stave off the onset of infantile jaundice that she's seen so many times. She plumps up the pillows, helps Katherine into a sitting position and lays the tray across her lap.

'Well! You're some woman to do this on your own! How are you feeling now?' She unpeels the swaddling towel. 'Oh, it's a little boy!' Her midwife eyes go straight up to the umbilical cord. 'Neat job there, whoever did that. Buttonhole twist?

Mmm, that was a good idea.' She pulls a little tub of powder from her pocket and sprinkles the contents onto the umbilicus. 'You don't have any scales, I suppose? I guess it's about five and a half pounds, maybe less. Bit premature by the look of him. Better keep him warm. Where are those nappies you said you got last week?'

Presently, she has everything tidied up. Baby dressed, mother fed and checked over and a fire lit in the tiny bedroom hearth.

The infant begins to mewl, and Katherine grabs him up before Marie can get another hold. As if she had been doing this all her life, she opens her nightshirt and holds him up to her breast.

Marie watches the infant sucking at the large, dark-brown nipple. It's getting to be a rare sight with mothers these days.

'You don't have to do that, you know; we could get some bottles sorted out, a little sterilizing unit, and some formula milk. That baby's pretty small. He needs nourishing. He's a bit blue too.' After a while, she takes him from his mother's grasp, joggles the wind out of him and walks over to the window to get a better look.

'He might have lost a bit too much blood at birth. That often happens when you aren't experienced; they can bleed out through the umbilicus if you're not careful enough about tying it off. Well, don't keep us in suspenders, then. Who was it?'

'Who was what, Marie? You know as well as anyone how it happened.' Tears appear in Katherine's eyes, and she is cross with Marie for turning the moment sour. She reaches out her arms and snatches the baby.

Marie's voice softens a bit, but she nudges on anyway. 'You know I didn't mean anything, well, you know, about that.' She sits on the edge of the bed, patting the dog rather than looking at Katherine's distressed face. 'You should have called me last night. I would have found some way to get over to you. Someone must have helped you, anyway; you didn't do this on your own, did you? And where's Bridget when you need her most?'

'I tried to phone you last night, but my phone was dead. She's over in Grainey. Her mother had a bad fall a week back, remember? Bridget's gone to settle in after the hospital. If I had the phone, I could ring Harry and tell him he has a son, too.'

It's an easy distraction. She knows that Marie loves talking about Harry but doesn't often get Katherine sufficiently off guard to have the chance. He's an enigma to her. She can't even picture him, although she has a vague notion that he must be tall, dark and handsome, like James Bond, perhaps. She cannot imagine any man who'd let his wife go off to another country for months on end. A man so ambitious for his own fortune that he could seemingly forget he has a pregnant wife in Ireland. Although, back in the fifties, the men left their families in droves to go off to London or Glasgow to earn money. They often even had a second family over there. Wives all over Ireland were left raising children on their own then, only seeing their husbands once a year when another baby would start. Marie saw it all the time when she was still practicing.

'What do you think he'll say when he hears the news? Do you think he'll come straight over? How will he take it? A son! You'd better not have that other fella here when he does come, though.'

'What other fella?'

'Whoever it was who helped you out last night. How anyone was able to get through that storm, I can't imagine!'

There is a brief and awkward silence while Katherine tries to think up some reply that will satisfy Marie. Then she laughs, looks out of the window and says, 'It was so awful, wasn't it? So good of you to brave it and come over this morning. Thank you, Marie. You are really good to me. I'll eat the breakfast later. I think I need to sleep now. I'm very tired.' With the baby in the crook of her arm, she pulls up the bedclothes and closes her eyes. 'We can talk later.'

'Of course. I'll come over with Daddy this evening and check up on you, anyway. You can tell me all about it then. He'll go up to Grainey on the tractor to fetch Bridget back.'

Katherine dozes lightly with one ear cocked for the sound of a tractor.

When it does come, it's Bridget who jumps down, landing in the yard with a muddy thud. Katherine hears her shouting to Jim. She does her best to fly up the stairs. Panting, she throws her long arms around Katherine, smothering her in kisses. She takes up the infant, holds him to the light and kisses him too.

'Well! My dotey little pet and my dotey little peteen! How are you? What is it? A boy or a child?' She spins him around the room and flops in a heap onto the bed. 'Well?'

'It's Jack. Jack Henry Francis Fletcher.'

'Oh, that's lovely! A little boy! Have you sent a message to Harry?'

'I think Marie was going to send a telegram on her way home.'

Bridget has tears pouring down her flushed cheeks. 'Oh my God, all on your own here. Katherine, I love you. Only *you* could do that by yourself! He must be at least three weeks early. Is he okay? What did Marie think? Jim knew nothing; he just said Marie had sent for me to come urgently. Whew! What a bonjarvey! I'm going to put the kettle on. Any of that brandy left? We'll have to wet the baby's head. Then we can give you a good wash and bath that little babe.'

'How is your mother, Bridgie? Will you have to go back up there again now?'

'My sister should be arriving this afternoon. She'll do till then.'

231

~

The question of who helped Katherine with the birth hangs in the air for several days. Marie tries to work it out of Bridget but finally admits to herself that not only does Bridget know nothing, but she is so engrossed in the whole wonderful scene that she doesn't seem to care who it was, as long they aren't here now.

Nicholas calls. Quite late on the third day, he walks into the house without knocking, nods to Bridget and walks straight over to Katherine, who is sitting in the chair with the infant in her arms.

'Well?' He pulls a little package wrapped in brown paper out from under his coat and holds it out to her. Their eyes meet.

'Something my mother knitted for the child.' His unusually shy smile and her warm response are enough for Bridget. The penny drops.

'You'll drink a cup of tea while you're here?' Bridget offers.

'Got anything stronger?' Sitting in the chair beside Katherine, he reaches out and takes the baby. 'He's not a great colour, is he?'

'What do you mean?' Bridget snaps. 'What would you know about babies? Here, give him to me before you drop him!'

'I know what I see, missus, that's all. He looks fair blue to me. Don't get me wrong.' He smiles again to the anxious mother. 'He's a fine child. Just not got his colour up yet, I suppose. I heard he came with the hurricane? Maybe that's what it is. He'll be a proper stormtrooper before you know it.'

Over the next few days, concern for little Jack gathers momentum. Marie wants Katherine to take him to a doctor to have his heart checked out. Bridget is terrified of anything that might signal problems with the dotey little peteen. Neither woman wants to think about what Nicholas had to say. Nor can they ignore it.

On the fifth day, the flood waters have subsided sufficiently to get the car out. Katherine, Bridget and Marie take little Jack to the hospital. An elderly paediatrician listens to his heart, nods gravely and pronounces, 'Something is seriously amiss, all right. I'm not sure exactly what it is, but he needs further tests. We don't have the equipment here. I'm going to refer him to a specialist in Dublin.' He starts writing a letter, and Katherine looks appealingly to the other two women. Both shrug their shoulders. Bridget has tears in her eyes.

'How long will that take?' Marie snaps aggressively.

'We'll post this off today, and you should get an appointment in a week or two.'

'A week or two! Here, give me that letter. I'll take it myself.' Marie snatches the envelope out of his hand and gathers her little group together, herds them out of the hospital and bundles them into the back of the car.

'We'll get a few bits and pieces together and go straight to Dublin this afternoon. I'll just have to clear it with Mammy. She can take care of things for me.' Marie mumbles on, jerking the car forward and back in the hospital car park, eventually getting it out on the road back to the Ryans' farm.

Marie rushes around organising her own family. 'Heaven knows how long this will take.'

Bridget rocks the baby in her arms, oblivious to all the commotion. She can hear Katherine's voice in the background. She's on the phone in the hall.

'You'll be there to meet us, then? Will you speak to him? You'll make the arrangements at the hospital?' Katherine stares at the other women. 'I spoke to Harry on the phone. He says I'm to bring the baby home right away. My mother's first cousin is one of England's leading paediatricians. Harry's going to make the arrangements with Uncle Tommy himself. He'll meet us at Heathrow. There will be tickets waiting at the airport.'

'So that's it, then? Harry just takes over when it suits him!' Marie can't believe how annoyed she is with Harry, when he is so obviously right.

Bridget's reaction is different. 'That's the proper place for you, pet. I'll tidy up the few loose ends here and follow you in a week or so. Do you think you can manage the flight on your own with the baby?'

Not sure how to answer, Katherine just says, soothingly, 'I need to do this one alone, Bridgie. This is my new life.'

'You're right, pet. I know that, really. I'll be praying for you both.'

However, when it comes to saying goodbye at the airport, Bridget's courage begins to ebb. When the stewardess sees her anguished face, she encourages her to go onto the plane and settle them into their seats. As they walk out across the tarmac, the weak remains of the sun slip behind soft, grey clouds. It looks like more rain. Handing over the little peteen and kissing them goodbye gives Bridget a pain in the pit of her stomach. Before she backs out of the narrow cabin, she takes a final look at them. They seem really small. Katherine is so pale that her freckles have almost disappeared. Bridget crosses herself and says a silent prayer that Harry will bring his best self to the airport and that God will be good to them. She, Marie and Marie's young daughter Fionnuala stand in the viewing tower, watching the propellers wind up, and the plane, with shamrocks on its tail, begins to taxi down the endless runway.

'But Mammy, what makes it take off?'

Marie hasn't a clue. She looks over to Bridget, who puts her hand into the soft, golden curls, gazes into Fionnuala's inquisitive blue eyes and forces herself to smile.

'It's all done by magic, darlin'. A bit like Santa, really, only without the reindeers.'

The plane rises and disappears into the clouds.

CHAPTER TWELVE

Harry, who was expecting Katherine to look much like she always does, but with a bonny little baby under her arm, is shocked by the sight of the figure who approaches him in the arrivals' hall at Heathrow. She appears to have shrunk. Her hair has lost its lustre. Her cheeks are gaunt. The pasty infant in her arms, smothered in a shawl, peers out at him with no hint of expression and, in fact, with very little sign of life at all.

She was expecting him to reprimand her for taking off on a whim, having the baby in 'that third world country', for ignoring his wise words and refusing to consult with a proper doctor before she left England; in fact, for bringing all this not only on herself but on him and his child as well. However, when faced with the reality, he melts. He gathers them both into his arms and herds them gently through the airport and into the car park.

Like a sleek black panther, the Bentley purrs through the evening traffic and glides smoothly into a parking place right outside the hospital reception.

Uncle Tommy's consulting rooms are on the first floor. Harry holds onto Katherine as the elevator jerks to a halt. He reaches out to take the baby from her, but that doesn't happen.

The examination is brief. The situation is grim. Harry and Katherine look helplessly at each other as Uncle Tommy leaves the room to call for a nurse. Their baby is lying naked in a clear plastic crib. His slatey-tinged skin is like translucent tissue paper, and his little navel has hardly healed. Katherine's fingers are poking through the holes in Bridget's crocheted heirloom, twisting and tightening, pleading with the creamy threads to comfort her.

Harry whispers, 'Don't worry, darling. They say he's the best there is.' He puts his hand over hers and tries to stop her torturing the shawl. She is grinding her teeth to keep from crying.

When he returns, Uncle Tommy has a young nurse with him. She nods to the frightened parents and puts a nappy on Jack, swaddles him in a blue aertex blanket and begins to wheel the crib away. Uncle Tommy puts out his hand to stop Katherine from going with them.

'Not exactly sure what the extent of the problem is. Can tell that it's serious. Child is underweight. Poor colour. Sounds like his heart is in trouble. Need to do more tests. Admitting him into the neo-natal ward.' These darts of information shoot across the room, piercing Katherine all over. She watches with a helpless hollowness as the door closes.

'I'll need you to sign some papers before you leave.' Uncle Tommy hands Harry the documents and a pen. 'Don't worry, my dear, he's in good hands. We'll do our best for him.' As he attempts to usher them out of the door, he says in as soothing a tone as he can manage, 'I've arranged for the hospital chaplain to come in tonight and baptise him.' When they reach the hospital lobby, he goes on, 'Best thing you can do now is go home and get some rest yourself, my dear.'

Katherine just shakes her head. She is staring at the deep-blue carpet and massaging the creamy fleece between her fingers. 'I'm not going home. I won't leave him alone with strangers.' Even the word 'home' no longer sounds right.

He looks appealingly across to Harry, who just shrugs as his wife embarrasses him yet again.

'Surely the hospital has some facilities for nursing mothers?' Katherine can feel her breasts tightening.

'Breast feeding? Oh, good gracious! I might have known, I suppose. I'll get them to find you a breast pump. Okay, look, why don't you two go over to the canteen and get a nice cup of tea while you wait for the nurse and the chaplain?'

'You can go to the canteen. I'm going to look for Jack.' Katherine gathers her skirt, puts up her chin and stomps back into the passage, leaving Harry standing in the doorway, shaking his head. She calls back over her shoulder, 'Can you bring me a cup of tea if you ever find that canteen, please, Harry?'

She is drawn by the distant echo of crying babies. Her long, cotton skirt flaps around her legs, and her sandals squeak on the polished linoleum. As she approaches the nurse's station on the children's landing, a voice calls from behind her.

'Is it you for the breast pump? Can you come with me, please?' The nurse has a musical Kerry accent. Staff Nurse Nuala O'Malley is printed on her name tag.

The two of them stand in the antechamber to the special care baby unit. Katherine scans up and down the rows of incubators and little plastic cribs. Nurse Nuala draws a curtain around them and manoeuvres Katherine into a chair. The contraption in her hands looks like a bicycle hooter with a little glass globe in the middle.

'Here, I'll show you how to do it.' She rubs it briskly up and down her apron a few times 'to warm it up a bit', then takes hold of Katherine's engorged breast, presses the wide mouth of the trumpet over her nipple and starts pumping.

'But why can't I just feed him myself?'

A little pool of milk is gathering in the globe; a lot of effort and not much to show for it. Nurse Nuala sees Katherine's tears. 'Okay, come with me, then, and we'll see what we can do.'

Sitting in the nursery, Katherine lifts her jumper and holds the tiny infant up to her breast. His suck is weak. His eyes seem to have slipped back in his skull. He is very blue around the lips. She can feel him giving up. She squeezes him tightly and wraps the shawl around him. She wishes Bridget were here to whisper life into the little ears the way she did so many times for her.

'When the priest has been, we'll have to put him on a drip and start the treatment.'

After a few futile attempts to prise the baby from his mother, Nurse Nuala gives up and brings Katherine a cup of sugary tea. She prays the ward sister doesn't come back on duty early. This is very much against the rules.

The baptism is a formality. A paunchy old priest mumbles away in Latin for a bit, asks for a name, calls Nurse Nuala to stand in as the godparent and makes her hold the baby while he sloshes the holy water onto the tiny, fluffy head, pressing the sign of the cross into his brow with his thumb. It's all over in five minutes. Jack is taken away and placed in an incubator. He is connected to a drip, which is tubed up his nostril and taped to the side of his face. He gags weakly as they ease it down the back of his throat. There are needles and monitors, charts, lights, pipes and sticky tape all over him. What is visible of his little body now has a kind of violet hue compared with the other babies. He looks so peaceful, even with all this activity going on. Katherine thinks his soul must be somewhere else. Harry finally catches up with her, a cold cup of tea in his hand. He doesn't linger.

'I'm not staying here. You can if you like. I've got work to do. I'll be back later to take you home.'

There isn't any place for mothers in the special care baby unit. Katherine hovers around between the nursery and the nurses' station, when the ward sister isn't around, or hides in the toilets as a last resort. When Harry does come back later that night, he eventually finds Katherine sitting on an upturned bucket in an annexe where they keep mops and brushes and the nurses come to smoke fags.

'What the dickens are you doing in here?'

'I'm trying to hang out where I won't be in the way, but where I can keep an eye on him in case he wakes up.'

'What will you do if he does wake up?'

'Be here,' she says feebly. 'I could feed him, if they'll let me.'

At the thought of which, her breasts begin to leak again. He resists pointing out to her that the baby is being fed through a tube now. Instead, Harry manages to talk Katherine into coming out with him for something to eat. 'You've got to eat to keep your strength up for when he gets better.' Then, giving Katherine a little ping of optimism, he adds, 'For when you need that milk again.'

'Oh Harry, I thought you'd given up on him too.'

'Of course, I haven't given up on him. He's my son. We Fletchers don't give up! We'll get some food, straighten you

240

up a bit and then come back later and see what we can do.'

The very act of stretching her lips sideways and feeling her eyes wrinkle with something other than tears puts her in a better frame of mind. She hooks her arm through Harry's for support, and they take one more turn past the nursery to stare at the helpless infant.

'You missed the christening, Harry. Nurse Nuala stood for him. I wanted Bridget to do it. Pity you weren't there too.'

'Oh, you know how I am about those sorts of things.' He glances into the special nursery. 'I suppose they mustn't hold out too much hope for him if they had to get the priest in. Poor little beggar. What a start in life, eh?' he says, quite cheerily, then, looking at his wife's tear-filled drooping eyes, he adds, 'I suppose it's routine procedure. All the same, it's a long way to pull himself up from. But look at the size of his hands and feet; he must have it in him. I'd say he's a full forward in the making!'

She squeezes his arm and lets him steer her out into the rain. He tucks her into the car and drapes the shawl around her.

There isn't much open at that time of night. They drive around a bit until they find a little Italian bistro. Picking through his tagliatelle, Harry looks across at the forlorn remains of his beautiful wife. Trying to stay upbeat, he says, 'That's a great shawl. Is it a family heirloom?'

'It will be, I suppose. Bridgie made it.' Another world, another life, it is all so far away now. She doesn't want to lose the memory of it from her mind. She knows it's a life she'll never share with Harry. Just like she knows she'll never tell him about Boxing Day last year when the Wren Boys came beating on her door.

'You must miss Bridget now?' he muses, trying to seem

241

sympathetic. But this is a mistake. It precipitates a fresh flood of tears. He reaches across the table and presses a handkerchief into her freezing cold hand. 'Come on, Katherine, let's go home. You can ring Bridget in the morning, and we'll go back to the hospital together and see how Jack is getting on after that.'

'No, Harry, I want to go back to the hospital now. We've already been away too long.'

As they walk the short distance from the restaurant to the car, in the rain, Katherine pulls the shawl up over her head. To her husband, she looks like a starving Irish colleen from another century. Her fiery red hair is frizzled into damp curls hanging limply around her little hollow face. Her mind is flitting back and forth from the pain and anguish of haunting the hospital corridors to a hot bath and a comfortable bed.

The Bentley is the only car left parked on the street. Even to Harry, it looks ridiculously opulent and out of place, sitting outside a downbeat Italian joint in Soho. For a second, Katherine expects to see her father sitting behind the steering wheel, his ginger-coloured driving gloves tapping out a tune for the girl he loved so well. The image of that pink dressing gown behind the bathroom door flashes into her mind.

'Who is the woman who was staying in our house?'

'What woman are you talking about? The only woman I know who sometimes stays over is your mother.'

'Why?'

'What on earth do you mean? She often comes to London. You know that.'

'But why does she stay in our house and not in the flat at the Albany?'

'Oh, that place has been let for months now; ever since your father was first taken ill. It's one of the many things we'll have to deal with when you get your strength back. That could be your project.' He smiles, thinking he might have turned a corner.

But Katherine says glumly, 'I'd rather she didn't.'

She can't imagine her mother in pink, and her mind isn't really able to cope with that kind of thing right now. Her breasts are leaking milk. Her womb is still bleeding.

'Okay, we'll go to the hospital and see how he is. Then we'll go home. You could do with a good wash and a night in your own bed.' He slides his left hand up along her thigh and gives it a squeeze. 'We both could.' Then he has another thought. 'We'd better give him a name, now he's officially a Christian.'

Katherine blows a lung-full of smoke into his face.

'Jack, Henry, Francis. Three names. Is that enough for you?'

The hospital is very quiet so late at night. The lights, which were glaringly bright earlier on, are now subdued. There are no visitors, no one at reception, no doctors in white coats with stethoscopes around their necks and most of the nurses have disappeared from the wards. Katherine and Harry go as quietly as they can manage up the stairs and down the many corridors until they reach the nursery. Jack's cot is missing. Katherine's heart nearly stops.

'Calm down. They won't have taken him too far away.'

It is some time before they discover that Jack has been taken to the operating theatre. They wait. Harry checks his watch every few minutes. He paces up and down in front of Katherine, who is leaning against the wall, chewing her fingernails. Eventually, Uncle Tommy comes down the passage towards them. There is a trail of earnest-looking students following in his wake. He is caught between his desire to impress his pupils and his surprise at seeing his cousin's child, tired, scruffy, but ready to pounce.

'We needed to do some tests.'

'Where is he now?'

'You can see him in the morning.'

'Did you find out anything that you didn't know already?' Harry asks.

The tall, white-coated figure shakes his head. Katherine stares at the spots of blood on his sleeve.

'Come to my office at ten thirty in the morning. We'll decide what to do then.' He nods his head to the two of them, lays his hand on Katherine's shoulder and adds, 'I'm sorry, my dear.' Then, looking at the ground, he walks on. The white-coated group all follow, averting their eyes as they pass, except for one female student who sneaks a glance at Katherine. Their eyes meet. No reaction.

'I'm not leaving the hospital again without him.'

'Don't be ridiculous. Nothing is going to change between now and tomorrow. You can't stay here, you know that.'

But Harry can see that he's beaten when Katherine sits down on the only chair in the corridor and refuses to look at him. He thinks of his warm bed, all the phone calls he has to make first thing in the morning and how he is going to shuffle meetings and appointments to be back here by ten thirty.

'Please yourself, then. I will bring some clean clothes for you in the morning.' He walks away, shaking his head, his hands buried deep in his coat pockets.

Katherine looks around and eventually finds an empty corner with some more chairs in it, where no one can see her. She shuts her eyes and doesn't wake until trolleys start clattering up and down and the sky is turning pink again. She stands outside the nursery and peers at the incubators.

Jack's is the one with the most contraptions attached. He is still covered with sticky plasters and bandages, wires and tubes. She watches intently to see if the ribcage is moving up and down. She's not sure. She can barely see any patches of skin left. When his eyes eventually open, he just stares for a while, blinks a few times and then closes them again. His feet twitch a little and his hand catches hold of one of the tubes. The nurses don't look for any more breast milk, although it is still leaking out and forming increasingly large dark patches on Katherine's tee-shirt. She pulls her jumper away from her chest in an attempt to stop everything from getting soaked again. She takes the breast pump into the toilets and milks off as much as she can, then sluices it down the sink. Nurse Nuala mumbles about Epsom Salts to dry up the milk, but Katherine is not ready for that.

Harry bounces in with sandwiches and a clean sweater, a jacket and a few smalls for Katherine.

'Let's put the best foot forward, eh?'

As the nursery door is open, they go inside and stand beside the incubator. Katherine tries to match up the shallow breaths with the wiggling lines on the screen of the monitor. Nothing makes any sense. Harry, determined not to be sucked into his wife's depression, says brightly, 'Who do you think he looks like? Has he got my nose, would you say?'

'He just looks like a visiting angel to me. Do you think he knows we're here?'

Katherine is sliding behind that faraway look that he dreads. He places his large, square hand on top of the incubator. Its shadow almost covers the child. Uncomfortable at being in the nursery, which he knows, instinctively, is out of bounds, he says, 'Come on, Katherine, it's nearly time to go and see your uncle.'

Arguing with Harry is too much for Katherine right now, so she follows him into the corridor, looking back over her shoulder.

'You go and clean yourself up a bit in the toilets. Brush your hair. You look a mess. I'll wait for you here.'

They sit on the two chairs in the hallway outside Uncle Tommy's consulting room. Katherine tries to drink tepid coffee from a plastic cup. Harry eats the sandwiches, checks his watch and glances at the *Financial Times*. Katherine stares at the sign on the door, trying to gain some solace from the bold lettering: MR T. BAGSHOT, a lot of capital letters and then CONSULTANT PAEDIATRICIAN.

'We are monitoring the situation. The signs aren't good. It appears that the child has a very rare congenital cardiac disorder. There could be other complications. To be honest, I've only seen something like this once before. In that instance, I think incest was involved. Of course, I'm not suggesting anything like that in this case.' He smiles dryly, looking at Harry, and then reaches out to touch Katherine on the shoulder. 'You really should go home, my dear. There isn't anything you can do for him here. It upsets the staff to have people hanging around the place.'

'Can I hold him? Feed him myself?'

'He's too weak. He'll have to be fed through a tube from now on.'

'What do you mean, "from now on"? He can't stay like that forever!' Her voice is rising and thinning to a pathetic whine.

Harry holds Katherine's hand firmly, trying to prevent her from leaping up, hoping to God she doesn't start that begging again.

'We'll keep you informed as we go along if you ring the staff nurse, or better still, ring me here, and I can tell you myself.'

'What happened to that other baby?' Harry's curiosity overrides his common sense, and he immediately regrets inquiring.

'Oh, I think it lasted a week or so; I can't really recall how long.'

Harry winces, expecting an outburst. Then Katherine surprises them both. She seems to pull herself together a bit and calmly asks her uncle, 'Is Jack going to die?'

The two men look at each other. Tommy Bagshot turns away first. After an uncomfortable pause, he stands up and walks around the desk. He puts his arm around her narrow shoulders and gives her an avuncular hug.

'You need to look after yourself now, my dear. You go home and have a good wash and a rest and leave the baby to us. He's in good hands.'

Harry stands up, but Katherine doesn't move.

'I need to know the truth, Uncle Tommy.'

Her uncle moves back to his side of the desk and sits down again. Looking his niece squarely in the eyes, he says, 'We are doing what we can for him. His condition is not treatable. He is unlikely to live for more than a few days.'

'Why are you doing all these tests if you know he can't be treated?'

At this, Tommy Bagshot turns to Harry. 'This is a very rare condition. Like I say, I've only seen it once before. We know very little about it. We are in a teaching hospital, and keeping your child alive like this is giving us the opportunity to learn a great deal more.' Then, as an afterthought, he adds, 'And you know, of course, the child is very premature. Should have been born in a hospital.'

'How would that have improved his chances?'

Katherine snaps.

'Well, for a start, it would have given us a bit longer to learn more. It's important for the students, you know. Like I said, this is a very rare condition.'

A large lump is lodged in Katherine's throat. It seems to be stopping all the other questions she wants to ask. Grasping the opportunity, Harry nods to Bagshot and scoops his wife onto her feet. He ushers her out into the corridor and, sensing that she might faint, leads her to a slightly open window. They stand together, looking out into a pleasant garden. It is surrounded on all sides by high hospital walls and blank windows, with ghosts in white coats floating around behind them. Some blackbirds are hopping about, rooting through the fallen leaves for worms.

Suddenly, a door swings open and the birth cries of a new baby pierce the silence and ring through the corridors.

Katherine turns to Harry. 'I'm not leaving the hospital until ...'

'Until what?'

He has run out of words. He desperately wants to escape the claustrophobia of his wife's anguish. He doesn't know how to react. He has no reference points, nothing to measure this against. For the first time in many years, he longs for his mother to guide him through it.

'Harry, they are just keeping Jack alive because they want to experiment on him!'

'Oh, Katherine, you are being so dramatic. They are doing what they can for him. You heard your uncle; little Jack is helping other babies to live, in the future. Anyway, what else could they do? Just let him die?'

Her eyes light up. Her nostrils flare like a wild horse. Her tangled red mane flies outwards as she spins round to face him.

'He's being used as a human guinea pig!'

She stomps off down the corridor and into the women's toilet. Weeping is so hard with great lumps of tension holding onto the tears. She sobs helplessly, walking round and round in the small space between the basins and the cubicles, then collapses onto the floor and sits in the corner. Sent by Harry to see what's going on, Nurse Nuala finds Katherine with her head on her knees and her hands locked behind her neck. Her hair is flopping up and down as she shakes in anguish. Nuala wants to sit down beside her but is afraid of getting her uniform grubby. She stands helplessly, looking on for a few seconds, then has a glimmer of inspiration.

'I think the baby is awake now. Would you like to try holding him again?'

The face that Katherine sees through her tears is like a rainbow against black clouds. Nuala smiles, holds out her hand and helps Katherine to her feet. 'Come on, we'll see what we can do for my godson.' Her gentle, undulating voice is soothing.

Harry is standing outside the nursery as the two women walk past. Nuala offers a little smile and nods. Katherine ignores him. He watches as the nurse opens the incubator, removes a few tubes and carefully lifts the limpid infant out. Katherine takes the shawl from her shoulders and, with the utmost tenderness, wraps it around her son. Harry is overcome by the picture before him. His wife, whom he has hitherto thought of with twinges of embarrassment and guilt, whom he considered only in terms of social position, sexual adventure and financial leapfrogging, has become a woman. She and Nurse Nuala are working together to encourage the infant to latch onto a grossly engorged breast. They are oblivious to Harry and everything else as well. Eventually, a feeble suck latches the baby to his mother. Harry can see them talking but can hear nothing. He knows that no matter what happens, by siding with the establishment, he has utterly excluded himself. He leaves the hospital quietly.

Harry had arranged that they would meet Georgina for lunch. It is impossible for him to envisage bringing his mother-in-law to the hospital under the present circumstances, even though she is sure to agree with him and her cousin. She is unlikely to be able to help put an end to this mewling over a child that hasn't a chance anyway. He goes to the restaurant and explains the situation to Georgina in terms that will, while acknowledging that she wants to see her daughter and her grandson, persuade her to stay away.

'Things aren't great at the moment. The baby is quite delicate and needs to be in an incubator. You can't really get near enough to see anything.' From the pained look on her face, he senses Georgina leaning her sympathies into that nursery. The possibility that she might get sudden pangs of motherly togetherness alarms him. 'Katherine is in a bit of a state, as you can imagine. Rather upset; well, almost hysterical, in fact. It's all quite messy at the moment.'

Georgina winces, 'Oh, poor you. Well done for coping with it all.'

Realising he's turned the corner, Harry boots his goal home. 'You could maybe ring your cousin and talk to him. He'll fill you in on the details better than I can.'

Georgina is picking over a leafy salad. She puts down the fork and says, 'I think it's best if I stay out of it, Henry. I'm getting my hair done this afternoon, and I'll take the early train home after that. You can keep me up to date with developments. Give Katherine my love.' She straightens her hat, checks her lipstick in a small, compact mirror and pats her cheeks with powder. Then she drifts away, leaving most of the greenery still on the plate.

Harry sits for a while, smoking a cigar and nurturing a familiar sense of connivance.

Two days pass in a blur. Katherine hangs around the intensive care nursery, dodging the ward sister, nibbling snacks from a machine and leftovers she can retrieve from the trays that come out of the maternity wards. Smoking fags in the toilets is her one indulgence. Nuala is the only nurse who will let her into the nursery, and that has to be when no one else is around. Jack is wheeled in and out of the theatre several times for tests, and every time he has to spend hours closeted in a secret recovery room afterwards. His condition has deteriorated so much that holding or feeding him is no longer possible. Occasionally, Katherine is able to slip her hand into the incubator and let him hold her finger for a few moments before the clear plastic bubble is closed up again to reduce the risk of infection.

Harry comes each day, but Katherine refuses to talk to him. A situation which is exacerbated by his mention of her mother and even more by the way he produces a hairbrush each time. Katherine tries to dodge him if she can.

Day five dawns. As far as she can tell, it's bright and sunny outside, although those coming in are saying it's bitterly cold and winter is setting in early. Jack has been almost in a coma for twenty-four hours. His colour is very poor now. Two nurses come to collect him from the nursery and start to wheel him briskly along the corridor.

'Where are you taking him?'

'More tests.'

'Please, don't take him away again. He's too weak for more

tests.'

They look at each other and pretend they haven't heard her. She is brushed aside, and the double doors open and swallow them up, closing with a muted thud.

Katherine goes into her sanctuary of the toilets. She gazes in the mirror at her eyes, which now look like blood-flecked poached eggs. Tears are blurring her vision. She feels weak and dizzy and knows she is getting near the end of the road herself. Something will have to give. There is lipstick smeared on the glass. It reads, 'God loves you, baby.' As she stares at it, the words begin to come alive. They glow and move around. She holds onto the edge of the basin and pleads out loud, 'Do you? If you love me, Lord, help me now.'

She doesn't wait for a reply. She splashes water onto her face and smears it around. There are grey smudges on the white towel where she has dried her drawn and lifeless skin. She pulls the brush through her matted hair and makes an effort to straighten out her clothes. Her fingers tangle with the rosary beads that Bridget had slipped into the skirt pocket during their last goodbye at Dublin Airport. She closes her eyes and mouths the rosary.

'Hail, Mary, full of grace, The Lord is with thee, blessed art thou amongst women, and blessed is the fruit of thy womb, Jesus …' Her own, empty womb, is still bleeding.

Katherine manages to corner her uncle before he too disappears behind the double doors. She steps between him and his entourage. 'I need to talk to you about Jack.' She straightens her hair with her fingers. 'I'm not happy for him to have any more tests.'

'Well, my dear, Henry has signed the consent forms, you know that.'

'But he's *my* child!'

252

'Henry is the child's father. That's what counts.'

'No, he isn't.'

Tommy Bagshot looks alarmed. He ushers Katherine into a corner and waves the students away. He looks at her. She looks at the floor. She takes a gulp of air to steady herself. She stares at her baby, who has re-emerged and is marooned in his space bubble in the corridor. The crucifix in her pocket is biting her fingers.

After a brief silence, she continues, trying to sound calm and reasonable but knowing that the thin remains of her voice betray her horrors. 'A violent crime was committed against me. That's how I got pregnant. Harry is not the father.' Katherine can almost still taste the blood from cutting her lip. With her tongue, she can feel the chipped front tooth. She is not yet able to say the word 'rape'.

By this stage, the two of them are sitting down on a visitors' bench.

'Does your husband know this?' Bagshot can think of nothing more appropriate to say. He takes her hands and squeezes them. She shakes her head.

'He isn't going to live long now, is he?' He looks away and mumbles something she doesn't want to hear. 'What if you removed the tubes and didn't keep reviving him each time his heart stops?'

'We'd have to call it a day, then.'

'How long would he live for?'

'Hours; maybe less.'

Katherine stands up. She tugs at her skirt, trying to flatten out the creases. 'I want you to do that. Now.'

Bagshot looks past her and out of the window. He mulls this idea over for a minute or two. Then he starts to stand up as well, but the sight of Katherine's tearless agony draws him back into the seat.

'You can't make him live or die to order, just because it's convenient!'

'The students are all so wound up over it. It is really important research, Katherine.'

Her green eyes shine now, like newly cut emeralds, from their bloodshot and tearful sockets. He puts his hands up to his face. The tips of his elegant, long fingers disappear into his fringe. There is a flash of light as a sunbeam catches his gold signet ring and bounces off the shiny wall.

'Okay. You understand what this means, don't you, Katherine?'

She nods.

'Come back in an hour, then. The necessary papers will be in the nurse's station. You can leave the remains; we'll deal with all that for you.'

So focussed now on her next few moves, she misses, or ignores, the last sentence.

'Please, don't say anything to Harry or my mother about this or what I told you,' she pleads.

He nods slowly as if to take in something he really doesn't understand.

Katherine takes her purse full of change to the public phone on the first landing. She rings Aer Lingus. She rings Bridget and then goes looking for the hospital chaplain. The old priest gives Jack the Last Rites and forgives him all his sins. None of the nurses is prepared to remove the tubes and pipes. Katherine has to do this herself. She prays the Lord will love her enough to forgive her too and to keep Harry at home. In the nursery, she is quick and methodical. Starts at the feet and works upwards; like taking the rug off a horse. The nasal tube is the last to go. She whips off the sticky plaster and gives the tube a gentle tug. Nuala watches, nodding nervously. He is as light as her change purse and a horrible colour, but to Katherine, so perfectly beautiful and, miraculously, still breathing. She wraps his punctured little frame snugly into the shawl, pulls a woolly hat onto his tiny head, grabs her holdall and stuffs the papers into it. Then, clutching him tightly, she runs down the stairs.

Nuala is skipping the steps behind her. 'You are doing the right thing,' she calls after Katherine as mother and child climb into a taxi outside the hospital. 'Good luck!' are the last words Katherine hears as she shuts the cab door.

'Heathrow, as fast as you can, please. We don't have long.' As the taxi struggles with traffic, she slips her hand inside the shawl. He is warm and—yes—still breathing. She kisses the top of his head, inhaling the powerful smell that bonds a baby to his mother. What to do next? A London taxi is not the right place. Jack will hardly make it back to Ireland alive. This was a mad idea. She knocks on the glass separating her from the cab driver.

'Can you pull into the park there, please? I think I'm going to be sick.'

He wheels the vehicle round in a terrifying U-turn with a screeching of brakes and hooting of horns and drives into the park.

'Wait here, please.'

She clambers out of the cab, holding the baby tightly to her. For a moment, she stands still, taking in the cold, dry air. It has almost turned to winter since she came to England nearly a week ago. The grass in the sheltered areas twinkles with a fine frosting of stardust. Katherine walks briskly until she is out of sight, then sits on a bench, snugly overshadowed by the low branches of a cedar tree. She peels back a corner of the shawl and lifts the infant to her face. As she caresses his forehead, the little eyes flicker, open briefly and catch hers, then close. He has taken his last breath. Katherine crosses herself and prays.

'Everyone has a right to live. And a right to die. Thank you, God, for hearing my prayers, and for giving me the most precious moment of my life. Please take his soul into heaven.' She crosses herself again and then tucks the bundle into her jacket next to her heart, buttons it right up, so just the top of his woolly hat is showing, and hurries back to the taxi.

Jimi Hendrix's 'Purple Haze' is thumping and twanging away on the radio. The cab driver is tapping the steering wheel, nodding his head and mouthing the words. Then he sees Katherine.

'You all right? You look right peaky.'

She stands for a moment, looking up at the bright blue sky above her. A group of white clouds coming over the trees from the west are like old men's shirts billowing on a washing line.

'Just excuse me while I kiss the sky.'

'Poor Hendrix, life was too much for him.'

'Yeah, that's it, isn't it? Life was just too much. Heathrow, please, as fast as you can. I have a plane to catch.'

In the privacy of the cab, as it sways and jerks its way through the traffic, Katherine unbuttons her coat and takes another look at Jack. She kisses the soft eyelids, then rolls him even more tightly into the shawl so that no part of him now is showing. When she gets to the airport, she goes into the ladies, locks the door on the cubicle and unbuttons her coat. She checks once more. The body is still warm, but the angel has flown. She takes out the bundle and packs it carefully into her holdall. She covers him over with her few bits and pieces and zips it up.

Travelling first class has its disadvantages. The stewardesses fuss over you. They want to take your bag and put it in the overhead locker. To their dismay, Katherine clutches hers tightly on her lap. She closes her eyes on England as it fades beneath them.

The customs hall in Dublin Airport is a rudimentary show of officialdom. Katherine has sailed through this airport with pounds of hash several times in the last year. A big smile and Irish eyes, together with an air of well-bred innocence, is usually enough to dazzle the dozy officials. However, this day is different—further troubles in the north. Everyone is getting twitchy. They have decided to open all bags. There is a long queue. The benches are strewn with personal belongings. Katherine tries to hide her inner panic by lighting up a cigarette. She offers one to the young officer and looks coyly up at him, really glad that she remembered to put on some lipstick and eye shadow and force the brush through her hair again before she left the plane.

'What's in the bag?'

'Nothing much, just a few smalls, really.'

'Where is your suitcase?'

'It's only a flying visit.' They exchange a small titter at the unintended pun. 'A funeral, actually.'

He looks at her for a couple of seconds. His superior is standing beside him.

'Can you put your hand luggage on the bench, please? Have you anything to declare? Open it, please.'

She is in the process of pulling the zip and shakes her head, praying they won't notice the tremor in her hands. Pretending it's stuck, she opens her mouth, runs her tongue across her bottom lip and gives the two men the biggest smile she can muster.

Just then, a few hippies with guitars over their shoulders, flowery bands around their hair and big frothy beards, rock up behind her. The two officers look at each other, shrug their shoulders and wave her through. 'Ah sure, go on then.'

They turn their attention to opening guitar cases and rucksacks instead.

Katherine swings the bag back over her shoulder and strides out, thanking the Lord once more and praying that no one else can hear her heart pounding.

CHAPTER THIRTEEN

Like angels at the Pearly Gates, Marie and Bridget are waiting in the arrivals' hall. Bridget is shocked when she sees Katherine. She knows the disguises that hide despair. She pretends her tears are those of joy at seeing Katherine home safely. Marie reaches for the holdall, but nothing will prise it out of Katherine's grasp.

'Where's the … the baby?'

Katherine nods downwards in the direction of the holdall.

'Christ! Come on, let's get out of here!'

The old car rattles and lurches through the evening traffic. Bridget curses at the wipers, which scratch, lazily slopping the rain from one side of the windscreen to the other, leaving greasy rainbows. She and Marie exchange glances as Katherine curls up on the back seat, cradling her precious bundle. They discuss stopping for a cup of tea before they leave the city, but the thought of the body in the bag spurs them on. Marie's mind is on the practicalities.

'Is there a death certificate?'

Katherine stares blankly out of the window. Even the word death won't register with her, never mind any talk of certificates.

So Marie goes on. 'Should we go to Dr Howard's surgery first or Father Fitzgerald?'

No response.

Bridget tries to concentrate on the driving, but her mind keeps slipping back to the baby in the holdall and the pain in her chest.

'Why is it baby boys are so unlucky?'

Once they get through Inchicore and out onto the Naas Road, Bridget pulls onto the verge. She can't contain herself any longer.

'Kate, my dotey little pet, I can't bear to think of him in that bag. We'll take him out.' She gets out of the driver's seat, walks around the car and climbs into the back seat beside Katherine. She opens the bag and rummages gently until her fingers feel the shawl. Like a doctor performing a caesarean section, she gently lifts out the bundle. But this baby is not squirming and slimy, gasping for its first breath in an alien world. It's like the dolls that Katherine played with when she was small and used to wrap up tightly to keep them warm. She peels back the wool and peeps at the tiny face. The eyes of the doll used to close when it was lying down and then pop open when you lifted it up. As she raises Jack to her lips, his eyes stay closed. His cheeks are cold like the silk of a ball gown in the early hours of the morning.

Marie drives the rest of the way, glancing occasionally in the mirror at the other two women huddled together on the back seat. Bridget is cradling the lifeless infant, and Katherine is staring straight ahead. Both have tears seeping slowly down their cheeks. She doesn't even attempt to talk. She makes a plan and then another but realises that getting home is all that matters.

When they eventually drive into the farm, the lights are on to welcome them. Josie has been over and lit the fire. She has left a few apple tarts in a cardboard box on the table; a box that later serves as a temporary coffin for Jack. There is a posy of late roses and dried lavender flowers standing up in a jam jar, their stems bound together with mirror foil. Marie reaches out and takes the body, astonished at how small and light he has become. Stiff and pale, a porcelain doll. She puts it carefully into the box and tucks the flowers into the folds of wool. She can't resist the temptation to bend and inhale their sweet scent before she turns her attention to Bridget and Katherine. They are standing in the middle of the room, clinging together. In spite of the fire, glowing in the range, the house is cold. She closes the back door firmly and turns on the light. They keep their coats on.

'I'll put the kettle on; it won't take long. We'll have a nice cup of tea and make a plan.' Marie's brisk voice and business-like approach snaps Bridget back to life. With cups of tea and slices of apple tart in their hands, Bridget and Marie sit, facing each other at the kitchen table. The makeshift coffin is between them.

'What now?'

'I'll see about organising a burial. I'll call over to the parochial house on my way home.'

From her seat by the range, Katherine suddenly comes to life.

'No, I'll do that myself. First thing tomorrow. I'm going over to visit Father Fitzgerald, and I'll talk to him about arranging a proper funeral for Jack.'

'I'll call over for you and drive you. Bridget can stay here

261

with the baby.'

'No, thanks, Marie. This is something I need to do for myself.'

That night, a few neighbours call to pay their respects. No one stays too long. Josie makes a few pots of tea; Fonsie and Jim crack into the whiskey. After an hour or so, they have all gone home, and Katherine is sitting on Bridget's lap beside the glowing range.

'Who's going to keep vigil with Jack?' Bridget asks rather weakly.

'I'm taking him to bed with me.' Katherine starts to carry the box upstairs. She walks very carefully, but the whole thing is too cumbersome in the narrow stairwell, so she ditches the box and takes the body in her arms, still wrapped in its crocheted shawl, up the stairs to her room. She contemplates sleeping with him in her bed, but the thought of waking up in the morning beside a dead body is too much for her, so she opens the bottom drawer of the chest of drawers and nestles him into it. When she is drifting into sleep, she hears rats scratching behind the skirting boards. She jumps out of bed and moves Jack to the top drawer, then she pulls the dog into the bed beside her. She listens to the sounds of Bridget washing cups and sorting things in the kitchen below. Watching shadows drifting across the wall, she realises she hasn't even drawn the curtains. The window is slightly open. She can smell the damp soil, hear a barn owl hooting from the tall trees and, presently, a timid moon climbs slowly above the horizon. The cold night air is blowing gently through the room.

Katherine finds the old priest in the church. The light of the morning is shining through the brightly coloured windows, casting streaks across the pale new pews. All around the inside are carved friezes of the passion of Christ. She hasn't noticed this before, having focussed her attention on the starkly modern altar with its huge gilded cross. Father Fitzgerald is dressed to leave. When she tells him why she is here, he lays his hat on a pew.

'So, the baby died. May the Lord have mercy on his soul.' He crosses himself with his right hand, using the left one to support himself on the side of the altar.

'I'd like him to be buried next to my Uncle Jack.'

'Well, now, first things first, my child. It's not as simple as that at all, at all, so it isn't.' He attempts to stand up straight but lists slightly to the right, a fact that is emphasised by the way his heavy silver crucifix hangs vertically down over his right breast. 'Do you have a death certificate? You can't bury someone without that, you know.'

She pulls the envelope of papers Tommy Bagshot had left for her from her handbag. Saying a silent prayer, she hands them all over to the priest. He lurches forwards down the aisle into a shaft of light from outside. Leaning against the door frame, he mouths the words as he reads them. He pauses a few times, coughs violently and rolls his eyes to heaven.

'So, he died because his heart wasn't properly formed. He had no chance, the poor little soul. Where did you register the birth at all?'

'I haven't got around to that, Father.'

'Oh, I see.'

The open church doors perfectly frame the picture of a bright blue sky, smiling over the rolling green and yellow fields of north Kilkenny. Father Fitzgerald's black form is now in silhouette.

'No birth certificate, eh? Died before you had the chance? And this'—he flutters the sheets of paper like a fan—'is all you have in the way of a death certificate too? Is it? I suppose they could hardly issue one without the other.' He mumbles, 'You could nearly say he never existed at all, at all. The trouble is, you see, that is consecrated ground. Was the child baptised, even? Any meaningful sign or gesture, a sign of the cross and a few prayers perhaps, before he, well, before he went to Jesus?'

'Jack was baptised by the hospital chaplain, a Catholic priest, Father, and he also gave him the Last Rites. I have no proof of either, though. You'll have to take my word for it. Or else phone my uncle at the hospital or even speak to the hospital chaplain.'

The old man smiles. 'Indeed, and I will. Well, thanks be to God. The baptism is all that really matters. Bring the child here to the chapel tomorrow, and we'll bury him after morning Mass. I'll call by the farm this evening, and we'll say a few prayers over him then. No need for a big fuss.'

Fonsie has made a little wooden coffin. The smell of fresh paint fills the room. Marie and Josie transfer the body from the cardboard box. They dress him up in a white, flannelette gown. The posy of flowers is laid at his feet as if it were the faithful dog of a medieval knight. They spread a damask cloth over the table in the parlour and arrange the open coffin in the middle. A few briquettes add a flickering glow from the fireplace, but nothing would really dispel the smell of damp. No amount of dusting and brushing the few bits of furniture can brighten the corners of the room that suck the memories of family tragedies deep into their dingy recesses.

'Oh, good God, we can't leave it there. It looks like the Christmas turkey!' Marie says, turning the coffin and moving it more to one side.

'Marie! How could you say such a thing?' Josie chides, but really, she knows that Marie is just trying to lighten the mood, as she always does. Bridget puts a few candles in jam jars and places them strategically here and there. She drapes a sheet over the mirror on the mantlepiece. The parlour becomes a shrine.

The day wears on; more visitors trail through. Some stop and drink tea or whiskey or both. Some eat cake and wedges of tart; some eat nothing but leave sliced pans of ham sandwiches for others to have later. It is hard to breathe in the kitchen with the mingling smoke of cigarettes and unsettled candleflames. Bridget opens the scullery window and quenches the candles; they sizzle between her licked finger and thumb. The visitors huddle closer to the open firebox in the range.

People chat and make harmless jokes, taking care not to laugh too loud. Katherine knows or recognises most, but not all, who file past and shake her hand.

Nicholas introduces his mother, Moira. He supports her carefully and helps her into the empty chair beside Katherine. She looks directly into the young mother's familiar, green eyes and says, earnestly, 'I'm truly sorry for all your troubles; your father, and now your little boy.' She takes both Katherine's hands in her cold grasp. 'I knew Frank well, once upon a time …' Nicholas catches sight of a far-away look on his mother's face. 'During the troubles. He was a fine man, knew what he stood for.'

He tugs her arm and hauls her to her feet. 'Come on, Mother. We don't want to go into that now. We won't hold up the queue.'

Katherine wants to talk more, to hear about her father, what Moira might have known about him, but Nicholas resolutely takes her to the door and out into the drizzle of the waning day.

Father Fitzgerald mumbles a few prayers over the

baby. He nods to Fonsie to close the coffin. When he sees the alarm on Katherine's face, he puts his hand out to her and says, 'He's at peace now, child. You must let him go.'

'Fonsie can do it later; in the morning, perhaps?' She looks at Fonsie, who is uncomfortable, caught between the grieving mother and the parish priest.

Bridget intercedes. 'Look't, I'll do it myself. Leave me the tools. Besides, her husband hasn't arrived yet. He has to say goodbye too.'

This invocation of Harry when she needs him at first seems smart, but quickly the thought of him turns sour in her mind, and she knows that the idea of Harry, showing up to say goodbye, is the last thing Katherine would want or consider important. Bridget knows he will come, though, sooner or later. He doesn't give up that easily.

'We can't hold onto people just because we want to. His place is with God now. The Lord giveth, and the Lord taketh away. It's not for us to pull them back.' The old priest makes a sign of the cross above the baby's head, touches it with his thumb and smiles. 'You'll have the comfort of knowing that you did your best for him, and you'll always have a little angel in heaven.'

He nods again to Fonsie, a little more firmly this time, holding out his long arm to keep the women back. As the lid is screwed into place, he leads them all into the rhythm of the Rosary. Finally, putting his hat onto his head, he says, 'Bring him to the altar before the Mass and sit in the front pew; that way, it won't be too unsettling.'

Nicholas returns sometime later, alone and considerably more drunk than when he left with his mother. By this time, the only people in the room are Bridget and Katherine. Bridget heads for the stairs to 'rest for a while' but sits on the step just around the return of the staircase, out of sight, to eavesdrop, in case she is needed.

Having been drinking on and off all day, Nicholas' conscience is riddling his common sense. He has decided, once again, to come clean and tell her the truth. He is feeling sorry and wants to make a clean breast of everything. Most of all, he wants to know if this was his child. He takes the whiskey bottle from the table and puts it to his lips.

'Don't you think you've had enough of that for one night?'

'Ah, don't fuss, woman. I came back to tell you something.'

'You can tell me tomorrow when you are a bit more sober.'

'I want to tell you now.' He sits by the hearth and takes a swig from the bottle. There is an unnatural chill in the room. He glances at the stairwell and over at the open door of the parlour. He knows that he is losing his nerve again. 'This house is haunted. Did you know that?' he says finally.

'Is that what you came all the way back to tell me?'

'Why are women so hard to talk to? Look't, girl, I came to say sorry.'

'Sorry for what?'

'Ah, sure, that's enough for now.'

Bridget reappears at the bottom of the stairs. Her shape fills the opening completely; in fact, she has to duck her head slightly to take the last step.

'Come on, my dotey little pet, you need to get to bed. It's been a very long day.'

'Okay, okay, I can take the hint. I'm going anyway. Good night to yees.' The two women listen as Nicholas tries to start his car. It hegs a few times, then eventually, it kicks. He makes several attempts to turn it. They hear it splash over the ford and rev off up the boreen. The moon glistens on the dewy fields beyond the yard, picking up trails the sheep have made over the years, wending their way up and down the hill.

'I'll stay up with the child. Try to get some sleep, pet. You look really tired out.'

Bridget opens the window in the parlour a small bit to let the wee one's soul go free and keep the body cool. She closes the one in the scullery, draws all the curtains, and soon she is sound asleep in the armchair beside the range. Underneath the table in the parlour, the dog keeps vigil for Jack.

On the third day … the sun rises early, bringing with it a chilly morning. Draughts gush in through all the cracks. Katherine, hoping not to wake Bridget, creeps around gathering up glasses and cups, dropping half-eaten sandwiches into the dog's dish. She makes a fresh pot of tea and opens the door to chuck the crumbs out for the birds. The sun is catching and lighting up the wet branches. The kitchen is full of dead fags and stale booze, so she leaves the door open and relishes the clean smell of this important day. A pale moon is still lingering low in the western sky. Some sparrows are hopping around the yard, gleaning crumbs and bits of corn left by Jim Ryan when he fed the animals earlier. They fly off in a flurry as the dog bounds out towards them. Everything seems so normal until she turns around and sees again the little white coffin on the table in the next room. Hesitantly, she walks into the parlour, closes the window and opens the curtains slightly. A shaft of light skips across the old, brown furniture, making it look warm and loved. She tries to visualise the peaceful face of her baby lying in his soft nest. Resting her hands on the coffin, she feels the grain of the wood on her fingertips. Bridget is now up and busily tidying and fussing around. Her practised hands sweep the curtains fully open and gather up the last few glasses and some saucers with butt ends in them, making a neat pile on her tray.

Katherine turns to her and asks, 'Do you think this house is haunted?'

'Haunted? I don't know. A lot has happened here over the years, I suppose.'

'Do you believe in death?'

'Oh, pet, what are you on about?' Bridget has a horror of this kind of conversation. She has no idea where it's going or what to say.

'Do you think perhaps people don't really die? They just change into something else; that really, they are all still here, everyone who ever lived; we can't see them or talk to them, but they are all watching us, now?'

Bridget shivers. 'God in Heaven, child, I hope not. Anyways, whatever about that, we need to get ready for Mass. Come on, pet, I'll help you sort out your clothes, and we'll do your hair.'

Katherine could have guessed that Harry would time his arrival perfectly. Even so, she is quite taken aback to see him standing on the porch of the church, waiting for the cortege to arrive, expecting them to glide up to the door in a big, black hearse. Ever since he discovered that she had taken the baby, he began the process of lashing himself into an epic temper. Via a series of phone calls to the Gardaí, the Ryans and Father Fitzgerald, he worked out that the burial would be this morning. He has gone over his speeches of wrath many times, tweaking the details during the starlight flight and polishing it up over breakfast in the hotel. All this time, he has been building a massive head of steam with which to belch rage and fury at Katherine, at Bridget and anyone else who crosses his path. However, the sight of his wife climbing out of her old Morris Traveller and carrying a miniature, white coffin completely disarms him. He is unable to manage a smile; nor is she, but the two of them nod civilly at each other and walk up the aisle side by side.

Marie is so captivated by finally setting eyes on Harry that she forgets to cry at the graveside. So much so that she gets annoyed with the children, especially Fionnuala, who is sobbing piteously at the sight of the coffin being lowered into the hole.

Bridget puts her arms around the child. 'There, there, pet. Don't be crying so. He's gone to a better place. He was never really meant for this life at all.' Crooning the comforting words helps her not to weep herself.

The farmyard is chock-a-block with cars, tractors and bicycles crammed in and many more backed up along the boreen. The women make tea. The men drink it and more besides. The children run around in the sun, relieved it's over. Having done all she can to avoid it, sometime during the afternoon, Katherine finds herself alone in the parlour with Harry. She gets the whiff of alcohol from his breath.

He is standing between her and the door. He kicks it shut behind him. Catching her by the shoulders and with his face inches from hers, he growls, 'Why did you do it? You killed him. You won't get away with it, you know.'

'What do you mean, Harry? We both know he was only being kept alive so they could experiment on him. Research, that's what Uncle Tommy called it.'

'You are a murdering bitch!' He starts to shake her violently.

Attracted by the raised voices and the prospect of a good row, Nicholas bursts into the room. 'Whoa, steady on there! That's strong language.'

Harry is well into his stride and isn't going to let some drunken paddy come between him and his outrage. He growls, still staring at Katherine, at point-blank range. 'You stay out of this, whoever you are! And as for you, Katherine, you murdered my son! I'll never forgive you.' He rakes her face, searching for any sign of remorse. Sucking in sharply through clenched front teeth with a hiss, he starts up again. 'It's all your fault. None of this would have happened if you hadn't run off like you did, coming here to this hovel, to play at farming and live like a … like a bloody peasant! No proper doctors, no decent hospital. I knew something like this would happen if I let you go. My poor son never had a chance! If your father was still alive …' His voice is going up again, and his face is purple between his bushy sideburns. There are white rims around his lips.

Nicholas throws in his haymaker. 'What makes you so sure he was your son?'

'Who is this impertinent …'

This is not at all how Marie pictured Harry behaving; but he is not disappointing her. Now he is a real entity, a *guerrier* with some fight in him. Delighted to get the chance to join the drama, she nudges Nicholas back out of the way and says, 'Calm down, everyone. Look't, you can see how upset Katie is; there's no need to make it worse.'

'It could hardly be any worse! And who are YOU?'

'We are all Katie's friends. We only want to help. Come on, come out into the kitchen and have a drink,' is Josie's contribution from the doorway.

This is Marie's prompt to lure Nicholas and a few other onlookers out of the parlour by brandishing the whiskey bottle.

With some difficulty, Bridget squeezes in between Katherine and Harry. When she is sure that the dotey little pet is out of danger, she talks quietly to him. 'I can see how upset you are. Clearly, you feel a strong sense of loss too. This has been a terrible shock for all of us. Katherine did what she

271

had to do. What any real mother would have done under the circumstances. It took a lot of courage. She couldn't bear to see the little mite suffer any more poking and prodding when it wasn't doing him any good. Mr Bagshot wrote as much in the discharge papers. He said the heart was seriously malformed, and the baby had no hope of living. Even with life support, it was only a matter of hours. I know it's really hard to accept, but he would have died in the incubator sooner or later, which or whether. She saved him even more suffering. You must see Katherine did the only thing she could do to be true to herself and true to her own values. She gave your son the chance to die with dignity in his mother's arms. We all have to accept that it's over now. Come on back into the kitchen and make your peace with our neighbours.' And then, knowing how it pacifies him to be called by his proper name, she adds, 'Please, Henry.'

By the time Bridget finally wins the battle and persuades Harry to come back and talk to the others more calmly, most of them have gone home. Marie and Josie are clearing up. The last embers of a turf fire smoulder away in the musty parlour alone. Katherine puts her head outside the kitchen door to breathe the frosty evening air and finds Nicholas, Sergeant Dawson and JJ Ryan all leaning against Harry's hired BMW, deep in conversation. Something about the way they look at her makes her think of crates of guns. And then of Wren Boys. A shiver runs through her, and she shuts the door again. So that's why Nicholas is sorry! She is glad not to be alone in the house tonight.

Bridget is gently folding small sheaves of dried lavender and rose petals into the crocheted shawl.

'We'll put this away safely and hope for a little girl the next time.'

'I don't want to think about a next time. Jack lived and died, and now it's over, as you said yourself. We've got to look for another reason to go on, Bridgie.' But Katherine can't see the tears in Bridget's eyes. She watches the long fingers, which are already becoming knobbly and misshapen, smoothing the wool and carefully layering it into the folds of tissue paper.

'Oh, really, Katherine, you do talk a lot of nonsense sometimes.' Harry rounds off that conversation, as he usually does, and goes to the window. 'What are those boys doing out there? Why don't they go home? If they scratch that car, I'll have to pay for it.'

He moves towards the door, but Bridget has the words to stop him in his tracks and bring him back to civility. 'I should leave them alone, Henry. They are discussing who will buy the farm now that there is no longer an heir.'

The women exchange glances, and Josie pours the tea. Marie chirps up, 'Come on, everyone. Let's sit down and look at the Mass cards. We still have Mrs Hayes's chocolate cake to get through!'

'I can't sit around and gossip. I have a plane to catch, and if I don't get that car back by ten, I'll have to pay for another day.' Harry buttons his overcoat.

Katherine goes with him to the car to say goodbye, hoping for some kind words and ready to give him a kiss on the cheek, but realises this is not going to happen when she sees the thunder still lurking in his bloodshot eyes.

'What did he mean, "How do you know you're the father?" This isn't over yet, Katherine. Not by a long stalk. You won't get away with this. I'll be back. Next time, you'll have to come with me and face up to what you've done!'

But really, he knows he has lost this battle before the longbows have even been drawn. He can see that Katherine has changed. He can no longer frighten her with growls and threats. He has already spoken to a divorce lawyer, but he will save that until the next time; until he has had a chance to work out his best position. The real war is yet to come. That one won't be about babies and women's nonsense. It will be about property, pure and simple.

CHAPTER FOURTEEN

Father Fitzgerald calls round a few days later. 'Well, child, how are you now? It's a grand soft day at any rate, thanks be to God.' The old priest lifts his hat and lets the sun peek in at his shiny scalp. 'I've given nearly forty years in this parish, did you know that? Sure, how would you?' He leans over a wooden gate that faces northwards up the hillside. Katherine does the same. They survey the pasture, emerging from a morning haze and scattered with sheep. The ram is busily taking any chance he can get while the sun shines. 'I've seen God's work in life and death. I've seen this village grow from a little crop of roughly thatched cottages, huddled around the old church, to the thriving community it is today.' He takes out a fresh white handkerchief and coughs into it, then stuffs it back into a pocket deep beneath the folds of his cassock. 'We'll walk a while.'

He opens the gate gingerly, like a man who is well used to old farm gates. They stroll out into the field, feeling the chilly morning breeze blowing the mist up from the river. The old priest is easily puffed out and needs to stop frequently to gather his breath. He coughs more vigorously as they start into the hill. He leans in with the strain. The sheep look up, and some begin to huddle, their short tails bobbing up and down. It takes a minute or two for him to regain his composure. 'I knew your father well, you know. Did he ever speak of me?'

'He didn't speak much about Ireland at all, really. He did mention you, though, shortly before he died. He said I should talk to you about the past to ask you about things that took place here during the troubles and the Civil War.' This little lie seems harmless, but Katherine knows she is pushing it; she just can't resist the chance when it's offered.

'Did he now? Well, some things are better left alone, child. We always kept in touch, how and ever. I looked after ... well, certain things for him here.'

'What sort of things?'

'Family business, politics; he never lost interest.'

'But what about his brother, Jack? Couldn't he have done any family business? Daddy never let on that he had any particular business interests in Ireland at all.'

'Jack was just a simple man, Katherine. He had no reading or writing to speak of; no interest in politics, just the farm and the odd game of cards. Your father wanted to keep his life in England separate; he would never have involved Jack.' He looks up at the sheep as they settle back to rutting and grazing. 'I think he really left a part of himself here, you know, a big part.'

Katherine searches the soft, pale skin on the old man's face for clues. They say the eyes can't lie. But she sees nothing helpful, and then he looks away.

'So, was Uncle Jack illiterate?'

'A lot of that generation were, you know. They left school

very young to work the land. Sure, someone had to. Book learning wasn't so highly regarded back then.'

'Would that explain why he didn't leave a note? Some kind of suicide note, I mean?'

'We mustn't speak ill of the dead, Katherine. He did his best. He was, well, how can I put it? He was out of his depth.'

'What do you mean, Father?'

'All things in time, child, all things in time.'

After walking around the curve of the hill for a while, the old man begins to slow the pace. They turn and let the rising sun warm their faces.

'I've little to show for my life, you know, but I said I'd build a new school so all the children of the parish would be educated in comfort. It was terrible hardship in our day, in those old buildings. They were cold and bleak, no facilities at all. I said I'd leave them something after me; the new chapel and a decent school. We built it big enough to accommodate my growing flock.' He sweeps his upturned hat in a wide arc, taking in most of the landscape and the grazing sheep. It seems like he's passing it around for a collection, as if coins are going to fall from heaven.

'This is just a farming community, simple people, you understand. They've had to fight for everything. It was hard won, every acre. Your father and I, we were part of that struggle here. Truth to tell, your family led the march, so to speak.'

Having more or less circumnavigated the hill, they are now back at the wooden gate. Katherine opens it this time; she understands its eccentricities. The old man is heaving and wheezing. He looks down at his wet shoes.

'Frank left you a wealthy woman, I believe?'

Feeling the wind change direction, Katherine catches a glimpse of what's on his mind.

'Well, yes, I suppose I am, really. But you know, Father, money is only money; it isn't love or truth, and it won't bring my baby, or my father, or for that matter Uncle Jack, back.'

'How well you can say that, child, you have always had plenty of it! Poverty was a daily reality for most people in this country.'

'Poverty is relative, Father. I've never experienced it, but I know how lonely and frightened having money can make you feel.'

'How so, child?'

'It robs people of their reasons for loving and needing each other. People see money and they don't feel the same need for love.' She is thinking of Harry, and how for him everything is measured and justified in simple economic terms. Love is incidental; a nuisance, even. It's only useful if it pays well. Feelings are like window dressing; Harry doesn't get them and wealth mixed up.

'That's a pretty well-worn path, Katherine, and you'd want to be careful who you tell that they don't need money. Your family didn't always have it, you know.'

'I don't think all the money in the world would have made Uncle Jack's life any better. He was a contented man and liked his very simple life. That's why I can't believe he would shoot himself.'

'Mmm, well …'

He stoops a little as he enters the kitchen. Katherine looks around for Bridget, but she must have gone out for some reason. Bridget doesn't like priests.

'Father Fitzgerald, what is really on your mind?'

'You know, you are very direct for a young woman!' He is about to sit down, but instead he hovers by the door. 'How and ever, as you ask so plainly, it's like this. I don't expect to live in this world much longer, and I couldn't leave the parish in debt on my account. The building funds; you know the way it is now.'

'How much is left to pay?' Katherine is relieved to know that it's only money that the old man wants and not some kind of a penance along with it. When he tells her the amount outstanding, she is amazed, not by how much but by how little it is. How such an inconsiderable sum can cause a man of God to grovel so. She writes a cheque and hands it to him. He folds it neatly and tucks it under the greasy ribbon on the inside of his hat, while she pours him a glass of whiskey. He lifts the glass to the light, crosses himself and tosses the whole lot back in one swig. He tips the ash from his cigarette into the turn-up of his trouser leg and, when finished, he quenches it between his thumb and forefinger and drops the stub, still warm, into his pocket.

'The money will be well spent, you may be sure of that, child. There will always be a memorial to your father now. We'll put a stone up near the school to the memory of Francis Butler, patriot.'

Katherine considers this for a moment, thinking of his knighthood and Jack and the other Butlers of Knocklong, and wonders how her father could be considered a patriot when he spent his adult life building a fortune in enemy territory.

'I would really like you to tell me more about my dad's story and all his political connections. What happened to the family here? He did try to tell me himself. But then he died before he got the chance. There is a lot I don't know.'

He bows his head as he replaces his hat. Katherine knows that means he's putting the lid on all discussions for today. He has got what he came for. She is sorry she was so direct, didn't spin him out some more. She is sure she could have drawn a lot more out of him if she had held off the giving him the money and if her own impatience hadn't goaded her tongue. A coughing fit takes hold of him, and he grabs his hat before it falls off.

'It's a long story, child. I will tell you, but that's for another day. Let the dust settle around here a bit first.' And then, with a gentle smile, he adds, 'You've had enough grief for the time being.'

~

Once the phone is reconnected, Harry rings a few times. He makes some attempts to persuade Katherine to focus her mind on selling the farm and coming home. However, his big opening shot, before resorting to threats and emotional blackmail, comes in the post. It is in fact the first serve in a volley of letters that fly back and forth between London and Knocklong for several weeks. He never mentions divorce, but instead opens with enticements such as, 'I won't expect you to live in London if you'd rather be at home in Suffolk on the farm ... the hunting season is starting soon. Peter tells me the cub hunting is well underway already ...' Developing his arguments with strokes like, 'Your mother misses you, she seems very lonely ... the house is so quiet without you and Bridget to give the char something to do ... I've had to let the others go because there isn't any point in having two maids and a cook in a virtually empty house ...'

As Katherine's replies don't give him any encouragement, the velocity of his attack increases. 'Your mother says she might put the manor house on the market if you don't come home. She is thinking of buying something near us in Kensington.' And when that doesn't do it, he tries a direct hit.

'Maybe it's time to try again for another baby. I think I would like that now.' However, far from achieving the desired effect, Katherine replies, 'Harry, I am not ready for another baby. There are still too many unanswered questions here for me to leave. I feel like I might be getting nearer to the truth about Uncle Jack, and I won't come back until I know what really happened.' What she doesn't say is that she has seen what kind of a father he would be and it shocked her. She has recurring visions of him shouting into her face, 'You murdered my son!' Every time that happens, she gets a pain in her stomach, like it's expecting the blows that will follow.

As soon as he speaks on the phone, Katherine hands it to Bridget.

'How long do you expect a man to wait for his wife to pull herself together and come home, where she belongs?' Harry demands to know. 'What on earth is she doing there? Can't you do something to talk her round? Surely, she isn't planning to spend another winter in that God-awful place?'

Bridget has no reply ready for him. She tries to think of something. 'Katherine needs time to recover. It's like I said, this has all been a terrible shock for her. You'll just have to be patient, Henry.' But they both know this is not the answer he wants.

What little patience he had has now expired. 'What on earth can I do? I'm at my wits' end.' His voice has sunk. But Bridget, very far from edging around to his point of view, is not convinced that he's suffered anything like enough.

'Wait. That's all any of us can do.'

'I'm not bloody well waiting for ever. Tell her that!' Harry has the uncomfortable feeling that he has lost the game, and although the match is still to play for, he could well lose that too. What's more, the legal advice he is getting is not encouraging. He has discovered that women have a lot more rights in England than he realised.

~

Every day, there is more in the news about the north: a lot of civil unrest, riots, murders and sectarian violence. Katherine tries not to listen but finds it increasingly compelling. She has nightmares about the guns, the river and moving scarecrows. Bridget is unable to pacify her, probably because she also has nightmares about the same things and more besides.

Today, however, Bridget has other interests on her mind. Unnoticed by anyone, she has reignited an old flame. Johnny Holland has been in the background forever. Not being a big one for writing letters, his candle had faded over the last few years while Frank was so ill, and more recently, with the dotey little pet being so needy. Katherine assumed that Johnny had either given up or found another love. Now it appears that during the last year of coming and going, he has been seeing Bridget quite a lot. Not wanting to alarm Katherine or encourage gossip from Marie Ryan, they have been meeting in Bridget's home place. There have been quite a few evenings when Bridget has slipped out 'for a walk' or to 'visit her mother', who has, unknown to Katherine, been moved to a home for the elderly in the village. Sometimes, she goes to the pub where Johnny just happens to be watching a match or playing darts. She never stays out late, just long enough to get a bloom in her cheeks. She is always home in time to settle Katherine with a hot drink and some soothing words.

When alone, Katherine potters around in the garden and on the farm. Against her own better judgement, she has taken to buying and reading the daily paper, which fuels her fascination with events in the north. She is trying to build up enough courage to go again along the river and have another look into that shed. In her heart, she knows there has to be a connection between the crates of guns, the Wren Boys and the violence up there; possibly even in Jack's untimely death.

As the last few days of autumn shine into the orchard, Bridget and Katherine gather windfalls and make crab-apple jelly. Fonsie raids the beehive and triumphantly puts a few jars of honey onto the kitchen table. The remaining cabbages are cut and potatoes dug and clamped, and the barn is packed with the golden straw bales and a stack of sweet hay.

For several days, a storm has been blowing up from the west. There are branches of trees falling all over the place and leaves blocking shores and forming waves around the corners of the farmyard. Some slates come jetting off the cowshed roof. A bunch of lambs have escaped through new holes in the ditches, and a water pipe is leaking, causing a pond to form in the haggard. While Katherine is outside with Jim Ryan, trying to fix things, shouting at each other about winter foddering arrangements as they plough through the mud, Johnny comes to call. With the gale behind him, he almost falls in the front door. He's dripping wet but ruddy-faced and full of cheer. By the time Katherine and Jim have found the missing lambs, mended the plumbing and fenced a few gaps, Bridget and Johnny are well into their second glass of whiskey. Apart from darts and hurling, reminiscing and tracing family trees are Johnny's favourite pastimes. His hat is steaming by the range, the creases in his trousers are beginning to dissolve and his wild, peppery hair is matted into curls by the wet weather. For all this, Katherine can see immediately what the attraction is. Johnny is bouncy and friendly with every sentence starting and ending on a positive note. He jumps to his feet when she comes in.

'Your Ladyship! And it's really well you're looking!' He bows dramatically and then shakes her hand vigorously. 'So well for someone who's after having such a sadness. Better days around the corner, no doubt about it.'

Bridget is glowing. She hasn't been like this since the days when Frank was well and taking 'his girls' for a spin around the lanes in the Bentley. Even Jim Ryan melts a little as he is plied with drink and drawn into chawing over old times. He perks up, especially when remembering the dead. Jim tries to drag the conversation down to basics—gloom and politics—but Johnny tosses in new ideas to keep it buoyant, like chucking fresh kindling into a dying fire.

'And did you hear they have a new captain for the under 21s?'

'Under 21s! Who gives a fig for their chances? They haven't a ghost. Not since they lost Fogarty to Killishmeesta. Now that was a black day in Knocklong. It's left the back line very weak.' Jim looks into the fire with a sad face.

Bridget lays on a few more sods of turf. Her cheeks are flushed and her bright blue eyes sparkling as they reflect the flames.

Johnny bounds on brightly, 'Sure, the All Ireland gave us all a lift. What harm if Fogarty deserted, good riddance to him anyway. It'll give some other young lads a chance to come on the team now. And, let's face it, Killishmeesta could do with a leg up!'

Katherine looks at Bridget. She hasn't a clue what they are talking about, and Bridget isn't much of an expert on hurling either, but she is watching the conversation intently with a broad smile on her face. She isn't keeping the score, but she knows her man is winning.

Jim is getting more and more cantankerous as the level in the bottle goes down. Finally, he rounds on Katherine. It starts off with the usual story. 'Don't tell me you intend staying on here now! At least give us the land. Surely, that's not too much to ask. We'll pay you fair and square for it.'

'Ah now, Jim, don't start that again.' Bridget can't bear to hear that wrangling going on. It's the same old broken record, but Jim Ryan has a new needle.

'Molloy is boasting all over that since he pulled you out of the river, you'll have to give it to him.' He thumps his knee with his fist. 'Goddamn it, girl, can't you see what he's up to!'

Johnny, sensing that he's blundered into a war zone, finishes off the whiskey and says bravely, 'Time we left, I think, Jim Ryan. Let the women get some rest. Come on. We'll go to the village and see if we can get some more drink into us.'

Bridget winks and smiles at Johnny as he gently herds Jim towards the door. The gale is raging outside, but the two men head off in Johnny's old van, bumping and thumping over the swelling ford and away up the boreen.

'Oh, thank God for that!' Bridget collapses into the armchair, and Katherine folds like a baby into her lap. She buries her head into the valley between Bridget's large, soft bosoms and sinks. Flakes of dope are rolled into a joint, and Katherine smokes it, inhaling the soft, aromatic fumes until she feels she can face the night. She takes the dog to her room with her but leaves the bedroom door open. It isn't until the next morning that she can put it all into words.

'I think I've got it now, Bridgie. If it was Nicholas who rescued me from the river, shortly before Jack was born, then he was one of the Wren Boys. He could have been the one who came back that night. Jack's father! He is obviously the one who's keeping guns in the shed. This is their headquarters! Maybe he shot Uncle Jack too, Bridgie. And to think, I thought he was our friend!'

Bridget's eyes glaze over briefly at the mention of Uncle Jack. She crosses herself and mumbles, 'Lord have mercy on the poor old dickens.' Then the thought hits her, and she blurts out, 'He must have copped by now that we know about the stash of weapons.'

'What are we going to do? Who can we trust?'

'You get dressed, pet, and go over to Father Fitzgerald. Tell him everything. He'll know what's best to do now.'

'Suppose he's in on it too?'

'Your father had great faith in him. He often said as much. When you first came over here last year, he told me not to worry about you, that Father Fitzgerald would look out for you.' Even though Bridget also has her suspicions about Father Fitzgerald, she can't think what else to do. 'And I certainly don't trust that Sergeant Dawson, anyway!'

'I don't trust any of them! Look what happened to me, and besides, my father was a Fenian too, Bridgie!'

'I suppose not all Fenians are rapists and gun runners.'

'No, maybe not, and we don't have much choice but to trust Father Fitzgerald. Do you think Marie and Josie are in on it too?'

'Probably. Maybe they all are. The whole lot of them and more besides. Who knows, but the whole bloody government is part of it! Everyone thinks Haughey and that slimy creature Blaney are guilty of gun running for the IRA. Why else would Lynch have sacked them from the government?'

Katherine hasn't a clue what Bridget is talking about. She is focussed on her meeting with Father Fitzgerald.

'Surely not Josie? That is criminal activity.'

'Yes, well, I rest my case.'

They both agree that it's unlikely that Fonsie is in on it, but you never know. Certainly not Johnny Holland. All of a sudden, Harry seems so tame and cosy. At least you know exactly where you are with him. Katherine feels utterly foolish. To think she trusted everyone, especially Nicholas Molloy, but didn't trust her own husband. Now it seems certain that Nicholas is the ringleader ... But then, even if he is, she's not frightened of him now, any more than she is of Harry. The worst has happened to her already, and she survived. She is stronger. She isn't the hapless girl she was a year ago. She is a *woman* now, and that is not the same.

'Where does Johnny live, Bridgie? I'll drop you off there first. I'm not leaving you on your own here, at least not until we get to the bottom of this.'

Johnny lives with his brother over their hardware shop in the village. Katherine stops the car outside the shop.

The two women sit in silence for some minutes. Then Bridget starts. 'Have you thought about what you are going to say?'

'I've turned it over in my mind so many times that now I think I'm just confusing myself. All I want to know, really, is what on earth is going on. I want the truth. And I want it to stop.'

'We agreed you'd tell Father Fitzgerald about the guns, remember? To see if he knows what to do about it.'

'But what if he is in on it too?'

'Then he'll know the game's up and deal with it himself.'

Passers-by scuttle past with their coats up over their heads against the rain, but can't resist having a peer into the car through the steamed-up windows. Katherine feels like an alien in a hostile land.

'Why do they all gawk at us like that, Bridgie? Don't they know us by now?'

'It's just their way. Gives them something to talk about. Don't mind them. You've faced worse than those old biddies! Look't, you can do this, you have to do it. Are you sure you want to go alone?'

'I don't want to go at all, but I know it's something I have to do. I don't think he'll talk to me if I'm not alone.'

'If he'll talk at all, the old fox that he is!' She smiles, and they both giggle nervously. Then Bridget gets out of the car before Katherine changes her mind. She goes into the hardware shop, head up, all business, as if she lived there already, and Katherine drives on to the parochial house alone.

A big part of Katherine hopes that Father Fitzgerald is not at home, that the mild-mannered Father Noel is there, and she can confide in him instead. But this is not the case. Their housekeeper answers the door and shows her into the old priest's office. He is surrounded by a miasma of papers, dog-eared books and cigarette smoke. The housekeeper hovers around, tending the fire with little pieces of coal and brushing the dust away.

'Thank you, Jean, you can leave that now. We'll take a sup of tea in here, please.' He nods to her and then looks at the door. Katherine senses something. It reminds her of the look that her father gave to Bridget when she would slip a hand beneath the rug to 'settle him' into his chair. She doesn't want to think about any of that now; she came here for help, not to be side-tracked by the needs of old men.

The priest gestures towards a reading chair beside the hearth. 'Sit down, my dear. It's a vile day to be out, but I'm glad you called. How have you been since?'

They watch the hopping flames. The fresh lumps of coal

fizz and sparkle as the outer parts succumb to the fire. The old priest coughs consumptively, leaning forwards and heaving from the depths of his threadbare lungs. Had he not been in such company, he would have spat the gloopy spume directly into the fire. Instead, he deposits it into a paper handkerchief first, folds it away and then pokes it into the flames.

Katherine wants to say brightly, 'Oh, I'm fine really, just getting used to things the way they are now, you know. It isn't easy.' But those words are blocked by the vision of gun crates and talk of the IRA. She can taste the river water glugging into her lungs. And besides, she doesn't want to get side-tracked. She stares at the patterns fashioned over the surface of the slate fire surround, swirling and polished to look like marble, and the blue irises on the Victorian tiles, yellowed around the edges with age. The fire makes them shine in the dim light of the room. 'I've been better.'

Jean puts her shoulder to the door and backs into the room with a loaded tea tray, which she lays down on a side table. She pours his first and adds a good splash of brandy from a naggin that she keeps tucked away in her apron folds. Six lumps of sugar follow and are stirred in well before handing him the cup. She pours for Katherine, places two lumps of sugar and two digestive biscuits on the saucer and passes it across the hearth. Her hand is perfectly steady, her forearm neat and strong.

After lubricating his throat with a few sips from the bone-china cup, Father Fitzgerald gestures towards Katherine and says, 'Jean, this is Katherine Butler, the late Sir Francis Butler's daughter,' leaning on the 'Sir' with a touch of irony. For a split second, Jean hesitates, not sure if that means the visitor is to be seen as friend or foe. She shoots a quick look at the priest. He nods; she nods back.

'Ah, yes, I've seen you a few times at Mass and, of course, the funerals. I'm sorry for your troubles. Lord have mercy on them all, especially the poor wee child.' She crosses herself, and when there is no more to be said about that, she does a little bob, 'Well, if that's all, I've the dinner to prepare. It's good to make your acquaintance.' On her way out, she leaves the door slightly ajar.

Katherine thinks the priest hasn't noticed, but he calls after her, 'Shut that door, please, Jean. There's a bit of a draught in here.' The door clicks gently closed. 'It's bound to be a difficult time. Losing a baby is never easy, especially after such a brave struggle.'

Before her eyes have a chance to fill with tears and her throat to seize up, she says boldly, 'Thank you, Father, but that isn't why I'm here. There is something else I need to talk to you about.'

The old man looks up. His face is shining a little from its proximity to the fire.

'What is it, child?' He takes out a cigarette case, opens it and offers one to Katherine. They both pull hard, sucking the soothing smoke deeply into them. 'What is on your mind?'

In one long sentence—lest she might lose her nerve—she relays her story. How she and Bridget have discovered a shed packed with guns and ammunition on the outreaches of her farm. How, considering all that has happened to her, they do not know who they can trust, and finally, that her own father, just before he died, intimated that if she ever needed help, she could turn to him, Father Fitzgerald.

The flames reflect from his red cheeks. He coughs, and this time his whole body shudders. When he has settled down again, he says in a carefully measured tone, 'Katherine, I find myself in a dilemma.'

'Did you know about this already?'

'In a way, yes. A priest hears things, knows things, is told things. These guns, I have reason to believe, are destined for the north, for the Republican struggle against the oppression of Catholics and civil injustice.' Katherine looks shocked, although truthfully nothing really surprises her anymore. The old man responds, 'But, my dear, you must know that our community is virtually under siege in places up there, with more troops arriving from England every day.' She hasn't considered it until this moment, but now she realises that she is part of 'our community'. She is one of them.

'But they must be meant for killing people, Father. What else are guns for?'

'Ah, there is the heart of the dilemma.'

'Surely, we should report the arms and hand them over to the authorities?'

'It isn't as simple as that, child. For a start, who are the authorities?'

'The police. The Gardaí, I mean.'

'Suppose they know about it already and are turning a blind eye? There is a lot at stake here, child. People are dying in the streets, being butchered in their beds, fathers slaughtered in front of their own children even, men and women. God-fearing Catholics like you and me, Katherine.'

She has a brief flashback to the image of Nicholas, JJ and Sergeant Dawson leaning on the BMW in her farmyard. Conspirators; no doubt about it now.

'The army?'

'Perhaps. What do you think the army does with guns?'

'Well, at least they do it under proper control.'

'That depends which army you are talking about!'

Then, with more courage than she thought she would

be able to muster, she challenges him, 'You know who is responsible for this arsenal, don't you?'

'Knowledge I would sooner not have. It doesn't make it any easier.' The priest heaves himself to his feet and stalks around the office, navigating his way between the piles of papers and heaps of dusty, old tomes. He chain-smokes and is gasping for breath on each lap between the chair and the window. He leans against a bookcase and goes on, 'Did your father ever speak to you about the troubles, Katherine?'

'He told me a bit about my Great-Uncle Daniel: the ambush, the Black and Tans, the murder of Daniel and his wife.'

'Did he tell you I was with him the day we burned Sunnyhill?'

With shivers running down her spine, Katherine realises she is right in the heart of the vipers' nest, but having come this far, she must plough on.

'I didn't make the connection. You mean Daddy was part of that too? Are you involved in this now, Father?'

The old priest decides to bind her to the truth with his secret ace. 'Did he tell you about Moira Madden?'

'He did mention her. She worked in the house at Sunnyhill, didn't she? What's she got to do with it?'

'That's right.' He looks even more pained than before and dramatically drops his head down into his left hand, while the right one is clutching his chest as if his lungs might burst through. His voice is crackling with phlegm. 'Did you know that she is Nicholas Molloy's mother?'

'No, I didn't make that connection.'

'What did he tell you?'

'That she was an accomplice of some sort, and that she worked up at the big house. I think he might have been a bit sweet on her, actually.'

'He was that, all right. He ran off with her afterwards. They went into hiding together. Eventually, her family caught up with them and dragged her home. By this time, she was pregnant. Your father wanted to marry her, but the Maddens wouldn't hear of it; he was a wanted outlaw by then. They fixed up for her to marry an old bachelor by the name of Tom Molloy, and that was the end of it. Frank and I did a stint in jail and then, when the civil war died down, all of us got a kind of amnesty. But you see, we were on the wrong side, and those feelings never went away. Your father scarpered off to England, and I went into the seminary. He sent money for the cause all those years. That was his conscience money. Moira had a son, Nicholas, and he took after Frank—another raw Republican.'

'So Nicholas is my father's son, my half-brother?'

He sits down opposite Katherine again and puts his hand on her arm. 'That's right, child, that's right. But he doesn't know this, and I gave my word to your father that as long as Moira was alive, I wouldn't tell him.'

'So, was it my father's money that has been financing the gun running?'

The old man nods gravely.

Katherine leans back and closes her eyes. Her head is a swirling mass of jigsaw pieces flying into place. 'But Nicholas doesn't know that either?'

He shakes his head. 'I don't think so.'

They sit in silence, broken only by fits of coughing, the wind smashing rain against the window and the ticking of an old mantle clock. Then Katherine, feeling increasingly uncomfortable and finding it hard to breathe in the stuffiness of the room, asks him, 'So, what is really troubling you about this now, Father?'

'The problem you see is this. I have heard on the grapevine, as it were, that they are planning to ship these guns up to the north in the next few days, but the Loyalists have been tipped off, and there is likely to be a very bloody ambush.'

'Will Nicholas be involved in this?'

'I think so. I promised your father I would see that no harm came to him, but I'm in a very difficult position.' There is a brief hiatus, another paroxysm of coughing. Unable to gauge Katherine's reaction to all this, he feels the need to pad in a few more details. Having brought her this far into it, he has to know where she stands. 'Your uncle apparently discovered what the boys were up to. He was tormented beyond his ability to deal with it. He knew, of course, about his relationship to Molloy. Up until the time he found out what they were doing, his intention was to leave the family farm to Nicholas. But Jack wasn't a sympathiser, and he knew also that arms dealing is a very serious crime, with dangerous consequences for everyone. When he found out about it, he felt implicated by association; caught between the sword and the wall. Between his family and his fears. Now I feel the same way. That sword has a sharp point to it.'

'So, it wasn't for the land that he was tormented. It was his own conscience!'

'That's it, Katherine. Living with all this going on around him, surrounded by active Provisional IRA supporters, in his own family and on his own land, frightened and anguished him out of his right mind.'

'Who else is involved in it?'

'That's something you would be better off not knowing, child.'

'I don't see why you can't just tell them they've been found out and be done with it.'

'A man in my position can't be seen to be involved in this kind of thing. I know far too much as it is.'

The sagging black clouds that followed Katherine to the parochial house have burst, and the rain is teeming down outside. The room is becoming increasingly gloomy.

'What'll happen to them if they aren't warned?'

'I can't even think of it, child.' He pauses, pokes the fire. 'Of course, now that you know of your family connection, you could, maybe, find a way to tell Molloy yourself?'

Feeling the sharp point of that sword herself, she stands up and walks over to the window. The view is smeared with rain. All she can make out is the outline of a few old tombstones and some gloomy yew trees. She is unsure of the wisdom of it, but under the circumstances, she decides she must explain her own suspicions about Molloy. Skating over the embarrassing details, she tells him about the Wren Boys. That she believes he could have been the one who fathered her child in an act of violation against her; that he was certainly an accomplice. She faces him directly, expecting him to melt in a fatherly show of sympathy.

Instead, he just stares back at her. He sees his opportunity opening up before him, and like a startled hare, he leaps for the gap. 'Katherine, you cannot take that hatred any further. It will eat your soul and force you to do things that would affect your chances of eternal salvation. You must seize this God-given opportunity to forgive your brother. Go to Nicholas Molloy right away and tell him about the very grave danger they are in if they persist with their plan. Tell him to bide awhile and, as a last resort, to surrender his arms to the commandant in the army barracks in Kilkenny so they don't fall into enemy hands. There are ways of doing it without recrimination. He'll know. But *do not* tell him how you know this.'

'Suppose he decides to shoot me instead? He's already shown that he is capable of acts of extreme violence against me. Even if he doesn't want to shoot me, he has no reason to believe me.'

The priest is flummoxed, but only briefly. 'Tell him this came to you from a trusted friend of the family. Use the code word "Sunnyhill".' But he can see that Katherine is still far from convinced. 'Tell him that you are coming to him in a spirit of forgiveness. That you want to put those things behind you both.'

'But I can't tell him that we are brother and sister?'

'All I can say is that your father would not have wished any harm to come to either of you; he loved you above all other things. Under the circumstances, I think that decision will have to rest with you, my child.'

Katherine feels like the sword is slipping in between her ribs.

'Go right away, before it's too late. No one else can do this but you. I'll say a special Mass for your intentions. Good luck.'

The rain hits her face with a welcome smack. The air outside is cold. She gasps it in like the first breath of the newborn. She throws her scarf around her neck, but it flies back and tangles in her hair. She grapples in her wet pocket for the car keys. When she finds them, her hands are so cold she drops them into a puddle. The surface of the water is being punctured by bursts of rain. She paddles around in it with her freezing fingers and pulls out pebbles, slime and, eventually, wet car keys. The rain slithers down the back of her neck.

At first, it seems like the car won't start. Then when it does get going, it coughs like Father Fitzgerald. It's as if everything around her is saying to her, 'Are you sure this is a good idea?' She knows if she speaks to Bridget first, Bridget will be afraid and try to talk her out of it. The wind is still battering the hedgerows. Large pools are beginning to merge into running floods on the sides of the road. In a deliberate act of defiance against the will of fate, Katherine forces herself to splash straight through the village without stopping and head on for the hills.

The Molloys' farm is two miles the other side of Knocklong. It's one of those places that seems to brood in an avenue of tall evergreens, like an owl peering out of a tree trunk. The car turns in off the road and bumps through potholes. When she reaches the farmyard, two hunting dogs bound towards her. They rear up, scratching at the car doors, snarling. Katherine's heart pounds. She is about to reverse out again when Nicholas appears at the back door and calls the dogs to heel.

She looks at him through the rain. His black curls are clinging to his wet face. He is no longer her attacker and her uncle's tormentor, nor a dealer in death. Not the hooded stranger who plucked her from the river and gave her the kiss of life. Now it's about something else. She has a brother, and he is in danger. She has to do this for her family. She must forgive him. She wants to let go, to be free of fear and anger. She says a silent prayer. She feels strong. Perhaps she has forgiven him already. Either way, she knows she has that choice.

Nicholas strides over to the car, opens the door and puts out his hand to help her stand up. He herds her into the corner beneath an overhanging corrugated sheet. Their backs are to the wall. The rain is streaming off the roof and gushing into a shore a few feet away.

'Well? It's good you called, actually, because I have something I want to show you.' He points to the stone buildings across the yard. Leaning up against the cowshed wall is a substantial slab of marble. 'What do you think of it?'

Feeling completely disarmed and wiping the rain out of her eyes, she says, 'What's it for?'

'It's for you. I found it the other day in a stonecutter's yard. I thought it would be ideal for the baby's headstone. You didn't put one up yet for your uncle, did you? They could both share this one, when the ground has had a chance to settle.'

'Why are you doing this, Nicholas?'

He just looks at her. His covenant with God is still incarcerated in his heart. But how do you say those things? Surely, she knows already? Surely, he doesn't have to spell it out?

'Come inside out of the rain. Mother would like to say hello, I'm sure.'

'I won't come inside now, thanks. This isn't really a social call.'

'Oh?'

'Does the word "Sunnyhill" mean anything to you?'

He looks down onto his brown leather boots. His hands are in his pockets, fiddling.

'Okay. Tell me, where did you get hold of that one? What is this all about?'

'A trusted friend of the family. It would seem that whatever it is you are involved in has been rumbled. The operation is no longer safe to proceed with. It's come to light, apparently, that an ambush is planned.'

'It was Father Fitz., wasn't it? Oh, you needn't bother denying it. The slooky old devil, getting you to do his dirty work for him.'

'How could an old priest like that be involved in any dirty work?'

'Look't, Katherine, how long have you lived here? You know nothing. That old man has set us all up. Now it looks like he's lost his nerve. Either that or he's got a sudden attack of conscience. No, I know what it is. He's not long for this world, and he's thinking of his interview with St Peter! He wants me to kick over the traces for him. Who else have you told this to?'

'This is just between you and me, Nicholas.' Then, suddenly remembering that it's guns and war she is really talking about, she adds, 'Except I have left, in a safe place, enough evidence to convict anyone who might think of bumping me off.'

'Well, you are no back of a clock, I'll give you that!'

'Look, it's time we were honest with each other, Nicholas. I know more than I want to know, but probably not as much as I should. I came here to tell you for your own safety that the … well, it's not cool anymore. You should hand the … well, the goods, shall we say, to the commandant in the barracks in Kilkenny. You aren't safe either. Whoever you are working with is also in danger. The game's up for all of you.'

'I'd say it took courage for you to come up here and tell me that. I thought you were a silly hippy when you blundered into our lives here nearly a year ago, but you aren't, are you? You are some woman!'

'I've told you what I came to say now, but I want you to know that I won't be involved in it. I won't be involved in any way, and I don't want anything moved through or stored on my farm ever again. That's all I ask. Please.'

'Are you planning on staying, then? You know your uncle had that place willed to me once upon a time?'

'Why would he do a thing like that?'

'I was good to him. He liked me, always did. I think he

saw me as a bit of a son to him.'

'What do you think made him change his mind?'

'I don't know. I only found out I wasn't getting it when you came along.'

'Did he really shoot himself?'

'We've been over this ground before. What do you think?'

'I think I know too much already.' There is a silence, interrupted by the panting of the hounds and the pounding of the rain on the wet concrete. 'I'm going to go now, Nicholas. Do you think we have an understanding?'

There was another brief silence. 'We do.'

Katherine dithers a little, listening to the relentless howl of the wind and the gusts of rain whacking off a tin roof. She is waiting for him to say it, to cross the unbridgeable divide of guilt and apology, so that she can tell him she's forgiven the unforgiveable. She turns away, as if not looking into his face will afford him the space to be honest with her. In the end, she is quite relieved that he doesn't say any more. There will be another time, she is sure of that now. What matters to Katherine is that she has the upper hand. The power is in knowing the truth, not necessarily in sharing it. Talking about forgiveness isn't that important, really, not now that she no longer holds the bitterness in her heart. She buried that along with her baby. It's all in the past. What matters to her right now is that she owns this moment.

'Thank you for the headstone. I really like it. If you call up next week sometime, we can decide what to put on it. You can help me.'

He nods, pinches up his lips, and watches her reverse out of the yard, turn the car and drive away.

Katherine is in the jungle, but now it feels okay. She is no longer struggling to find a way out.

Phyllida Taylor

Stand still, the trees around you are not lost. The forest knows where you are, you must let it find you.'
—David White: Presenting the Soul

A Note from the Author

If you enjoyed this book, I would be very grateful if you could write a review and publish it at your point of purchase. Your review, even a brief one, will help other readers to decide whether they'll enjoy my work.

If you want to be notified of new releases from myself and other Alkira Publishing authors, please sign up to the Alkira Publishing email list. In return you'll get a free ebook of short stories and book excerpts by Alkira Publishing authors. You'll find the sign-up button on the right-hand side under the photo at www.alkirapublishing.com. Of course, your information will never be shared, and the publisher won't inundate you with emails, just let you know of new releases.

Acknowledgements

This story has been a very long time incubating, and my family, teachers and friends have given me the support and encouragement I needed to persist. I thank them all, especially those who read it during its various incarnations along the way.

9 781922 329684